MOTHER'S LOVE

"You have a pearl of a daughter, Duchess, to throw such a gala to celebrate her mother." Lady Clarendon looked around her at the crowd of people standing together in clumps chatting gaily and nibbling hors d'oeuvres in the Duchess of Ashford's gold salon.

"You are kind to say so, Lady Clarendon." The Duchess of Ashford smiled and raised a quizzical eyebrow. "Shall we hope it catches the fashion? Mothers need to be appreciated every now and again."

—"A Betting Affair" by Marissa Edwards
in A MOTHER'S JOY

And what better time to appreciate mothers than during the month of May on Mother's Day. From Regency England to modern times, the joys of family love are wonderful indeed. Matchmaking mamas, well-meaning mothers-in-law, expectant mothers, stepmothers—with kindness and wisdom these wonderful women often care so much for their loved ones they forget about themselves.

And thus we set aside a special day to honor mothers, and we celebrate that day with this charming collection of six Regency stories. So let Carola Dunn, Marissa Edwards, Jo Ann Ferguson, Cindy Holbrook, Lynn Kerstan, and Joy Reed whisk you away to a most proper historical period where conventions ruled society and love ruled the heart.

A Mother's Joy

Carola Dunn
Marissa Edwards
Jo Ann Ferguson
Cindy Holbrook
Lynn Kerstan
Joy Reed

ZEBRA BOOKS
KENSINGTON PUBLISHING CORP.

ZEBRA BOOKS are published by

Kensington Publishing Corp.
475 Park Avenue South
New York, NY 10016

First Printing: April, 1994

Printed in the United States of America

TABLE OF CONTENTS

The Dower House

by Carola Dunn

"The best thing about being a grandmother," said Catriona placidly, "is that if Donald falls in, you have to fish him out, not I."

Letty laughed. "Unfortunately, Daphne is just as likely to fall in. If they both take the plunge at once, Mama, you may be called upon to help."

Lady Catriona March and her daughter stood on the bank of the ornamental lake. Among the reeds, in an aged rowboat tied to a rickety jetty, Letty's seven-year-old twins played at pirates. With bulrushes for cutlasses they hacked harmlessly at each other, the August sun bright on their copper curls.

Even as the ladies watched, the boat began to sink with a bubbling sigh.

"The water is not very deep," said Letty with her usual optimism, "and it is a warm day. I hope they can manage without me, as I foolishly put on my new gown." She glanced up the slope at the sprawling manor of Lincolnshire stone before moving to the near end of the jetty.

Knee-deep in muddy water, Donald and Daphne argued about whose fault it was that their pirate ship had sunk. Dearly as she loved her grandchildren, Catriona's thoughts were on their mother, slender and graceful in lavender-green sprigged muslin. She had not missed Letty's backward glance at the manor house, nor its connection with her new gown.

The new heir to the baronetcy and to Marchbank had arrived last night. Catriona knew little about Sir Gideon March, except that the lawyers had at last found him in Canada a year after

Jeremy's death. He was Jeremy's uncle's grandson, a distant cousin, and though there had been no positive breach, the two branches of the family had lost contact. She did not know Sir Gideon's age, nor even if he had a wife. Whether he would bring life and gaiety back to Marchbank, she could not guess.

Letty deserved a little gaiety. Wed at seventeen to her childhood sweetheart, widowed after three weeks of married life, she was a devoted mother and seemed content with their quiet life at the Dower House. Yet she was too young, too pretty to resign herself to widowhood.

Catriona herself found a proper resignation difficult to attain. She, too, had married at seventeen and borne her only child not a year later, but she had had Jeremy's love and support for long years thereafter. His absence now was an aching void in her life.

At her age, that void was not to be filled. Letty was another matter. Somewhere in the wide world was the man who could mend her broken heart and who would not flinch at taking on a pair of energetic twins.

"My feet are stuck in the mud, Mama," said Daphne gleefully.

"So are mine," Donald clamored.

"I can't move a single inch."

"Perhaps we'll grow roots, Daph, and turn into plants like in that story Grandmama read us."

"You mean Narcissus? I can't see my face in the water, though."

"There's too many ripples. Keep still."

"For heaven's sake, children!" Letty took a tentative step onto the dilapidated jetty. "Lean this way and hold out your hands, Daphne. I shall try to reach you and pull you out."

"May I be of assistance, ma'am?" The deep, amused voice came from behind Catriona.

With a startled gasp, she turned. A tall, powerful gentleman in buckskins and a walnut brown coat raised his hat to her, revealing thick black hair with the merest hint of gray at the temples. Dark eyes smiled down at her from a sun-bronzed face.

"Thank you, sir. I daresay my daughter will be glad of your aid."

"Your daughter?" For a moment he looked surprised, then his gaze went beyond her. "Perhaps introductions had best wait," he exclaimed, and strode past her.

Letty crouched on the edge of the jetty, precariously reaching toward Daphne. Their fingertips were a good six inches apart. If they met, Letty was more likely to land in the water than to pull the child out.

"Wait!" called the stranger imperatively. "I believe I can reach her, ma'am."

Looking round, Letty rose from her undignified position in one graceful movement. "Do you think so, sir? That is very kind of you. You may be splashed, I fear." She stepped back to be out of his way.

"A little water won't hurt me."

"And mud," said Donald with relish.

"And pondweed," Daphne chimed in, draping a strand of greenery around her neck. "Look at my necklace."

Undeterred, the gentleman set foot on the jetty. He had taken two paces when his foot went through the rotten wood. The whole structure promptly disintegrated, dumping him and Letty to flounder in the water among floating planks.

The twins, overcome by giggles, clutched at each other and both sat down. Catriona bit her lip, her chin quivering in her struggle to suppress unseemly merriment. She was undone when a shout of mirth behind her announced the arrival of another newcomer. Her laughter escaped her control, and she was breathless when she finally managed to give her attention to the second stranger.

Ten or twelve years younger than the first, in his late twenties, he was nearly as tall, equally strong-looking but tending more to a lean, sinewy build. His complexion, too, was browned by the sun. Fair hair, blue eyes, and a broad grin completed the picture of a handsome Buck.

"Need a hand, Gideon?" he called.

So the older gentleman was the new baronet. "Not unless you fancy a swim, coz," he answered wryly. Finding his feet, he rose from the shallows like a Triton from the depths. He took Letty's hand, pulled her up, and disregarding the muddy water cascading from their persons, he said with gallant courtesy, "Permit me to offer you my arm, ma'am."

She cast a laughing glance up at him and accepted. Her straw bonnet sagged about her ears, but far worse, her gown clung to her body, the thin muslin almost transparent. As they made their way to the bank, Catriona wondered despairingly what she could use to cover her daughter's scarcely decent form.

"If only I had worn a shawl, or even a spencer!"

No longer amused, the young man beside her tore his wide-eyed gaze from Letty. "Take my coat, ma'am," he said in a slightly unsteady voice. Stripping off the bottle-green garment, he handed it to Catriona.

She hurried forward with it. Sir Gideon heaved himself out of the water and turned back to haul Letty onto the bank. With a smile for her mother, standing by with the coat, she reached up to take his hands. A moment later she was on dry land. Her eyes widened as she caught sight of the second gentleman, now in his shirt sleeves.

A flush mantled her cheeks. "Mama, pray let us go home at once," she begged, hastily pulling the coat on and buttoning it.

"Will you not come up to the house to dry off?" Sir Gideon invited them. "The children, too, of course."

They all turned back to the lake, where Donald and Daphne were now wrestling in the muddy water.

"We cannot possibly inflict those two on you!" Catriona exclaimed. "In any case, they all need dry clothes and the Dower House is not much farther off."

"Then you *are* Lady Catriona March?" said the baronet. "We enquired for you at the Dower House, and your servant said you had walked this way, but I couldn't believe . . ." He glanced from Catriona to Letty and back. "I took you for sisters. To tell the truth, I had supposed the dowager to be an older lady."

"You don't look a bit like one's notion of a dowager, ma'am," his cousin agreed.

"Lady Catriona, I'm Gideon March, as you will doubtless have guessed. Allow me to present my cousin, Harry Talgarth."

Mr. Talgarth bowed. Catriona's lips twitched as she gravely introduced the dripping Letty to the dripping baronet and his dry but shirt-sleeved cousin. "My daughter, Mrs. Rosebay."

"How do you do, Sir Gideon, Mr. Talgarth." Letty was beginning to shiver. "I am most grateful for your help, but pray excuse us now. I want to go home! Daphne, Donald, come out at once."

"We can't, Mama."

"We're not pirates anymore."

"We're sea serpents."

"We'll die if we leave the water."

Harry Talgarth reached the water's edge in two strides. "Out!" he commanded.

Four bright blue eyes turned on him with more speculative interest than alarm, but after a moment the twins decided to obey. They slithered up the muddy bank à la serpent, completing the devastation of their clothes.

However lively and argumentative, they were well-taught. Daphne curtsied and Donald bowed. The sight was almost too much for Catriona, and then she met Sir Gideon's twinkling eyes. They both burst out laughing.

The children glanced at each other and shrugged their shoulders.

"Let's be racehorses," Daphne proposed.

"I'll get home before you."

They dashed off. "Straight home, and go in through the kitchen," Letty called after them. She looked chagrined.

"Come on, darling, you will take a chill," said Catriona. "Excuse us, gentlemen. We shall be happy to receive you later this afternoon—at four, say?—though I cannot promise your coat will be fit to return to you by then, Mr. Talgarth."

"No matter, ma'am. I only hope it preserves Mrs. Rosebay from a chill."

"We shall see you at four," said Sir Gideon, "without fail. I'm badly in need of a lady's advice."

So he was not married, Catriona thought as they parted. Gallant and charming, with a splendid sense of humor, he would suit Letty to a T. To be sure, he was considerably older, but Jeremy had been twenty years older than herself and she had come to love him dearly.

She had been shocked, though, when her father, the Earl of Dunshannon, had insisted on wedding the youngest of his many daughters to a suitor she considered positively elderly. Best not to say anything to Letty until she was better acquainted with Sir Gideon. It had not passed Catriona's notice that Letty had been instantly at ease with him, amused by their mutual mishap. Not until she saw Harry Talgarth had she shown any sign of embarrassment.

"What must they think of us, Mama?" Letty wailed. "I have never been so mortified in my life. I made an utter cake of myself, and then the children misbehaving . . ."

"They were no worse than high-spirited and their usual imaginative selves. Indeed, I was quite proud of them when they remembered their manners, even if I could not help laughing. And it was Sir Gideon, not you, who demolished the jetty, though I do think you would have had a ducking anyway," she added to be fair. "I must say, he took his soaking very well."

Letty sighed. "Yes, he was all that is gentlemanly. But Mr. Talgarth stared at me *so!*"

"And lent you his coat. Come, let us forget the incident and start afresh."

"If only they will forget. Still, I daresay Mr. Talgarth will soon go away and Sir Gideon will be a pleasant neighbor."

"I am sure he will." Catriona heard the note of hope in her own voice and chided herself for being a matchmaking mama. Not to mention overhasty: she had taken an instant liking to Sir Gideon, but after all, she still knew very little of him. A pleasant manner and attractive person by no means proved him to be a man of character and principle.

Standing in the sun at her chamber window, Letty brushed her long, damp hair and wished it were more like Mama's, a rich, chestnut color, instead of her own paler hue. Papa had called it titian, but to Bart she had always been "Carrots." Perhaps if she had been blond, or if her eyes were green like Mama's rather than commonplace blue, he would have . . .

With a deliberate effort, she shook off the unwonted mood of self-pity. Bart was six years gone, buried on a Spanish mountainside, and she had long since learned to live with the memory of those three disastrous weeks.

"Mama?" Daphne peeked around the door, then came in. Dressed in a clean white pinafore embroidered with ivy leaves, her red curls combed into a semblance of order, she was a sight to lighten a mother's heart. "Mama, Betsy says she's nearly finished with Grandmama and is your hair dry enough to braid?"

"Tell her yes, lovie. You are looking very pretty."

"My hair was tied in *knots*. Betsy thought she'd have to cut it all off. I could've worn a wig, like Grandpapa did when he was young. Mama, Grandmama says me and Donald . . ."

"Donald and I."

". . . can take tea with you, but I have to ask you first."

"If you both promise to behave yourselves."

"We'll sit ever so quietly in our corner and look at picture books."

The twins had never been known to sit quietly in a corner for more than ten minutes, but Letty decided that, as a close neighbor, Sir Gideon must accustom himself to them. As a visitor, Mr. Talgarth's opinion mattered not a whit to her, she thought defiantly. How stern he had sounded when he ordered her children out of the lake!

Daphne added a proviso. "Except when we're eating. Sarah's making jam tarts."

Twenty minutes later, her hair braided and pinned up beneath a lace cap with a ribbon that matched her blue gown, Letty joined her mother in the sitting room. Mama was still wearing half mourning, though it was eighteen months since Papa died. Her dark lilac gown trimmed with black ribbons suited her remarkably well. Nonetheless, her eyes opened by Sir Gideon's and Mr. Talgarth's comments, Letty resolved to persuade her it was time she put off black gloves. She was too young to dress like a dowager.

She looked up from the smock she was embroidering for Daphne. "How well that gown suits you, Letty. Sir Gideon will quite forget his last view of you. I am sadly flustered, I declare, to be entertaining gentlemen again. Other than the vicar, few have called since we came to the Dower House."

"You flustered, Mama? Fustian!" She glanced about the room, bright with flowered chintzes and gleaming wood. Surely Mr. Talgarth would find nothing here to criticize. Not that his gaze had been precisely critical when she emerged from the waters like a naiad, but unlike Sir Gideon, he had not been smiling. Too far off to read the expression in his eyes, she only knew that something in his look had made her blush.

Her mother's voice was a welcome distraction. "The kettle is on the hob and Sarah has been baking."

"I see you have set out the madeira."

"Gentlemen often prefer wine. You recall your papa's opinion of tea-drinking in the afternoon."

"Chatter-broth!"

They both laughed.

Daphne came in, still reasonably clean, followed by Donald, equally angelic in his blue skeleton suit and short jacket. On their best behavior, they settled in "their" corner, furnished with two footstools and a shelf of children's books. A moment later the door knocker sounded. Letty discovered she was bracing herself and forced herself to relax.

"Sir Gideon March and Mr. Talgarth, my lady," Lois announced.

As Sir Gideon bowed over her mother's hand, Letty met Mr. Talgarth's eyes. Now his regard was warm, appreciative, even admiring. Disconcerted, she hastily turned away to greet Sir Gideon.

After the usual polite exchanges, Mr. Talgarth said to Letty with a sympathetic smile, "Unless appearances deceive, you have quite recovered from your wetting, Mrs. Rosebay. The children have taken no ill?"

"They positively enjoyed the experience, sir." Eager for him to see the twins for once looking well-bred and tidy, she gestured toward them. He nodded and went to speak to them in their corner. Watching, Letty saw them pointing out to him something in their book. He responded seriously, then glanced up and smiled at her again.

There was something curiously disturbing in Mr. Talgarth's smile. Letty managed an uncertain smile in return. Then Donald asked him another question, and with relief she gave her attention to her mother and Sir Gideon.

"In view of the circumstances," the baronet was saying soberly, "you will excuse my belated expression of my condolences on your late loss. I greatly regret that I never knew Sir Jeremy."

"We miss him." Catriona blinked away the mist that suddenly obscured her vision. "How foolish it is to let family ties lapse. I know your relationship to my husband, but little else. You have been in Canada, I collect?"

"For a year or two. Before that, we were for some time in India."

"You had no home in England?" Letty asked. Catriona was pleased by her interest in his history.

"My father was a doctor, Mrs. Rosebay, and while he did not leave me penniless, he owned neither house nor land. I had always longed to see the world, so I joined the Navy when I left school."

Letty glanced at Mr. Talgarth. "And your cousin?"

"My mother's nephew. Harry's parents died when he was a small child, and my parents brought him up. He happened to leave school just when I was feeling the tedium of blockading France's Channel ports, so I left the Navy and we have been adventuring together. China, India, Canada, South America, even to Russia. You might call us the proverbial rolling stones."

A little dismayed by his unsettled life, Catriona said, "You had no notion you were heir to Marchbank?"

"None. My grandfather was a third or fourth son, I believe. I still sometimes wake up and pinch myself to see if I'm dreaming that I'm a baronet."

As Catriona and Letty laughed, Lois carried in the tea tray and set it on the small table by the window. Letty went to pour, reaching the table three seconds before the twins.

"Not a nibble," she said severely, "until you have passed the cups and handed round the plates. Sir Gideon, will you take tea or do you prefer madeira?"

"A drop of madeira will do me, thank you."

"Shall I pour the wine, ma'am?" offered Mr. Talgarth, who had followed the children. "I'll drink tea, though."

Donald brought a glass of madeira for Sir Gideon, and Daphne, concentrating hard on the cup and saucer in her hands, brought Catriona's tea without spilling a drop. They returned with plates of jam tarts and almond cakes. Sir Gideon took one of each.

"I've sampled many interesting foods on my travels," he said, "but there is nothing to beat English pastries warm from the oven. And that reminds me, Lady Catriona. I'm hoping to obtain some information from you. The manor is in excellent condition—the lawyer tells me you have been keeping an eye on it? I am most grateful. Indeed, I was dismayed to hear that you had removed so promptly to the Dower House. There was no need . . ."

"It seemed advisable. We knew nothing of your disposition."

"True. I might have been the sort of villain who evicts grieving women and children from their homes."

Catriona shook her head at him in mock reproach. "Well, you might! In any case, we are perfectly comfortable here. Jeremy had the house set in order, expecting that . . . expecting . . ." Her throat tightened, blocking the words.

He came to her rescue. "A wise precaution, and it's a charming house. However, I trust you will continue to make use of the Marchbank park and gardens as if they were your own."

"You are very kind, Sir Gideon. To tell the truth, I doubt we could keep the children away if we tried," she added candidly. "But we have wandered from the point. What is it you wish to consult me about?"

"I want your advice about hiring servants. Though the present staff has kept the place well, now that we are in residence, they are too few if they are not to be grossly overworked. For a start, I need a cook, preferably one who has as light a hand with pastry as yours."

"You cannot have Sarah, but do have another jam tart. Daphne, pray—oh, *twins!*"

Unseen by their grandmother, and by their mother, who sipped her tea with bowed head, listening to Mr. Talgarth, the children had taken the entire plate of pastries to their corner. The last crumb disappeared as Catriona spoke, and they looked up with jammy beams. Sir Gideon grinned.

"We've been ever so quiet," said Daphne with an air of conscious rectitude.

"We don't like almond cakes," Donald explained.

"It's all right, Grandmama. Sarah made loads of jam tarts."

"We'll get you some more."

"How could you!" Letty sprang to her feet, far more agitated than their minor naughtiness warranted.

Surprised, Catriona said calmly, "Pray ask Lois to bring more tarts, children. Wash your faces—I expect your fingers need it, too—and go and play in the garden."

Subdued by their mother's unexpected outburst, Daphne said, "Yes, Grandmama."

As Letty subsided into her chair, Donald ran to her, flung his arms round her, and kissed her. "We're sorry, Mama. We didn't mean to vex you."

They dashed from the room. Mr. Talgarth took a handkerchief from his pocket and gravely handed it to Letty. Her face almost as red as the jam, she scrubbed the sticky smear from her cheek.

Once more the poor girl had been put to the blush before Harry Talgarth. If he had seemed amused, as Sir Gideon was, she could have laughed it off instead of being horridly embarrassed. Catriona decided it was time to end their tête-à-tête.

"Letty, you know the village people as well as I do. Come and help me advise Sir Gideon as to what servants can be hired locally and which he must advertise for."

Mr. Talgarth produced a notebook and pencil and wrote down names as they talked. When at last they had discussed all available positions, Sir Gideon thanked his advisers.

"I am glad you intend to take on so many," said Catriona. "I hated having to let them go when we left the manor. Am I right in supposing this means you are going to settle at Marchbank?"

"We are. We have seen a good part of the world, and now it's time to settle down and tend my acres. To begin with, would you object if I had a new jetty built and obtained a boat that will actually float?"

"Object? Good heavens, why should I object?"

He turned to Letty with a smile. "I was thinking of your enterprising offspring, Mrs. Rosebay. I fear a seaworthy vessel might prove an irresistible temptation to a couple of pirates."

"Then I had best teach them to swim," Mr. Talgarth unexpectedly proposed in a practical tone.

Letty stared in astonishment. "Teach them? Both of them? But they are so full of mischief!"

"That's why they need to learn," he pointed out, "and the sooner the better, while the water is warm enough. They are good-natured and loving despite their mischief. I have no qualms if you have not, ma'am."

"An excellent suggestion," said Catriona since Letty still looked stunned.

"You'd best start tomorrow, Harry, if the weather holds." Sir Gideon stood up to take his leave and a few minutes later the gentlemen were gone.

Letty started to collect cups and plates. "I cannot believe it," she said, stopping dead with the wineglass in her hand. "I was convinced that he had taken the twins in dislike and held me to blame for their naughtiness."

"I could see you were ill at ease with Mr. Talgarth." Catriona brushed some crumbs off the table into her hand and deposited them on the tray. "However, since it sounds as if he is to make his home at Marchbank with Sir Gideon, you must strive to overcome your dislike."

"I don't precisely dislike him, Mama. How can I, when he has so kindly offered to teach Donald and Daphne to swim? He just . . . makes me uneasy."

"It is a pity that he did not turn it to a joke when Donald bedaubed your cheek with jam."

"Oh no," Letty exclaimed with fervor, "that would have been worse than anything!"

"Then it seems the poor fellow can do nothing right," said Catriona, smiling. "How fortunate that Sir Gideon is so charming."

"Indeed, he is most agreeable."

With this temperate praise Catriona contented herself. Letty must have time to get to know Sir Gideon before marriage was to be thought of—always supposing that the baronet was in the market for a wife.

As twin red-headed sea serpents splashed toward the new skiff, Sir Gideon shipped his oars. "They have learned amazingly fast," he said.

"They are clever children," said Catriona with a proper pride in her grandchildren, "and they have an excellent teacher."

"It is good of Mr. Talgarth to go to so much trouble." Letty dabbled her hand in the water. "Daphne told me they always do exactly what he says because otherwise either they swallow water or he threatens to stop teaching them."

"Daphne, Donald, that's far enough," came Harry Talgarth's incisive voice. The twins turned at once and paddled back toward the bank. "Mrs. Rosebay," he called, "we'll be getting out now. The water is not as warm as it was."

"I shall come and fetch them," Letty called back, averting her gaze from the wet-shirted figure.

Catriona smiled and waved at him. At the advanced age of forty-two, she was, she felt, exempt from the demands of bashful modesty. She had only come out in the boat to chaperon her daughter. Not that she thought for a moment that Sir Gideon would take advantage of being alone with Letty; he was by far too gentlemanly.

With long, lazy, powerful strokes, he rowed toward the new jetty. Beneath the blue Bath superfine of his coat, his muscles flexed, driving the boat smoothly through the water without haste or wasted motion.

The way he rowed was typical of him, Catriona decided. Always tranquil, unhurried, good-humored, he had already restaffed the manor and taken the reins of the estate management into his capable hands. Hilton, the bailiff, had dropped in to see her at the Dower House the other day. Sir Gideon, he reported, was a fair man who realized his own ignorance but knew what he wanted.

"And among other things, my lady, that's a new roof for Ben Welter's farmhouse," he had said with satisfaction. "Them lawyers wouldn't let me spend the blunt, but Sir Gideon dubbed up wi'out a murmur."

He was generous to his dependents, amused by the children's antics, as vigorous as a man half his age—what more could Letty want? She was comfortable with him, making a laughing reference to the demolition of the old jetty as he handed her out of the boat onto the new.

Over the past month, he and his cousin had called at the Dower House nearly every day, or they had met in the park or gardens. Baskets of plums and pears and vegetables arrived regularly. Surely kindness alone was not enough to explain such assiduous attentions. Sir Gideon must be attracted to Letty. Several times in the last few days, Catriona had almost spoken to her daughter about the possibility of a second marriage.

Yet she had hesitated. The Dower House would be sadly empty without Letty and the twins, to be sure. The manor was no more than half a mile off, though. They could see each other daily. So why did her heart ache at the prospect?

"Shall we go round the lake again, Lady Catriona?" Sir Gideon smiled down at her.

"I beg your pardon, I was woolgathering! The boat is excessively comfortable, but no, thank you, I ought to be getting home, and I must not keep you." Cautiously she stood up. He took her hand, steadying her as the boat rocked a trifle.

"Careful now. The sun is warm, but the water is colder than when Mrs. Rosebay and I took our ducking."

With one foot on the jetty, Catriona realized that Letty had already left. "Oh, where is she?" she cried. "My stupid heedlessness has prevented your walking with her."

In her dismay, she tried to step up too hastily and lost her balance. Instantly Sir Gideon's arm was about her waist, lifting her as though she weighed no more than a child. She fell against him, or he caught her to him—what did it matter which? She was clasped to his chest, his mouth mere tantalizing inches from her own. Gold flecks danced in his brown eyes. Her pulse racing, she moistened suddenly dry lips as a flood of heat washed through her.

Her face was aflame. She pulled back out of his arms, stepped back, turned away, fleeing danger. But the danger was in herself, not in him. She dared not look at him lest he read the desire in her eyes. It was indecent for a respectable widow of her years to feel that way.

"Are you all right?" He sounded shaken. Had he read her mind? No, of course, she had narrowly escaped falling in the lake and had nearly pulled him in with her.

"Yes, quite all right," she said in a stifled voice. "Thank you for saving me. I am sorry."

"Whatever for?" Now he seemed deliberately to misunderstand. "I had no intention of going with Mrs. Rosebay," he went on calmly. "She has the twins for company. If you permit, I shall walk with you back to the Dower House. Will you not take my arm? You have had a shock."

His obliging offer was impossible to refuse. Catriona laid her hand lightly on his arm, and they turned down the path along the bank. Whatever he guessed to be the cause of her agitation, he set out to distract her.

"The skiff is comfortable," he said, "but less stable I believe than the canoes we used in Canada. I should not care to trust it on a whitewater river."

He went on to talk of the natives' skill with canoes, their wretched treatment at the hands of the Northwest Company, and the treatise on the subject Lord Selkirk was writing.

"When we met his lordship in Montreal, we promised him to do what we can to influence the government to pass laws protecting those unfortunate people. Harry and I have been writing letters, and next month, when Parliament sits, we shall go up to Town to speak to people face to face. Money talks. I ought perhaps to tell you," he added awkwardly, "that I returned from India something of a nabob."

Her discomfort thoroughly dispelled, Catriona stared at him. "A nabob! You have been sailing under false colors, sir. Did you not claim to be a rolling stone? Don't laugh at me, you odious man! A sailing stone may be an infelicitous image, but you know very well what I mean."

"To complete the confusion of metaphor, you must not tar all of us rolling stones with the same brush. Some of us do gather moss. What would you have thought of me had I announced on entering your sitting room that, far from being saved from poverty by my inheritance of the manor, I am well able to buy an abbey?"

"I would have thought you a vulgar, ungrateful braggart."

"Well, I cannot quite afford an abbey, and I'm proud to be a March of Marchbank."

"And I think you a truly gallant gentleman," said Catriona softly as they reached the Dower House's back gate. "I shall not invite you in, Sir Gideon, as the turmoil attending on the arrival of two wet children is no place for a visitor. But I would have you know that I am most sensible of your kindness—"

"Gammon!" he said roughly, and turned to stride away.

She stood for a moment in the shade of the great elm and watched his tall figure until he was lost to sight in the copse. With a sigh, she went through the gate and into the house to see that water was heating and towels were warmed for her grandchildren.

The first frost of autumn came that night. Leaves began to change color, and clouds of swallows gathered to fly south. The first russet-cheeked apples arrived from the manor orchards. Winter clothes were brought out to be aired.

Several days of constant, chilly rain kept the twins indoors.

After their lessons, they were unable to work off their energy in the small house. Up at the manor, they would have raced up and down the corridors with their hobbyhorses, or built and attacked fortresses of tables and chairs and old sheets. Here at the Dower House, they fussed and whined and squabbled.

It was enough to ruffle anyone's spirits, Catriona convinced herself. Her megrims had nothing to do with the absence of visitors from the manor.

She persuaded Letty to allow Daphne and Donald to go out for a while, well wrapped up. They came back sniffling, and Sarah complained about the wet clothes hanging in her kitchen. Letty's silently reproachful glance both irritated Catriona and made her feel guilty.

Fortunately the sniffles came to nothing. The wind veered to the northeast, frigid, blustery gusts off the North Sea that split the clouds and sent them scurrying. Leaves whirled from the trees, and the twins returned pink-cheeked from an expedition to the copse, with pocketfuls of brown shiny horse chestnuts.

"For cannonballs," Donald explained.

"To shoot at paper ships."

"We met Mr. Hilton in the wood."

"He showed us a badger's set."

"That's what you call its hole."

"Where it lives."

"They only come out at night."

Daphne gave him a repressive look and changed the subject. "Mr. Hilton says it's shaping up to a rare blow."

The bailiff's prediction was borne out by the rising wind. A tile slid off the roof and crashed to the ground, and Lois's bonnet blew away as she returned in the late afternoon from visiting her family. By nightfall a gale whipped the trees and moaned eerily around the Dower House.

Catriona and Letty ate their early dinner with the twins, put them to bed, and settled for the evening in the cozy haven of the sitting room. Letty read aloud from *Waverly* while Catriona sewed. The howl of the wind and the creaking of the house timbers were punctuated by an occasional bang or clatter from outside. A splintering crash made them both jump.

"There goes the cucumber frame," said Catriona with a sigh. "Everything which is not tied down—"

A thunderous shock rocked the house. Plaster fell from the ceiling, and a porcelain shepherdess dived from mantelpiece to hearth, shattering in a hundred pieces. From the hall came a wail.

Paling, Letty set down the book and jumped to her feet. With a shaking hand, Catriona stuck the needle in her work and laid it aside. Lois rushed in.

"Oh, my lady, I was that startled I dropped the tea tray. It was an earthquake, that's what it was."

Betsy appeared in the doorway, Sarah's round face visible over her shoulder. "The elm's down, my lady," she said grimly. "Hit the roof square on, from what we could see out the kitchen window."

"The twins!" White as a ghost, Letty pushed past the servants and ran to the stairs, Catriona at her heels.

Before she reached the landing, Letty stopped with a cry of despair. The upper flight of the narrow staircase was a jumbled, impenetrable tangle of splintered elm branches, their yellow leaves stirring fitfully in the gusts that blew down from above.

"Daphne!" Letty screamed. "Donald! Answer me!"

Only the roar of the wind answered.

"Oh, ma'am, they're dead." Lois began to cry as Letty frantically pulled at the obstruction.

"Be quiet, you silly girl," Catriona commanded, a cold, unnatural calm enveloping her. "Go and fetch the hatchet from the shed. Hurry." She stood behind Letty, helpless, the stair too narrow for her to lend her aid. They could not be dead, her darlings! They must be too frightened to call out. "They are too frightened to call out," she said, trying to convince herself.

With a reverberating *cr-r-a-ack* the tree shifted as a beam gave way beneath its weight. A huge limb shoved the tangled mass of smaller branches at Letty.

"It's not safe, my lady," cried Betsy. "The whole house'll be down next."

"Outside with you. Keep Lois out. Letty, my dearest, you cannot reach them this way. We must see what we can do from outside. Come, love."

She took Letty's scratched, bleeding hand and forced her down the stairs and out into the garden. The moon shone bright between fleeing clouds, then disappeared again. Stumbling through a litter of fallen tiles and broken branches, they sped round the side of the house.

The teasing moon illuminated the scene with pitiless clarity. Its roots riven from the sodden soil, the elm's massive trunk angled up to the shattered roof of the Dower House, its ravaged crown centered on the crushed wreck of the twins' chamber.

Letty tore her hand from Catriona's clasp and rushed to the tree. As she reached it, it moved again, another overloaded beam failing. She scrabbled at the creviced bark, straining for a fingerhold to pull herself up onto the only pathway to her children.

Catriona could not deceive herself any longer. Donald and Daphne were dead. Letty was all that was left to her. She ran to seize her daughter round the waist, to tear her from the deadly destroyer.

"No, Mama! Let me go!" Letty fought her with the strength of desperation. "Donald! Daphne!"

And then the men were there. Harry Talgarth easily pulled Letty away from the tree. Shrieking, she pounded him with her fists, then collapsed against his chest, tears coming at last, glinting in the moonlight. He held her as she shook with sobs.

Somehow Sir Gideon was atop the trunk. Catriona held her breath, fists clenched beneath her chin, as he balanced his way up the slope, wavering in every blast of wind. As he reached the first branch, the moon once more hid its face. When it returned, he was past the branch. On hands and knees he crawled up the narrowing trunk.

He slipped. Catriona's fingernails bit into her palms, an involuntary cry breaking from her throat. He caught himself, slithered past another limb, reached the house, and vanished into a jagged chaos of boughs and timbers snapped like matchsticks.

Darkness again. Suddenly the wind dropped. Into the stillness came a small, anxious voice.

"Mama?"

"Daphne!" Catriona swung round, trying to pierce the black night with her eyes, trying to believe she had not imagined the sound. "Daphne? My God, is it really you?"

The moon sailed clear of the clouds. There beside the shapeless mass of the elm's roots stood the twins, hand in hand, in coats, hats, and boots, consternation on their small faces.

Letty fainted.

Harry Talgarth lowered her to the ground and knelt beside her. "Mama!" wailed Donald.

"Grandmama!" Pulling her brother behind her, Daphne scrambled over the flattened fence and ran to meet Catriona. They both burst into tears as she convulsively hugged them to her. "What's wrong with Mama?"

"Is she dead?"

"Did the tree fall on her?"

"We didn't know it was going to fall."

"We only went to see the badger."

"Will she be all right?"

"Yes." She forced the words out. "Yes, she will be all right."

Miraculously Sir Gideon was beside her. "I'll look after these two. You go and see to your daughter." He gathered the twins into his arms and began to explain to them what had happened and why their mother had fallen into a swoon.

Letty was already stirring when Catriona reached her. She looked up and whispered, "Mama? The twins?"

"Perfectly safe, darling. I have half a mind to beat the little imps within an inch of their lives. They went to see the badgers, if you please!"

"But if they had not!" Letty cried, sitting up with Mr. Talgarth's assistance. They all glanced up at the ruin of the twins' chamber. A sudden dizziness hit Catriona as reaction to the horror set in.

"All's well that ends well." Harry Talgarth, prosaic but comforting, helped Letty to stand.

"Mama, Sir Gideon says we can live at the manor!" The twins dashed up to cling to their mother.

"Till the Dower House is mended."

Their voices seemed to come from a long way away. "Your turn to swoon, I think," said a soft, faintly amused voice in Catriona's ear. Sir Gideon took her arm. "Come, sit down and put your head between your knees."

"I never . . . swoon," she gasped, obeying the light pressure of his hand on her shoulder.

"I don't suppose Mrs. Rosebay makes a habit of it, either. You both have every excuse. While you are about it, so as not to waste time, let me tell you that we came across your maidservants on our arrival and I sent them up to the house to give word of your coming."

"What . . . brought you here?"

"The force of the wind made us uneasy, though I cannot claim to have foreseen anything like this near catastrophe. It seemed unwise to bring out a carriage, or even horses, in that gale, so we walked down—avoiding the copse, unlike your intrepid grandchildren."

"Intrepid? Foolhardy!" She raised her head to smile at him. "But thank God for it. I wonder whether they saw any badgers."

Sir Gideon laughed, his teeth gleaming white in the moonlight. The sky was clear now, a vault of stars, and the wind was no more than a fitful breeze. Catriona shivered.

"You're cold. Dash it, I took off my greatcoat before performing my circus act. Harry," he called, "where did I drop my coat?"

Harry came to join them, shrugging out of his coat. "I've no idea, coz. Pray take mine, Lady Catriona."

"We keep cloaks in the hall cupboard . . ."

"I cannot think it advisable, ma'am, to enter the house before we are able to assess the damage in the morning." Harry helped her don his warm, caped coat. "Gideon, shall I go home and bring a carriage?"

"The wind may rise again." The baronet had found his coat and was holding it for Letty to put on. "If the ladies feel up to it, we had best walk."

So they set out on foot up the hill to the manor. The twins raced ahead, still astonishingly full of energy. Letty walked briskly at Sir Gideon's side, chatting to him with her usual cheerfulness restored. In the rear Catriona trudged along, glad of the support of Mr. Talgarth's arm, for she was still shaken by the terrifying incident. She felt old.

The Dower House was unsalvageable. The builder Sir Gideon called in refused to vouch for the safety of the ground floor and advised razing the whole. Rebuilding was best started in spring, he said, and might with luck be completed by this time next year.

Catriona raised only a token protest to Sir Gideon's offer of hospitality. Not for a moment did she doubt the sincerity of his assurance that he'd be delighted to have her family about the place. *His* family, too, he reminded her. And to be still more closely related, she hoped. With him and Letty living in the same house, her matchmaking could not fail.

A wing was set aside for their use. Farm carts carried up the hill all of their belongings that could be safely rescued from the ruins. Within a week they had settled into the manor almost as though they had never left.

As the news spread, neighbors came to commiserate. Some of them, Catriona had scarcely seen since moving to the Dower House after Jeremy's funeral. Marchbank was some five miles from the nearest sizable house, and while ladies had occasionally called at the Dower House, the distance and their lack of a carriage to return calls had deterred visitors.

On the other hand, since Sir Gideon's arrival, several gentlemen had already ridden over to the manor to make the acquaintance of its new owner. Returning these calls, Sir Gideon and his cousin had made the ladies' acquaintance and had more than once been invited, in the country way, to stay and take potluck.

"It's time I gave a dinner party," he said to Catriona one afternoon, seeking her out in the small parlor where she was writing letters to her sisters. "Dare I hope that you will be my hostess?"

She set down her pen. "I don't know, Sir Gideon. *Do* you dare?"

"I do. Without a hostess, I might conceivably contrive, but I'm aware of my limitations. I've not the least notion of how to plan a dinner party."

Catriona laughed. "That is something of a backhanded compliment! Is the invitation to act as hostess a bribe to persuade me to plan for you?"

"Lord no, you teasing creature. You know me better, I trust."

"All the same," she said seriously, "it might be better if Letty and I simply joined your guests. I have no wish to figure among our neighbors as an encroaching female, unwilling to recognize that my time is past." She saw that he was about to protest and hurried on. "But that can be decided later. Have you a list of those you wish to invite?"

"Of those I wish to invite, and those I feel obliged to invite. Here. Harry has kept a tally of our visitors."

She ran her eye down the list, which was much as she expected except . . . "Lord and Lady Rosebay! I did not know you were acquainted with the Rosebays."

"His lordship called, and we returned his call. A most formal quarter of an hour! Is there some difficulty? If their coming will distress Letty—Mrs. Rosebay, I can perfectly well . . ."

"Oh no. You must not suppose that they have ever been unkind to her, only rather distant." She wanted him to understand Letty. "Her husband, Bartholomew, was one of several younger sons, you see, a handsome, hey-go-mad boy. He had a sister Letty's age and she had known him for years. She thought herself in love with him as soon as she was old enough to take such a romantic notion into her head. Jeremy and I hoped nothing would come of it, for he had no prospects and not a great deal of sense."

"You don't believe in romance?" he asked.

"Yes. No. I am not sure!" she said, flustered. "Not as a basis for marriage at that age."

"But you yourself must have been very young when you married."

"That is no argument for romance. I did not choose my husband, though I came to love him very much. But this is beside the point. I am attempting to explain to you any slight awkwardness with the Rosebays."

"I beg your pardon, Lady Catriona." The smile in Sir Gideon's eyes belied his grave apology. "I shall endeavor not to interrupt. So Letty fancied herself in love with this scapegrace?"

"She was just seventeen when Bart announced that his father had bought him a pair of colors and he was off to fight with Wellington in the Peninsula. At once Letty resolved to wed him before he left. His parents were not averse—there were Marches at Marchbank when the Rosebays were still peasants. Besides, as you have discovered, Jeremy was far from poor and her portion was good."

"A potent argument. How did you feel?"

"I was dismayed, I own. Bart seemed to me a care-for-nobody, and Letty too young to know her own mind. But, after all, I had never regretted marrying young. I decided I was being an overprotective mother. Jeremy was very much against the match but unable to hold out against Letty. How she persuaded Bart himself to take on such a responsibility remains a mystery!"

"Not at all. As he was about to leave the country, the responsibility was far in the unimaginable future, and I daresay he was flattered by her eagerness."

Though startled by his acuity and suspecting he was right, she said severely, "Or perhaps he was desperately in love. Be that as it may, they were wed scarce three weeks before he went off to war. Letty stayed with the Rosebays, but she was very unhappy, and when she discovered she was with child, she came home."

"And the Rosebays were affronted?"

"Not then, I believe. After all, it is natural to want to be with one's mother at such a time. However, after the twins were born, when the news came of poor Bart's death, they invited her to return. A matter of duty, I am certain, not of any affection for her or even for their son."

"The proper place for a widow is with her husband's family?"

"Precisely. My family would be horrified if I wished to return to Dunshannon." Never having considered the possibility, Catriona was saddened by this insight. She sighed. "Naturally Letty preferred to stay at Marchbank, where she was loved. Her refusal offended the Rosebays, though not deeply. They have continued to send the children birthday gifts, and when Jeremy died, they paid a visit of condolence. They even renewed their invitation to Letty."

"Which, of course, she once more refused."

"Of course. The reminder of Bart disturbed her deeply. I believe she had at last become reconciled to his death."

"She seems to me a cheerful young lady."

"Oh, she is." She did not want Sir Gideon to think Letty was still mourning Bartholomew. "She is quite recovered now, and she was never wont to let low spirits affect her demeanor or depress those of others."

"Admirable. She is delightful, a credit to you. She and the children have brought a much-needed liveliness to the house."

Such praise ought to have left Catriona elated. Instead she felt a horrid, inexplicable, sinking sensation. Hastily she returned to the plans for the dinner party.

Letty was miserable. Sir Gideon's dinner party, postponed several times for various reasons, was at last to take place the evening before his departure for Town. Tomorrow Harry Talgarth was leaving for London, and she was afraid she was going to miss him desperately.

Her struggle against her attraction to him, difficult enough at the Dower House, had grown a thousand times harder now that they lived at such close quarters. She was constantly conscious of his nearness, of his tall, lean, quiet strength, so different from Bart's swaggering impetuosity. His thick fair hair tempted her fingers to touch it. His intent blue eyes made her shiver inside.

If only he were not also amiable, sympathetic, and chivalrous! He had even befriended Donald and Daphne, and he had just that blend of firmness with kindness and interest in their concerns that they needed. Nonetheless, even for the children's sake, she would never marry again.

Of course, he might not offer for her. That would solve her problem neatly. Yet somehow the thought failed to cheer her.

And tonight she must wear a cheerful face. The last thing Mama needed was a mopish daughter. Serene, competent Mama, with her ready sense of humor, was in high fidgets over the dinner party. She had taken it into her head that in playing Sir Gideon's hostess she might be considered encroaching. As though the daughter of an earl could ever be thought encroaching! Even Lord Rosebay was only a baron.

Mama's other worry made more sense to Letty. They were two women sharing a household with two single men, even if their chambers were in opposite wings of the extensive manor. Sir Gideon's relationship with Papa made it acceptable—as long as no one discovered how distant that relationship was.

"It is silly to worry," Mama had said anxiously, "for I am past the age of being a subject for scandal, more than old enough to be your chaperon. All the same, pray wear a dark, simple gown—your forest green sarcenet will do very well—and strive to appear as *widowish* as possible. I shall wear my dark gray silk."

So Letty had Betsy pin up her hair and conceal it under a cornette cap with a minimum of lace. The maid went to help Lady Catriona. Letty stared at her despondent face in the looking glass. Practicing a smile, she recited to herself a list of her blessings, as Mama had taught her long ago. She had two healthy, happy, adorable children, a loving mother, a comfortable home, agreeable company, employment enough to occupy her time without ever becoming a burden.

And she'd never again have to lie in bed waiting with despair in her heart for—

"Mama?" Red curls poked around the door, then Donald came in, in his nightshirt, followed by Daphne in her shift. "We're ready for bed."

"Grandmama told us a story."

"We need a kiss."

Daphne examined her seriously. "I hope I'm pretty like you when I grow up, Mama."

As she kissed their soft, soap-scented cheeks, Letty's smile became genuine. "Off to bed with you now. I shall see that Cook saves a slice of chocolate gâteau for each of you." Those dreadful nights had been worth enduring since they had given her the twins.

Sleepy-eyed, they went off. Fastening around her neck her gold locket with a curl of Papa's hair inside, Letty went downstairs.

The dinner party went very well. For all her unaccustomed fidgets, Mama was accustomed to entertaining, for Papa had been a sociable man. Sir Gideon was a superb host, affable, solicitous of his guests' comfort without fussiness, readily taking his place among the gentry and not toadying to the Rosebays. And Harry moved from group to group, conversing with young and old, dividing his attention equally between plain and pretty . . .

Letty caught up her thoughts. It mattered not a jot to her whether Harry Talgarth spent his time chatting to the Master of Foxhounds about the local hunt or to the Master's flirtatious daughter about the next Assembly.

To her surprise, she enjoyed the occasion. She had known most of those present all her life. Contented though she had been at the Dower House, she had missed the social intercourse more than she had realized. When the front door closed behind the last guest, her spirits were still too high to think of seeking her bed.

"I shall not go up with you now, Mama," she said. "I am too restless to sleep. I believe I shall play the pianoforte for a little while. Tell Betsy not to wait up for me."

"Do not stay up too late, my love, if you wish to bid the gentlemen goodbye in the morning. You mean to leave early, do you not, Sir Gideon?"

"Yes, but not for the world would I drag you from your well-deserved slumber. I don't know how to thank you, Lady Catriona. You have established my credit for hospitality without the least effort on my part." He raised her hand to his lips.

Letty was astonished to see a blush on her mother's face—or perhaps it was a trick of the light, for the servants were moving about the hall snuffing candles. The color ebbed as quickly as it had appeared. She must have imagined it, she decided, as Mama and Sir Gideon said good night and went their separate ways.

She returned to the drawing room. She and one or two others had played after dinner, so the pianoforte was open. Searching out the slow movement of a Mozart sonata, she began to play. As she had expected, the music soothed her, and by the time she played the last chord, she was ready to retire.

"Bravo."

The quiet voice startled her. "Mr. Talgarth! I had no notion you were there."

He lounged by the fire, his long legs stretched before him, a glass in his hand. The rich red of claret shimmered as he raised it to her. "A last drop of wine for a nightcap. I beg your pardon for not warning you of my presence, but I did not wish to interrupt. You play well."

The simple compliment pleased her inordinately. To conceal her pleasure she said, "I should play better if I practiced more often. I am going up now. Shall I leave these candles for you?"

"No, I am done."

Setting down the half-full glass, he extinguished the candles on the mantel while she did the same for those by the pianoforte. Together they went out to the hall. Their bedside candles awaited them on the table at the foot of the stairs.

At the lamp that burned all night in the hall, he ignited a spill. He lit one of the candles, waited until the flame burned steady, then turned to hand it to Letty. As she reached for it, he abruptly set it down again, fumbling behind him, and pulled her into his arms.

His lips were on hers, warm, gentle, yet insistent. His hand caressed the nape of her neck, sending tremors down her spine. Then he pulled off her cap, scattered her pins so that her hair cascaded about her shoulders.

He raised his head long enough to murmur, "Glorious!" His eyes burned into hers, and then his mouth met hers again and her bones melted.

Time stood still.

"Letty. Laetitia. Gladness."

Was it his passionate whisper that brought her to her senses? She wrenched herself out of his arms. "Don't! Don't touch me! Don't *touch* me!"

She fled up the stairs, along dark passages, to the safety of her chamber, *her* chamber, hers alone, with a key in the door.

For hours Letty sat on the window seat, gazing blankly into the night. At last the chill penetrated her daze. Slowly, with numb fingers, she began to undress.

Her locket was gone. And her cap! Her hairpins, scattered on the floor of the hall.

With a dry sob, she wrapped a warm shawl about her and crept back down the stairs. The polished oak of the floor was bare, no betraying sign of cap or pins. Her locket, which could have dropped off at any time by chance, lay on the table, beside the flickering lamp. She picked it up.

The catch was undone. He had looked inside, had seen the lock of steel gray hair that must be her father's, that could not possibly be her young husband's.

What Harry might make of it, she was beyond guessing.

He was long gone when she awoke in the morning. When she rang, Betsy brought her tea and toast instead of the hot water she expected.

"Her ladyship said she's set the children their lessons, madam, and you're to lie abed long as you want. Oh, and here's a package Mr. Talgarth asked me to give you." She delved in the pocket of her apron.

Flustered, Letty took the small parcel. "I daresay he has left something for the twins. They will miss him. Thank you, Betsy. I shall get up in half an hour."

As soon as the chamber door closed behind the maid, Letty tore open the parcel: her cap, of course, and the hairpins—had he really called her hair glorious?

And a letter. She unfolded it with trembling fingers.

My dearest Letty—Give me leave to call you thus!—I depart for London with a heavy heart. Were our errand less important, were I able to tell my cousin the true reason I wish to stay—but I will not lie.

You are deeply offended, and rightly so, yet I meant no offense. Such ungentlemanly conduct is inexcusable, yet I dare to hope your tender heart will excuse me. I can only plead that you were irresistible. You must be aware of my admiration, and you surely cannot suppose that I would toy with your affections! My aim is honorable—to offer you my hand and my heart. If Laetitia will be my wife, Gladness will be mine forever.

Forgive, my love,
your most devoted humble servant,
Harry Talgarth

He did not understand! How could he understand? How could she tell him that marriage was what she feared?

At first Catriona was quite pleased to see her daughter moping. Letty undoubtedly missed Sir Gideon. So did Catriona. One quickly became accustomed to having gentlemen about the house, she told herself.

Then, one evening, returning to the drawing room with a book from the library, she found Letty in tears. Damp patches on the blue muslin she was embroidering showed where the drops that trickled down her cheeks had fallen.

"My darling!" Without another word, Catriona took the sewing from her, sat down on the sofa beside her, and drew her into her arms. Just as when she was a child with some childish hurt, she sobbed on her mother's shoulder. Just as when she was a child, Catriona ached for her grief.

Gradually the sobs stilled. Letty fumbled for a handkerchief and Catriona pressed one into her hand.

"Tell me."

"Oh, Mama, I am so unhappy!" Letty wailed. "He kissed me the night before he left for Town."

A cold shock took away Catriona's breath. So Sir Gideon did love Letty.

It was what she had hoped for. If she felt her heart had been riven in her breast, it was because she had not thought him so ungentlemanly as to force his attentions on Letty before they had come to an understanding. Had he proposed, a kiss would not make Letty cry. She was no inexperienced maiden.

Catriona struggled to calm herself and to gather her scattered wits. Letty, still sniffling and with an occasional hiccup, awaited comfort. "I cannot believe he is dishonorable. He must have meant to make an offer. Did you give him a chance?"

"I ran away . . ."

"There you are, then. He had to leave in the morning—he had appointments with several influential men. He will ask for your hand when he returns. Such matters are not to be entrusted to a letter."

"He left me a letter, Mama. He does want to marry me."

Catriona was baffled. "Then why are you unhappy, darling? Surely I am not mistaken. You are fond of Sir Gideon, are you not?"

"Oh yes, I am, but it was Harry—Mr. Talgarth who kissed me."

"But . . . but . . ." The weight that lifted from her was quite out of proportion to the discovery that Sir Gideon had not, after all, taken advantage of Letty. "Oh dear, and you have always disliked Mr. Talgarth, though I must say I have come to like him very well, and to respect him. However, I have frequently noticed that you are uncomfortable with him. My poor child, no wonder you are overwrought."

"I do not dislike him, Mama." Letty's voice was so soft as to be almost inaudible. "I . . . I hold him in great esteem. If he makes me uneasy, it is because . . . I think . . . I think I *wanted* him to kiss me."

"Gracious heaven, then why . . . ?"

"I don't want to *marry* him!" A huge sob shook her and tears again began to flow.

Catriona held her again, but she said quite severely, "You cannot marry Sir Gideon while you yearn for Harry Talgarth's kisses."

"I don't want to marry Sir Gideon. I don't want to m-marry anyone. I *h-hated* being married."

As light began to dawn, Catriona felt a terrible guilt. Why had she never guessed? She had failed Letty when she was most needed. Was it too late to heal the hurt? She held her close, rocking her and murmuring nursery words of comfort.

"I love him, Mama," Letty whispered into her shoulder, "but if I married him, he would . . . he would expect to . . . to share my bed, wouldn't he?"

Once she started, the sorry story poured out. Bart Rosebay, nineteen years old and off on a great adventure, had come drunk to his marriage bed. For Letty, losing her virginity had been painful and humiliating enough to make her cry. Bart had cursed her for a watering-pot and gone to sleep.

Every day of the three weeks before his departure, he had spent carousing with the friends who admired and envied his smart new uniform. His bewildered bride was left to face the curiosity and pity of his sisters, the polite indifference of his parents. If he came home at all at night, he was foxed and the dreadful experience repeated itself.

"I was going to kill myself before he came back from Spain," Letty blurted out. "But then there were the twins. And then he was killed. I was *glad* when he was killed, Mama. It was almost the worst of all, being happy that he was dead because I'd never have to . . . to let him do that again. Only the twins have made it bearable. Was I . . . was having me enough for you?"

"Oh, my darling, you would have been, had I needed compensation. You were an added joy. Your papa was the gentlest, most considerate, most loving of lovers, and from the first I. . . ." Her throat was too tight for speech. It was her turn to weep, for Jeremy and for the tender, passionate intimacy she would never know again.

Shocked, Letty put her arm around Catriona's shoulders and said helplessly, "Papa was different. Papa was the dearest man in the world."

Catriona fought for composure. What she said now might alter the entire course of her daughter's life. She took Letty's hands in hers.

"Papa was special, Letty, but not, I am certain, unique. You must not judge all men by your husband. He was young and heedless and in a ferment over going off to war. Papa and I should never have let you marry him."

Letty's lips quivered. "It was my fault, Mama. I, too, was young and heedless, and would not listen to you."

"That is what parents are for, to protect their children from their youth. We failed. It is not always an easy task."

"I know!" said Letty feelingly, and Catriona returned her smile, memories of the twins' scrapes flitting through her mind.

"Donald and Daphne obey Harry Talgarth," she observed.

"Yes." Letty was silent for a moment. "He is not a bit like Bart, is he?"

"Not a bit."

"You think I should marry him."

"You said you love him."

"I do. I do, but . . . I'm frightened, Mama."

"I cannot make up your mind for you," Catriona said gently.

"What if I accept him and then I find I cannot bear to . . . to be a proper wife to him? He will not understand. He will be hurt—I don't want to hurt him!—and he will hate me."

Catriona nodded thoughtfully. "Did Bart ever kiss you before you were married?" she asked.

"Yes, once," Letty admitted, puzzled.

"What did you feel?"

"A bit breathless. As if . . . as if something more ought to happen."

"And when Harry kissed you?"

Letty crimsoned and looked down at her hands. "As if the world had gone away and there was nothing left but him, and I only existed where he touched me."

"I doubt you will have any insuperable difficulties being a proper wife to him," said Catriona dryly. "Nonetheless, it is only fair that he should be warned before you accept his hand."

"Tell him about Bart?" Letty was appalled. "I cannot!"

"I shall, if you wish, but I believe you ought. His reaction will tell you a good deal about him, and you may change your mind. If he changes his, then you will be well rid of him! If not, then he will understand your fears and take care to dispel them."

"I will try, Mama." She kissed Catriona's cheek. "Shall I ever be as wise as you?"

As they tidied away their sewing, Catriona felt exhausted and far from wise. Letty's long-delayed disclosures were forcing her to confront her own feelings.

She was sorry for Sir Gideon's disappointment when he learned that Letty loved his cousin, but her chief emotion was relief. She could not have borne to see him married to her daughter, because she loved him herself.

And could anything be more foolish than a middle-aged widow in love?

"Fireworks?" squealed Daphne. "Real fireworks?"

"Sshh." Harry Talgarth grinned. "It's a secret. We've been abroad so long we haven't celebrated Guy Fawkes Day for years, but it's Gideon's birthday and I want to make a proper do of it."

"His birthday tomorrow!" Catriona dropped her sewing in dismay.

"His fortieth. I took the liberty of writing from London to invite those of our neighbors who have children."

"Heavens, I must speak to Cook. I wish you had told me sooner."

"You are not to do a thing, ma'am. Gideon has already made arrangements for the traditional gathering of tenants and villagers as Mrs. Rosebay described it to us."

Ignoring his slight flush as he spoke Letty's name, Catriona cried, "Yes, but a bonfire and mulled ale are scarce sufficient entertainment for our . . . for *your* other guests, even with fireworks."

"Can we have the bonfire, too?" Donald asked anxiously. "As well as the fireworks?"

"We've been building it."
"And making a guy."
"In *splendid* clothes."
"And we've got chestnuts and potatoes to roast in the ashes."
"But if you want just fireworks, that's all right," Daphne assured Harry earnestly. "That will be a special treat, even better than a bonfire."
"We've never seen fireworks," Donald confirmed.
"We shall most certainly have both," Harry promised. "In fact, Gideon insisted upon inspecting the bonfire the moment we arrived, before coming into the house, which is why he has not yet put in an appearance."
Daphne heaved a deep sigh of pure joy. "Thank you, sir. Grandmama, please may we go to the stables and finish the guy?"
"Yes, but put on your coats first." As they ran off, Catriona started to rise, saying again, "I must go and speak to Cook."
"Indeed, ma'am, there is no need. Besides mulled ale there will be potatoes and chestnuts, not to mention gingerbread, apple turnovers, meat pies, and cocoa for the children. I warned the people I invited to expect simple fare, and I brought from Town the ingredients for punch for the gentlemen and negus for the ladies."
"I see you have everything under control." She subsided, inviting him to sit. "All the same, I wish you had told me sooner about Sir Gideon's birthday. I should have liked to give him some small gift. He has been so very generous to all of us," she added self-consciously and hurried on, "are not fireworks dangerous?"
"They will be set off down by the lake, to avoid any possibility of fire, and I have hired a man from Vauxhall Gardens to be in charge."
"How efficient you are, Mr. Talgarth! You must have gone to considerable expense, I fear."
"Nothing I cannot afford, ma'am. When Gideon made his fortune in India, I was not idle." Abruptly he stood up and moved to lean on the mantel, gazing down into the fire. "I am well able

to support a wife," he said in an agitated voice. "Is Mrs. Rosebay very angry with me?"

Catriona chose her words with care. "Not angry, no. She is . . . disturbed and afraid."

"Afraid!" He groaned. "That I should have made her fear me!"

"She does not fear you, but herself. She will explain, but you must be patient with her."

He swung round eagerly. "Then I may hope? When may I see her?"

"At dinner, if not before," she said, smiling. "She is not trying to avoid you. However, if I may advise you, treat her as no more than a friend for the present. Let her choose her own time for explanations. Do not press her, Mr. Talgarth."

"I shall not, I swear it." He took her hand and raised it to his lips. "You are the best of mothers, and I pray I may soon call myself your son. Will you not call me Harry, ma'am?"

She acquiesced, and he departed, a spring in his step, leaving her feeling unutterably aged. His mother! He was near thirty. And she was two years older than Sir Gideon—two years eight months to be precise. Nearly three years. What would be nothing if he were the elder was in fact an impassable gulf.

The weather was perfect, clear, with a hint of frost and a crescent moon sailing in the starry sky. Warm in her old cloak, Letty had to admit that with an excited twin hanging on to each hand, she was enjoying herself.

She stepped back as the seven-foot tower of kindling, faggots, and logs flared up. The heat from the bonfire was intense. Its ruddy light shone on a circle of small, thrilled faces and, behind them, on the parents enjoying their offspring's rapture. The Marchbank servants passed among the crowd with trays of food and drink.

Every now and then, Letty caught a glimpse of Harry. With her mother and Sir Gideon, he was circulating among the guests, gentle and common, making sure everyone had what they wanted. He stopped to exchange a few words with her, as casual and noncommittal as he had been since his return to Marchbank the day before. Had he changed his mind before she even revealed her secret?

"The guy's on fire!" someone whooped as the flames reached the top of the pyre.

"We made it!" Donald screeched. "We made the guy."

"Aahhh." There was a collective sigh of satisfaction as the center of the fire gave way and the traitor Guy Fawkes dived to his yearly doom.

"Look!"

The cry was taken up. "Look, down by the lake!"

Those on that side of the dying fire turned. The rest moved to join them. Down by the lake, three Catherine wheels spun, sparkling red, yellow, and green. Daphne and Donald were by no means the only children jumping up and down and squealing. Indeed, Letty barely managed to limit herself to a gasp of delight. She, too, had never seen a firework show.

"So that's what you were up to!" Sir Gideon's laughing voice came from behind her. She glanced round, saw Harry Talgarth standing there, and quickly turned back to the fireworks.

"Ten years' worth of birthday celebrations wrapped into one," he said. "My man has been scurrying about to set them up since darkness fell, to keep the secret from you."

As if the man from Vauxhall Gardens knew he had everyone's attention, he set off a flurry of fire-lances, gold and silver stars, and Roman candles. Rockets whizzed glittering into the sky; squibs and crackers banged; serpents crawled along the ground, spitting sparks; the smell of gunpowder drifted up the slope. Even as Letty wondered at the ghastly, ghostly sight of faces illuminated by the glare of blue lights, she was very much aware of Harry standing close behind her.

At last there came a pause. "Keep your fingers crossed," he murmured in her ear. "The fellow wasn't sure he could get the set piece right in a hurry in the dark, with untrained men helping him."

Then to one side appeared the French tricolor. Beside it a ship in full sail blossomed. Opposite, another ship took shape, followed by the white ensign of the Royal Navy flying from its stern. The ships shot balls of fire at each other until *le drapeau tricolore* winked out. The French ship faded and a cheer went up from the audience. The British ship spluttered out, and then the ensign, but before it was quite extinguished, a fiery red, white, and blue Union Jack flourished in the center.

The crowd roared a huzza.

"Capital!" said Harry. "Gideon fought at Trafalgar, you know."

Letty turned and impulsively held out her hands to him. "It was simply splendid, Harry—Mr. Talgarth," she said as he took them in a gentle clasp. "I shall never forget it."

The twins, having watched the last spark die away, hung on his arms, forcing him to drop her hands, to her relief. "It was . . . it was *slap up,*" Daphne breathed.

"Famous, sir," Donald agreed.

"Mama, may we go and see if the potatoes and chestnuts are done?"

"Don't burn your fingers."

"We won't." They dashed off.

"I must go down to thank the men," Harry said, adding tentatively, "will you walk with me?"

He had not changed his mind! Letty froze, thoughts racing frantically: she loved him; by going with him alone now, she would prove that she trusted him; it was not fair to keep him waiting for an answer; perhaps—surely!—telling him her doubts and fears would be easier in the dark; she loved him.

"Yes, I will come," she whispered, and despite the chatter of the crowd, he heard her.

He took her hand again, holding it as if she were a child, making her feel safe and protected. Hand in hand, in silence, they walked down the hill. As he distributed thanks and shillings among the undergardeners and stableboys, she added her words of praise, scarcely knowing what she was saying.

Harry sent the men to get their share of meat pies and mulled ale. Letty found herself strolling along the edge of the lake, her hand on his arm.

"You had my letter?" he asked, his tone conversational on the surface, yet with an undercurrent of deep feeling.

She nodded, realized he could not see her, and said, "Yes. Th-thank you for returning my locket and . . . and the other things."

"I have nothing to add to what I wrote to you, except that I shall not press you for an answer, but if you choose to honor me with your confidence, I shall hold it infinitely precious."

As they reached the jetty, she stopped and turned away from him to face the lake. The still surface was bright with reflected moon and starlight; beneath, the dark depths lay undisturbed. Then a fish jumped, falling back into a widening circle of ripples. The reeds rustled, and from the far side of the lake came the whistle of an otter.

The brief disruption of the fireworks was over. The night world returned to its familiar course.

Hugging her cloak about her, Letty took a deep breath and let it out on a long sigh. "I was only married for a very short time," she said without looking at the silent figure who stood beside her, not touching her. "Only three weeks, really, before he went away. But then I had the twins, so . . . so you know that I . . . that we. . . ."

"I know, of course. I have always known, and that in itself makes no difference." Harry paused, then went on hesitantly, "You never speak of him, as your mother does of Sir Jeremy. Do you still mourn him so deeply?"

"No!" The denial exploded from her, followed by the dreadful confession. "When I heard of his death, I felt like a bird set free from a cage."

"What did he do, that his death came as a release?"

The suppressed violence in his voice reminded her that he had survived in the wild places of the world. She felt almost as if she ought to protect Bart.

"He was . . . not very kind. I suppose he did not find me attractive. He was out a great deal, and when he did come home, he . . . he hurt me. Not on purpose. I cannot believe it was deliberate. He just . . . took what he wanted without . . . without caring . . . without even noticing that he hurt me." She bit her lip hard to stop a sob.

"My poor, poor girl," said Harry very quietly, not moving.

Letty turned and moved into his arms. She laid her cheek against his chest. The gentle, undemanding strength of his embrace comforted her, kept her safe, protected her from harm. He held her, and the tension ebbed away, the memories faded. Her whole reality was his warmth. A sense of vitality held in check, of passion under firm control.

"I lovc you," hc whispered into her hair. "I want you. You are beautiful, and I cannot pretend I don't want you in every way. I shall never hurt you. Can you learn to trust me?"

She looked up at him, his shadowed eyes, resolute mouth, face pale in the faint reflected light. With one finger she touched his cheek, then his lips. "Harry," she murmured, "I love you." Her hands crept to the back of his neck, pulled his head down to her.

His kiss set her on fire.

White ash, black charcoal, and a few red-glowing coals were all that was left of the bonfire. Charred potatoes and sweet, floury chestnuts had been consumed with gusto. While tenants and villagers thanked Sir Gideon for the treat, Catriona shepherded the gentry back to the house.

She had provided light refreshments in the drawing room. One or two ladies took a cup of tea, and one or two gentlemen a glass of wine, but most had eaten and drunk their fill by the bonfire. It was time to take weary children home to bed—the twins sat nodding in a corner, for once exhausted by the excitement. The guests were just waiting for their host's return to the house before taking their leave.

Catriona moved from group to group, chatting with her friends and neighbors, her mind elsewhere. Harry Talgarth and Letty were missing. Harry might be with Sir Gideon, bidding farewell to the local people, but Letty had no reason to do so. More likely the two were together.

All Catriona could do now was pray she had given the right advice.

Sir Gideon came in. Meeting her gaze across the room, he smiled. She wondered unhappily how cast down he would be if Letty and Harry came to an understanding. Her answering smile must have reflected her thoughts, for he frowned in concern. Then his guests surrounded him, and the vicar's wife spoke to her, demanding at least part of her attention.

The first carriages had just been sent for when the missing pair entered the drawing room. Letty's radiant face told her mother everything.

Departing guests fell silent and stopped their movement toward the door as Catriona met Letty in the middle of the room.

"Mama! You were right."

They hugged each other, tears in green eyes and blue, hearts too full for words. Harry spoke briefly to Sir Gideon, who joined mother and daughter while Harry went to the twins' corner. He knelt there talking to them for a moment, then brought them with him, an arm about each sleepy, confused child's shoulders. Catriona took their hands, and Harry moved to Letty's side, putting an arm about her waist.

Sir Gideon held up his hand to ask for a silence he already had. "As you may have guessed," he said dryly, "I have an announcement to make. It gives me the greatest pleasure to inform you that my cousins, Letty Rosebay and Harry Talgarth, are engaged to be married."

"Grandmama, does that mean we'll havc a daddy?" Donald piped up.

"Will Mr. Talgarth be our daddy?" Daphne asked.

"Yes, my loves."

The twins exchanged a glance. "Bang *up!"* they chorused.

Everyone laughed and crowded round with felicitations. Gradually the good wishes turned into goodbyes, and Sir Gideon ushered his guests out to the hall. Letty and Harry together took the twins up to bed.

Catriona lingered in the drawing room, standing by the fireplace, warming her hands. She felt cold, hollow, more alone than she had ever been in her life.

Sir Gideon was losing both the girl he loved and the cousin who was more like a younger brother, with whom he had traveled the world. He had taken the news well, his disappointment well-hidden. Catriona vowed that Letty should never see her loneliness, only her joy in her daughter's happiness.

From the hall came a last flurry of goodbyes, the sound of the front door closing. Catriona recognized Sir Gideon's footsteps behind her, but she continued to gaze into the flickering flames, her head bowed, unwilling for him to see her despondency. He came to stand beside her, leaning against the mantelpiece.

As if he read her mind, he said, "You won't lose her, you know, her and the twins. Harry means to make his home here at Marchbank. There's plenty of room for two families."

"Two families?" Startled, she glanced up to meet the steady regard of his dark eyes. "What do you mean?"

"Well, I shan't insist on children, but if we were to produce one or two, I shan't complain."

"We?"

"I'm hoping you'll marry me, Catriona."

Her heart began to race, thundering in her ears. "But I am forty-two!" she cried tragically.

"An excellent age. I look forward to it."

"Nearly forty-three."

"I trust I shall reach that, too, in the not-far-distant future."

"But you are only forty and you can never catch up."

"Not catch up, but grow closer and closer. At present my age is roughly ten-elevenths of yours. When you are forty-eight and I am forty-five, I shall be eleven-twelfths your age. And—"

"You are laughing at me, Gideon!" she said, indignant. "I never learned fractions."

"Then let me explain. Imagine cutting a cake into twelve slices. Each slice will be smaller than if—"

"Pray don't trouble yourself to explain." She looked away from his mirthful face. "Do you truly wish to marry me?"

"I do." He sounded utterly serious.

"Because you cannot have Letty?"

"Letty! Good gad, woman, she's young enough to be my daughter."

"Not unless you were excessively precocious," she said tartly. "Anyway, that is no barrier to love."

"Catriona, why in heaven's name should you think me in love with Letty?"

"You have told me several times how charming you find her and how much you enjoy having the twins about the house."

"My dear, I was under the impression that the way to a woman's heart is to praise her children, not to mention her grandchildren."

"Oh." Feeling foolish, Catriona peeked up at him sideways. He looked just as good-natured and gallant and altogether attractive as always. "I thought you would be the perfect husband for her," she confessed.

"Not for her; for you. I have written proof, my skeptical love." Gideon took a paper from the inside pocket of his coat and unfolded it, handling it with care. "See," he said, holding it out to her, "a special license. I obtained it while we were in London, and the names on it are Gideon March and Catriona March."

"Gideon, how could you!"

He grinned. "You may justifiably condemn me as precipitate and overconfident, conceited even." He paused, but she failed to take advantage of the permission. "However, though the banns will do very well for Harry and Letty, at our age we cannot wait so long."

"You said you do not mind about my age!"

"*Our* age, my sweet, or our ages, if you insist. Catriona, my dear love, will you marry me?"

Jeremy had called her his dear love. She felt tears rise to her eyes, and she whispered, "I want to, oh, so very much, but I feel dreadfully disloyal."

"To Jeremy? My dear, I know you loved him, and I don't expect you to forget him. I do believe you have room in your heart for me, too."

"He always wanted me to be happy."

"Then I shall do my best to fulfill his wishes," he said gently, "if you will marry me. Have you any further difficulties to raise?"

"You don't just need me to be your hostess?"

"Catriona, you try my patience! *That* is a role you fill very well without my needing to wed you. Any more reasons against marrying me?" As she shook her head, he enquired hopefully, "I suppose you cannot think of any reasons *for?*"

"Only one." Her face burning, she turned away from him. "I love you."

"That will do for a start," he said philosophically, but with a laugh in his voice. He came up behind her and put his arms around her waist.

A frisson of desire shook her, and she leaned back against him. "There is another reason," she admitted in a strangled voice. "I *want* you."

"My odds are improving." His hands slid up her body to cup her breasts.

"And I cannot imagine life without you."

He bent his head to nuzzle her neck. Passion exploded within her. With a moan, she turned in his arms. "I can't wait, Gideon. Must we?"

"No, love. After all, we are both *mature* adults." He picked her up, and disregarding the scandalized servants, he carried his respectable widow up the stairs.

A Betting Affair

by Marissa Edwards

"You have a pearl of a daughter, Duchess, to throw such a gala to celebrate her mother." Lady Clarendon looked around her at the crowd of people standing together in clumps chatting gaily and nibbling hors d'oeuvres in the Duchess of Ashford's gold salon.

"You are kind to say so, Lady Clarendon." The Duchess of Ashford smiled and raised a quizzical eyebrow. "Shall we hope it catches the fashion? Mothers need to be appreciated every now and again."

Lady Clarendon laughed and agreed. "Most of your friends are here and all of the family, I think?"

"Yes. Jessica was very thorough in her invitations. It seems everyone has come save one of the duke's brothers. His gout was acting up too much for him to travel, poor man."

Lady Clarendon tsk-tsked. "A shame. But Lady Jessica is—"

The duchess's sharp ears heard her major-domo announce the name she had been waiting all evening to hear. Glad to escape Lady Clarendon's questions, the Duchess of Ashford smiled sweetly and said, "Would you excuse me, Lady Clarendon? Stomes has just announced a late guest I must see to." She reached to clasp one of Lady Clarendon's hands. "I am so pleased you were able to come, my dear. I shall speak with you again in a bit." She patted Lady Clarendon's hand and made her escape, moving through her guests, speaking here and there as she made her way regally toward her major-domo and her late arrival.

With difficulty, Lady Clarendon nodded and prevented frustration from appearing on her face. She craned to see who the late arrival was. She had almost put her question about Lady Jessica and her new husband to the duchess. Everyone knew there was something havey-cavey going on between the two, and Lady Clarendon wanted to see what the duchess might say about them.

Lady Clarendon stifled a gasp. Speak of the devil: the late arrival was none other than the tall, attractive, chestnut-haired Marquess of Blackburn, Lady Jessica's husband—by the Church's books at any rate. Lady Clarendon turned to her husband, just coming up with a glass of orgeat for her, and whispered in disapproval, "If he were going to come, he could at *least* have been punctual! How very rude."

In an undertone, her husband asked her the question most of the duchess's guests, also surreptitiously surveying the marquess, were wondering: "Do you think Lady Jessica invited him?"

The Marquess of Blackburn stood, resplendent in a Spanish-brown coat, buff breeches, and shining Hessians, quizzing glass raised.

Aware that many eyes were on them, the duchess greeted the marquess. "Blackburn! It was good of you to come and honor an old lady."

The Marquess of Blackburn let fall his glass and bowed over the duchess's hand. "Never call yourself that, Duchess. It doesn't do you justice."

The duchess tucked her arm in his and took him round to speak to several groups of her friends. Finally she drew him toward the tables of food and drink against the wall. There she signaled a footman to pour the marquess a glass of wine.

The marquess gave the duchess a wry face and lowered his voice. "As I suspect you know, I fear I've an ulterior motive for presenting myself here tonight. I'm certain you can guess what it is since I assume you are behind the fact that I received an invitation? And may I thank you for this opportunity to speak to Jessica, though I'm equally certain this is not the place to try to do it? I take it you're aware I've had no luck trying to meet or speak with her elsewhere. Nor have notes carried to her served me any better." He sighed with a trace of exasperation and almost ran his hand through his chestnut curls.

The duchess shook her head and also sighed. She placed several small cakes on a plate for her son-in-law. "She can be stubborn when she gets her mind made up, Blackburn. Like her mother there, I fear. And you, unless I miss my guess." She gave him a penetrating look.

The marquess grinned back at her and chuckled. " 'Tis so."

The duchess returned his smile. "She went to check on replenishing the tarts ages ago. She should be back any moment." The duchess started to call Lord Tremaine over to join them, very conscious that she did not want Blackburn to appear excluded even for an instant, when she saw her daughter come through the doorway with a footman bearing a large tray of tarts. "Ah. Here she is. Gently, Blackburn.

"My dear, you've been an age. People are complaining they haven't gotten more than three words out of you all evening. Now. I shall attend to the tarts and the rest of the hors d'oeuvres for a time while you play more of the hostess. Yes, yes, go. Don't look at these tables for the next hour! I won't have you in the kitchens the whole evening." She gave her daughter a slight push in Blackburn's direction and turned to direct the footman in putting out the tarts.

The Marquess of Blackburn observed his wife's shock, quickly masked with polite indifference, as she came face to face with him.

"Good evening, Blackburn." She gave him her hand.

He was also surprised at her coolness, and her use of his surname rather than his first name struck him with the force of a blow. "Hello, Jess." He bowed smoothly, playing her little game, and obediently kissed her hand. "You're as beautiful as ever." He raised his eyes to pass admiringly over her tawny tresses, her large blue-gray eyes with their long, dark lashes, and her slim, curvaceous figure, outlined to perfection in her gown of dark rose silk, cut low to set off her creamy shoulders and bosom.

The Duke of Ashford lounged over to his duchess's side and asked quietly, "Elsa, what are you up to? You did not, surely, invite him here. They will end by brawling in the center of the room and knocking down who-knows-how-many guests."

"You sound as if you already know the answer to your question, Judson. So why do you ask? Have you had a tart, dear? Cook truly did surpass herself."

The duke sighed with a slight smile. "I quite agree. I've had two."

The duchess cast him a glance under her lashes. "Besides, I knew you would be keeping your prudent eye upon them."

"Hmph." Without saying whether he would or he wouldn't, the duke lounged away to mingle with more of his guests.

The duchess smiled after her husband and returned her attention to the tarts.

Jessica's blue eyes, to the Marquess of Blackburn's disappointment, remained emotionless except for a faint questioning look.

In answer, Blackburn said, "I wonder if I might have a few minutes in private with you, Jess. You must know I've been trying to speak with you for some time."

"As you must know that I have been trying to avoid such a communication. I don't believe we have a thing to speak about, Blackburn. If you'll excuse me?" She gave him a polite smile and began to move off. "I have guests to attend to."

The marquess laid his hand on her arm and drew her back to his side. He bent his head toward her and lowered his voice. "Listen to me, Jess. When are you going to stop being in a pelter and come home? You know you are just living with your parents long enough to goad me into dancing attendance on you. What is it you want me to be? A fop who caters to your every whim?"

Jessica's blue eyes began to flash. "I don't give a fig what you are, Blackburn!" she whispered fiercely. "You err. I'm not doing this to goad you into paying me more attention. To put it simply, living with you makes me unhappy. I do not want to be unhappy. Therefore, I do not wish to live with you any longer.

"I am going to find a gentleman who *wants* to spend his time in my company because he enjoys being with me—because he likes *me*. Not a cavalier whose true first home—the place he can usually be found, day or night—is White's!

"If I'd known what it would be like being married to you—if I'd known what you thought marriage was—I wouldn't have married you. Now I fear we are resigned to the marriage, for neither my family, nor I myself, nor, indeed, your family would countenance the scandal of a divorce.

"Tomorrow, I am moving into my own town house. I consider our marriage one of convenience only. I am sorry for it. You shan't ever have a legitimate heir now, but I give you leave to find your pleasure where you may. I certainly shall!"

In the shocked silence that followed her words, Jessica tried to shake off Blackburn's restraining hand. Her blue eyes locked with his dumbfounded hazel eyes. Icily she whispered, "Release me!"

"Is everything all right here, my dear?" asked the Duke of Ashford pleasantly. "Blackburn, can I get you another tart? The duchess has made me eat two already." The duke eyed Blackburn's grip on his daughter's wrist pointedly.

Reddening, Blackburn relinquished Jessica's arm.

"He has another engagement to attend, Father. He was on the point of leaving. Good night, Blackburn. I really must tend to my guests." Jessica brushed past her husband and began to mingle among her guests, fluttering from group to group.

The duke clapped Blackburn on the shoulder and began to move with him toward the salon door. "That's too bad. I wanted to chew over with you the points of that new filly Tattersall's just got in."

They stepped outside the salon.

"Another time, perhaps. Good evening, Blackburn. You still know your way out, I think?"

Under his father-in-law's cool regard, Blackburn felt a fool. Grimly he replied, "I do, sir! Good night!"

The duke watched his son-in-law stalk down the staircase and leaned to see him snatch his cape from Stomes. "Poor devil." He chuckled and reentered his salon.

His son-in-law's thoughts were not so generous.

Spoiled! He has spoiled her abominably! thought Blackburn, grinding his teeth as he leapt up in his carriage and the footman slammed the door behind him. "Oh, t'hell with her." He banged the ceiling of the carriage viciously with his knuckles and let down the window to shout, "To White's! A guinea if you get me there in five minutes!"

The marquess sat back with the lurch of the carriage as John Coachman slapped the reins and attempted to win his guinea. But Blackburn didn't wish to go to White's for once in his life. He knew if he wasn't stepping over the threshold in five minutes, he was very likely to change his mind and go home. And there he'd make a morose evening out of it, just he and his decanter, mooning over Jess. Surely she could not mean the things she had just said!

"Devil take her!" The marquess raised his arm and thumped the ceiling again, hard. "Faster, man!" he shouted at the window, though he doubted the fellow could hear him. It was just as well he couldn't, for he knew he was acting like a madman.

The carriage pulled up, careening before White's, and the marquess flung open the door himself and jumped down before the footman could run out and let down the steps.

Without consulting his watch, Blackburn tossed a guinea at his coachman and all but ran inside almost before the footman could open the door for him.

His coachman shook his head after him, bit his guinea, and slapped the reins again, easing the horses down the street to the spot where he usually waited for his master.

As the marquess strode in upon his friends, he allowed the clouds of smoke and shouts and greetings of "Blackburn!" to soothe him and push his encounter with Jessica to the back of his mind. Someone pounded him on the back and thrust a drink in his hand, and he gulped thirstily. She *couldn't* have meant what she said. She was simply still angry with him. All he need do was continue to wait, until she got over her anger.

He called for his drink to be filled and moved to stand behind a good friend of his and watch the card play. He shook his head when Lord Endicott signaled that he could enter the play if he wished. He knew better than to gamble when he was in this humor—better just to watch and talk and perhaps drink.

The game ended, and Lord Wainsby rose, throwing down his cards and yielding his place at the table. "Too high for my luck this night," the stout gentleman muttered.

"Wainsby, my good fellow." The marquess claimed his friend in conversation.

Wainsby's boyish face lit at the sight of the marquess, and he clapped Blackburn on the shoulder and shook him. "Blackburn, I didn't see you come in. Intent on my cards, I s'pose. What news? Ho! Do I see you looking a trifle bedeviled?"

The sudden gleam in the marquess's hazel eyes warned Wainsby off the subject of Blackburn's mood. Quickly Wainsby answered himself. "No, no. Of course not. Must be the light in here. 'Tis casting tricky shadows over everything. Or you could, of course, be sickening for something, eh? That could be it. Been out in any downpours of late? That always gives people the ague or some such silly ailment, and first thing you know the thing's carried them off. And Lord! It's easy enough to get caught out in a downpour this time of year—"

"Wainsby." Ignoring his friend's nervous blathering, the marquess cut him off to change the subject to a safer topic. "I hear there's a new filly at Tattersall's. Have you seen her?"

Wainsby smiled with relief and nodded. "I have indeed."

Blackburn indicated a table with two empty chairs, and they seated themselves. "Is she anything to look at? Tell me about her."

"She's a beauty, and she'd be a good addition, my friend. I'd buy her if I had the blunt."

Wainsby began to describe the filly, and the two gentlemen embarked on a profound discussion of horses that kept a footman busy keeping their glasses filled. Thus they dispatched agreeably the better part of three hours.

Some time around one o'clock in the morning, Wainsby called it an evening.

Blackburn looked about him and, not seeing anyone else he felt like keeping company with, slowly agreed with Wainsby, drained his glass, and offered to drive him home.

Having dropped his friend off, the marquess still did not want to go to a house that was empty save for servants. However, since he could see little alternative, he went, hoping he had drunk enough to send him to sleep as soon as he removed his clothes and lay down. He had had his fill of lying awake, restlessly tossing and turning, remembering and thinking of Jess.

He did go to sleep as soon as his dark head touched the pillow. But it was only to have a nightmare about living the rest of his life without his tawny-haired, blue-eyed, usually fun-loving Jess.

The Ashford family, gathered in their sitting room before going to bed, sat talking over the evident success of the evening's party.

"And Mother," asked Jessica, eyeing the duchess suspiciously, "did you invite Blackburn? I know it wasn't Father, and I don't believe even Blackburn would barge in upon a rout given in honor of someone's mother unless he'd been invited."

"My dear, you did not tell me not to, and he *is* a member of the family," replied the duchess innocently. "I suppose I thought he'd been left off the invitation list by accident."

"Coming it a bit strong there, Elsa," commented the duke, intent on lighting his cheroot.

His wife threw him a scowl.

"Oh, Mother! How could you! You of all people know what an impasse we're at. I've been living with you for the past I-don't-know-how-many months rather than with him, and you know I've denied him admittance and declined every note he's sent in. You must have known I left him off the list deliberately. How *could* you! What possible purpose could you have had in mind?"

"But he is a member of the family, Jessica. It would have looked exceedingly odd if he hadn't at least put in an appearance at a party everyone knew you had planned."

"Faugh!" exclaimed Jessica rudely.

"I know you don't give the snap of your fingers for what society may think—and neither do I—but you must at least give the *illusion* that you are observing the proprieties, my love, or you will find yourself being cut everywhere. And that is *not* the fate I wish for *my* daughter.

"I hope you will strive to remember that little piece of advice at the end of this week after you are set up in your little town house. I cannot think that is a good idea." The duchess put up her hands to forestall her daughter's protestations. "Yes, I *know* you have hired a companion. It's just that the temptation to— Temptation is just too great, my dear, that's all. I hope I am not going to be sorry I sanctioned this," she murmured, as if talking to herself.

Jessica flung out of her chair. "Oh, Mother. There is nothing in that to worry about. I am going to bed. I'll see you both in the morning. Good night."

"Good night, Jessica. I do hope you know how very proud I was tonight of having a daughter who thought so much of me she gave a party in my honor," answered her mother softly.

"Oh, Mother," Jessica choked. She ran to bend over her mother and kiss her cheek. "I do know."

Jessica dropped another light kiss on top of her father's head and left the sitting room.

" 'Night, Jess," returned the duke. He puffed on his cheroot in silence for several minutes and then complimented his wife. "That was a nice bit, that bit about 'hoping you wouldn't be sorry you sanctioned her town house.' Wild horses couldn't keep her from moving in now."

"Did you think so? Thank you, my dear. Nothing will set up Blackburn's back more. Once they both discover how much opportunity she has to misbehave in the freedom of that house, Blackburn will appreciate that he needs to *do* something to make her come home."

"You're playing with fire," intoned the duke, taking his last puff on the cheroot and stubbing it out.

"Pish. Don't be such an old woman, Judson. Come. Are you finished with that thing? Let's go to bed. My back is killing me." She waved the duke before her out of the salon.

"Oh?" he said. "I happen to know just the trick to improve aching backs!"

Chuckling together, the Duke and Duchess of Ashford retired.

Jessica woke early the next morning and, not being able to go back to sleep, got up. She had not slept well, for seeing her husband again had disturbed the peace of mind she had been able to achieve by cutting him out of her life and pretending he did not exist.

She slipped on her light blue wrapper, sat down at her dressing table, and began to brush her hair. He *had* looked handsome, she thought unwillingly. What was it he had said to her? "Beautiful as ever, Jess." Or something close to that. She couldn't help a little smile of flattered pleasure. She could've said the same to him—but she wouldn't give him the satisfaction.

She frowned. He could at least have had the decency to gain a paunch or allow his muscles to become loose and flabby so he wouldn't be so devilishly attractive. If that weren't just like him! A handsome blackguard.

But there was still no talking to the man—he had proved that again last night. She had talked and talked and talked at him, she felt, trying to explain how she felt about all the time he was spending at his clubs. He had just laughed, joked, "The honeymoon is over," and kissed her goodbye. Gentleman Jack's during the day, White's at night. It had got to the point that she felt he was never home, though she also felt ridiculous, at first, complaining about it: how could a husband never be at home?

And, at first, she thought the reason he went out so much was due to something she was or wasn't doing. She thought if she could discover what that something was and remove it or provide it, he would spend more time at home or, at any rate, with her, the way he had when they were courting. She really did not understand. When they were courting, and during their honeymoon, they had been inseparable. What had changed? What had she done? Or not done?

She had wracked her brain trying to think of entertainments

and worn herself to a thread trying to search out invitations to functions that would appeal to him, regardless of whether she herself might want to partake of them or attend them.

Then she had realized that it wasn't anything she was or was not doing. What it was, was her husband's view of married life: he thought he was doing what a married man did. And as she looked at the husbands around her, Jessica was shocked to discover that he was only spending his time the way most other husbands did. It seemed to Jessica, as she observed other couples, that once one was married and the honeymoon over—just as her husband had laughed and declared—one ceased spending time with one's spouse and spent it instead with one's cronies, one's cicisbeo or doxy, or one's court of the same, if one were fair enough (or wealthy enough) to be able to muster such a court.

But that wasn't what marriage meant to her, and she didn't want hers to be like that. She knew Blackburn didn't keep a mistress, but if he continued to spend his time the way other husbands did, how long would it be before he *did?*

She had explained and explained. All he need do was be a bit more like her father. The duke did the same things most husbands did; he just spent a trifle less time doing them and a little more time doing things with her mother. And not because the duchess forced him. He just seemed to like her mother's company as much as he liked going to his clubs or to Tattersall's or to wherever else gentlemen went.

But Blackburn would not understand. Gradually, day by day, Jessica had said less and less and gotten more and more furious. The week he truly did go to White's, or wherever, every single night—she kept count—she left him.

She could see him now folding up *The Chronicle* and getting up from his armchair in the drawing room just as if he had done it yesterday. And she could feel her misery once more envelop her as she realized he was going out for the evening *again*—after an entire week of it!

He had leaned to give her a perfunctory kiss, and she, unable to help herself, had slowly followed him out of the drawing room, stopped as if turned to stone, and watched him descend the stairs to the front hall. She had stared as McHenry had handed him his cape and hat and heard her husband tell the major-domo his valet need not wait up for him.

She had heard the latching of the door as McHenry closed it, and she continued to stand as if made of marble. Then her misery and fury had erupted, and she had fastened on the first object within her grasp—the large decorative vase on the Chinese stand—and hurled it over the balustrade after her long-gone husband.

If McHenry had asked her what happened, she hadn't heard him. She had just stood and stared at the broken pieces on the polished floor below. She knew the servants would have them swept up almost immediately, and someone would place something else on the lovely Chinese stand. Her husband would never know.

She had gone to her bedchamber then, dismally certain that she had all the time in the world, and called her maid. Together, in all too short a time, she and Maisie had packed a portmanteau and left. The following day Jessica had sent Maisie back with her mother's servants to collect the rest of her things.

She hadn't seen her husband since then, until last night. And sadly, he didn't seem to have changed his viewpoint one iota. What had he said? "A fop who caters to your every whim."

Jessica wondered if he thought her father such a fop.

But truly, she didn't believe Blackburn had ever *heard* anything she had been trying to explain. "It can't get through his thick brainbox. Faugh!"

She threw down her brush and rang for Maisie. They had a beautiful town house to move into, and she didn't want to be all week about it.

Two days later, Jessica had transferred all her things from her parents' house to her own and had her new home in polished, shining order. Her companion, a very amenable, pleasant-spoken woman called Mrs. Darby, in age somewhere between that of Jessica and her mother, had also arrived and settled in. Jessica noted with satisfaction that Mrs. Darby's graying chignon, plump figure, and matronly manners would lend her new household all the respectability anyone could require.

I must remember to thank Mother and tell her she surpassed herself in the choice of Mrs. Darby, thought Jessica, making a mental note as she and the subject of her thoughts ate a companionable dinner.

Jessica smiled as she finished her raised pigeon pie and mushroom fritters. It was almost as though, she felt, her mother suspected her of being about to commit so many peccadilloes that she must needs discover the most respectable-looking woman alive from one side or the other of the family to scotch whispers of gossip before they had even begun.

Mother must believe I am going to take a cicisbeo! thought Jessica and almost laughed out loud. For though she had threatened Blackburn with just that, she hadn't meant it. At least, she didn't mean to do it right away. She might consider it in a year or two, but she couldn't think about it yet. It was too soon after Blackburn—she would just compare and miss him dreadfully, she was certain, the entire time if she tried to make love with someone else. And she had a sneaking suspicion that Blackburn would be hard to rival in that arena. Not only did he have a beautiful body—strong, lean, and muscular—but, from little remarks her married friends had let drop, she had gotten the impression that Blackburn spent more time and took more care with her than the majority of husbands did with their wives.

That was one area in which he certainly didn't seem to mind deviating from the practices of other husbands! thought Jessica, scowling. Hmph!

They had never had any disagreements between them on that front. In truth, their compatibility there had only made everything else worse, to her mind. For it seemed that her husband was willing to spend time on her body in bed, but he wasn't willing to spend it on her mind, keeping company with her. Those priorities had made her feel like his doxy, especially toward the end. Though he was spending most of his days and nights out on the town without her, he would still come home and expect—but she had put a stop to that by moving into her own bedchamber to sleep and locking the communicating door. And it had taken every ounce of her willpower to do it, too!

But even that curtailment hadn't made him understand how unhappy she was, she thought sadly. She doubted he understood even now, after she'd left him, how much she loved him and how much she hated the way he had treated her. Indeed, if she loved him less, the way he had treated her wouldn't matter nearly so much.

"A shilling for your thoughts, my dear," asked Mrs. Darby gently.

"Forgive me, Ann. I fear I've been exceedingly rude."

"Fiddle. We're all entitled to our own thoughts every now and again. I am only concerned that you looked a trifle sad."

"Oh, 'tis nothing that signifies. I should ask you if you found a chance to lie down and rest this afternoon. I don't want the Yorks' ball tonight to overtax your strength after all the unpacking and shifting of furniture we have been doing."

"Yes, I did, thank you. But I fear you did not."

"I did manage to lie down, but not to rest." Jessica smiled. "And if there is one thing that vexes me, it is tossing and turning on one's bed. I got up soon after."

"I do feel the same way, my dear. But here, if we keep on in this vein, we may talk ourselves out of going, and I, for one, was looking forward to the ball! I don't mind telling you, Jessica," Mrs. Darby confessed happily, "I haven't attended such things since my come-out as a girl. Come, shall we change our gowns? I'm certain it will take me longer, for I don't move so fast as I once did." She pushed back her chair and rose.

Jessica smiled and also rose. Mrs. Darby's excitement was infectious. It appeared her companion, despite her years, was going to prove diverting to live with. Jessica grimaced inwardly—more diverting than living with her husband.

"I imagine a lot of things have changed," continued Mrs. Darby, leading the way toward their bedchambers.

"Perhaps more fantastic and assuredly more extravagant."

"My! I can scarcely wait!"

The ladies laughed at Mrs. Darby's sally and entered their respective rooms to change.

Two hours later saw the women entering the York town house and greeting their host and hostess. Jessica introduced her new companion about, and they mingled and socialized together for the first part of the evening.

Finally Mrs. Darby shooed Jessica off to the dancing, declaring she would go and try her luck with the cards for a time.

A quadrille ended just as Jessica entered the ballroom and spotted a good friend of her husband's. "Wainsby! I *know* you feel like dancing now, don't you?" She pressed him into service.

His response was delayed by several gentlemen who wanted to sign Jessica's dance card. But obligingly he finally answered, "I'd dance with you anytime, Jess." He held out his arms and grinned. "I'm certain sure you won't tread on m'feet."

"Hmmn. I am going to take that as a compliment, I think," Jessica replied, placing her hands in his.

They moved in unison to the music of the gavotte that was starting.

"And so you should," agreed Wainsby. "Can't say that for half the ladies in this room. The gentlemen either for that matter, I dare say." He looked around them at the whirling couples and nodded at them. "If you watch closely, Jess—you should do that some time—you can see 'em stepping all over each other. Yes, sir. Little twitches and grimaces here and there, here and there, all over!" He laughed heartily. "Vastly entertaining!"

Jessica laughed with him.

Abruptly Wainsby stopped smiling. "Lord, but your husband," he complained, nodding in Blackburn's direction, "is giving us the queerest look. What ails him? Makes me nervous when he does that. I don't like it, don't like it by half."

"Well, ignore him then. I certainly shall."

"Yes, well. A house don't have to fall on me. I'm changing the subject now. I say! Didn't I hear you'd set up in an establishment of your own?!"

"Goodness, gossip travels fast!" Jessica's shock was evident in her expression.

The gavotte came to an end, and she said, "Indeed, I've brought my new companion with me tonight. She's in the other room playing cards."

"That gossip certainly would travel," laughed Wainsby. "Scintillating morsel, that: a marchioness setting up without her husband. Not to mention, they've been wagering in the clubs for weeks on the date Blackburn would get you to move back in with him. Instead, you move into a house of your own! Lord, that's famous!" he laughed.

Then a thought struck him, and he stopped. "Ah. So that's what was bluedeviling him t'other night." He explained, "He came into White's looking morose as the devil."

Jessica held up her hands. "Stop! If you're going to start trying to make me feel sorry for him, Wainsby, it's time for us to part company. And don't I just see Redley over your shoulder!" She began to move off.

"Well then, I'll dance with you again later, Jess, if you've room on your card." Wainsby smiled, a trifle sadly for his two friends who couldn't seem to work out their marital difficulties, and also moved off.

"Redley, how do you?" called Jessica.

"Jess! Hello, you're in looks tonight, and you well know you shouldn't be, my dear." Redley smiled wickedly. "You should be pining away for that husband of yours."

Jessica frowned and pouted. "Oh, don't read me another lecture, Redley. I just had one from Wainsby. Lud!" she cried in disgust. "You two are worse than my mother."

Redley laughed and quizzed her. "Well, what do you expect, my dear? We're his bosom bows. Though if he can't keep such a delectable creature as you happy, he must be the greatest cod's head alive. Correct me if I err. Your courtship was simply torrid, was it not?"

"How ungallant of you to remind me!"

"I heard you've moved into your own house. Is it true?" he asked, changing the subject accommodatingly.

"Yes, it's true," she moaned. "And at the rate that little tidbit of gossip is traveling here tonight, the whole of London will know of it by morning!"

"Yes, I quite understand why it would," he declared, much as Wainsby had. He bestowed a look of sympathy upon her. "My poor girl."

"Finally, a little sympathy!" Jessica sniffed. "Thank you."

"Ah, Jessica! You're a minx," Redley laughed at her. "Well, now that I've pumped you mercilessly for all your news, who else shall we gossip about? Shall we dance as well? I hear the orchestra striking up a minuet, and I can execute that one tolerably well." He grinned at her and took her hands, leading her out in the dance. "You don't want to be paired with me for a mazurka, take my word."

Jessica laughed.

The steps of the minuet parted them.

When they came back together again, she said, "Really! You and Wainsby. I suppose he has also advised you to observe the couples on the floor and discover them treading all over each other."

Redley looked pained.

The dance parted them again.

As they joined hands, Redley said, "My dear woman, *I* brought Wainsby's attention to that little item."

"Well, I might have known you would say that! Very likely the pair of you were unable to secure dance partners one evening, so you stood about pointing out to each other every couple that stumbled!" Jessica teased.

"Take care, Jessy," Redley warned gaily. "If you tease me too far, I shall inflict your great brute of a husband upon you!"

"Oh Redley! Don't bring him up again!" cried Jessica as they finished the steps of the minuet.

"I dare say that's all you both require anyway," Redley continued as if he hadn't heard. "To be locked up together until you work out whatever your differences are, as m'mother is fond of saying. Grab him by his neckcloth, Jess, and *make* him listen to you, if you have to shout in his face."

Jessica took a breath and tried to be patient. "I thought I did that, Redley."

"Do it *again* then, my dear."

"No!"

Redley observed the mulish set of Jessica's jaw and smiled ruefully. "He won't take my advice either." He gave an exaggerated sigh. "What a pair! If either of you had just listened to a little friendly advice, I could've had you back together months ago, living happily ever after!"

"Hmph! The only thing I am certain of is that your life would have been considerably shorter!" Jessica retorted.

Redley laughed. "Are you attempting to tell me I am trying your patience, Jess?" he asked sweetly. "In that event, I shall yield to your next dance supplicant," he declared. He bowed and took himself off into the crowd.

"Good evening, Lady Blackburn."

"Good evening, Lord Newcomb." Jessica placed her hands in Lord Newcomb's and allowed him to guide them gracefully around the dance floor.

Lord Newcomb was older than Jessica and many of her friends, but he waltzed better than almost any other gentleman she knew. He was as smooth and graceful as Blackburn, though her husband's movements were more sensual. As was only proper. She would've been horrified if Lord Newcomb had attempted to make his movements sensuous! But both Lord Newcomb and Blackburn knew the steps of the waltz well enough to be assured in them and, more importantly, to bring a lot of creativity into their execution.

Almost as if to illustrate her thoughts, Lord Newcomb smiled at her and twirled her about. And Jessica laughed out loud, though she felt sorry for the poor man, for his own wife did not like to dance at all.

The waltz came to an end, and a dainty tinkling was heard in the immediate silence that followed the cessation of orchestra instruments. The low roar of voices as people broke into conversation again drowned out the tinkling.

Lord Newcomb spoke. "There is the bell for supper, Lady Blackburn. Shall I take you in?"

"Yes, indeed, unless you are spoken for elsewhere. Oh! How I do enjoy dancing with you, sir!" answered Jessica.

"Likewise, madam, I do assure you." Lord Newcomb smiled and presented his arm. "Shall we?"

He escorted Jessica to her place in the supper room and moved down the long table to discover his own place.

Jessica found that she was glad to sit down and rest. After all, she had been standing or dancing all evening. Apparently her two days of moving had taxed her more than she would have thought possible. She looked around the long table and was both glad and somewhat amused to note that her hostess had had the forethought to seat her at the opposite end of the table from Blackburn.

Seated far from where she need acknowledge her husband's existence, between Lord Concord, whom she had not known previously, and Lord Lethbridge, whom she liked for his unflagging humor, Jessica enjoyed the light meal.

The handsome Lord Concord, she discovered, had just bought out his commission. He had come to London to sample some of its social whirl and relax and entertain himself a bit before traveling on to his estate farther north. And Jessica judged, since Lady York had seated her very marriageable young daughter on his other side, he and his estate must be worth a substantial sum. Her supposition was further supported by the many feminine glances she had been surprised to notice being surreptitiously directed at him since the meal had begun. No doubt, any number of matchmaking mamas and their daughters hoped to fix his interest before he returned north.

Jessica speculatively regarded Lord Concord's sun-burnished brown curls and the dark blue eyes he turned on her. It was plain to see why the ladies were all hanging out for him. He was a virtual Adonis. If she weren't married herself, she would also be interested. Prodigiously interested.

Suddenly Jessica realized that Lord Concord had addressed some remark to her. She fumbled to give a noncommittal answer, vague enough that it could sensibly apply to almost anything he might have said.

Farther down the table, Blackburn's interested hazel eyes noted her speculative look as well as her flustered answer. The marquess felt his heart leap up into his throat and choke him. Suddenly, waiting for his wife to get over her anger toward him seemed to him the strategy of a chucklehead. Clearly he needed to act immediately to frustrate those speculative gazes and, more importantly, the behavior that was apt to follow them. But to command Jessica to stop was to ensure that she would go out of her way to flirt. No, of a certainty, he couldn't approach Jessica, but he could address those around her!

The supper broke up, and Jessica, making her way back to the ballroom, was intercepted by Lady Clarendon. That lady, ostensibly thanking and praising Jessica for the celebration of her mother, was intent on gaining the information on the state of affairs between Jessica and Blackburn that the duchess had previously denied her.

The orchestra struck up a mazurka, and Jessica glanced through the guests wondering where Lord Massey, her next dance partner, could have got to. Fending off Lady Clarendon's none-too-subtle questions, Jessica pulled out her dance card and checked it. Just as she remembered, Lord Massey had written himself in for the first dance after supper.

Oh well, Jessica thought with disappointment, I suppose he simply forgot, and she evaded another of Lady Clarendon's inquiries. Jessica would have much preferred, however, to dance. She felt rested after having supped, and mazurkas just made one want to dance. Even now, it was difficult to keep her foot from tapping to the music. Moreover, dancing would have helped her escape Lady Clarendon.

By the end of the mazurka, Jessica was close to mentally cursing Lord Massey. But she believed that she would be rescued at any moment by Lord Gadsden, her partner for the next dance. She asked Lady Clarendon a question, hoping to distract her.

A cotillion began, but no Lord Gadsden appeared to claim his dance. Jessica's cheeks pinkened in mortification, but she supposed it was possible for two gentlemen to have forgotten they had engaged themselves to her for a dance. She sighed. Lady Clarendon was back to her inquisition.

When she was stood up a third time as the next dance began, Jessica's cheeks turned a bright red, and she wondered if someone were playing a cruel joke on her. She must appear ridiculous standing on the edge of the dancing obviously waiting to dance. Unexpectedly, she became profoundly thankful for Lady Clarendon's presence. How much more absurd she should appear without that lady! Gratefully, feeling some sort of reward was due Lady Clarendon, Jessica gave her a tidbit of what she desired and told her conspiratorially she had just moved into her own establishment and hired a companion.

Lady Clarendon was in alt. She decided to give her subject a rest and search out a seat. She would admit to being weary herself. It had taken her forever to get that little crumb out of the chit!

Jessica, her cheeks still bright, went in search of Wainsby to press him into dancing again.

He saw her coming. "Oh no, Jessica. Go away. Can't dance with you!"

"Go away? *Can't?"*

"What I mean is, I won't."

"Why? You said you would. Have I offended you in some manner? What have I done, Wainsby?" Jessica cried. *"Three* gentlemen in a row have just stood me up, and now you won't dance with me either!" Her large gray-blue, stricken eyes began to fill with tears.

"Oh now. Don't do that, Jess. It's nothing to do with you—dash it! Demmed Blackburn! But I don't believe he realized it would be this cruel."

"Blackburn! What has he got to do with this?!" shot Jessica angrily. She wiped at her eyes.

"Well, I really don't think he meant it that way, but it *is* cruel, so I shall tell you," said Wainsby, as if explaining himself to Blackburn. " 'Tis only fair. Come away. Come over here by the flowers." He took her arm and fairly dragged her over against the wall where a large potted palm had been placed for the best decorative appeal.

"I'm certain he was only thinking of it from his end of things—"

"As usual!"

"Now, Jess. I'm sure he never considered how it was going to make you feel. And he looks a damn fool, too, doing it, as I tried to tell him! But, well, he's been going up to a lot of fellows and threatening to pummel them or call them out or some such rot if they dance with you."

"What!"

"I told you when we were dancing earlier he was giving us a queer look."

"You mean he threatened you, too! You're his friend!"

"Yes, well, he appears to have gone balmy. Let's just say I took it as the special request of a good friend. Besides, he's an excellent shot. And I truly don't think he realized it would leave you looking as if you'd been stood up. I truly don't, Jessica."

"Oh! Just *wait* till I—" She left her sentence hanging and lifted her skirts.

"Whoa, Jessica!" Wainsby grabbed her arm and pulled her back. He knew her well. "Wait a bit. Wait till you cool down a trifle." He smiled at her persuasively. "In the meantime, you can think up something that will really get his goat. Come. Let me take you home."

Discreetly, Jessica struggled and then gave up. "Oh, all right, Wainsby! Go call for your carriage. I will collect Ann."

He held onto her a few moments longer and then gave her a penetrating stare. Apparently satisfied with what he saw, he released her arm and left her, skirting the dance floor.

Jessica smoothed her sleeve and searched out Ann, taking care to note Blackburn's location.

"Hello, Ann. I expect I shall want to depart in a few moments. Is that acceptable to you? Please don't feel you must accompany me. If you would prefer to remain for a time, I can leave the carriage for you."

"Oh no, my dear. In truth, I am growing a trifle weary. So

much excitement! No, no. I shall be more than ready whenever you are."

Jessica squeezed Ann's hand and smiled. "You're a dear. I shall be back for you directly."

Slowly, her anger reawakening, Jessica strolled to the punch tables. Pointing to a large bowl that contained a pink liquid with sliced limes floating upon its surface, Jessica indicated that the footman behind the table should pour her a cup.

Coolly, she thanked the footman and, taking a sip, strolled to stand directly behind her husband. She spoke his name, watched him turn to face her, and just as slowly raised her cup high and dumped its pink liquid over his dark head.

Her eyes flashing, Jessica observed her husband's bushy brown eyebrows rise in shock as the punch spread over his hair and ran down his face in little rivulets that broke up and dripped from his chin onto his broad, black-coated shoulders.

There was a concerted gasp from those around them as the guests hastily drew back to avoid being splashed.

Jessica continued to look wrathfully into her husband's hazel eyes, but her anger began to turn to amusement. As she observed her punch drip from his strong, clean-shaven jaw, she couldn't prevent herself from smiling. Then she saw his eyebrows come down and snap together, and a giggle escaped her. She knew she better take herself off quickly before she began to laugh uncontrollably.

She noted Redley grinning over Blackburn's shoulder, nodded to him, and fled, clapping a hand over her mouth.

Blackburn spun to face Redley and barked, "You were looking right at her! You must have seen what she was up to! Why the devil didn't you warn me!"

"I fear I didn't see the cup of punch until the last moment. But in truth, Blackburn," he said slowly, as if he were only realizing it himself, "had I seen it, I doubt I would've warned you, for I rather feel you've been deserving that since you threatened me to stay away from her. I didn't care for that by half. Makes a fellow feel you don't trust him."

"Go to the devil!" exclaimed Blackburn.

For the benefit of those around them, Redley shrugged and raised his eyes heavenward. "All right. But I suggest you accompany me. You look a fool."

Tittering, Lady York's guests believed for a moment that Blackburn was going to hit his friend.

But in a lightning change of mood, as if he couldn't help himself, Blackburn's scowl became a grin, and he threw back his head and laughed heartily. "Sorry, old man," he apologized.

"I believe I am ready to depart now, Ann," Jessica remarked, beaming upon her companion as she calmly approached her again.

"Yes, I can understand why!" retorted that lady tartly, directing her eyes pointedly toward Blackburn. Several people were still trying to mop him off as he appeared to shout at a gentleman standing at his elbow. "That was necessary?" asked Mrs. Darby.

"Mmmm. Most necessary." The laughter Jessica had stifled moments ago bubbled up over her lips, and she found she couldn't stop.

"I can see we need to get you out of here immediately, my dear," said Mrs. Darby, smiling herself.

Jessica nodded vigorously, laughing helplessly.

Mrs. Darby began to chuckle. "Oh dear, I am doing it, too. But he did look so shocked!" She put her arm around Jessica, and they bolted for the door.

Wainsby bundled them both into his carriage and signaled Jessica's carriage to follow.

The ladies had stopped laughing. It was quiet as they rode along, jolted every now and again as the wheels met some imperfection in the road. Wainsby began to fidget as the silence continued overlong.

"This quiet bodes ill and more for Blackburn," he muttered, breaking it finally himself, scarcely realizing he had spoken.

"You're being fanciful, Wainsby," answered Jessica. "We are all tired. That is all."

Wainsby had more sense than to argue, but he nodded to himself in the dark: yes, it did. Then he shook his head the other way: poor devil.

* * *

The next morning saw Jessica visited by the usual number of her female friends. Her male friends, she discovered, had all decided to respect Blackburn's "wishes"—whether out of friendship or cowardice she couldn't be certain. She did know she was going to have to contrive some manner in which to make Blackburn rescind his threats and stop, in essence, prescribing whom she could and couldn't see.

Devil a bit! she thought angrily as she dressed for Lady St. John's gala. *He* doesn't want to spend time with me, but he won't let anyone else! Hmph! There is assuredly a way that two can play at his little game, and I intend to find it! It is going to become much more difficult for him to even speak with another woman!

She applied several dabs of perfume to her wrists and her throat, patted a curl in place, and went to see if Mrs. Darby was ready to go.

That lady was indeed ready, seated in the sitting room, turning the pages of *The Chronicle* while she waited for Jessica.

"You look so cozy and comfortable here, I am almost persuaded to join you and forego Lady St. John's party."

Mrs. Darby looked up and smiled. "I suspect the operative word in that is *almost*."

Jessica laughed. "How do you know me so well in such a short acquaintance, Ann? Shall we go? I hope you did not wait on me long."

"Not at all, my dear. I was catching up on the paper," answered Mrs. Darby, folding the *Chronicle* and gathering up her shawl. She rose, smiling at Jessica. "Let us go!"

They were soon standing on Lord and Lady St. John's stone staircase waiting among a throng of other new arrivals to enter. For at the height of the Season, the large affairs were attended by almost everyone.

"What a crush! How tedious. We should have stayed in the sitting room and been cozy, Ann," sighed Jessica.

"I am certain we'll be inside in a few moments, my dear."

Jessica appraised the crowd of people ahead of them on the stairs. "I don't believe so, but I hope you may be right."

But it was Jessica who proved to be correct, for they stood another quarter of an hour, inching their way up the steps, before they reached the top and greeted Lord and Lady St. John.

Once inside, Jessica decided to get something to drink and then stroll through the other guests and locate her husband. The way matters stood there was no point in even entering the ballroom, which is what she might ordinarily have done. "Ann, I see negus in people's glasses, and I believe I shall procure some. Would you care for a glass?"

"I haven't had negus in years, Jessica. How lovely! But I believe I'll just follow along behind you, for I don't know the half of these people. I vow I feel quite cowed."

"Never let them think so, Ann, and you'll do famously," advised Jessica with a grin at her companion. "I see the negus! This way."

" 'Tis a good thing you're taller than me," muttered Mrs. Darby, struggling to squeeze through the small space between bodies that the slim Jessica had just slipped through. "We might never have found the negus."

Jessica passed a glass behind her to Mrs. Darby and reached for a glass for herself. Then they began to wrestle their way free of the tight crowd around the negus tables.

But even when they had distanced themselves from the negus tables, strolling through the different rooms was arduous. They were all full to overflowing with guests.

Blast! thought Jessica, after three-quarters of an hour strolling and speaking to friends she happened upon. I'll never discover Blackburn in this crush.

The next moment, as if her curse had conjured him up, Jessica saw him ahead of her. He was standing in the ballroom doorway talking to Lady Kittrell, a small-boned, quiet, dignified woman who had never acted any thing but courteous and well-mannered in all of Jessica's acquaintance with her.

Knowing full well that Lady Kittrell was married and had no designs upon Blackburn, Jessica descended upon them and draped herself over Blackburn's arm. "Oh, *here* you are, *Gordon*. I've been looking for you for *ages*."

In her best imitation of a jealous wife, Jessica continued coldly, "Oh. Hello, Lady Kittrell. Don't let me interrupt you two. I'm certain you were having a simply *fascinating* conversation." She made no effort to fill the embarrassed silence that had fallen over the pair. She merely waited, leaning all over Blackburn and looking from one to the other expectantly.

The two were so astonished at her behavior that it took them a moment to recover their wits and stammer out a greeting.

Jessica recollected that she had had Mrs. Darby in tow before she had descended on Blackburn. Leaning heavily upon Blackburn's arm, she shifted her weight so suddenly that she unbalanced him for a moment as she craned to see what had become of her companion.

Blackburn's curse, as he righted himself, was audible.

Mrs. Darby was standing at Jessica's elbow with the same flabbergasted expression on her face that Blackburn and Lady Kittrell had succeeded in masking only moments before.

Drawing Ann forward into the group, Jessica asked sweetly, "Did I introduce my companion, Mrs. Darby? Ann, this is my *adorable* husband, and this is his friend, Lady Kittrell."

The three greeted one another politely, and another awkward silence fell.

Again, Jessica did nothing to dispel it. She swung upon Blackburn's arm and looked intently from one to the other in the group.

The three started talking at once.

They stopped, with blushes and stammers of "Pardon me!"

The hateful silence reigned once more.

Then Mrs. Darby laughed gaily.

Lady Kittrell and Blackburn regarded her warily. Blackburn was uncertain if what was going to follow was going to be as crackbrained as the manner in which Jessica was behaving. Lady Kittrell was trying to think of a polite way to escape the group.

Mrs. Darby said, "You know, something of this nature happened to me only the other night at Lady York's ball. There were five of us in the group, and would you believe we all started to talk at the same time on three separate occasions?"

Relieved the woman had come out with something so normal, Blackburn went to her aid. Before Jessica could come out with some other daft remark, he commented, "They say that the average subject of conversation endures for about twenty minutes." He smiled at Mrs. Darby. "After that, I suppose you get that moment of silence, and then everyone starts talking at once to attempt to fill it."

Mrs. Darby returned his smile, quite liking her employer's husband. "Oh, now I didn't know that. What an interesting notion."

Lady Kittrell began, "Do you know, it is almost time for dinner, and Lord Kittrell is very likely looking for me. I believe I had better go and see—"

She was interrupted by a loud gong.

In the silence that followed, a footman announced, "Dinner is served! Be pleased to follow Mr. Tiffin into the dining room."

Mr. Tiffin, the major-domo, resplendent in a black and gold uniform, threw open the double doors to the dining room and stood ready to aid those who couldn't find their place cards.

There was a concerted gasp as guests viewed the sumptuously laden tables and then the low roar of conversation began again as people made their way toward the long tables.

"We will see you in to dinner, Lady Kittrell. Won't we, Gordon," commanded Jessica. "You will never find your husband now."

"So kind," murmured Lady Kittrell.

Placing both hands in the crook of Blackburn's arm, Jessica led the way regally.

As soon as they were through the double doors, Lady Kittrell made her escape. "I have an idea that my place card is on one of the tables over here," she said, waving vaguely at the tables to her left. She hurried off in that direction.

Jessica dropped Blackburn's arm as if it were a hot poker and turned to link her arm through Mrs. Darby's. Leading her off to the right, she suggested, "Shall we find your place first, Ann?"

About to berate Jessica and ask her what the devil she thought she was doing, the astonished Blackburn sucked in his breath and clenched his fist at his side. "I miss your feather weight already, my love," he called after her, hoping to vex.

He grinned and went to find his own place. She'd heard him; he'd seen her back stiffen.

Jessica saw Mrs. Darby safely seated and then searched out her own place. As she sat down, she looked to discover where Blackburn was seated.

When she found him, above her at the next table over, she had to bite her lip to keep from exclaiming angrily. The man had the luck of the devil! He was seated next to the voluptuous widow, Lady Thompkins, who had set her cap at him from the moment she had clapped eyes upon him. And since she was a widow, she hadn't minded in the least when he had gotten married. Apparently, an affair had been what she had in mind—and no doubt still did—from the first.

Lud! Just look at that décolletage! thought Jessica. I am amazed he can keep his eyes from it.

She watched Blackburn answer Lady Thompkins and smile genially at her, looking directly into her eyes. Not even a glance at her bosom.

Jessica's respect for Blackburn, having been on a steady decline for the last several months, rose ever so slightly.

The widow leaned close to Blackburn to whisper something to him, thereby positioning her bosom where it would be difficult to overlook.

Blackburn was not proof against that ploy. He glanced.

That old trick! thought Jessica scornfully. Lud! What a tart.

Jessica tore her eyes from Blackburn and Lady Thompkins and turned her attention to the conversation at her own table. There was nothing she could do about Lady Thompkins and Blackburn while they were at dinner a whole table and many seats away from her. But *after* dinner, Blackburn had better confine himself to speaking with the gentlemen!

Jessica smiled. Even if he did, she wasn't certain she could restrain herself from descending upon him again to vex him. She had loved every minute of acting the jealous wife and hanging all over him. The shock on his face when she had first draped herself over his arm and called him Gordon, a name she hadn't used in several months, still made her want to laugh.

The first course of Lady St. John's dinner, a pair of dressed partridges with several side dishes, was done to perfection. The second course of scalloped oysters was equally good. But Jessica found that a feeling of anticipation was tingling in the bottom of her stomach and taking her appetite. As each course drew her closer to the end of the meal, the tingling grew.

This anticipation, she knew, was due to the expectation of being with Blackburn again after dinner, and that, she also knew, was a bad sign. She tried to squelch it with no success. To get so involved with him again that she would look forward to seeing him was to set herself up to be disappointed and hurt all over again. It was better to cut him out of her life and see nothing of him, and she had done that until her mother had invited him back in. And now she knew she should leave Blackburn alone after dinner and find someone else to occupy her interest for the remainder of the evening. But she knew she wasn't going to do that.

I am being a fool, I *know* I am being a fool, and I am doing it anyway! Jessica thought in disgust as she tasted her Savoy cake.

Then the dinner was breaking up, and people were rising from their chairs and spreading back into the other rooms.

Jessica observed Lady Thompkins rise and pull Blackburn out of his chair so that she could link her arm through his. As they left the dining room together, the widow was hanging upon Blackburn quite as lasciviously as Jessica had done earlier.

Faugh! thought Jessica, forgetting her anticipation and her disgust. Does he believe he is the support of all womankind?! He seems to allow simply everyone to hang upon him! *She* needs a good, strong cane!

With an idea taking shape in her mind, Jessica rose herself and walked purposefully from the dining room back to the negus tables. When she arrived at them, she discovered that the negus had been exchanged for champagne and that small cakes had appeared beside the champagne.

No matter, she told herself, eyeing the thick layer of frosting that adorned each cake. She chose two and took a glass of champagne. Then she began to circle back through the crowd to the vicinity in which she had last seen her husband and Lady Thompkins. No doubt the woman will *still* be hanging upon him, she thought.

And when Jessica discovered them, the widow was still leaning on Blackburn's arm.

Ah well, smiled Jessica, 'twill simply make this all the easier for me.

Slowly Jessica began her approach. They remained unaware of her until she was almost upon them. When she judged she was close enough, it was the simplest matter in the world for her to pretend to stub her toe, stumble, and spill her napkin of little cakes upon that magnificent bosom as she fell into Lady Thompkins.

That lady could not untangle her arms from Blackburn's fast enough to save herself. Both she and Blackburn recoiled, to no avail.

The little cakes were mashed upon Lady Thompkins's chest, and a third of Jessica's champagne flew from her glass and splashed upon Blackburn's crisp, white shirt front.

There were several gasps from those standing close, as they also recoiled.

"Oh my! Oh my goodness, I'm so sorry!" cried Jessica, wiping ineffectually with her napkin in a manner that was effectively spreading the thick white frosting.

"What are you doing! Stop! You are making it worse!" Lady Thompkins exclaimed angrily. She knocked Jessica's napkin away, glared at her, and looked down at the front of herself, aghast.

"There's nothing for it," commiserated Jessica. "You'll have to go to the retiring room. Let me go with you and help. I just feel terrible about this. How *could* I be so clumsy?"

"Here, take this," said Blackburn, offering Lady Thompkins his large white handkerchief.

"Oh, thank you!" Lady Thompkins bunched the handkerchief

up and placed it over the worst of the frosting so that unless one looked closely, it appeared that she was trying to still heart palpitations.

Lady Thompkins smiled gratefully at Blackburn, turned to Jessica, and said coldly, "Don't *dare* to accompany me!" and marched off in the direction of the ladies' retiring room.

Jessica grinned and raised her champagne glass at Blackburn. "What a shame." She took a sip of her remaining champagne and laughed gaily.

Blackburn brushed at his damp shirt front and clamped a hand on Jessica's free wrist. His hazel eyes glinted. "Well, Jess. It is dawning upon me that you would like to dance." He pulled her close and spoke in her ear. "And since *I* am the only one I sanction to do that with you . . ." He left the sentence unfinished.

"No!" cried Jessica as his intent became clear.

"Better get rid of this," he remarked, taking her glass from her and quaffing the remainder of her champagne. Setting the glass down on the first table they passed, he began to tow her through the crowd toward the ballroom.

"I don't believe I wish to, Blackburn," Jessica called politely, struggling discreetly and trying to maneuver people between them so that Blackburn would have to let go of her.

To circumvent her, he pulled her up abreast of him, kept his grip on her wrist, and put his other hand on the small of her back, pulling and pushing her body to avoid running into other guests.

They reached the ballroom in short order.

"I said I don't want to dance, Blackburn!" cried Jessica furiously as Blackburn turned her to face him and transferred one hand to her shoulder, the other to her waist.

The orchestra started to play.

"Ah, 'tis a waltz. You won't be proof against that, Jess! It's a long time since you've had my arms around you." Blackburn drew her closer. "Feels good, doesn't it."

Jessica panicked. It felt entirely too good, and she didn't trust herself. Heaven only knew what starry-eyed visions of Blackburn she'd have if she waltzed with him. She wouldn't be able to see past loving him, and then she would do something she'd regret mightily. By cutting him out of her life these past several months, she'd been able to distance herself from the relationship and maintain a fairly cheerful frame of mind. But the effort of distancing herself had cost her much. If she were going to keep her hard-won peace of mind, she couldn't lose that distance.

At the same moment Blackburn swung them into motion, Jessica wrenched herself from his arms. "And it will be a sight longer before you get them round me again!" she cried.

The force with which she wrenched herself away sent her careening sideways.

Blackburn, believing she was about to fall, lunged to catch her and planted a heavy boot squarely on the hem of her skirt.

Jessica took another step to steady herself and found with dismay that she was also stepping on her skirt, already pulled taut under Blackburn's weight. With no footing to be had, she went down to the sound of tearing sarcenet. She reached for Blackburn, who was extending his arms to her, but she wasn't able to hold on. Her hands slid down his coat sleeves, and she landed painfully on her hands and knees.

A young couple, talking furiously and paying no mind to where they were waltzing, collided with Blackburn, almost knocking him down next to Jessica.

The force of their collision tore the young couple apart. The young woman spun away from her partner and fell backward over Jessica. The young man was spun into another dancing couple, knocking them rudely apart, before he also fell down.

Wiser couples, observing the mêlée developing on the floor, slowed their pace as they whirled by to avoid becoming part of the turmoil. Others actually stopped momentarily to stare and chuckle at the ridiculous figures on the floor.

Jessica tried to stand and grimaced with pain as she felt her right knee buckle. It had taken most of her weight. She turned over and sat down upon the floor.

"Come on, I'll pull you up," said Blackburn, holding out his hand.

"No, go away," Jessica said wearily. She brushed away his hand.

"Don't be absurd, Jess," he returned, coming round to stand behind her.

"Don't touch me! I can manage!" She swatted at him.

"Or stubborn." He put his hands under her arms and hauled her to her feet. "You can barely stand. Come. Let's get off this infernal dance floor. We're in the way. Lean on me."

As they neared the edge of the dance floor, several people broke from the crowd of people watching to ask what had happened and if Lady Blackburn had hurt herself.

Blackburn grinned at them and then answered for Jessica, " 'Tis merely a slick floor. I don't believe she's hurt anything save her pride. Thank you for your concern."

"Hmph! Their curiosity, more like," muttered Jessica.

Mrs. Darby, carrying her shawl, materialized out of the crowd. "Oh, my dear! However did it happen?" She draped her shawl around Jessica's shoulders and tied it loosely, spreading the lengths of it out over the front of her gown. Then she stepped to support Jessica's other side, and the three of them continued their slow progress toward the front door.

"Oh dear. Thank you, Ann. The skirt has probably come away from my bodice. Has my shift been showing since I stood up?" wailed Jessica.

"Nothing so bad as that, my dear," comforted Mrs. Darby. "Did you hurt anything else besides your leg?" She looked anxiously at Blackburn.

He shook his head. "I don't believe so. But I'll wager she'll have to stay off that leg for a couple of days."

Jessica choked and said crossly, "Don't answer for me as if I were a child. I can still talk! It is my knee, not my leg. And thank you, but you can take yourself off now. I've Ann to help me, and we shall manage famously."

"Please don't scold him, my dear. 'Twas my fault for asking him," said Mrs. Darby, looking distressed.

"A pity," muttered Blackburn.

Mrs. Darby frowned at him.

"What did you say, Blackburn?!"

"Of course we'll let him come with us. He only wants to be certain I get you home safely." She twinkled up at Blackburn.

"I shall see you home, Jessica," Blackburn said firmly. "You cannot lean on Mrs. Darby alone for the entire distance, not to mention getting up and down from your carriage, or up your front steps. You will exhaust her."

"Oh, stuff!" retorted that lady.

But Jessica silently acknowledged his point and made no more complaints about his accompanying them.

Blackburn and Mrs. Darby found Jessica a chair and left her to make their goodbyes, and hers, too, Mrs. Darby assured her, to Lady St. John.

By the time they came back for her, her knee was aching unmercifully. The two took one look at her pale, strained face and hurried to support her to the carriage.

Blackburn suggested they take his, thinking Jessica would fare better on its plump cushions and in its well-sprung body. But her own carriage was closer to the St. John entrance, so they bundled her into that.

The carriage soon pulled up before Jessica's house, and Blackburn and Mrs. Darby got Jessica down and inside.

In the face of the stairs that led up to her bedchamber, Jessica hesitated.

"Up, I presume?" asked Blackburn, his eyes twinkling.

Jessica nodded miserably.

Blackburn picked her up in his arms. "Which way?" It told him much when she didn't protest or argue with him over it.

Mrs. Darby answered, "Up the stairs, down the hall, and it's the second door on the left. I'm going to go and see about a poultice. I'll be right there." She hurried off to the kitchen.

Blackburn took the stairs.

"My feather weight," murmured Jessica with a half smile.

Blackburn chuckled. He climbed slowly, liking the feel of her in his arms again.

Jessica closed her eyes and laid her head against Blackburn's shoulder. She'd forgotten how secure she felt in his arms. A tiny sigh for the future they might have had escaped her.

"Just a little farther now," said Blackburn, hearing the sigh.

He rounded the doorframe and crossed her bedchamber to the fourposter bed. Laying her gently on the feather tick, he sank down beside her.

They were both silent, regarding each other.

Blackburn put his hand on Jessica's as it lay on the quilt and slid it up her bare arm. "We could try to patch it up, Jess," he suggested softly.

"Oh, Blackburn," she answered, her voice a blend of weariness and irritation. "Please." She closed her eyes.

"We could try harder," he persisted.

For answer, she shook his hand off her arm and turned her face away from him. A tear slipped out of the corner of one eye and rolled to meet the pillow, unobserved by Blackburn.

"All right," he growled. *"I* could try harder."

Jessica's heart leaped at his words. She turned to face him but made no answer. She was afraid to trust words. He was very likely feeling carried away by the closeness she'd allowed him due to injuring her knee. On the morrow, all would return to normal.

He read her answer in her eyes: she was not about to invest more effort in patching things up between them unless he gave her a very good reason for doing so.

Her blue eyes hardened. And she didn't believe he could.

"All right, Jess. I guess I'll have to show you I mean what I say. But will you at least promise me one thing?"

She looked wary. "What."

"Promise me you won't bar your door against me or my notes. For if I cannot get in to talk to you, 'tis a ridiculous attempt on my side. You can see the sense in that."

"I suppose so," she answered.

"Good girl!"

"Don't patronize me, Blackburn," she retorted crossly.

But her crossness couldn't dampen Blackburn's exuberance. He leaned over her, pinning her shoulders and bringing his face nose to nose with hers. "I know you love me, Jessica Ashford," he growled.

Jessica's gray-blue eyes opened wide in surprise.

"And I know I love you, even if you don't know it. We just aren't good at living with each other. But we will be. We *will* be!" His mouth came down on hers, and he kissed her thoroughly.

His kiss surprised Jessica as well. It felt so good and natural between them that at first she simply enjoyed it and kissed him back with equal passion. Then, thinking that he was trying to seduce her, since his words hadn't done so, she began to struggle and protest against his lips.

He released her mouth and grinned at her. "Not so cold as you led me to believe, Jess! I don't suppose you could see your way clear to calling me Gordon again, could you?" He released her shoulders and sat back quickly as her right hand just missed the side of his face. "No, I was afraid not," he answered for her, still smiling.

Jessica was breathing rapidly and looking up at him with angry, flashing eyes.

"Well, one promise a day is enough for me. 'Tis enough for hope." He rose. "Certain you don't want me to stay?" he suggested, moving strategically closer to the door. "I could, ah, help you off with your dress?"

"No!" Jessica raised herself on one elbow to snatch a pillow and fling it at his head.

Mrs. Darby, on the point of entering with several cloths and a bowl of something hot that smelled spicy and herbal, was brought up short as the pillow landed at her feet. "If you can do naught but aggravate my patient, Lord Blackburn, I'm going to have to ask you to go home," she scolded. "And you've been such a help up till now, too," she continued, as if talking to herself. "I don't understand it."

"But ma'am! I was merely continuing to be helpful," complained Blackburn, smiling.

"Oh?" replied Mrs. Darby, ready to hear an explanation that refuted the evidence of the pillow on the floor before her.

"Never believe it, Ann," muttered Jessica, lying back down.

"I'd only just offered to stay and help her get her gown off. You'll have the devil of a time getting her into her nightrail after you've spread that concoction all over her knee," he said plausibly.

His logic struck Mrs. Darby. Turning to Jessica, she suggested, "The poultice is growing cold. Perhaps, since he *is* your husb—?"

"No!"

Mrs. Darby turned back to Blackburn. "Thank you for your kind offer, Lord Blackburn," she said smoothly. "But as you can see," she nodded at the angry Jessica, raised up on one elbow again, "I believe we can manage."

Blackburn chuckled. "From what I've seen of you tonight, ma'am, I believe you could manage almost any situation."

Mrs. Darby blushed with pleasure.

Jessica scowled. Blatantly flattering her so that he can gain any number of favors later, I've no doubt! she thought. What a complete hand!

"Thank you indeed, sir, but go along now. We need to be spreading this on the knee before it gets any more swollen."

"Well then, ladies, I bid you good night. Look to see me tomorrow, Jess." He bowed and left, closing the door after him.

"Let me put this on your knee first, and then it can be soothing it while we get you out of your dress," Mrs. Darby addressed Jessica.

Jessica grimaced and nodded, gingerly removing the slipper and stocking from her injured leg.

"Don't worry, my dear. It won't hurt, and it will do a world of good for your knee."

A moment later, intent on spreading the thick mixture over Jessica's bruised knee, Mrs. Darby gasped and exclaimed, "Oh my! I should have rung for someone to show Lord Blackburn the way out. Tut, tut. How remiss of me."

"Hmph!" Jessica snorted. "Don't distress yourself over it. I doubt he had the least difficulty. Do you know, I believe it is just as you said. My knee is already beginning to feel better."

"Good. I suspect you will be able to walk about as freely as usual tomorrow, as long as you do not try to climb the stairs too often."

"Oh, Ann, that is wonderful! You are much too good to me! I don't know where my mother can have found you. I could hug both of you."

Mrs. Darby blushed again with pleasure. "Now, Jessica, stop. Between the pair of you, you and Lord Blackburn will turn my head."

They both laughed.

"That's all of the poultice," Mrs. Darby said, scooping the last of the herbal mixture from the bowl with two fingers and patting the dab on Jessica's knee with the rest. She used one of her cloths to wipe off her hands. Another she wrapped, being careful to keep the poultice from oozing out the sides, around Jessica's knee. Dabs of excess poultice at the two ends of the bandage were wiped off, the bandage was pinned in place, and she was finished.

"There! Now let us see about getting that gown off you so you can get to sleep before the sun dawns upon us. I expect a good night's rest will do that knee quite as much good as the poultice. Shall I call Maisie to help us?"

"No. I'm certain she's been in bed for ages. With your help on the hooks, I think I can manage." Jessica sat up and turned her back as far toward Mrs. Darby as she could.

Mrs. Darby leaned to undo the long column of hooks down Jessica's back. Then, as Jessica squirmed and wriggled from side to side, Mrs. Darby drew the gown from beneath her until they had got it bunched about her waist.

Mrs. Darby pulled the last lengths of material over Jessica's head, and Jessica exclaimed, "Lud! Perhaps we should have called Maisie. What a struggle!"

Mrs. Darby smiled in agreement and hung the dress in the wardrobe. "Here is your nightgown, my dear." She transferred the nightgown from the foot of the bed, where Maisie had laid it out, to Jessica's lap. "Is there anything else I can get you? I believe I shall take myself off now and leave the rest to you."

"No. But I thank you from my heart, Ann, for all your help tonight. I shouldn't have managed half so well without you."

"You are most certainly welcome, my dear." Mrs. Darby

stooped to pick up the pillow Jessica had flung, brushed at it, and deposited it back on the bed. "Sleep well. She smiled and left, closing the door softly.

Jessica kicked off her remaining slipper, unrolled her other stocking, tossed it after the slipper, and changed her chemise for her nightgown. All the while, a tiny frown played over her features. Her knee had begun to feel better and better since Mrs. Darby had spread her poultice over it. It was Blackburn's words that were causing the frown. She wanted dearly to believe his avowal. Yet she also feared hoping for it. It would be too wonderful if they could patch things up between them. She would be too happy if that occurred. She wasn't sure anyone was ever allowed to be that happy.

She wriggled under the bedclothes and lay back on her pillows. She wondered if Blackburn was really going to visit her the next day. Well, he had said to expect him. He didn't say things he wasn't going to do, she'd give the devil his due. Wonder what he was coming for? she thought, and couldn't help a tingle of anticipation.

She turned on her side, keeping her hurt knee uppermost, and drifted off to sleep, dreaming of her life with Blackburn the way it had been on their honeymoon. A small smile curved her lips in her sleep.

Blackburn himself left Jessica's town house, having no trouble finding his way out again and feeling more lighthearted than he had felt in days.

He climbed up into his waiting carriage and, oblivious of the fact that he had not told his coachman where to drive him, knocked on the ceiling with his cane.

John Coachman was perplexed for a moment. But, at the second impatient knock, decided to take his master where he habitually went first after a ball or some such entertainment. He started the horses.

He pulled them up in front of White's and watched the alert footman run to open the carriage door and let down the steps.

Blackburn bent his head, took the first step down, and realized he was not in front of his house as he'd expected to be, but about to enter his club. He did not, for once, feel in the least like going in. It seemed to him a more frivolous and wasteful manner to spend his time than it usually did.

He recollected that he had given his man no directions and felt the weight of some of Jessica's accusations. The fact that his man would feel sure enough of his lord's destination not to question it told Blackburn that he might indeed be frequenting his clubs more than he was consciously aware of doing. With a wry smile, he twisted on the carriage step and called, "My apologies, John Coachman. Take me home, please."

He returned to his seat inside his carriage. He wasn't certain why he didn't feel like going to White's tonight, except that he didn't want to be distracted from his thoughts about Jess. He wanted to concentrate all his faculties on mending his fences with her, what it might take to do that, if it were possible to be successful, and if that was truly what he wanted. He realized abruptly that, for the first time, he wasn't running away from his thoughts about his wife.

John Coachman pulled up to his house, and his lordship got down. When his major-domo opened the front door for him, he said, "Have a bottle of brandy brought to me in the library, McHenry."

"Very good, my lord."

Blackburn sank into his favorite armchair before the fire in the library and waited for his brandy. He wished Jessica was there with him.

A footman brought a bottle and a glass and poured his lordship's brandy. "Close the door, my lord?" he asked.

"Yes." Blackburn lifted his glass and drank. He put the glass down on the table next to him and struggled with his boots for several minutes. He let them fall to the floor as he got them off and then turned to open a drawer in the table beside him. He pulled out a cheroot, lit it, and took a few puffs, then picked up his brandy again, settling himself. Now he could think.

He sipped his brandy. He felt good about Jess. He had talked with her, and he had gotten past that cold, indifferent front she'd been putting up for weeks and touched something at the core of her. If that kiss was any judge, she wasn't indifferent, and she wasn't interested in anyone else, even if she had looked that Concord fellow over pretty damned carefully.

He was pleased with himself, too. He was finally addressing his problem: first, his unhappy wife and, then, the absence of his wife. He wished he'd addressed the problem sooner. Facing it felt much better than anesthetizing himself from it at his clubs, only to return home and have drunken nightmares about it. He felt certain he would sleep well tonight for a change.

Now, he thought, to the problem. He took another swallow of brandy. I suppose the kernel of the problem is that my beautiful Jessica wants me to spend every waking moment with her and, though I love her dearly, I don't want a lifetime of that. I will admit I was spending a trifle too much time at the clubs and, possibly, as a consequence, not enough with her.

If she wanted me to simply stop going to the clubs, I suppose I could manage that, though I wouldn't like it by half. But literally every moment together? Even her paragon of a father don't do that!

He finished his glass and poured another. He wondered if he had it right. Surely no person in her right mind would want to spend every single moment of the day with another person? The woman must be daft!

He took a large gulp of brandy and was assailed by doubts. Perhaps he didn't have the kernel of the problem right. Women were such cagey, complicated creatures. They said one thing, and then he discovered that they meant something entirely different. Possibly he was missing something here. Although that was one reason he had liked Jess from the start. She meant what she said; there were no hidden meanings. Unless he'd misread her from the start? No, that was not possible! he thought. He gulped his brandy. Look at how she'd let him know she was unhappy. She'd waited till he came in one night and then just told him to his face, in direct language. No manipulating, no tears.

If he hadn't misread her, could she have changed? Could she now be speaking in subtleties that were going over his head?

Blackburn asked himself. He poured and drank again. He doubted it, but it was possible.

Who could corroborate what he thought Jessica wanted? Blackburn wondered. Wainsby? Assuredly not. But Redley might serve. He'd always been good at knowing what women meant, despite whatever they said. He'd proved it numerous times. But Blackburn did not want to admit to his friend that he was uncertain about what was troubling his own wife.

Then Blackburn remembered the Duchess of Ashford. She was certainly desirous of seeing them back together, or, he assumed, she wouldn't have sent him the invitation to Jess's celebration honoring her. He could trust her to be discreet, and he'd wager she knew her daughter pretty well. Not to mention the fact that Jessica had spent her first months after moving out with her parents. She must have discussed at least part of their problems with her mother!

Done! thought Blackburn. I shall pay her a visit tomorrow before I see Jessica, and then I shall know better how to go on with my beautiful, spoiled wife. For the memory of the duchess's celebration party had put him in mind of the spoiled behavior of his wife that night and the coddling behavior of his father-in-law.

Blackburn drained his glass, corked the bottle, and picked up his boots unsteadily. Thinking that the duchess would assuredly know and was never wrong, he made his way upstairs to his bed.

Dropping his clothes where he stood as he removed them and changing into his nightshirt, Blackburn's thoughts returned to Jessica's kiss. Once again, he felt comforted. He might miss some subtleties of women's speech, but that was not the kiss of an indifferent woman! He'd stake his best team on it.

He climbed into bed and, as he had predicted, got one of the best nights of rest he'd had since Jessica had moved into her own bedchamber.

He woke at the advanced hour of eleven o'clock, eager to speak with the Duchess of Ashford. Throwing off the bedclothes, he got up and went to yank on the bellpull, bellowing, "Bailey!" at the same time.

While Blackburn waited for his valet, he strolled to his wardrobe and considered what he would put on. "Bailey, old man. Where are you?" roared Blackburn again, pulling a black coat out and tossing it on the foot of the bed.

Bailey knocked and threw open the bedchamber door grinning and crying, "Yer lordship! And a good morning to you, too, my lord!" It had been some time since his master had gotten up bellowing his name. Some fellows whistled when they got up feeling good; some fellows sang. His master bellowed. It seemed to be his manner of singing, and Bailey hadn't heard it in much too long.

"Hot water's coming right up, sir," said Bailey.

"The black today, I think, Bailey," remarked Blackburn, nodding at the coat on the bed.

Bailey followed his master's nod and gasped with horror. He ran to scoop the coat up gingerly and place it back on its hanger. Turning from the wardrobe to his master, he scolded indignantly, "You could at least wait till I get it on yer before yer wrinkle it!" When he was excited, Bailey's language suffered, bespeaking his origins.

A footman came in bringing hot towels and hot water. Bailey pointed to where he wanted them and signaled the man out.

Blackburn flung himself into a chair. "Sorry, old man," he said, smiling. "I forgot. You can cut my throat if you wish as long as you begin shaving me now. I've some important negotiating to do today. I want to be off."

"He forgot, he forgot. Again, he forgot!" muttered Bailey, placing a hot towel on his lordship's face. "Hmph! If that isn't just like you, too—so generous, you'll let me cut your throat. So the constable can arrest me and hang me up for a pretty bauble at Tyburn! Cut your throat, indeed."

"Bailey!" his lordship bellowed. "Bailey! Bailey!"

Bailey's mouth began to crook into a smile.

" 'Twas a little humor, man!" Blackburn continued to roar. "I'm sorry I forgot!"

"You forget rather a lot, my lord, if I might be allowed to say so," replied Bailey. He accepted his master's absent-minded approach to the finer points of clothing himself and grinned back at him. It was his only flaw, in Bailey's eyes.

"You may," intoned Blackburn magnanimously. "I probably do," he sighed, agreeing with his valet. "What say we raise your wage a couple of guineas to take care of it, eh? Done!"

"My lord. I was not hanging out for an increase."

"I know that. But you're an excellent man, Bailey, and I'm certain I'm a trial to you. I'm a trial to Jess, too. She's told me so any number of times. I must keep you happy in my service, mustn't I?"

"I'm content, my lord. Without the increase, I'm content."

"Well, it's done now, and if you don't have done about it, you're going to make *me* cross."

"Then, if you'll stop wagging your jaw, my lord, I can get you shaved. I thought you said you wanted to be off?" Bailey bestowed a smug smile upon his lordship.

Blackburn choked. "A hit, Bailey!" He threw back his head and laughed. "A demmed fine hit!" Then he closed his mouth in a most obvious manner and signaled for the shaving to begin.

Bailey had his master shaved in a trice and dressed immaculately in a black coat, buff breeches, and shining Hessians in a trifle longer than that.

The valet admired his handiwork as Blackburn left the bedchamber to breakfast and set off for the duchess's town house. Bailey heaved a great sigh. "If he would only take a little more interest, with that figure we could be greater than Beau Brummel!" Bailey shook his head and began picking up crumpled cravats and discarded towels.

Blackburn made short work of his breakfast and was in his curricle on his way to see the duchess some three-quarters of an hour later.

Dismayed to see a barouche, obviously waiting for its owner, before the duchess's house, Blackburn pulled up his horses and got down. He gave the reins into the hands of a footman in the duchess's livery who sprang from nowhere.

Knocking upon the door, he unconsciously put his hand to his cravat and squared his shoulders. The Lord only knew how long it was going to take to get the duchess off alone, he thought. If fortune were with him, he had come at the end of her visitor's call.

Fortune, however, was not disposed to be kind to Lord Blackburn that morning. Lady Bathurst had only just sat down and settled herself on the divan across from the duchess.

The two ladies had inquired after the other's health. The duchess, not being one of those ladies who derive entertainment from discussing any ill health she suffered, had answered briefly that her lumbago had been better of late. Lady Bathurst, who derived a great deal of enjoyment from comparing aches and pains, had nodded sympathetically. Then she had launched herself on a description of her latest complaint, shingles, conquered only the week before with a powder her daughter-in-law had procured for her. Her description had gone on quite long enough for the duchess's taste and had been much more detailed than she cared to hear. The duchess was searching about in her mind for another subject to present whenever next Lady Bathurst paused long enough to take a breath.

Both ladies were surprised by the announcement of Blackburn, the one glad of the interruption, the other annoyed by it. Lady Bathurst, however, forewent easily enough further description of her shingles and their miraculous cure, for she had planned in the course of her visit to sound the duchess on the state of affairs between her daughter and her husband, if one could still call them that. Blackburn's arrival meant she could glean her information straight from the horse's mouth!

Blackburn suffered the ladies to ask after his health and then inquired after theirs. The duchess almost moaned aloud, believing she must now be treated to a second recital of Lady Bathurst's description of her shingles. That lady, however, served the duchess a shock when she gave one of the briefest descriptions of her ills that the duchess had ever known her to give. But Lady Bathurst's next question told the duchess why.

"How is your lovely wife, Lord Blackburn?" asked Lady Bathurst innocently.

Blackburn's bushy brown brows snapped together in a frown,

swiftly replaced by his blandest expression. "Well ma'am, if you must know . . ." He hesitated.

Lady Bathurst sat forward in her chair.

The duchess observed him with curiosity.

Blackburn continued in a matter-of-fact voice, "I am about ready to have her poisoned and be done with it."

Both ladies gasped and looked at him in astonishment.

"Did you say, *poisoned,* my lord?" repeated Lady Bathurst, as if she felt she could not have heard aright. She laughed uncertainly. "You are joking, surely?" She looked at the duchess. But the Duchess of Ashford was not laughing. She looked as shocked as Lady Bathurst felt.

"Yes, I suppose I am," answered Blackburn in a voice that made Lady Bathurst believe the exact opposite. "Though heaven knows, my wife deserves to be poisoned—begging your pardon, Duchess."

"She has her flaws," replied the duchess faintly.

Blackburn continued in outrage, "Do you know that she was making eyes at Wainsby—a good friend of mine!—while she was dancing with him at the York ball? She ogled another fellow during supper there. And then she had the gall, at the St. John affair, to follow me around all evening and hang on me every time any woman attempted a conversation with me—Lady Kittrell, for one!"

"Lord Wainsby? And Lady *Kittrell?"* breathed Lady Bathurst. "Yes, she's irreproachable. No reason for jealousy there."

"You can see why I've almost gone stark staring mad over what she's been doing to me," said Blackburn, pleading for Lady Bathurst's understanding.

"Almost?" whispered Lady Bathurst. She gave the duchess a look of sympathy.

The duchess blushed and looked at her feet. Her lips were trembling.

Blackburn ran a hand through his chestnut hair and sat forward to lean his elbows on his knees and stare at the flowered pattern on the carpet. In a low voice, he remarked, "I suppose I shouldn't be talking about poisoning her so openly. I can't seem to keep from it. I beg you won't repeat it, Ladies. It's just that—well, I'm afraid she's getting under my skin."

"Oh, Lord Blackburn, I am sorry," commiserated Lady Bathurst. "You do appear a bit . . . obsessed."

Blackburn was quiet, and the duchess did not seem inclined to present another topic.

"Well!" said Lady Bathurst as if coming to a grand decision. "It must be time for me to go. I don't want to overstay my welcome." In addition, she was anxious to relate to Lady Mortimer what Lord Blackburn had just said.

She took her leave of Blackburn, and the duchess saw her to the salon door and gave her into the care of Stomes to see out.

Coming back in the salon and closing the door behind her, the duchess remarked dryly, " 'Twas wise of you not to mention the Widow Thompkins, Blackburn. She would quite have ruined the effect."

Blackburn grinned. "So I thought, Duchess."

"Really, Blackburn," the duchess scolded. "That was not well-done of you." Then she threw back her head and laughed. "But awfully diverting! Now, to what do I owe the unique pleasure of your visit, you wicked boy," she asked, her laughter subsiding. "You are as bad as Jessica. I can quite see why she likes you."

"Indeed, I fear so. And it is about her that I've come, Duchess. I would like a few moments to speak privately with you, if I may."

The duchess walked back to the door thoughtfully, opened it, and called, "Stomes, I am not at home for a bit." She closed the door again and returned to her chair.

Blackburn hesitated and then began, "This is going to sound as absurd as the Banbury tale I just told."

"I'm not certain," answered the duchess. "I've been hearing some exceedingly fantastic stories about the pair of you—something about knocking each other down on the St. John dance floor and bringing down half of the other dancers with you. Must have been quite a turn up," smiled the duchess.

"I fear so," Blackburn smiled back wryly.

The duchess's eyes twinkled. "I'm sorry I missed it." She continued, "You're making every hostess's party that you both attend."

"Making every party—?!" exclaimed Blackburn in disbelief.

"Yes, for your entertainment value," explained the duchess. "I must admit, it would be highly diverting to see half a ballroom's dancers rolling around on the dance floor." She chuckled. "And Judson tells me they're betting on you in the clubs."

"I was aware of that." Blackburn shifted uncomfortably in his seat.

"In truth, Blackburn, Banbury tale or no, at the moment I believe there are more stakes on your killing each other than on your making up. I am not a betting woman. I leave the gambling to Judson. I prefer taking steps to see that the outcome I desire is the one that turns up." The duchess paused and regarded Blackburn intently.

He felt the hair on the backs of his arms rise and was suddenly very glad the duchess wanted him back with Jessica. Most certainly, his mother-in-law would be a formidable woman to oppose.

He addressed the duchess. "Then tell me what you know. Tell me why Jess left. What is it she wants before she'll come back home?"

"Oh lud, Blackburn!" exclaimed the duchess in mild disgust. "You know that better than I. You might think you don't, but trust me, you do. Jessica isn't the kind that bares her soul. Never has been. She's not the kind to dissemble, either! If she has an argument with you, she simply corners you and tells you to your face what her difficulty is. Then, if you don't change something, she tries once or twice more. Then she doesn't have anything more to do with you. What did she say to you?"

"If I heard it aright, she said I was spending all my time at my clubs. That I wasn't spending any time with her, and she didn't understand why I married her if I didn't like being in her company. But I couldn't have been spending every night at my clubs. That's just not possible. She must have been exaggerating."

"You don't need to defend yourself to me, my boy."

Blackburn recollected uncomfortably John Coachman's driving him to White's, though he had had no instructions to do so. "I believe she wanted me to spend all my time with her instead of at the clubs."

"Then nothing could be easier. There!" cried the duchess. "I told you that you knew what the problem was. Give her precisely what she wants, Blackburn."

"Spend every waking moment with her? You're as daft as she is! Er, begging your pardon, of course, Duchess." He took several turns about the middle of the salon and returned to stand before his mother-in-law. "I can't do that. I don't want to do that. And more, I don't believe that's healthy for either of us!"

"Don't shout at me, Blackburn. I agree with you."

"You do? Then why tell me to give her what she wants?!"

"Because, you great looby," the duchess smiled affectionately at Blackburn and got up to pat his arm, "sometimes you must obtain what you want in order to discover that, in fact, you do not want it."

"What the devil does that signify?" asked Blackburn in exasperation.

"Think about it." The duchess smiled again and linked her arm through his, beginning to walk toward the salon door.

Blackburn gathered with frustration that his interview was at an end.

The duchess put her hand on the doorknob. "One impression I did receive from Jessica that you haven't mentioned, Blackburn," she said quietly. "She didn't believe you were making much of an effort."

"To keep us together?" Blackburn finished.

The duchess nodded. She turned the knob and opened the door. Fixing Blackburn with a steely eye, she asked, "If I *were* a betting woman, Blackburn, which wager would you have me stake?"

"Perhaps I'll tell you that, Duchess," replied Blackburn, his hazel eyes flashing, "when I've discovered what your mysterious statement signifies."

"Fair enough. Stomes," the duchess called.

Stomes approached and bowed. "This way, my lord."

Blackburn followed the stately major-domo to the front door.

Women! Blackburn thought with aggravation as he climbed up in his curricle and took the reins from the footman. They made you think they knew the answers to even the gods' questions. So, you took your questions to them, these women, and what answers did they give you? He whipped up his horses. Riddles! Absurd statements that made no sense! "Sometimes you have to obtain what you want to discover that you don't want it." Demmed women!

Hold, he thought, and slowed his horses. That did make a modicum of sense. If he gave Jess *exactly* what she thought she wanted—if he never allowed her to do anything without him—the duchess was right. He smiled. He perceived possibilities. He could also understand now why the duchess had been so oblique and mysterious. It was an easy matter to plague most people by being always at their elbow. He doubted Jessica was any different, and he'd lay a monkey that that was what the duchess was suggesting he do! If he made it a point to be constantly at Jessica's elbow, indefatigably underfoot, she would realize that always being together was not as desirable as she thought it.

Blackburn smiled again. Oh, the duchess was a downy one! He chuckled as another thought struck him: now that was what a mother was for—doing something she knew you wouldn't like to ensure your happiness. If Jess hadn't already thrown the duchess a party, he thought, I should want to. Indeed, if all comes right, I believe I'll throw her another!

He pulled up in front of Jessica's door and jumped down. Taking the steps two at a time, he was at the door in a trice banging the knocker exuberantly.

The door swung open to reveal a burly gentleman in butler's livery.

Blackburn raised an eyebrow and presented his card. "Is the lady of the house at home?"

The fellow took his card, ran his eyes over him, and shut the door in his face.

"Demmed unsociable fellow," muttered Blackburn, turning about on the top step to admire the sunshine and blue sky of a beautiful day. He began to whistle.

A polite cough interrupted his whistling, and Blackburn jumped and spun around to discover the large butler observing him noncommittally. "Follow me, please," he requested and led Blackburn to Jessica, seemingly absorbed in *The Chronicle,* seated in a large leather armchair in her small, colorful sitting room.

"Lord Blackburn!" barked the butler and withdrew.

Jessica put down the paper. "Well, and if you didn't pay a call, just as you said you would," she remarked, looking up with mock surprise.

"Like a bad shilling, Jessica, my love," he smiled, approaching to take her hands, pull her to her feet, and drop a light kiss on her lips. "How does your knee fare?"

Surprised, Jessica drew back but did so too late to avoid the kiss. "Oh, it feels almost as though I never fell on it. I shall have to discover what Ann put in that poultice. She is abovestairs resting at the moment," Jessica said uncertainly. "But I do believe it would be best if she joined us." Jessica edged toward the door. Ann could assuredly help with the conversation, Jessica thought nervously, and added, "I will just go and call her—"

"Thunder and turf, Jess!" exclaimed Blackburn. "If you're uneasy about me, you would do better to call that great oaf of a butler of yours and have him toss me out on my ear. Where in the world did you find the fellow? I believe he could do it, too, for he's as large as I am."

Jessica laughed. "Well, I didn't know but what I might have to ask you or someone else to leave someday, and I thought the request would be more inclined to be recognized if it were seconded by Moncton. Don't you agree?" she asked sweetly.

"Moncton, is it? Indeed, I do. He doesn't seem to have much of a sense of humor. Don't seem to have much of a personality, if it comes to that. But, Jess! I'm hurt. You had *me* in mind when you hired that oaf?"

"Well, Blackburn, two ladies living alone? We must needs have some kind of protection."

"But how could you think I would ever hurt you?" he asked, looking disappointed in her.

"Oh, Blackburn!" cried Jessica defensively. "Take that look off your face. You know very well I know you wouldn't hurt me. You are exaggerating. And you also know very well that if I asked you to leave and you didn't want to, you wouldn't. That is all I was thinking of—mercy!" Skirts swishing, she took several short turns about the middle of the room.

Blackburn stepped in front of her and stopped her, taking up her hands again. "You're right, Jessica," he said contritely. "I was but teasing. I forgot you're so easy to provoke. I'm sorry. I got carried away. I came to ask you to come out for a drive in my curricle, and now I've very likely riled you so that you won't come. Am I right?"

She shook her hands free of his. "In truth, I don't believe it is a good idea. We shall only argue the entire time," Jessica agreed, shaking her head.

"We could drive round The Ring in Hyde Park," coaxed Blackburn.

Jessica smiled but continued to shake her head.

"We could race it," he cajoled. "There was a time you liked to do that."

"That was a very long time ago, Blackburn, and two very different, very ignorant people, I fear," answered Jessica sadly.

Blackburn persevered, teasing her. "I have it! You can drive, Jess. You can race us around The Ring."

She sucked in her breath and narrowed sparkling, skeptical eyes at him. "You wouldn't! You're just saying that to lure me into going, but I know you won't really let me race it," she said.

He knew he had her. " 'Pon rep, Jess, I'll give you the reins if you want 'em. Come on," he smiled engagingly, "go get your hat or your shawl or your vinaigrette, and let's go. It's a beautiful day."

Jessica stood uncertainly, biting her lip.

Blackburn put his hand on her waist and gave her a push. "Go on! No doubt Mrs. Darby must have a note, so that she does not believe I have kidnapped and murdered you?" he grinned. "I will do that while you collect yourself."

She stood irresolutely a moment longer and then capitulated.

"Oh, dear. Oh, all right, I will!" she exclaimed, picking up her skirts and running to the door. There she halted abruptly and ran back a few steps to point and breathe, "Paper, quills, and ink in the writing desk there. I'll be back in a trice!" She hiked up her skirts again and fled.

Blackburn chuckled and sat down at the desk to scrawl a short explanation.

As he sanded the paper, Jessica reentered the sitting room.

"Got your vinaigrette then?" he grinned, observing the chip straw bonnet tied becomingly beneath her chin with red ribbons.

Jessica laughed excitedly. "Indeed! For assuredly, if I don't need it, you will!"

He waved the note in the air with a questioning look.

Interpreting that motion as if she'd lived with him for thirty years, Jessica answered, "Put it on my chair. She will be certain to see it there. And I will also tell Moncton."

"Lord, yes, tell Moncton!" exclaimed Blackburn in mock fear, giving Jessica his arm. "I cannot have him stalking me." He smiled down into Jessica's eyes.

Her gray-blue eyes laughed back up at him. She put her arm through his and, in her anticipation, hugged him close just for an instant the way she used to do. "Oh, I can't wait! I haven't driven anything since I moved out! What I should have done," she teased, "was buy myself a new high-perch phaeton and have the bill sent to you!"

Blackburn chuckled. "I believe," he said, "if you had done that, you would have received a visit from me well before your celebration for your mother!"

"Oh dear," retorted Jessica. "We better stop there, or we'll be embroiled in an argument before we even leave the house!"

"In that event," said Blackburn, "I'd better get you out of the house and into the curricle before you change your mind again—either before I accidentally provoke you again or before the wind blows!" He pulled her from the sitting room into the hall.

"Hmph! You mean before you say something tiresome and rude that would put anyone out of all patience with you. Quick! We better run!" she laughed, suiting actions to words.

Both ran noisily down the hall of Jessica's town house.

Moncton dispassionately held open the front door.

As the pair ran through and continued down the front steps, Jessica called, "Moncton! Please tell Mrs. Darby I've gone for a drive with Lord Blackburn."

"Very good, Lady Blackburn," replied Moncton. But it was doubtful if she heard him, for Blackburn had tossed her up into his curricle, leapt up himself, and the horses were pulling away.

Several minutes later, Blackburn pulled up before the gates of Hyde Park and held out the reins to Jessica. "Better get used to the horses before you try to race 'em," he remarked.

"And they to me?" Jessica asked, reading his mind. She took the reins from him.

"Well, I wasn't going to say so," he grinned, "but yes!"

Each laughed at the other one.

"Oh, Blackburn," said Jessica with mild scorn, clicking her tongue at the horses and slapping the reins. "I am not going to hurt your precious blacks."

They passed through the gates of the park.

"It was Lady Warren, was it not, that said something of that nature to her husband last week and then promptly tried to run over a water trough with the carriage and lamed one of his animals in the process?" asked Blackburn pointedly. "Poor devil had to shoot the beast, and he'd only just purchased him at Tattersall's."

Jessica laughed. "Yes, it was. But I am not as totty-headed as Lady Warren by half—nor her husband either, for allowing such a flighty creature to drive in the first place. Your animals are in no danger. Shall I prove my mettle?" She slowed the horses and looked around them for something to test her skill on. "Let's see how close I can drive to that iron bench without scraping it."

Blackburn's eyebrows flew up, and he began shaking his head.

"Or," continued Jessica, still looking around, "let's see how fast I can drive through that little stand of trees without nicking anything. They look to be nicely staggered for that sort of thing?" She turned to Blackburn for a moment to see if any of her suggestions were meeting with approval.

He was still shaking his head.

Jessica took one look at his expression and burst out laughing. "Coward! All right, we'll make do with only a race today."

He breathed a sigh of relief and sat back. "The gods are merciful! Thank you, my dear," he said in heartfelt tones.

Jessica patted his arm. "Now. Whom do we see that will race me?"

"Lady Bartlesville?" asked Blackburn hopefully, nodding in that lady's direction.

Jessica followed his nod. "In a phaeton, Blackburn?" she asked in disgust. She smiled and waved at Lady Bartlesville as they drove past.

"Lord Monroe," suggested Blackburn persuasively. He raised his hand at a portly, white-haired gentleman sitting his horse complacently and observing all those who passed before him.

"Lord Monroe! Faugh!" exclaimed Jessica rudely. "He is sixty, if he is a day!" She brought the curricle to a stop as she saw Lord Monroe spur his horse in their direction. She observed his approach and turned to bestow a quick scowl upon Blackburn. "And that poor beast must be one hundred! Really, Blackburn."

Blackburn had time to shrug sheepishly at Jessica before Lord Monroe was close enough to greet them.

"Hello! Didn't expect to see the two of you here today," Lord Monroe hailed them. "At least, not together!" he laughed. "No doubt your dancing will improve, too, eh, Lady Blackburn?" he asked with a sly wink.

"I doubt it, my lord, unless she continues to dance with me," answered Blackburn, turning a placid look upon Jessica. "It's dangerous to ask her. She is difficult to lead, don't you know, Lord Monroe." Blackburn smiled blandly at Jessica.

Jessica gave him a sweet smile in return and delivered a small pinch which she hoped went unnoticed, to Blackburn's thigh.

"Ow!" Blackburn glared at her and turned to explain to Lord Monroe. "Bumped m'knee on the side of the carriage."

"Yes, I can see," remarked Lord Monroe, his eyes twinkling. Nevertheless, he decided it was time to take his leave of the pair. By all accounts, to remain too long these days in the company of Lord and Lady Blackburn was to risk becoming an accidental casualty in their private war. With the wisdom that had helped him achieve his white hair and twenty years of marriage with a wife of his own, Lord Monroe judged by that pinch that it was past time for him to depart. "Well, good day to you both," he said, doffing his hat and turning his horse's head to amble back the way he had come.

Blackburn stared after him. "Bit abrupt, that. Don't you think?" He turned to Jessica with a puzzled expression.

"Perhaps." Jessica slapped the reins, and they started to move. "But, you know, eccentricity runs in that family. The older they get, the more peculiarly they behave."

Blackburn thought a moment and frowned. "I don't think that's it."

Jessica gasped and slapped the reins again harder, sending the blacks into a canter. "There's Wainsby! He will race me I'm certain!"

"Oh, Lord," moaned Blackburn. "He's mounted, Jessica," he pointed out.

Ignoring Blackburn's remarks, Jessica called, "Wainsby!" She drew the curricle up beside her husband's friend.

Lord Wainsby, astride a beautiful golden stallion, looked from Jessica to Blackburn and beamed upon the pair of them. "What! You've made it up between you—finally? Well, jolly good. I don't believe it!"

"As well you shouldn't, for it isn't true," retorted Jessica.

Wainsby's face fell. With disappointment, he looked to Blackburn for an explanation.

"We are, ah—negotiating only, Wainsby," Blackburn said blandly.

"Negotiating?" Wainsby appeared confused.

"Yes, you know. Negotiating matters," said Blackburn. He gave Wainsby a large wink that Jessica was certain to see.

"Blackburn, don't do that," she said crossly. "And wipe that look off your face as well. You will give him notions."

Blackburn laughed. "I want him to get notions, Jessy, my love. I want everyone to get notions about us." He put his arm about

Jessica and hugged her to him. "Including old Monroe," he added magnanimously. "Wainsby! Do you know, the fellow was—"

"Oh, Blackburn, don't tell him that *now!*" interrupted Jessica, struggling out of his hug. She wanted to get Wainsby to race.

"—prating along," continued Blackburn as if Jessica hadn't spoken, "and then, suddenly, as if he were on some deuced timetable, he stops, says good day, and turns his horse about. Doesn't that strike you as dashed odd behavior?"

Wainsby considered the question, stroking a smooth chin. "Old Monroe, you say? Never done anything like that in my presence. But you know that madness is the curse of the Monroe family?"

Jessica and Blackburn looked at Wainsby with the same arrested expression on their faces.

Wainsby nodded solemnly. "Oh yes. The last two earls were mad as hatters."

Jessica and Blackburn burst into laughter.

"Here now! I don't think that's the proper response at all," said a shocked Wainsby. "Don't see anything laughable about it. Poor blighter's—"

"It isn't that, Wainsby. It's just that that's exactly what Jessica said," interrupted Blackburn, still smiling. A puzzled frown replaced the smile. "But I really don't think that's why."

"Why not, Blackburn?" asked Jessica impatiently. "And what does it matter anyway?"

"I just have this feeling. I'll lay you a monkey 'the curse of madness' or, as Jessica so politely put it, 'eccentricity' isn't the cause."

"And speaking of wagers, Wainsby," interrupted Jessica, neatly changing the subject and grinning at Blackburn as she did so, "I'll wager that you can't beat me in a race around The Ring."

Wainsby was affronted. "Devil a bit, Jess! I'm on horseback."

Jessica looked accusingly at Blackburn.

Blackburn shrugged. "Well, he is. However," he went on, as he saw Jessica's countenance fall, "if I remove my great weight from the carriage and start Wainsby two or three furlongs behind you, we can even the race up a trifle. Does that interest you, Wainsby?"

"How many furlongs behind Jess?" he asked warily.

"Three."

"Three! She's not exactly ham-fisted with the ribbons, you know."

"Two?" amended Blackburn.

"Done!" exclaimed Wainsby. He trotted his stallion the short distance to the large dirt ring known for the many races that occurred on it daily and waited excitedly for Jessica and Blackburn.

Blackburn jumped onto the curricle's step, and Jessica tooled them over to join Wainsby. She drew up next to the golden stallion, fidgeting restlessly beneath Wainsby.

"Start out hell for leather, Jess, and don't let 'em flag for an instant," murmured Blackburn, smiling at her and jumping down from the carriage step. He blew her a kiss and turned to walk off to the side of both horse and curricle.

Taking his white linen handkerchief from his coat pocket, Blackburn shook it out and raised his arm high. "The first time I bring my handkerchief down is your start, Jess. When I've judged she's gone two furlongs, Wainsby, I'll bring it down again. That's your start. Good luck to you both. Ready?" He raised his handkerchief.

Jessica sat forward, butterflies in her stomach, and regripped the reins.

Blackburn's arm came down.

Jessica slapped the reins and cried, "Giddap! Giddap!" She continued to slap the reins, whipping the two blacks to a gallop and giving them their heads.

Behind her, the stallion danced beneath Wainsby, eager to follow the two blacks.

Blackburn's white handkerchief came down again.

Wainsby's heels dug into the stallion's sides, and they were off in a rain of pebbles.

Blackburn shielded his eyes from the sun and growled, "Come on, Jess. Come on, you can do it. Don't let 'em flag now. You can do it. You can *do* it—! By George, she's going to do it! She's going to—!"

He watched her take the last curve and start down the straightaway toward him. She was slapping the reins for all she was worth. Blackburn laughed heartily and threw his handkerchief on the ground. "She's *got* him! He'll never catch her now!"

Blackburn windmilled his arms at Jessica and picked up his handkerchief to wave her across the finish line as the winner. He let out a loud whoop and grinned at her as she flashed by him.

Jessica crowed and stood up to pull back on the reins and slow the two powerful blacks.

Several moments later, Wainsby, bent low over his stallion's mane, streaked by Blackburn, and Blackburn brought his white handkerchief down again, shouting, "Second!"

Jessica succeeded in stopping the blacks and turned the curricle around. She trotted the horses, snorting and blowing and shaking their harnesses, back toward Blackburn.

As soon as Wainsby galloped past him, Blackburn abandoned his role as judge and ran to meet Jessica.

Beaming, as if she were going to burst out laughing at any moment, Jessica slowed the blacks to a walk as Blackburn neared the curricle.

He came abreast, and Jessica, beginning to laugh and exclaim excitedly, stopped the horses. Her face was flushed becomingly, and her chip straw bonnet, long since blown off her tawny hair, was hanging down her back by its red ribbons.

Laughing himself and keeping up with the curricle, Blackburn shouted, "Well done, Jess! You didn't let them slack off for a moment!" The carriage came to a halt as the horses stopped, and Blackburn, in his excitement, grasped Jessica about the waist and dragged her from the curricle. She gave another whoop as her body went over the side and swung into Blackburn's. He captured her against the solid length of him and delivered a resounding kiss. "Jolly well done!" he repeated, beaming upon her. He laughed again and teased, "You have the most nonsensical look upon your face!"

" 'Tis the mirror of yours, I suspect!" Jessica agreed, laughing back at him. "Put me down! People will begin to stare!" She continued to laugh but started to struggle.

"Too late!" remarked Wainsby, grinning at the pair as he walked up, leading his stallion by the reins. He directed their gaze toward several clumps of people who had gathered not too far distant and were looking their way and pointing. "You're already tonight's morsel for dinner!" he said and laughed.

"Oh lud," groaned Jessica ruefully, turning her back to the crowd and fumbling to put on her bonnet.

Blackburn pounded Wainsby on the shoulder. "Good race, Wainsby," he said, smiling warmly at his friend. "I believe I gave her too much of a lead over you. If I'd known she could hold her own, I'd have allowed her only one furlong."

"Indeed, were we to race again, I'm not certain I'd give her the one," Wainsby said, turning to Jessica. He teased, "What have you been up to, Jess? Coming out at the crack of dawn to practice?"

Jessica laughed. "No. In truth, as I was telling Blackburn earlier, I haven't had anything to drive, or ride, since I, ah, set up my own establishment."

"Hah!" Blackburn snorted in disapproval.

"Well, I'm fortunate I didn't wager anything," said Wainsby. "Lord! Do you know I was ready to wager m'stallion against one of your blacks? What a near thing!"

Jessica and Blackburn laughed, and Jessica remarked, "Pity, for I should have been halfway to having a conveyance of my own!"

All three laughed.

Blackburn took Jessica's arm and began to help her back up in the curricle. "Well," he said, "since the horses still need to be walked and since you, Wainsby, kept yours by the skin of your teeth, thereby depriving poor Jess of half a conveyance, I propose we walk the horses to Gunther's and you buy us all ices. Will that satisfy you, Jess?" he asked, climbing up into the curricle.

Jessica smiled. "I think that's a capital idea, Blackburn." She smiled at Wainsby and teased, " 'Tis only fair."

Wainsby grinned back and mounted his horse. "As I happen

to like ices myself, Lord and Lady Blackburn, and as I am in the funds today," he held up a warning finger "—not always the case—I am in a position to accommodate your suggestion. You are fortunate," he finished in the tones of the Prince Regent.

They all laughed again and set off for Gunther's.

The ices did not take long to consume, and Blackburn and Jessica were soon teasing Wainsby with the promise of another race and bidding him goodbye. Equally soon, Blackburn was drawing the curricle up before Jessica's house and climbing down to help her out.

He saw her to the door and bowed over her hand.

" 'Twas amusing, Blackburn. Thank you," said Jessica, smiling warmly into his hazel eyes.

"You raced well, Jess," returned Blackburn simply, causing Jessica to blush with pleasure. "And if we cannot get old Wainsby to race you again, I'll race you myself," he grinned.

Jessica's eyes lit. "Done!" she agreed and whisked herself through the front door.

The next thing he should ask me to do, I shall have a previous engagement, Jessica thought defensively and hardened her heart as she climbed the staircase to her bedchamber to change her walking dress.

Blackburn descended the steps out front musing, 'Tis better to wait two or three days before I ask her to anything else. I don't want to look like I'm rushing my fences.

This dancing at cross-purposes went on between the pair for several weeks. Finally one evening, when the moon was particularly white and full and the late roses in Lady Sudbury's front garden were especially fragrant, as Blackburn and Jessica departed their hostess's ball, Blackburn asked Jessica to attend a musicale with him the following evening, and Jessica's heart overruled her head. She said yes.

Thus gradually, bit by bit over the next several weeks, Jessica came to accept Blackburn's invitations on every occasion he asked, and Blackburn began to invite her five and six times a week.

During this last, happier period of weeks, the post brought

Jessica a formal invitation from Blackburn to "Dine and While Away the Evening's Hours at Home in the Fashion of True Husband and Wife."

Though Jessica was not precisely certain what Blackburn meant by that, she accepted with a tingle of anticipation up and down her spine and mailed back the response card, smiling at his formality.

The bespoken evening arrived, and Blackburn came to get Jessica in his crested coach. They alighted in front of the door Jessica had left unhappily a good many months before and entered, Jessica unconsciously squaring her shoulders as she did so. The rooms looked exactly as they had when she left. There was not a speck of dust or dirt to be seen, everything shone with a well-polished gleam, and fresh-cut flowers and spicy potpourris adorned select tables.

Unable to stop herself, Jessica's eyes rose to the Chinese stand outside the door to the drawing room. She could just see it through the balusters. A vase of white flowers stood in place of the decorative vase she had last seen in fragments down here on the polished floor.

Blackburn put his hands on her shoulders and kneaded gently. "Don't think of that, Jess. Please," he asked softly.

Jessica's head snapped up, her gray-blue eyes wide in astonishment.

"Yes, I knew of the broken vase."

"But who would've told you of that?" she asked.

Blackburn smiled ruefully. "Who, but Bailey? He apparently felt it was not a detail I should be ignorant of. Now, let's not think of it again. Here, let me have your cloak."

Jessica untied the front and let Blackburn draw it from her shoulders. He removed his own cape and handed both wraps to McHenry, standing woodenly, as if he were but another column in the front hall, and waiting patiently to receive them.

"Dinner?" Blackburn queried his major-domo.

"Ready to be served, if you care to sit down now, my lord," responded McHenry, withdrawing.

"Yes. Come, Jessica." Blackburn held out his arm and allowed his eyes to travel over Jessica's form-fitting blue lustring as she approached to place her hand on his arm. His hazel eyes halted appreciatively at the décolletage and continued until they met her blue eyes. He bent and whispered wickedly, "Have we dampened our skirts just the tiniest wee bit?"

"Certainly not!" Jessica exclaimed. Her cheeks, already pink from his perusal of the lines of her gown, blushed rosily, and she blinked in surprise at his acuity. "And if we had, we would not expect you to be so rude as to notice it!" she remarked tartly, starting toward the dining room. She was not about to admit that she had, in truth, scandalized poor Maisie by dampening her skirts, though she had done so only ever so slightly. For, as she had told Maisie, who better to try such out on than one's husband?

Jessica wasn't about to repeat Maisie's answer: " 'Tisn't any better to tease yer husband than any other poor fool. And yer haven't been calling him that for many a week, or so I noticed." It made her feel a trifle guilty about dampening her skirts. And she knew if she examined her motives for doing so they wouldn't be very pure.

"I am not complaining, mind," Blackburn interrupted her thoughts.

They entered the dining room, and Blackburn stopped her to raise her hand to his lips. "Beautiful as ever, Jess," he said softly. He left her to sit in the chair the footman pulled out for him at the end of the table.

That, thought Jessica fleetingly, as pleasure and guilt both flamed in her cheeks again, is why I dampened them! She took her seat in the chair a footman pulled out for her at the opposite end of the table from Blackburn.

They took their time over the dinner, relating the latest *on-dits* to each other and laughing about them over the lentil soup, arguing the politics of Prinny over the chicken à la tarragon and French beans, and comparing further thoughts they had had about the play they had attended two nights previously over the apple tarts.

When they had eaten the last bit of apple tart, Blackburn came round the table and took Jessica's hand, leading her into the library. "Cozier than the drawing room, for just us, don't you agree?" he asked.

Jessica regarded the leather spines of the books lining the walls, the plump pillows upon the divan, and the fire crackling behind the ornate grate in front of the fireplace. "Indeed, 'twas always a cozy room, I thought," she smiled.

Blackburn sent for a bottle of dessert wine and challenged Jessica to a game of piquet. She accepted with relish, and they immersed themselves in the give and take of a card for several hours, each loath to stop while the other was ahead.

Finally Jessica, looking to the clock on the mantel for the time, sat back and picked up her wineglass. Sighing contentedly, she sipped. "Well, I would be willing to cry off now, if we can pick up just here next time," she proposed magnanimously.

Blackburn raised his bushy eyebrows at her. "If you yield, then I win."

"I don't yield! 'Tis late. That's the only reason." Jessica sipped again and nodded toward the clock.

Blackburn looked. "Lord, where did the hours go?" he exclaimed. "Very well," he agreed. He put his cards down and stood up. Drawing Jessica to the divan with him, he said, "We'll begin at these scores next time." He put his arm around her shoulders. "Right now, we will just sit here and be cozy for a moment or two while we finish our wine. Then I'll take you home. Does that suit you, Lady Blackburn?" he teased.

"It does," Jessica replied regally and smiled.

A thought struck Blackburn. "Ah, I shouldn't assume so much, no doubt. Is there going to be a next time?"

"I'm not certain. You tell me, Blackburn. It wasn't high stakes at White's, but I thought it entertaining," Jessica replied bitterly.

"Oh, Jess," Blackburn commiserated, hugging her apologetically to his side. "It was entertaining." He looked at her intently. "I would like there to be a next time."

"So would I," she whispered, regarding him steadily.

They sat in contented silence for several minutes, both staring at the flames in the fireplace, both of the same mind, thinking, This is how it should be.

Jessica frowned and broke the spell, withdrawing herself from Blackburn's side. " 'Tis time to go, I think," she said coldly.

Surprised at her tone, Blackburn looked at her carefully. "Only a few moments more?"

"Now."

He sat forward. "Lord, you can change humor like the wind, can't you?" he exclaimed, marveling. "What's the matter, Jess? You were happy a moment ago—weren't you?!" he asked with a sudden and ludicrous doubt of his previous assessment.

In spite of herself, Jessica laughed, tears springing to her eyes. "Yes," she corroborated, putting her hand to his cheek. Love and tears glistened in her eyes before she took her hand from his cheek to dash the tears away. She looked at him with distress and began hesitantly, "Blackburn, this is just what we did when we were courting. These past several weeks—nothing is different. I'm afraid nothing *will* be different." Another tear escaped and slid down her cheek. It was dashed away. "You'll just fool me again. You'll convince me you've changed, you'll persuade me to move back, and then, sooner or later, you'll spend all your time elsewhere—just like before." She stared miserably at him, her eyes filling again.

Her distress wrenched Blackburn's heart. He growled and pulled her close, folding her in his arms.

A sob escaped Jessica.

Blackburn hugged her tightly and began to rub her back soothingly. "No, Jess. As you once said to me: you err. We—I am not going to repeat the same mistake." He raised her flushed, tear-streaked face and kissed her salty lips thoroughly. Then he set her away from him, looked into her eyes, and said, "Give it time, Jess. That's all we can do." He paused and pulled her back under one arm, close to him. "Will you trust me long enough to let time prove me right?" he asked softly, his eyes on the flames.

Unhappily Jessica gulped and nodded, laying her head on his shoulder.

"Good," he said, fumbling in his coat pocket to pull out his large white handkerchief. He did a miserable job of wiping her cheeks, which made her chuckle, and continued, "Because if you won't," he said slowly, tightening his hold on Jessica's body and looking down at the beautiful face lying against his shoulder, "I really don't know what I'd do without you." His lips found hers. "Jessy, my love."

Jessica's arm crept up around Blackburn's neck.

"Mmmmmmn."

It was not immediately clear whether the comment was made by the lady or the gentleman.

After some time, a bemused Jessica offered, "I really should go. I'm not even going to look at the clock. It's probably frightfully late."

Blackburn gave her a look of disappointment.

Jessica mentally gave herself a shake. "Yes, please, Blackburn! I should go." She disentangled herself from him and stood up, smoothing her skirts and pushing her hairpins back in place.

Blackburn yawned and stretched. "Very well, Jess. I'm highly against it, as I'm certain you know," he stood up, grinned at her, and dropped a light kiss on her cheek, "but if you wish it."

Jessica gave a last pat to her hair and faced Blackburn to ask, "Do I look mussed?"

"Sadly, no," answered Blackburn, smiling ruefully. "Are we ready then?"

"We're ready."

Blackburn held out his arm, Jess linked hers through it, and they set out to retrieve their wraps from McHenry and reenter the Blackburn coach.

Blackburn delivered Jessica to her front door and bowed over her hand. "Good night, Jessica," he grinned. "I hope you don't sleep any better than I fear I'm going to!"

Jessica laughed and gave him a moue as Moncton opened the door. "Good night, Blackburn," she said pointedly, fluttered her hand at him, and disappeared inside.

Blackburn was left grinning at Moncton.

"Will there be anything else, my lord?" Moncton asked imperturbably.

"Decidedly not!" retorted Blackburn and retreated to his

coach shouting, "Home, John Coachman!" He leapt inside and slammed the door behind him.

His driver set the coach rolling with a small lurch, and Blackburn settled back against the cushions for the short ride back home.

Well, he acknowledged, Jess has brought home the first half of the lesson admirably. I will admit (if only to myself) that I've enjoyed myself prodigiously in her company these last few weeks and I am a cod's head not to have been amusing myself in this fashion since we married.

Indeed, at that moment, he could not have told anyone, had any cared to ask, why he had previously spent so much of his time at his clubs. For he had enjoyed this evening, when they had done nothing save stay at home, as much or more than their other evenings together at the balls, musicales, and plays they had been attending.

The coach pulled up and remained motionless.

Blackburn realized he was home just as a footman flung the carriage door open. Yawning, his lordship got out and entered his house. Yes, Blackburn told himself again as he climbed the stairs to his bedchamber, I am a cod's head not to have been amusing myself this way all along. Then Jess and I could simply have moved from the divan up here, he thought, entering his chamber to stand before his big fourposter.

Gazing at the large expanse of coverlet, he pulled off his cravat and missed, feeling almost a physical pain, the small lump that was Jessica curled up under the bedclothes, which had once adorned the far side.

He struggled out of his coat, sighed, and sat down upon his side of the big fourposter. Well, we both had lessons to learn, he told himself sleepily. I have dutifully learned what Jess wanted me to know.

He yawned and addressed his left boot as he attempted to remove it: and now, you, my beautiful Jessica, must learn what I want you to know. He gave up on his boot, swung both legs onto the bed, and lay back. Telling himself he'd try his luck with the right boot in a moment, he pulled the bedclothes from Jessica's side up over his shoulders and promptly fell asleep.

Over the weeks that followed, Blackburn slowly, unnoticeably, increased the number of social affairs to which he asked Jessica to accompany him. Occasionally he invited Mrs. Darby to come with them; occasionally he brought Wainsby or Redley; occasionally the pair went out in a group of other friends. But, in time, they were spending the better part of every day and evening together.

Blackburn knew he was close to bringing home his point one afternoon when Jessica snapped at him during their afternoon drive in the park after he made an altogether innocuous—even a rather humorous, he considered—comment concerning Lord St. John and his mastiff.

Jessica passed a hand over her brow and apologized profusely. "I don't know what can be the matter with me, Blackburn. I vow I've felt simply . . ." she searched for the proper word, *"cross,* this entire week. Perhaps I'm coming down with something." She looked at him with a puzzled expression. "Could we go back now? I think I should like to lie down and rest for a time."

"To be sure," answered Blackburn, giving her a concerned look back. He turned the horses' heads, and they started to retrace their drive.

Blackburn was soon pulling his blacks up in front of Jessica's house.

"Shall I come in, Jess?" he asked before jumping out of the curricle to come round and help her down.

"No, I fear I wouldn't be very good company just now."

He swung her to the ground and looked crestfallen. "As you wish, Jess."

"Oh, Blackburn! Don't look like that, please. You'll be back here for dinner in a very few hours, and we shall be together all evening long at the Rowan ball. Can't you do without me for just a few hours?" she pleaded as they climbed the steps to her front door.

Blackburn tried to sound sad and a trifle offended. "Certainly,

Jessica, if that is what you wish." He bowed over her hand, turned on his heel, and walked smartly down the steps.

Moncton opened the door.

Astonished at Blackburn's behavior, Jessica called after him, "Blackburn? Wait!"

Blackburn leapt up into his curricle, snapped the reins, and tore off. As soon as he was several meters down the street, his back solidly to Jessica, he began to grin.

"Oh, blast!" cried Jessica, stamping her foot.

"Shall I send someone after him, Lady Blackburn?" inquired Moncton politely.

"No, 'tis all right," Jessica answered wearily, entering the house. She dragged herself through the hall into the sitting room and flopped down into the nearest armchair.

Mrs. Darby looked up from *The Chronicle.* "Well, you seem to have run down, my dear," she smiled. She put the paper aside and got up to ring for Moncton.

When he entered a few minutes later, Mrs. Darby ordered tea. "A nice, hot cup of tea will make you feel much more the thing," she told Jessica as Moncton left to see to it.

"No, it won't, for I am the greatest beast alive!" wailed Jessica.

"Oh, my dear, I only wish you were!" replied Mrs. Darby. "If you were the vilest creature on the face of the earth," she explained to an astonished Jessica, "London would not be half as wicked a city as it, in fact, is. The world would be a much more Christian place to live in, dear, for you are not very beastly."

Moncton brought in the tea and withdrew.

Mrs. Darby poured out a cup and handed it to Jessica. "I realize that you believe you have done something to distress Lord Blackburn. But we must keep whatever it was in perspective, mustn't we?" She sipped from her cup of tea.

"I cut short our afternoon drive to come home and rest, and he looked so hurt that I would rather lie down than be with him that I wish to heaven I had simply gone on with the drive as usual. I feel like a blackguard," explained Jessica morosely.

"Oh, Jessica, if I may say so, that is trifling! Truly, it is a piddling matter. I am certain Lord Blackburn has enough sense to know that the pair of you cannot be together every minute! He knows you must rest. Aren't you attending the Rowan ball tonight? Then resting is a very reasonable, intelligent thing to do. Indeed," she continued, as if thinking aloud, "I have marveled that the two of you weren't at daggers drawn before this, you have been so constantly in each other's company of late. I know—if Mr. Darby hadn't already passed to meet his Maker—I should've killed him by now, had we been so incessantly together."

Jessica laughed in spite of herself. "Oh Ann! Not you, I don't believe you."

Mrs. Darby chuckled and smiled. "Oh, indeed yes. Talk about a beast, my dear!" She pointed to her breast and rolled her eyes. "You are a mere lamb in comparison," she said, eyes twinkling.

"I only wish Blackburn agreed with you. But I fear I've hurt his feelings," said Jessica, shaking her head gloomily.

"Well, and if you have, I guarantee you he will have forgotten all about it by the time he returns for dinner. Why, I'd wager anything you'd care to lose," said Mrs. Darby matter-of-factly.

"Ann! I am shocked," cried Jessica, laughing.

"What! That an old lady gambles? Don't be so naive, my dear Jessica. You will end by being fleeced by one of us old ladies!" she teased. "Truly, my dear, I doubt you would believe the wagers I have heard proposed over some of these old ladies' card tables. *I* was shocked, I can tell you." Mrs. Darby recollected specifically the wager she'd heard proposed regarding Jessica and Blackburn, before it was learned she was companion to Jessica.

"But my tongue is running away with me, I'm afraid," finished Mrs. Darby. "For you told me yourself you came back early to rest. So, shoo! Go on upstairs, and I shall see you at dinner."

Jessica excused herself, deciding to take a long, relaxing bath before she lay down to reduce, perhaps, her irritability and increase her chances of actually napping. Her guilty conscience over Blackburn's hurt feelings, however, despite the bath, prevented her from drifting off to sleep. And soon, her irascible mood much the same as it had been before she lay down, it was time to rise, dress for the ball, and go down to dinner.

She found Blackburn, having arrived early, and Mrs. Darby in the sitting room enjoying a lively conversation.

"Feeling more the thing, Jess?" Blackburn asked, eyeing her with concern as she entered. "You look famous," he said, admiring her deep rose ball gown.

"Oh. Yes. Thank you, Blackburn," Jessica answered, giving him a rather wan smile. "Ann," she exclaimed, frowning in some surprise as she noticed Mrs. Darby's gown. "Are you not coming with us to the Rowan's ball?" For the gown was an elegant black dinner dress only.

"No, my dear, I fear not," Mrs. Darby replied. She held up her hands against both Jessica's and Blackburn's protests. "I don't know where it has come from, but I have the unmistakable feeling that tonight I would be a third wheel. I shall go with you another time."

Mrs. Darby linked her arm through Jessica's, and the three began to stroll toward the dining room.

Raising her brows meaningfully, Mrs. Darby fixed Jessica with a pointed look and said, "Lord Blackburn has been telling me about his afternoon."

"Oh?" asked Jessica, affecting little interest.

"Yes. He's been at Tattersall's, inspecting horseflesh." She winked blatantly at Jessica and remarked, "I *knew* I should have pressed you to make that wager! You are very fortunate I restrained myself, my dear."

"Why do I feel like I've just lost the battle?" asked Blackburn, eyeing the ladies astutely.

Both ladies laughed, and Jessica replied, "Because you have, you poor dear."

Blackburn smiled crookedly. "As long as 'tis only the battle and not the war."

Mrs. Darby patted his arm approvingly. "Quite the most sensible attitude a gentleman can take."

The three sat down to the polished, cherrywood dining table, and if either of Jessica's table companions considered her quieter than usual, neither thought it best to mention the fact. They made short work of Cook's tenderones of veal with truffles and fresh peas and rose from the table an hour or so later amply fortified for the evening ahead.

Mrs. Darby bid Jessica and Blackburn have a diverting evening at Lord and Lady Rowan's ball and removed to the sitting room to spend a tranquil night with her embroidery.

Jessica and Blackburn set out for the ball.

John Coachman deposited them before the Rowan entrance seemingly during the very peak of guests' arrivals.

"Oh, dear," groaned Jessica as she got down from the coach and saw the crowd of merrymakers gathered on the wide staircase. She envied Ann suddenly, at home in the peaceful solitude of their sitting room.

"Courage, Jess," Blackburn chuckled. He pulled her arm through his and led her to take their place at the back of the crowd.

For twenty minutes of jostling and polite conversation with their neighbors in the crowd, they inched their way up the staircase and finally across the threshold.

Blackburn kept his arm through Jessica's and steered them to the punch tables. Cup in hand, they mingled, stopping to chat with acquaintances and friends and enduring much teasing about their recent amicable relations.

After some time of rather aimless comingling, they found themselves in the ballroom. They stood and watched a minuet, and Jessica began to notice, just as Wainsby had remarked, little twitches and grimaces of pain here and there among the dancers' limbs and faces. She smiled but did not pass the tale on to Blackburn, for right at the moment the task seemed to require too much effort.

When the next dance the orchestra struck up was a waltz, Blackburn turned to Jessica. "Shall we dance this one, Jess? 'Tis nothing can compare with a waltz." He smiled affectionately at her.

Jessica did not feel like dancing, but to please Blackburn she acquiesced.

When a mazurka followed the waltz, they left the floor by mutual consent.

Blackburn chuckled as they came off, and Jessica looked at him inquiringly. "I am surprised they let us stay on the dance floor, recollecting the last time we danced!"

Jessica returned his smile wanly and, suddenly, violently craved a moment of solitude. She looked about her distraughtly and sighted a French door. Looking back to Blackburn, she discovered him engaged in greeting Wainsby. She waved briefly in greeting at Wainsby and, believing Blackburn would remain well-occupied in speaking with his friend, leaned close to say, "I'll be back in a few moments, Blackburn."

She hurried through the crowd, dodging to avoid running into other guests, and imagined herself already out on the terrace overlooking the quiet, peaceful lawn. It wasn't until she had almost reached the French door that she realized Blackburn was right behind her, dodging as she dodged.

She stopped abruptly and turned around to exclaim angrily, "Blackburn! What are you doing?!"

Bowling into her, Blackburn reached to steady her. "Lord, don't stop and turn on a fellow like that, Jess! You'll have us both on the floor again. I'm going where you're going, of course. Where *are* we going?"

"But what have you done with Wainsby?"

"I left him. He's back there—ah, he appears to have followed us."

"Hallo again!" exclaimed Wainsby, bouncing into them. "Where the devil are you haring off to?" He noticed the French door. "I say, they're not having fireworks! And you're going out early to nab the best seats! Famous! I'll come with y—!"

"No, they are not! I was going outside for a, for a breath of fresh air!" cried Jessica.

"Well, I'll come with you," said Blackburn, stoking the fires of Jessica's anger.

Wainsby's face fell. "Blast! I knew it was too fortunate to be true. Oh, I'll come, too, but I don't know why you would want to go out in the cold when there's not a demmed thing to see!"

"I," Jessica said awfully, "was going outside to be *alone* for a few moments. Blackburn, can't I leave you for a moment?"

she exploded. " 'Tis no wonder I've been cross beyond bearing. You are ever at my elbow!" She stopped abruptly, gasping in wide-eyed surprise as the truth of her own exasperated statements went home.

Wainsby, astonished at her outburst, then recognized all the earmarks. "Uh-oh. Wrangling again, are we?" he declared, looking from Blackburn's intent face to Jessica's outraged face, her outrage allayed and frozen in the throes of some Momentous Perception.

Wainsby took advantage of Jessica's pause. Edging gingerly away, he remarked politely, "If it's all the same, believe I sh'll just take m'self off now," and made his escape.

"You said you wanted someone who wished to spend all his time with you," answered Blackburn reasonably, oblivious to Wainsby's departure.

Jessica, also oblivious to Wainsby's departure, fixed Blackburn with an astonished blue stare as a second realization dawned on her. For a moment, she was bereft of speech. Then she burst out, "So! You have been *deliberately* denying me a moment's peace!"

"With some advice from your mother, I was trying to give you exactly what you wanted," answered Blackburn patiently.

A hot wave of anger washed over Jessica. "Oh, you are a blackguard. And to think that I have been feeling *guilty* for hurting your feelings this afternoon! I could scream!"

"Jess. Jess. Calm down now." Blackburn attempted to stave off the imminent storm. "You'll do yourself another—injury." He caught Jessica's wrist deftly as her hand flew up to slap him.

Looking round quickly, Blackburn spotted the forgotten French door. He put his arms about Jessica and whisked her through it, away from the curious eyes of those close to them who had begun to watch speculatively.

Once the altercation appeared to be over, those in proximity to Lord and Lady Blackburn dispersed, eager to be the first to sow that scintillating morsel of gossip among their friends and acquaintances: Lady Blackburn attempted to slap Lord Blackburn! They're fighting again!

Out on the terrace in the semidarkness, Blackburn grinned and asked, "Feel better, Jess?"

Jessica was standing stock-still with her hands balled into fists at her sides. Her eyes were still flashing angrily, her chest heaving.

Blackburn advanced on her, reached hastily to pin her arms to her sides, and backed her against the wall of the house. "Listen to me, Jess. You said you wanted someone who liked to spend his time with you. You have every right to be furious with me, but I hope you won't be. I only wanted to show you that you might not really like what you thought you wanted." Softly, he said, "It is possible to spend too much time together."

"I got your point!" Jessica retorted, struggling to bring up a hand. She sorely wanted to box Blackburn's ears.

"And I got yours," Blackburn parried. "Jess, stop struggling and listen to me! I wasn't spending enough time with you, and you showed me how agreeable that can be—just the two of us."

His last words caught Jessica's attention, and she stopped straining against his unyielding iron arms to listen, her anger fading.

"Remember that evening we spent at home—at our home—just us, having dinner together and playing piquet? That's how I think it should be, Jess," Blackburn said earnestly. "Just, mayhap, not every single night."

Blackburn was silent, regarding Jessica's face intently as she digested what he had said.

"I too," she answered solemnly at last.

"Can I let you go now?" he asked, a smile quirking his lips as he released her arms. "I think you wished me at my clubs tonight."

Jessica's own lips curved into a smile. "Yes. I wished you at Jericho."

They were silent, regarding each other intently.

Blackburn broke the silence. "I love you, Jess. I think it's time you came home and we endeavored to strike a balance."

"Oh, Gordon!" Jessica surged against him and threw her arms

about his neck. She pressed her lips against his and kissed him passionately.

Her kiss left Blackburn in no doubt that she loved him back, but he wanted to hear it. "Say it, Jessy," he asked softly.

She knew precisely what he meant, but she teased him with an inquiring look and waited to hear him ask again.

"Say it, Jess!"

"I love you abominably, Gordon," she whispered.

He pressed her to the wall with a hungry kiss.

Raising his head, Blackburn remarked, "We'll have your things moved back home tomorrow."

"And we'll hire Ann as nurse, if she'll have us, for our forthcoming and very legitimate son," murmured Jessica.

"Or daughter," amended Blackburn, rubbing his cheek against Jessica's. "And now," Blackburn suggested huskily, "I believe we should take our leave of Lord and Lady Rowan and go home to, ah, perfect the finer points," he traced her jawline with a gentle finger, "of our compromise."

"A capital idea," agreed Jessica just before Blackburn's lips descended upon hers once more.

"Mmmmn."

Those few of Lord and Lady Rowan's guests who noticed the pair come in through the French door and make their way toward their host and hostess were left in no doubt about the new understanding between Lord and Lady Blackburn. The guests' thoughts immediately flew with small sighs of disappointment to the next opportunity to wager on the pair. They would win that next wager, but, sadly, it would be the last wager proposed on Lord and Lady Blackburn.

Lord Chartley's Lesson

by Jo Ann Ferguson

"Do you need some help?"

Lily Armstrong knew her cheeks were turning the same shade as her hair as she looked over the lowered ears of her donkey toward the man who had shouted to her. When she had heard the clatter of carriage wheels on the stone bridge arching over the creek where she was mired on this want-witted beast, she had hoped it would pass by. Instead it had stopped.

Tilting back her head so she could see past the brim of her straw bonnet, she saw a dark-haired man leaning on the curved wall of the bridge. His features were lost to the brilliant rays of the spring sunshine, but she noted his collar was cut stylishly high. That and the tenor of his voice warned her he was of the *ton.*

Her hands clenched on the reins. It was bad enough that she might be embarrassed by being discovered in the middle of the creek by one of her neighbors. Worse was having a stranger find her in such an asinine scrape.

"Thank you," she called back, "but I am fine." That was false, but she did not wish to own to the truth that she had been trying to convince Trickster to climb out of the creek for almost a half-hour. The stubborn donkey refused to budge, and the water, still holding onto its cold from the winter that had vanished months ago, was creeping up the hem of her blue riding habit.

She was determined to be just as stubborn, for she had no desire to wade through the water to reach the shore. Although she was less than a mile from her home at Knowles Park and the day had the lusciously soft warmth of mid-spring, she was determined that she would not return drenched. She tried again to coax the donkey to move, but neither her gentle pleading nor her heels against Trickster's side gained her anything. The donkey could have been a lifeless statue.

"Miss, I suspect you need some help."

Lily turned in the saddle to see the man sliding down the steep bank rising above the creek, his hand holding his tall beaver hat in place. His gray coattails flapped against his pale breeches as he edged toward the narrow band of pebbles on the shore. When the sun glinted off the silver buttons of his blue striped waistcoat, she blinked and shadowed her eyes with her hands.

"Sir, as you can see," she called back, "I am exactly in the center of this creek. There is no escape from this watery prison, I fear, save convincing Trickster to lift his legs and take us out."

The man clucked his tongue, and the donkey's ears wiggled. Lily added a pat on the beast's rump, but Trickster was unwilling to shift more than his ears.

"By Jove," muttered the man as he shed his coat and reached for his right Hessian boot.

As he pulled it off to reveal his muscular leg beneath a white stocking, Lily gasped, "Sir, you shouldn't—"

"And who else shall help you? Do you expect to sit here until sundown?"

"I had planned to convince Trickster to continue."

"Your powers of persuasion seem quite lacking." He pulled off his other boot and dropped it next to its mate, rattling the pebbles. With his coat draped over a prickly shrub, he shook his head. "I have always failed to understand the proclivity women have for getting themselves into untenable situations."

"Well, I never—"

"Apparently you have. At least today."

Lily could not keep from smiling. The man's wit was as sharp as a fishwife's tongue. She sought some sign of a smile on his face, but the glare off the water swallowed any hint of his features. He might be amused or just exasperated.

One thing was clear. He intended to be as intractable as Trickster, and, she realized as he strode into the water, he apparently had as little sense. When he almost slipped and succeeded in righting himself at the same time he splashed her from head to toe, he swore vividly. He did not apologize, and Lily was glad. She thought the words quite appropriate for the situation and had considered saying them herself more than once since she had found herself in this predicament.

When he stopped in front of her, Lily was amazed that she could meet his cool, smoke-blue eyes evenly, although she still sat on the donkey's back. True, Trickster was not a high mount, but this man was tall. Ebony hair curled across his forehead, and he pushed it aside impatiently. A hint of whiskers shadowed the assertive line of his jaw, and she guessed from his wrinkled waistcoat that he had been traveling for some time.

Without asking her permission, he reached for her, sliding one hand under her knees and grasping her about the waist with the other. "Lock your hands behind my neck, miss," he ordered.

Taking a deep breath, Lily obeyed. She raised her hands to his shoulders. They looked sturdy enough to support her. As he hefted her from the saddle as if she weighed no more than his discarded coat, she regretted her agreement. His firm chest pressed against her, warning that any breath would bring them into far too intimate contact. She wondered how long she could hold her breath without turning as blue as her habit. Fortunately, it would take no more than a few steps for him to wade out of the creek.

"Ready?" he asked.

"As ready as I ever shall be."

He flashed her a frown, and she bit her lower lip to keep from smiling. What a grim gentleman! He acted as exasperated as a father with a recalcitrant child!

Keeping the hem of her riding habit out of the water seemed an impossible task, but she bunched as much as she could in one hand. She wobbled when her rescuer set her on the pebbles at the edge of the creek, but his hand on her elbow kept her from pushing them both back into the cold water.

"Thank you," she said, brushing her dress back over her low riding boots. The damage to her skirt was less than she had feared.

She could not say the same for her unnamed champion. From a hand's breadth above his knees, he was soaked, his breeches clinging with an unseemly closeness to his legs. She looked away hastily, not wanting to be accused of being bold, although she had to own the man, with his deep tan and compelling eyes, offered a pleasing sight.

"Wait here," he ordered as he strode back into the water.

"You won't get Trickster to move," she said to his back. She tried to jab her hairpins back into place. Her thick hair fought her, falling about her shoulders.

"We shall see about that."

Lily almost laughed at the clipped sound of his retort. Why had he made this into a personal challenge? Trickster was sure to protest every inch of the way.

"You need not go back," she called. "Trickster soon will tire of standing in the middle of the creek and come out on his own."

"If you have no concern for your beast, I do."

Lily clamped her lips closed abruptly. She cared deeply for Trickster, but she knew well the donkey's inflexible nature.

Her eyes widened when, as the man took the reins, he bent and whispered in the donkey's ear. Fidgeting, as if bothered by an insect, the ears rose. The man turned the donkey and led him toward shore.

"Bravo!" cried Lily, clapping her hands. Her smile faded when she saw her rescuer was still frowning. He simply handed her the reins as he stepped out of the water. "Thank you, sir," she added in a more restrained voice.

"You are—" A puff of wind plucked his hat off his head and swirled it into the water. "Damn!"

"Stay here with Trickster."

She raised her skirts high enough so she could wade into the creek and snatch the hat from the eddy. It twirled like a child dancing in a summer meadow. Kicking water from her high-lows as she climbed back onto the shore, she shook water from the hat before holding it out to him.

"You were wise, sir," she said with a laugh, "to select a chapeau made of the fur of a beast accustomed to such a watery jaunt."

"Look at you!" He grumbled something under his breath, something she suspected was another curse. The man certainly was skilled at that!

Lily obeyed and realized she looked a complete rump, but that did not explain his exasperation. What else could he presume when they had met under such trying conditions?

Before she could answer, he continued, "I toted you out of the creek as if I was the lowest caste servant, and you trot right back in."

"I thought you might wish to retrieve your hat before it got snagged on a bush." Gathering a handful of the wet skirt of her wool riding habit, she wrinkled her nose. "I am unsure which of us will raise the worst stink before we dry. However, I thank you for your gallantry, sir."

"Allow us to give you a ride to your destination, miss."

"Us?" She glanced up the hill to the carriage and, for the first time, noticed a child peeking out of the window. A flash of pity raced through her as she imagined the life the golden-haired moppet must have with such a stern father.

"Deirdre and me," he answered, drawing her eyes back to his.

Lily knew she should look away, but she searched his face for any sign of softening. There was none. She started to tell him she could manage quite well on her own, but one step in her wet boots warned her that the walk home—for Trickster was unlikely to cooperate if she remounted—would be most uncomfortable.

"Yes," she said. "I would appreciate your generosity."

"Allow me."

When he held out his hand, she wanted to tell him that she had scampered up and down these hills since she was younger than the child in the carriage, but he had been such a gentleman for keeping his temper under such strained circumstances, it behooved her to be as gracious.

Before they were halfway up the hill, Lily regretted her decision to acquiesce to convention. She suspected Trickster was following compliantly only to enjoy watching their awkward parade. Resisting her urge to tell her rescuer that she could have managed much better without his assistance, she let the gentleman hold her hand until they stood side by side at the edge of the stone bridge.

"Thank you, sir," she said again.

He did not release her hand as he regarded her in silence. His gaze moved along her from the top of her straw bonnet, which was by now awry on her messed hair, to the bottom of her mud-soaked habit. Instead of a quick dismissal, which she had expected after his curt remarks, his gaze was slow and intense, leaving a warm tingle in its wake. Glad that her clothes did not cleave to her as openly as his breeches did to his sturdy legs, she drew her hand away. She must endeavor to keep this conversation from becoming any more familiar . . . and prevent her mind from wandering in the same direction.

She feared her thoughts might be bare on her face, but the man said nothing as he motioned toward the carriage. The door came open, and the child looked around it.

"This is Deirdre," the man said as he led Trickster up onto the bridge in Lily's wake.

The donkey's hoofs clattered on the wooden board, but Lily paid no attention. Instead she smiled at the child.

The little girl, who must be no more than six or seven years old, nodded and spoke a polite greeting, revealing the gaps left by several missing teeth. Her blue eyes were dim with fatigue. Slippers of rose silk that matched the ribbons in her sleeves emerged from beneath her pale pink dress.

"How do you do, Deirdre?" Lily asked kindly.

"Very well, thank you."

Lily did not believe that. The child was struggling to swallow a yawn. "I would appreciate some company for tea if your father is willing to pause in your journey long enough to join me." When the little girl sat straighter and started to answer, Lily added, "You should ask your father's permission first."

"She is not my daughter," the man said in his even voice. "She is my ward."

Lily refused to be embarrassed by a mistake that anyone might have made. A pinch of relief raced through her. Mayhap the child was not always afflicted with the company of this grave gentleman. How long could anyone go without a smile? Forcing that irreverent thought from her head, she said, "Then, Deirdre, I extend the invitation to you and your guardian. A pause for a cup of tea and a cake would certainly make your journey less onerous, and it will allow me to repay you, sir, for your assistance."

Again the man answered. "We appreciate your kind invitation, but we must not delay. I am uncertain how far we yet have to travel before we reach our destination." He put his hand on her elbow to assist her into the carriage. "Mayhap you can tell me how far it is to Knowles Park, miss."

"Knowles Park?" She laughed and paused on the single step into the carriage. Turning awkwardly, she pointed past him. "If you look carefully, you can see its chimneys over that copse." She included Deirdre in her smile. "I had no idea I should be expecting a look-in today."

"You?" asked the man.

She sat on the lushly cushioned seat and held out her hand to him. She ignored the splotches of damp and dirt on her kid gloves as she said, "My name is Lily Armstrong."

"You are Miss Armstrong?" The man took a deep breath as if he was about to shoulder an immense burden, then released it. He shook her hand swiftly. "It is my duty, Miss Armstrong, to tell you that I am Randall Montgomery, Lord Chartley."

"Then thank you, *my lord,* for rescuing me."

"And this," he gestured toward the child, "is your niece Deirdre Armstrong."

Lily's smile vanished as she pressed her hand to her breast. She gasped, "My niece? I have a niece?"

Randall Montgomery cursed under his breath when he saw all color vanish from Miss Armstrong's cheeks. Tying the donkey to the boot and shouting to his coachman to make best speed to Knowles Park, he threw himself into the carriage, heedless of the damage his wet clothes would do to the velvet seat. He hushed the child's questions as he took Miss Armstrong's hand between his. Chafing her wrists, he chided himself.

Only a beef-headed boor would have broached the subject so thoughtlessly. Two days of traveling on these wretched roads after a sea journey halfway around the world from India still did not grant him the right to shock the woman. He must never allow himself to forget that Miss Armstrong was unaccustomed to the rough life and rougher manners that he and Deirdre had considered normal until her father's death. Yet how could he have guessed that Miss Armstrong had no knowledge of her niece?

When Miss Armstrong began to pepper him with questions, he glanced meaningfully toward the child. Miss Armstrong nodded and yielded to proprieties, although, after seeing her behavior in the past few minutes, he doubted if that was something she did often. This was not an auspicious beginning to the business ahead of them.

Uncomfortable silence swarmed through the carriage as they continued in the direction she had indicated. When they passed through the high gates of Knowles Park, he concealed his surprise. He had known from his commanding officer, Capt. Thomas Armstrong, that the Armstrong family seat was ancient, but Randall had not guessed that the house might go back to the years just after William the Conqueror. Massive walls with narrow windows, that looked like afterthoughts, presented an exterior as formidable as his captain's.

This was the perfect setting for the proper upbringing of a child, he decided, as he noted the well-kept gardens flowing down to a sapphire-eyed pond with a gazebo set on its farthest bank. Clusters of roses were aflame with blossoms, and a symphony of birds sang in the trees shadowing the luxuriant grass. He could understand why Captain Armstrong had wanted his child to return to Knowles Park. He just did not understand, he owned with a furtive glance at the rumpled Miss Armstrong, why her brother wanted this flighty woman to have a place in his daughter's life.

It was puzzling . . . most puzzling, and there was nothing Randall Montgomery liked less than a puzzle.

* * *

Lily was anxious to change out of her soiled, damp riding habit, but one look at Deirdre's face told her the tired child needed something to eat right away. Leading the way past her footman, Flagg, who could not hide his curiosity about her callers, to her sitting room, she whispered an order for tea and cakes to be brought straightaway. She looked back to see the short man in the bright green Armstrong livery staring after them. Offering him a weak smile, she watched him hurry away across the polished stone floor toward the back of the house.

Dear Flagg! She could depend on him to save his questions until later . . . when she might have some answers.

The room was bright with sunshine, which was rare in the old house that had been built to repel invaders and any hint of daylight. Added many years after the original hall, the sitting room gloried in the light that splashed through the tall, wide windows. Heavy, time-darkened oak benches and tables were topped by yellow checkered cushions, and flowers were scattered throughout the chamber. It was, without question, Lily's favorite room. She loved the cheerful colors and the memories that permeated each piece of furniture. Even the ceramic temple dogs on the mantel recalled the day her father had brought them from London to her mother. This was home, and she could imagine no place else she would want to be.

Offering a smile to Deirdre, who was on closer examination the image of Tommy Armstrong from the pale hair to the freckles spotting her nose, Lily motioned for her guests to make themselves comfortable on the benches which were nearly as old as Knowles Park itself. Lily sat and reached for the porcelain Chinese teapot when it was placed on the table between her and Lord Chartley. She paused as Lord Chartley lifted the teapot to fill cups for all of them.

She fought not to frown. The man had an imperious air that she found bothersome, and he acted as if he was the master of Knowles Park. Then she realized she still wore her dirty kid gloves. He might have mentioned the fact as lief assume she would prefer him to pour. Pulling them off, she silently sighed.

If for no other reason than because he was her niece's guardian, she owed Lord Chartley the duty of hospitality.

Lord Chartley handed her the tea and said, "Forgive me for breaking the news of Deirdre's relationship to you in such a heartless manner, Miss Armstrong. That had not been my intention."

She waved aside his apology. "Forgive *me,* my lord, for nearly swooning like a thorough block. I am delighted with the news of a niece." Flashing a smile at Deirdre, she flinched when the little girl regarded her with no expression. She held out the tray of frosted cakes. "Would you like a cake, Deirdre?"

"No, thank you."

The child's voice was a somber miniature of her guardian. Lily was unnerved, then scolded herself. Deirdre was fatigued and grieving for the loss of her father and mother. Lily knew nothing of her brother's wife, save her name and that she had been of a military family. Tommy had filled his few letters with details of his work—sparse detail at that—so they read like communiqués.

"How was your voyage from India?" Lily asked.

Lord Chartley answered, as he stared down at his tea, "It was long."

"You must be pleased to be back in England."

Although she had looked at the little girl, again Lord Chartley spoke. "A soldier goes where he must."

She wondered if he always used such banalities or if exhaustion made his words so terse. When Deirdre tried to conceal another yawn, a spasm of guilt raced through Lily. She should not have asked her guests to join her for tea until they had had time to recover from their lengthy journey.

Taking the silver bell from the tea tray, she rang it. The housekeeper, Mrs. Lewis, appeared before the tinkle had vanished, warning Lily that her household was as curious about the purpose of this call as she was. The plump housekeeper smiled uncertainly as Lily rose and held out her hand to Deirdre. The little girl looked at it uncertainly, then at her guardian. He nodded, and slowly she raised her short fingers to set them on Lily's palm.

"Mrs. Lewis, be so kind as to find Miss Deirdre a room where she can rest." Bending, so her eyes were even with Deirdre's, she smiled again, but still was unrewarded for her efforts. "I know, Deirdre, that you are too old for a nap, but I have found that a rest in the afternoon is necessary when I want to enjoy a pleasant dinner with my guests. You will join me for dinner, won't you?"

"Yes, Miss Armstrong." She dropped into a curtsy.

Lily put her hands on the little girl's elbows and drew her up. "No need for such formality here. I am your father's sister, so you should call me 'Aunt Lily'." Something about the child's reserved stance compelled her to add, "If you wish."

"I would be glad to call you 'Aunt Lily'."

Lily watched the child walk out of the room with Mrs. Lewis. *Walk,* not trot, not skip. Lily had never met such a controlled child. Even Tommy had been mischievous as a lad.

Don't judge unfairly, she reminded herself. Deirdre must be bone-weary. Once she rested, surely the child would be more spirited.

Lord Chartley sat as Lily did, and she noted anew the exhaustion carved into his bronzed face. No sign of fatigue shone in his gray eyes, however, as they aimed their authoritative gaze at her.

The silence was stifling, and she hastened to say, "My lord, I hope you realize that you and Deirdre are welcome to make Knowles Park your home as long as you wish."

"I plan to stay only until I have ascertained that the child is settled into her new life here."

"Here? You want Deirdre to stay here?" Lily could not have been more astounded . . . or pleased. The child needed someone to draw her out of her melancholy, and Lily could imagine no one better than she to do it. "But why? *You* are her guardian!"

"Financial guardian only, Miss Armstrong. It was your brother's wish that his daughter be raised here at Knowles Park as he was."

"Tommy told you that?" She raised her cup to hide the smile tugging at her lips. Now *this* was a surprise.

"Capt. *Thomas* Armstrong was most definite on that."

"Odd he would want her raised here and by me."

"Miss Armstrong," Lord Chartley said, his lips in a straight line, "I can assure you that your brother left his child enough blunt to tend to her every need. You need not be down-pinned on that account."

Lily had not considered that her attempt to conceal her amusement at his stiff pronouncements would be labeled dejection. He was a most inflexible man. Tapping her finger against her cheek, she wondered if Lord Chartley ever smiled.

A smile would do him a world of good, and it certainly would accent the strong lines of his face. She suspected a dimple hid in his cheek. If he was always so grim, she doubted if it had been seen in a long time. What a shame! It would be the perfect complement to his blue-gray eyes which should be sparkling.

If she was to share guardianship of Deirdre with Lord Chartley, he must be willing to smile . . . at least occasionally. When Tommy had become as serious as a thief with his head in a noose, she had vowed never to waste her life grieving for what might have been. She had considered Tommy an absolute chucklehead for hoping to heal his jilted heart by fleeing to India and a military career, and she was determined not to make the same errors of the heart herself. She had avoided Town and the flirtations of the Season, keeping herself from believing court promises that were merely nothing-sayings. Here, at Knowles Park, she was happy, and having Deirdre with her was sure to make her even happier.

If she must deal with Lord Chartley, she would have to convince him not to be so gloomy. Mayhap if she made him feel more at home, he might relax.

Rising, she walked across the room. She turned to see him set himself on his feet, a cross expression on his face. *Dear me!* she thought. Persuading Lord Chartley to smile and leave his stern demeanor behind might be more difficult than she had thought.

"This is Papa," Lily said as she paused in front of the portrait over the mantel. "You can see he passed on his need for glasses to Tommy." She clasped her hands and raised her chin to keep the tears from flooding from her eyes. "They told us Tommy died a hero."

"He saved the lives of all his men, including me, as well as his daughter's."

She whirled, astonishment honing her voice. "Do you mean to tell me that Deirdre was *with* you in the midst of battle? Blast Tommy! He always thought of his career foremost, but I would have guessed that he might give thought to the safety of his only child."

"We were attacked by the Pindaris. They are marauders, Miss Armstrong. They strike in the middle of the night and slink away like the serpents they are." He folded his hands behind him and stood as straight as if he was on parade. "I assure you that the captain would have done nothing to risk his daughter."

Lily was instantly contrite. If this dashed man would act like a real person instead of a tin soldier, she might not be so quick to judge. "Forgive me for my thoughtless words."

"Of course, Miss Armstrong." He eased his stance slightly and glanced down at the mud caked on his boots. "May I further infringe on your hospitality to ask for a place to clean myself?"

Although Lily fancied that Lord Chartley wished for any excuse to escape her company, she must not fail to be an accommodating hostess. "Mrs. Lewis will be glad to order a bath for you, if that is your wish. Leave your boots outside the door, and they shall be taken care of as well."

"Thank you."

She inclined her head in his direction and hid yet another smile when she noted, from beneath her lowered lashes, the relief on his face. What a peculiar man! He was even more staid than Tommy had become. Had he been a naughty lad, too, or had he always—?

His finger beneath her chin halted her in mid-thought. When he tilted her face toward him as if she was no older than Deirdre, she was caught anew by his forceful eyes. Warmth billowed from where his finger brushed her skin, wafting along her like heated winds before a building storm, pleasurable but potentially dangerous.

"We have much to talk about, you and I," he said in a voice no louder than a whisper.

"Yes." She was startled by her breathless answer as much as her reaction to his brazen touch. Stepping back, she folded her arms in front of her. Her pose was scanty defense against him, and she was relieved when he turned on his heel and left her alone in the room, which no longer seemed as secure from the world beyond the walls of Knowles Park.

As sunset washed across the stone floors in a ruddy river, Lily walked into the parlor to find it empty. No, she corrected herself quickly, for she saw a shadow by the tall windows. Crossing the large room, she called softly, "Deirdre?"

The little girl sat straighter on the bench, although sleep still clung to her eyes.

Lily said with a sympathetic smile, "If you wish to be excused from dinner, I will give Lord Chartley your regrets."

"I shall join you as you asked."

Wondering if there was anything left of a child in that small body or if Deirdre had become a marionette, merely performing to the orders of others, she forced another smile. "Lord Chartley may be delayed in joining us for dinner."

"He is always punctual."

"I'm sure." Her smile wavered, but she coerced it back into place. Did the haughty viscount have any faults other than lacking a sense of humor? That, in her opinion, was the worst shortcoming he could have. "While we are waiting for him, why don't we sing?"

"Sing?" Deirdre's tired eyes focused on her for the first time. Bafflement glowed in them.

"Why not? The song is simple." She sang a few notes, then motioned for Deirdre to join in. The little girl hesitated. "Do try."

"Yes, Miss Ar—yes, Aunt Lily." She opened her mouth, but no sound came out. Color raced along her cheeks, a flattering color in Lily's estimation. Hanging her head, she whispered, "I forgot the words."

"That's all right. Listen now, and you shall be able to sing along in no time."

Lily smiled as she sang and strolled around the room. Stopping in front of Deirdre, she continued to sing as she drew the little girl to her feet. She swung their hands in tempo to the music. When a suspicion of a smile tipped Deirdre's lips, Lily felt as if she had won the most formidable battle. There *was* childish joy within the little girl. She had been sure of that, but after seeing Deirdre earlier, she had begun to doubt she could reach it.

"Now you," she said softly. "You sing it."

"I don't know if I can."

"Then we shall sing it together."

Lily began the song again and gave an encouraging smile as Deirdre's sweet voice wove through and over hers. Grief tugged at her heart when Tommy's voice echoed in her memory. When Lily had been of an age Deirdre was now, her brother had sung this ditty with her. Blinking back tears, she knew she must not cause more grief for this little girl.

Deirdre clapped her hands and smiled as Lily took her light green silk skirt in her hand and bowed to an imaginary suitor. Whirling about the room with the gaiety of a May dance, Lily laughed. She motioned for the child to join her, but Deirdre shook her head, still too shy.

Lily refused to let her small victory end here. Taking Deirdre's hand, she spun her into a dance between the tables and the benches. Deirdre began to sing another verse of the silly song, astounding Lily. Had Tommy taught his daughter the song he had disdained when—as he had told her—he had become too old for such frivolity?

Clapping her hands, she laughed when Deirdre whirled so that her white dress belled around her ankles.

"Deirdre Armstrong!" The sharp words cut through the sitting room like the lash of a whip.

Lily gasped as Lord Chartley stormed into the room. His hands fisted at his waist. His pristine black coat and white breeches might be the ideal attire for dinner, but she suddenly had no interest in sharing her table with a tyrant who denied a child even this small bit of amusement.

Deirdre stiffened and curtsied in Lord Chartley's direction before dropping to perch on the edge of the closest bench. All animation vanished from her face.

Lily looked in astonishment from Deirdre to Lord Chartley. His lips were taut with outrage. Clenching her hands at her sides, she forced vicious words back down her throat.

She coerced her fingers to unfold from fists and put her hand on Deirdre's shoulder and said softly, "Cook must be frosting the cake for dessert just about now. I'm sure she would appreciate it if you would let her know if there is enough sugar in it."

"Aunt Lily—"

"Hush," she ordered with a smile. "Go and help Cook."

Another child might have argued. Lily *would* have argued when she was younger, wanting to see the course of the conversation between the adults, but Deirdre nodded compliantly. As she had earlier, the child glanced at Lord Chartley for permission. When he motioned with the tips of his fingers toward the door, she hurried out without looking back.

Lily walked after her and closed the door. Trying to rearrange her hair, for her hairpins had a frightful habit of popping out at the very worst times, she turned to face Lord Chartley.

"Miss Armstrong," he said coolly, "I trust I shall not be greeted with such a display again."

"Display?" She laughed without mirth. "Is that what you call happiness?"

"It was unsuitable deportment. Captain Armstrong would not have approved."

"For me, mayhap, but not for Deirdre."

If possible, his lips became even straighter. "I have no say in your behavior, so my comments are only for the child's welfare."

"Child! Finally you and I agree about something, my lord." When she saw his surprise at her retort, she pressed her point. "She is not a soldier. She is a child. You can't expect her to act like anything but a child."

"She is Captain Armstrong's daughter. I believe she should be raised as he would want. He established certain standards I expect you to continue. He would not have approved of what I just saw."

Folding her arms over the lace dripping from her bodice, she did not let his icy gaze daunt her. He was such a fine-looking man, and she had seen the fire from his soul in his eyes. If he would vent a bit of it. . . . With a shudder she could not suppress, she decided she would as lief not see that. His touch had unnerved her, and she suspected that those strong emotions would completely undo her.

Quietly she said, "My lord, I do as both you and my brother would wish. Didn't you tell me yourself only a few hours past that Tommy sent Deirdre to Knowles Park to be raised as he was? That song was part of a game we both learned from Papa."

"This was, indeed, a mistake."

"Why?"

"Do you wish me to be honest?"

She frowned. "I can imagine asking you to be no other way."

"Then I must say I find you a frivolous woman, Miss Armstrong."

"Thank you."

Randall was amazed she did not take insult at the words he had been trying not to speak since he had rescued her from that silly tableau in the creek. Somehow he must disabuse his head of the assumption that she would react as her brother had. Never had he seen two siblings so opposite. Captain Armstrong was precise. His sister was a flibbertigibbet. Why hadn't he been warned?

When she smiled, he was further astonished to hear her ask, "Why don't you help yourself to some brandy, my lord? It will oil your throat for the rest of our argument."

"The rest?"

She sat gracefully on a long bench, folding her hands primly in her lap. "I cannot imagine us speaking more than a few words without our conversation dissolving into a brangle, for I believe we are diametrically opposed on just about every subject."

"Especially the child."

"Deirdre. Her name is Deirdre. Can't you call her by it instead of calling her 'the child?' "

As he turned away, he sighed with regret. She had sounded—for a moment—so much like her brother. But Lily Armstrong was not like her brother. He must never forget that or the fact he owed Captain Armstrong his life. In return, he would be certain his captain's child had the life her father had been determined she would have. He must concentrate on that—and that alone—although he knew how difficult that could be when he looked into Miss Armstrong's enticing eyes and noticed the tendrils of chestnut hair curving along her throat.

Damn! Why did she have to be so appealing when her ways were so appalling? He suspected—for the first time—that this mission to see Deirdre Armstrong settled into a suitable life might prove to be the most onerous task he had ever undertaken.

And, he had to own as he saw the stubborn tilt of Miss Armstrong's chin, one he would have to use all his wiles to win.

Randall was still glowering as he walked through the garden the next morning. It was a bright splash of color, as outrageous and uncontrolled as Lily Armstrong. What an utterly absurd woman! One moment perched atop a disobedient donkey, the next scampering about like a caper merchant. He had planned on escorting the child here, making the appropriate arrangements for a monthly allowance until the child went to school, and then leaving to return to London.

He could not abandon his duty now when he was unsure if he should leave the child with this outrageous woman, although Deirdre clearly already adored her eccentric aunt. But if he did not let the child remain at Knowles Park, he would be going against his captain's wishes. That was the quandary he had battled all night, and he was no closer to an answer than he had been when he had sought his bed.

He heard laughter and Miss Armstrong's voice reaching across the lawn to him. He turned to see two slim silhouettes coming out of a small gazebo that was topped with a Chinese roof. They walked in his direction. By Miss Armstrong's side, Deirdre bounced on each step, obviously recovered from the strains of their long trip. Although the ocean voyage had left the little girl with a tanned face, she carried a parasol . . . a copy of the one her aunt held over her shoulder.

By Jove, but she's a lovely woman! The thought refused to be silenced. Nor would his eyes stop from admiring the gold ribbons of her gown and how the color accented her beauty. The lace on her parasol and edging her sleeves floated on the breeze like a silken aura. Unblemished kid gloves could not hide the slender length of her fingers as she held the child's hand.

They presented the perfect scene of familial tranquillity, but he had been forewarned. Nothing could be tranquil when Miss Armstrong was involved.

Deirdre glanced in his direction when Miss Armstrong gestured toward him. Some decidedly unpleasant sensation pinched Randall as the little girl altered her steps to a more sedate pace. Yes, this was what the captain had expected—the little soldier—but, for the first time, Randall could not keep from questioning that. The little girl had seemed so happy before. Now. . . . He *must* do as the captain wished. Deirdre Armstrong should have the life her father had planned for her.

"Good morning," Randall said, bowing toward them.

"Will you join us, my lord?" Miss Armstrong asked in a tone as aloof as his.

He suspected she, as much as the child, hoped he would excuse himself, but he asked, "Where are you bound?"

She looked at her charge. When Deirdre did not answer, Miss Armstrong prodded her lightly.

"We are going to see the polliwogs in the pond," the child said. She faltered, then hurried to add, "It would be most pleasant if you joined us, sir."

Chasing wisps of frogs about brackish water did not interest him, but he could not forget his obligation to Captain Armstrong. He must assure himself that Miss Armstrong would provide a proper education for the child. Mayhap this outing would prove as enlightening to him as to Deirdre.

And Miss Armstrong did look a vision in that golden dress.

Lily turned away to let the parasol come between her and Lord Chartley as his gaze edged along her, stoking the now-familiar warmth. There had been no warmth during dinner last night. That had been nearly intolerable, because she had been constantly aware of his disapproval of everything she said to Deirdre. She could not guess what was wrong with asking her niece about her life in India, but the viscount apparently had, for he excused Deirdre from the table right after dessert was served.

Meeting him here so few hours later was distressing, but she refused to let his somber countenance ruin the day she had planned for Deirdre. She took the little girl by the hand again and walked toward the pond.

As she squatted by the reeds at the edge of the water, Lily noticed Lord Chartley walking after them. Her breath burned in her chest when she watched the easy strength of his movements as he swept the grass aside with each step. Such a disturbing man he was! When he paused to rub the toe of one immaculate boot against the back of his other boot, she lowered her eyes. He was ever the strait-laced soldier, determined to be without blemish in appearance or actions. How boring it must be always to be correct!

She hid her smile as she had so often since Lord Chartley had swept into her life yesterday. When Deirdre had removed her slippers and stockings, Lily handed her a bottle and told her how to run it through the water to capture tadpoles. The little girl's eyes sparkled with anticipation as she held her dress up with one hand and the bottle in the other as she waded into the water beside the reeds.

"Be careful," Lily cautioned.

"I shall, Aunt Lily. Oh! There they are!" She bent to her task.

"You have made her feel at home so quickly," Lord Chartley said as he came to stand behind Lily.

She accepted his hand to bring her to her feet. "Knowles Park has that magic, my lord. No one can come here and not be delighted by the flowers and the birds and—"

"The frogs?"

"Even the frogs." She waited for him to smile, but he was gazing across the garden toward the house. "Are you looking for something?"

"Just trying to envision Captain Armstrong here. He seemed most comfortable in his field tent."

"I'm glad Tommy was happy at the end."

"Unquestionably," he said, his gaze capturing hers.

She was taken aback by the potent emotions clouding his eyes. She wanted to take his hand and thank him for being such a good tie-mate to her brother, but she resisted. Not only would he be distressed by such overt compassion, but she recalled how he had unsettled her last night with no more than the brush of his fingertips against her face. The memories of those sensations had colored her dreams with delight and teased her into setting aside her pledge never to risk her heart. Although she knew she was want-witted, she yearned to know more about this man who camouflaged his true feelings behind his military bearing.

"Thank you for telling me that." Her voice was no louder than a whisper.

"If there is anything else you wish to know—" He closed the distance between them until they were almost as intimate as when he had carried her from the creek. "—you need only to ask me."

She almost spoke the words burning on her tongue. His quiet words hinted at a promise of pleasure she had only sampled last night. When his hand rose to curve along her cheek, she shivered with the sensations that swept over her, precarious and beguiling. He tilted her face, and she closed her eyes as his mouth lowered toward hers.

"Help!"

Lily whirled away from Lord Chartley. Deirdre was flailing her arms as she fought not to fall into the water. Before Lily could move, Lord Chartley pushed past her. With a single, long stride, he reached the little girl and plucked her out of the clinging mud. He set her on the shore and grimaced as the mire sucked at his boots.

Lily looked at Deirdre and began to laugh. She could not contain her relief or amusement. Lord Chartley had been immensely worried about the shine on his boots only minutes ago. Now they were filthy again.

"You find this humorous?" he asked, his tone once again

sharp, as he stepped onto more solid ground. "The child could have hurt herself. You should be watching her more carefully instead of allowing yourself to be diverted. I can tell you that Captain Armstrong would not have approved."

She knew the foolishness of reminding the viscount that *he* had been her distraction. Then she might have to speak of how completely he enthralled her with his touch and the anticipation of a kiss. What was wrong with her? She had vowed long ago that Lily Armstrong would not be addled by passion.

"Deirdre," she ordered quietly, "go up to the house, and have Mrs. Lewis clean you up. Just carry your stockings and slippers." As the little girl nodded, she added, "Use the kitchen door. Flagg would not want you trailing mud through the front foyer."

Lily sighed when Deirdre waited again for the viscount's permission before she obeyed. For just a few moments, she had believed Deirdre was unfolding like the lovely blossom she could be, but the little girl had closed up more tightly again than a flower after sundown.

Setting her parasol on her shoulder, Lily put her hand on the arm Lord Chartley held out to her in a silent command. She muted the sweet cadence of happiness spiraling through her like the first birdsong of spring. Now was not the time to think of her own happiness. She must think of Deirdre. Lily had much to say to Lord Chartley on that subject, and she would not waste her breath arguing that she did not need him ordering her about as he had his soldiers.

"She was perfectly safe," she said as soon as the little girl was out of earshot. "The water is not deep in this pond."

His jaw worked, and she knew her hope that he was struggling not to smile was worthless. "A child is like a raw recruit. She must be watched every moment. The lessons she learns now will be important for the rest of her life."

"I realize that."

"Then you must realize, as well, that your duty is to drill her in those lessons until she knows them instinctively."

"This is not a parade field. It is a home."

"Practice guarantees that lessons are learned, Miss Armstrong."

Lily swallowed her frustration with his ridiculous assumptions. Although she longed to ask him if he had spent his childhood suffering such constraints, she said instead, "Come, my lord, there is no need for such formality on a beautiful spring day. I shall call you 'Randall', and you shall call me 'Lily'. That shan't insult your sensibilities too much, I daresay."

"I daresay you are correct."

"Could I have heard a hint of a jest there?"

"I suspect you often hear things that are not there."

Again she accepted his sharp comment with a laugh. "How true! I hear music in the waters of the creek and along the winter winds tugging at the eaves. I have been told many times that there is no music, only the splash of water against rocks and wind against stone. But I believe I am right. There *is* music."

"You are changing the subject."

"Am I?"

"We were speaking of the child, not your imaginings."

"You may wish to spend the remainder of your days mired in the mud." She chuckled as she glanced at his boots. "However, I shall seek every bit of joy with every ounce of my being."

"I believe you shall."

They climbed the hill and followed an exultant Deirdre toward the house. When Randall's hand settled over hers on his arm, she feared her heart had forgotten how to beat. The warmth of his fingers oozed through his gloves and hers to bathe her in enchantment. Quickly she told herself to stop acting silly. Randall was a dour man who needed desperately to learn to smile. Although she had thought today's outing might persuade him to give up his dreary ways, even rescuing Deirdre from the mud had brought no grin to his taut lips. Somehow she must convince him to be less strict with the little girl.

Softly she asked, "Can it be possible that, as we have agreed on two things today, we might agree on a third?"

"Mayhap on a third, for I would be less than honest if I did not tell you how charming you look today."

Knowing she should turn the conversation back to Deirdre, Lily hesitated. She rarely found herself at a loss for a retort, but Randall's compliment astonished her. She had not expected anything but more disparagement from him, for she sensed he was as unnerved as she was by their mutual near capitulation to the yearning for a kiss. Mayhap, if he was unsettled, he was not as hopeless a student as she had believed.

Tilting her parasol back over her shoulder, she raised her gaze to meet his. The gray of his eyes had become a smoldering smoke, warning of the banked fires within him. They could consume her in their potent heat and sweep aside thoughts of keeping her heart safe from being overmastered by a man who never smiled.

Hastily she looked away. Her life was just as she wanted it. Deirdre would be a pleasant addition, but Randall Mont-gomery. . . . With only a side glance, he threatened everything she had planned her life to be. His touch mesmerized her. She closed her eyes and fought down the captivating fantasy.

Suddenly she was sure the only way to safeguard her heart was to rid Knowles Park of Randall Montgomery as swiftly as she could. Dismay pricked at her, but she would have to pretend to accede to his demands about Deirdre.

It would not be easy, but it would be simpler than owning that she was ready to break her pledge to stay far from *affaires de coeur.* That vow she must never forget.

Lily walked through the nursery on the uppermost floor of Knowles Park. Although the rooms had been opened yesterday to air, the musty, warm scent of chambers too long unused curled around her. She could not remember the last time she had been up here.

The walls needed a fresh coat of paint, but otherwise the warren of rooms was as welcoming and wonderful as when she had spent her childhood here. By the round window which looked out over the porte-cochère, her dollhouse still sat, its furnishings spilling out onto the floor. She had kept each of her playthings, although, until now, she had not comprehended why. Deirdre had brought no dolls with her, so she could have Lily's.

Pausing, Lily stooped to look out the window. Tears blurred the scene, stealing the sunshine and leaving darkness in its wake. She could almost see the parade of carriages, each accompanied by a rider holding a torch, coming up the drive to a ball in the grand room directly under her feet. She and her brother had left their governess asleep in the other room while they crept to this window to enjoy the cavalcade.

"Tommy," she whispered as she dropped to sit on the padded window bench. Here in the nursery his shadow was strongest. His voice, his laugh, the muffled sound of his footsteps, she could hear them all most clearly here.

"Aunt Lily?"

Her smile was genuine when she saw Deirdre standing in the arch to the bedchamber. "How do you think you will like living up here under the eaves where you can hear the whispers of the wind and the dancing rain?"

"It is so different."

"From what you knew in India?"

The little girl knelt next to her on the bench and peered out the window. "Father told me a good soldier needs no more than the sky for a roof and soft earth for a bed."

"That may be all a soldier needs, but I can assure you that even a good soldier enjoys the comfort of a house once in a while." Folding her arms on her knees, she leaned forward. "After all, Randall has made himself quite at home here at Knowles Park. Did he enjoy his life in India?" She ignored the twinge of guilt that she was asking the child for information about Randall.

"I suppose he did." Deirdre sat and picked up a stuffed dog. Running her fingers along its matted wool fur, she said, "I think he must have, for he has been so sad since he left."

"He wasn't like this before?"

"Like what?"

Lily chose her words with care. "He always acts like a good soldier."

"Because he is!" Putting the dog back on the cushion, she said, "Lieutenant Montgomery is the bravest soldier I know."

"Is he now?"

The child must have sensed condescension in Lily's voice, because she snapped, "He is! Even Father said so!" She whirled to look out the window again.

Lily sighed. Deirdre obviously had a great deal of respect and mayhap even affection for Randall. Wanting to apologize to the child, she was unsure what to say. So many questions taunted her.

"I believe you," she said quietly to Deirdre's back.

"You should!" Deirdre relented enough to add, "Didn't you ever read Father's letters? He must have told you how Lieutenant Montgomery saved all of us from an ambush last year."

"Mayhap he was too busy to write that week." She did not want to tell the child the truth of how infrequently Tommy's letters had arrived at Knowles Park.

"Then, the night the Pindaris tried to overrun the camp, he halted them, nearly on his own."

"The night your father died?"

Tears glittered like shards of glass in Deirdre's eyes, and the sight sliced deep into Lily's heart. When not a single one fell, she was astounded. The child should be able to mourn.

She was about to put her arm around the little girl, but Deirdre slid away as she said, "Lieutenant Montgomery is the bravest soldier I know."

"I am glad you brought him to Knowles Park so I could know him, too," Lily said, because she could think of nothing else.

The words must have been the right ones because Deirdre smiled as the tears vanished. "I like it here," the little girl announced as she turned to look out into the room. "But I do miss my pony."

"If you wish to ride," she answered, startled by the abrupt change in the course of the conversation, "I'm sure we can find a mount in the stables for you."

Her nose wrinkled. "Not the donkey."

Lily stood and held out her hand. "I daresay Trickster is still irritated with me after our last ride. Let's see what other mounts we can find."

"Now?"

"Why not?"

"It is time for my rest period."

Although she winced inside, Lily kept her smile in place. "Did no one ever tell you that your grandfather's favorite saying was that rules are made to be broken?"

Deirdre stared at her, amazed, then she began to giggle. Pressing her hands to her lips, she giggled until tears bubbled at the corners of her crinkled eyes. Then she put her hand in Lily's, and they walked down the stairs together, looking, Lily was sure, as if they had known each other for years instead of days. Deirdre's arrival had revealed an emptiness that had been in Lily's life since Mama had died only a few weeks after Tommy had left for India. Now that void of family was filled again. She had someone to care for and about, and she wanted nothing to interfere with this happiness.

Not even her longing for Randall's touch.

The stables were set on a low rise behind the house. As ancient as the original sections of Knowles Park, they were weathered by centuries of rain and sun. The stone floors had been smoothed by uncounted feet and hoofs to the dull sheen of unpolished marble. Warm scents washed over Lily as she walked into the building which was dim after the enthusiastic glint of the sun.

Deirdre's hand tightened in hers as the shadows coalesced into a bent form. With a smile, Lily called a greeting to Perkins, the head groom. If he had another name, she had forgotten it years ago. Nor did she have any idea how old he was, for he had seemed ancient the first time she had met him when she was younger than Deirdre. A crooked, little man, barely able to see over the stalls, he leapt about the stable like a maddened leprechaun, always busy, always with a smile and a silly tale.

"G'day to ye, Miz Lily," he said with a grin. Although the rest of the servants had come to call her "Miss Armstrong" when she had assumed responsibility for Knowles Park, Old Perkins refused to change his ways. She was glad. "Who's this ye have with ye?"

"This is Deirdre, Tommy's daughter."

"Tommy's gal, eh?"

Lily watched as Perkins charmed Deirdre in the same way he had teased both her and Tommy when they were young. Discovering that Deirdre was interested in finding a horse she could use, the groom chuckled.

"Jes the thing for ye, young miss," he crowed as he waved for Deirdre to follow him.

She glanced back. Lily motioned for her to go ahead. Following, Lily realized she must convince Deirdre not to be afraid to make a decision on her own. If the little girl simply transferred her unquestioning obedience from Randall to her, it helped nothing. Deirdre must be willing to take chances and have fun . . . all on her own.

Deirdre selected a horse with Perkins's assistance, a small roan that was just the right mount for a young girl. When Perkins assured Deirdre she was welcome to come and visit the horse anytime, she dimpled with pleasure. Lily promised to take her for a ride the next afternoon, and the little girl rushed back to the house to rest and dream of her ride across the park.

Thanking Perkins, Lily followed at a more sedate pace. The day was too freshly warm for hurrying, and the air was fragrant with the promises of adventures in the copse on the far side of the meadow. So much of spring waited to be explored. She loved this time of year, but never more so than this year when her quiet existence had been jolted by the arrival of Deirdre and the enigmatic Lord Chartley.

As if her thoughts could take life of their own, she heard Randall call her name. She looked up to see him coming down the steps of the house. Easily she could imagine him leaping without thought of his own safety into the mad fray. The staid navy coat and nankeen trousers he wore did not suggest the uniform he must have found more familiar in India, but the image of him drilling his men upon the parade field was easy to visualize.

When she saw he was carrying a folded parasol in one hand, she resisted laughing. She could not halt herself from saying, "I would suggest something with less lace for you, Randall."

"This is for you," he said gruffly, and she sensed that her teasing had embarrassed him. "I thought you might want it while we were walking."

"Thank you." She opened it and settled it over her shoulder. "Where are we walking?"

"To the pond?" he suggested.

"To catch tadpoles?"

She wished—more than she had before—that he would smile at her jest. Instead he said, "We must talk about Deirdre's future."

Lily sighed. Randall made it clear that he intended to speak only business, even on this spring day when the air was so deliciously warm. Wandering by his side across the garden, she listened while he outlined the list of requests her brother had left for his orphaned daughter's upbringing. Shade and sun altered the variegated patterns across his face, but his expression did not change.

"I am sure you will wish to do as your brother requested," Randall finished.

"I shall . . . within reason."

"Lily, I must insist that you try."

"I think the only misdeed you will ever be able to accuse me of is spoiling the child."

"I can think of other aspects of your guardianship that I might disapprove. I know Captain Armstrong would not approve."

She tilted her parasol so she could see his face, expecting his mouth to be in a straight, uncompromising line. When a smile tipped it slightly at the very corners, she was astonished. A smile? From the formidable Lord Chartley? Not a true smile, mayhap, but it was indeed an auspicious beginning.

"You need not look so astonished," he said.

"But I do!" She laughed when he glanced at her, amazed at her answer. "I am most unaccustomed to the sight of a smile on your face."

"Mayhap I gave you the wrong impression from the onset, Lily."

"No, I think you were very much the loyal lieutenant tending to the concerns of his captain. I admire that."

"Thank you."

She laughed. "But I don't agree with it." She grew serious. "Deirdre is not an assignment you must complete. She is a little girl who is very confused by leaving the only home and family she has ever known to be deposited here with me."

"She will adapt."

"Of course she will, but that doesn't mean it will be easy for her." Taking a deep breath, she released it slowly. Although having this tempting man far from Knowles Park would be simpler for *her,* she must think of Deirdre. "Stay, if you would, another few days. You are her only connection with what was. Mayhap if you are near, she will acclimate herself more readily to this life."

With a sigh, he clasped his hands behind his navy blue coat. "I have obligations in Town."

"I am sure, but what can be more important than Deirdre?"

For a long moment, the silence between them was broken only by the call of the birds darning the clouds together in an intricate pattern of invisible threads. They continued along the winding path toward the pond, drawn by the call of the geese among the reeds.

"Are you going to be intolerable if I own you are correct?" Randall asked as they paused far enough back from the pond so their shoes were safe from the mud.

"Like Tommy?"

She was startled by a low rumble. When she realized he was laughing softly, she was glad her parasol concealed her shock. What surprises this day held for her! Not only was Randall smiling, but he was laughing.

"The captain did have a frightful way of gloating when he was correct."

"Which Tommy usually is . . ." She added in a whisper, "Was."

"Do you miss him?"

Sitting on the sloping bank, she leaned her parasol on her shoulder and stared up at the delicately blue sky. "Tommy has been gone for so long that he was out of my life more than in it."

He squatted next to her. "He spoke of you often."

"And called me a silly chit, no doubt."

"No doubt."

"Then I'm baffled about why he wanted Deirdre to come here. Mayhap you misunderstood him."

Shaking his head, he pulled a blade of grass from the earth. He held it between his thumbs and blew gently against it. The single note, rough and barely formed, drifted away on the breeze. With a sigh, he tossed the stem aside.

"No," he said as he stared across the pond. The wind, which teased his hair into his eyes, sculptured the water into ripples. "The captain was definite about Deirdre coming here until she was of an age for school. Of course, he expected that she will be sent to the best school. Your brother wanted her to be given a regimen that would be what she will know in school."

"Unlikely."

"Unlikely?" he repeated. "It would be best for Deirdre to practice such habits here, so she finds the transition to school easier."

"I would as lief have a tutor come here," she answered. "Then there is no need for her to *practice* anything save being a child. When are you going to accept that she is not a diminutive soldier, Randall? She is a child."

"Are you going to argue every point?"

"If it is in Deirdre's best interest, yes."

"You have become very attached to her very quickly." He sat back on his heels. "And she to you."

"She is very fond of you, too, Randall."

Once again, she was astonished by his reaction. She had thought he would be pleased. Instead he sighed. "I had hoped to keep her from suffering another loss."

Lily put her hand on his, because she could feel his grief deep in her own heart. She had forgotten that he had lost a dear friend when her brother died. "Is that why you treat her so coolly?"

"Yes."

"You have failed then, for she has a great deal of affection and respect for you. She says you are the bravest man she knows."

His laugh was terse. "What she considers bravery others might call stupidity. When a man isn't smart enough to run away from danger, he's labeled a hero. I am glad to be away from that madness."

"Does that mean that you intend to sell your commission?" Her heart paused as she waited for his answer.

"I don't know, Lily." He looked across the pond again as if he could find the truth in its gleaming surface. "I honestly don't know."

Randall was amazed to see an open carriage waiting in front of Knowles Park when he crossed the grass that was still damp with morning dew. An early morning stroll had brought him no closer to deciding what he wished to do when he met with his superiors in London. This sojourn in the country had convinced him that he wished a different life. Not this one, that much was certain. He would go insane with *ennui* here. If only he could be as convinced of what he should do with his life.

He whirled as he heard a squeal. Deirdre! He raced toward the sound. Chagrin halted him when he realized, as Deirdre pulled a kerchief from her eyes, the child was playing a game with Lily. Although he harbored the hope they had not seen his wild dash across the grass, he discovered they had when Deirdre pressed her hand over her mouth to hide her giggles.

"Good morning, Randall!" Lily called and gestured to him. "Do join us."

"What are you doing?" he asked.

She held up the square of silk. "You don't know how to play blind man's buff?" She arched a brow.

Randall met her challenging stare steadily. He would not allow Lily to make him feel as if the child had received a faulty education. Once again, he was confident that the captain must have been totally bereft of his senses to put Deirdre in his sister's care. And the captain had not been the only one who had taken a knock in the cradle.

He could have left yesterday. Nothing remained for him to do here. Lily had agreed—mostly—to the terms her brother had set forth for his child, and he could see she already doted on the little girl.

Yet he had stayed. He had to own he was fascinated with the undoubtedly unconventional Lily Armstrong.

"I suspect I am about to play blind man's buff now," he said drolly.

With a laugh, Deirdre took the silk kerchief from Lily. "You must tie this over your eyes, sir."

He wrapped it into place and fumbled with the knot, but paused when slender fingers drew the silk out of his. As Lily tied it, the scent of her perfume drifted over him like an eager caress, alluring and innocent at the same time. Lily of the valley, he realized. He turned toward it, drawn like a bee to sweet pollen. Stretching out his hands, he found only air. He heard the soft sound of muffled laughter and knew Lily and the child were enjoying his bafflement.

If you are lost in battle at night and cannot see a thing, use your other senses. Captain Armstrong's admonition resounded through his head. How many times had he heard the captain say those very words to his men?

Randall froze and strained to listen, to feel, to smell. The scent of the perfume . . . that he had already noticed. Beneath his feet, the ground was soft and lush with grass. Overhead, the sun was hot on his shoulders and the top of his head. That did nothing to help him. There! To his left. The sound had been no more than the brush of a slipper against the earth, but he had heard it.

He leapt forward and grasped a thin arm. Deirdre! "I have you now!" He reached to enfold the child in his arms. He gasped when his arm closed around nothing. If he held her hand, his arm should now be around her waist. Silk brushed his face, wafting the fragrance of lily of the valley over him.

Ripping off his blindfold, he heard a trill of laughter. He shook his head in disbelief when he saw Deirdre perched on Lily's back like a sack of vegetables a farmer was taking to market.

"You minx!" he snapped. "You should have warned me you were going to do something like this."

"Then it would not have been funny," Lily said as she let Deirdre slide down her back and patted the girl on the head. "Right, Deirdre?"

"It *was* funny," the little girl agreed with another barely stifled laugh.

"There will be more games at the village fair," Lily said with what he guessed was feigned nonchalance as she led the way toward where the open carriage was waiting. When Deirdre giggled again, he was even more certain the two were plotting something.

"Fair?" he asked cautiously.

"It is only a mummery now, but once the gathering celebrated a quarter day." Lily settled the silk kerchief over a basket of cakes on the floor of the gig. "Sometimes I find it difficult to believe that at one time Knowles Park oversaw the tenants on most of the farms in the shire, and they came in Knowleston to pay their rents. I like it better this way, for I, instead of playing the lady of the manor, can enjoy the day."

"I cannot imagine Captain Armstrong's sister shirking her duty."

"Nor can I." Lily saw his astonishment at her quiet answer, but she gave him no time to speak before she added, "But I shall always do them in my own unique way."

"That I never doubted." He stepped back as Deirdre scrambled onto the seat. "As you have orchestrated this day at the fair."

"Exactly. Certainly you would not wish to leave today when you can attend the Knowleston quarter-day fair." With a laugh, she put her hand on his arm and let him assist her into the carriage. She was rewarded when she saw the faintest of smiles on his lips.

When he had been so open yesterday while they sat by the pond, she had hoped he would set aside his dour ways. Instead he had embraced them again. She just was going to have to do something about this whole situation today. He was going to have a good time at the village fair, whether he wished it or not!

The common in the small village was bustling with excitement. Striped tents were a bright quilt on the green, and the scents of roasting meats and fresh bread urged fairgoers to think of dinner, although the hour was still far in the future.

Deirdre turned to look at a group of children tossing a ball in the air, then sighed and sat quietly on the seat between Lily and Randall.

Stretching behind the little girl, Lily tapped Randall's arm. "Stop here, please."

"Here?" He drew back on the reins, but pointed to the green. "I thought the gathering was over there."

"For us." She opened the low door.

Randall jumped down and came around to her side to assist her to the ground. "Do you want to explain why we are stopping here then?"

Lily handed him her white parasol that Deirdre had told her was the perfect match for her gown of sprigged muslin. With a smile, she thought of the times *she* had sat on a stool while her mother dressed for the Knowleston quarter-day fair. Now Deirdre was here to continue the tradition.

Taking Deirdre by the waist, she lifted the little girl out of the carriage. She flashed Randall a smile, then motioned to the group of children.

Randall watched as the children swarmed over to Lily, jabbering like a collection of monkeys, each of them calling her name joyously. This was no surprise. As childlike as she could be with her unconventional ways, he should have guessed that no child could resist her . . . or gentleman either.

His hand tightened on the door of the carriage as he tried to silence the thought. Captain Armstrong had been urging him for years to think of something other than soldiering when they were in garrison, but his work had kept him occupied. Then, during the interminable voyage home from India, he had seen no reason for being anything but polite to the two young misses who had ogled him, clearly considering him fodder for their aspirations of marriage. He had been thinking only of discharging his duty to see Deirdre delivered safely to her aunt.

Now he should be en route to London and his responsibility of reporting to his superiors. He should be deciding on his next billet or if he wished to sell his commission and take his place in the Lords as his father had implored in his last will. His whole future lay before him, but he lingered here at the Knowleston quarter-day fair, which seemed to be no more than an excuse to celebrate spring.

By Jove, you are definitely queer in the attic to stay like this. Even as he thought that, he could not keep his gaze from riveting on Lily's glowing face. She was laughing with the children, teasing them, urging them to say hello to Deirdre. Beside her, Deirdre was smiling more broadly than he had ever seen. With a start, he realized he could not remember the last time she had been with children her own age.

Lily clearly knew what the little girl needed while he had been inept at keeping the child from becoming just a wraith. Lily possessed, he had to own, a magic that spread out around her like the colors of a rainbow from a single raindrop.

With a low curse, he looked away. He would be an addle cove to mix himself up with her jobbernowl ways. All his life he had prided himself on his good sense. He must not lose it now simply because he could not keep his eyes from her loveliness.

"Shall we go on?"

He did not look at Lily when she came to stand beside him. Opening the door, he held out his hand to assist her into the carriage. This was going to be a most uncomfortable day, and if he had an ounce of sense, it would be his last one at Knowles Park.

Lily sat on a low stone wall beside the church. On the far side of the green, she could see Deirdre playing with the village children. She heard an intricate whistle and smiled. She would recognize that sound anywhere. Reverend Jones had used it to call children to enjoy icy lemonade during the fair since before Lily was born. She and Tommy had vied with the other children to be the first in line for the refreshing drink. Now it was Deirdre who was laughing and holding out her hands for an icy glass.

"Thirsty, Lily?"

She silenced her first, awed thought that Randall could read her mind. He held out a tin cup of iced tea to her, not the lemonade of her memories. Thanking him, she put her empty basket on the wall beside her while she sipped. The ladies from Reverend Jones's church had been delighted with the donation of cakes from Knowles Park's kitchen.

"Perfect," she whispered as the coolness oozed through her.

"Just like the day."

"Are you enjoying yourself?" she asked.

Randall smiled and sat next to her. "You need not sound so amazed."

"I am. Your face on the way here suggested you had little interest in attending our fair day."

"I had forgotten the pleasant monotony of life in an English village." He set his cup next to her basket and locked his hands around the knee of his buckskin breeches.

Looking up at the bell in the steeple, she said, "But this can be a dangerous place."

"Dangerous?" His question was sharp.

"Papa told us when we were small that if we went widdershins around the church, the fairies would pop out of the bushes and spirit us away into their dark land."

"Nonsense."

"True." She smiled at him. "But when I was young, I truly believed if I walked the wrong way around the church, I might be snatched by the fairies. Don't you see, Randall? It is so important for a child to have something fantastic to believe in."

"Captain Armstrong—"

"Would not approve." She set herself on her feet and gripped the basket tightly. When lighthearted music drifted from the green, she raised her voice over it to snap, "By all that's blue, Randall, you do have a tiresome habit of repeating that. Mayhap Tommy would not have approved, but what of Deirdre's mother? Do you think *she* would wish her daughter denied the joy of music and laughter?"

Anguish raced across his face, shocking her. "She was denied everything of her daughter, for Deirdre was but a few months old when my sister died."

"Evelyn was your sister?" When he nodded, she let her knees fold to drop her back onto the stone wall. Her voice was no stronger than a whisper. "I knew Tommy had married the sister of one of his fellow officers, but I had no idea *you* were Evelyn's brother. I never even knew when Evelyn died."

"That I am Deirdre's uncle was what urged Captain Armstrong to name me as her financial guardian."

Confusion taunted her. "If Tommy was your brother-in-law, why do you persist in calling him 'Captain?' "

Again his shoulders straightened in the pose she had silently labeled his soldier stance. "He was my captain, Lily."

"He was your friend and the husband of your sister."

"When we served by each other's side, he was my captain. It was best never to forget that, so I tried to form no bad habits I would have difficulty breaking."

"You have a bad habit?" She sniffed gracelessly. "I cannot imagine that from the exemplary Lord Chartley. You are so unrelentingly correct." Not giving him a chance to retort, she asked, "Have you always been so prosaic?"

"Prosaic?" His dark brows lowered, and she knew her choice of words had dumbfounded him.

"Were you never a naughty, nasty lad intent on putting a mouse in your governess's slipper or pepper in the headmaster's tea?"

"You did that?"

"Actually Tommy spiced his headmaster's tea with the hottest pepper he could find, but I helped him with the mouse for Miss Webster."

"The captain did such a thing?"

"Regularly." She smiled. "He nearly was sent home from school on more than one occasion for his misdeeds."

"Amazing."

She put her hand over his on the stones. "Some people are not exactly as you might think they are."

"Is that meant to be a warning?"

"About me or about you?"

When he took a sip of his iced tea and did not answer, Lily looked back toward the village green. The music swirled through the dancers whirling to the country reel. She watched the dancing and sighed.

It was impossible even to imagine spinning about with such abandon in Randall's arms when he was determined to withdraw from any attempt she made to dismantle the wall he had built around him. How she had hoped that a day at the fair would bring out in him the joy she had found in Deirdre! It must be there. She had never been more certain of anything. She had succeeded with Deirdre . . . and she must succeed with Randall. Even though she knew how she jeopardized the serenity of her heart, she owed him this much to repay him for bringing Deirdre into her life.

And because, sap-skulled though it might be, she feared she was falling in love with a man who considered her a silly widgeon. If she did as she planned, she was sure to prove that to him and to herself.

Deirdre bounced into the breakfast parlor, a layer of strawberry jam ringing her lips. "Is today the day, Lily?"

"Good morning," Randall said sternly, lowering the newspaper.

Instead of replying as she ought, Deirdre repeated, "Is today the day, Lily?"

When he flashed Lily a scowl that announced the child's lack of manners was her fault, Lily hurried to say, "Deirdre, if you wish to speak with us, you should do so politely. And, today *is* the day."

"For what?" asked Randall. He folded the newspaper so neatly it looked as if it had not been opened and put it beside his plate. When Deirdre seated herself on the opposite side of the table from him, he turned his eyes back to Lily.

"An outing. I thought the three of us might go for a ride about the park. Deirdre has been anxious to try her new horse, and I know the perfect place for an alfresco luncheon."

"Lily, I must think of returning to London. I am certain I told you that."

"Another day will not matter."

Deirdre added her voice to the argument. "Do stay, Uncle Randall."

He started at the name, and Lily realized it was the first time she had heard Deirdre call him anything but "sir" or "Lieutenant Montgomery".

"Mayhap," he said slowly, staring at the little girl, "as I have dallied here this long, another day will not matter."

When his gaze swept over her, Lily bit her lip. The emotions in his eyes were so potent, but she could not decipher what he might be thinking. The glance was a warning that what might be his last day at Knowles Park would matter a great deal to her.

The first drops struck the brim of Lily's favorite straw bonnet. Holding up her hand, she watched rain pock her palm. She laughed as she called, "We are going to have to race the storm back to the house."

Randall looked up from where he had been leaning against a tree, his hat pulled down over his eyes, while Lily had been telling Deirdre about other outings along the creek. Had he fallen asleep? He could imagine no other way the storm clouds might have gathered without him noticing.

Jumping to his feet, he grimaced when the wind swept into his face. He started to give an order, but realized that Lily already had rolled up the blanket and was packing the remnants of their luncheon in a basket.

He went to get the horses which had been tethered in the shade.

A gust of wind tugged at his coattails as he looped the reins around his hand and led them out into the clearing. A curtain of rain dropped over him, and he swore under his breath.

Seeing Lily with a blanket folded over her arm, he grasped her hand and tugged her back toward the protective branches of the tree. She gasped and stumbled. When he caught her, she stared up at him, her soft lips parted and ripe for his kiss. Quickly he set her more firmly on her feet. He was mad to be thinking of such things.

Lily laughed shakily as she set the basket and blanket on the ground. "I swear there was nary a cloud in the sky an hour ago."

"I should have kept a better watch on the sky."

"Seeing the sky is not easy through closed eyes and felt." She tapped the brim of his tall hat. "Did you have a good nap?"

"I was not asleep," he argued, although he suspected she was correct.

"You gave a good show of it then." She smiled wryly. "Tommy never told you that you snore, Randall?"

"I do not—" He bit off his words as she laughed. Dratted woman! She was always a test for the most patient man, and he was far from the most patient. If she had not proven to be such a good guardian to the child. . . . He glanced away, startled. "Where is Deirdre?"

Lily shrugged, pleased she could make the motion appear so unruffled. Her arm still tingled with the brush of Randall's fingers against her. Speaking of Deirdre was certain to lead them to a dagger-drawing, and that would prevent her from thinking the unthinkable about his eager touch and how wondrous his mouth would be against hers.

"She probably sought shelter under the trees over there." She pointed to a copse farther along the creek. "She was watching a turtle down on the shore."

"I'll get her."

"Why? She will be fine."

"She is just a child."

Coolly, she retorted, "I thought you considered her a little soldier, able to take care of herself in enemy territory."

"You do like to twist my words and throw them back in my face, don't you?"

"I wouldn't if you would own that you are mistaken."

He pulled his coat collar nearly as high as his cravat. "We can argue later. Now I must get her."

"Oh, Randall, do leave off. It is a rain shower, nothing more."

"The child will catch her death of cold."

With a laugh, Lily stretched her hand out from beneath the tree. "The rain is as warm as mother's milk."

"Really!"

She laughed again. "You might as well smile. You know you wish to."

"You are an incredibly irascible woman." His voice deepened to a growl. "But you are wrong. Smiling is not what I wish to do."

Before she could retort, he seized her arms. He pulled her against him and captured her mouth. She gasped as the heat of his lips burnished hers, setting them afire with delight. As he held her so tightly that the gold buttons on his waistcoat pressed into her hammering heart, his hands slipped along her. She softened against him when he sampled the curve of her cheek before caressing her ear with his tongue.

His hands framed her face, his fingers combing through her hair and loosening the hapless pins. He gazed down at her, not speaking. Slowly her hands rose to slip across his shoulders and behind his nape. Guiding his mouth to hers, she saw his smile in the moment before she closed her eyes to savor the full sweetness of his kiss.

The kiss was not sweet. It was hard and deep and replete with the craving she had seen in his eyes. The passions he had tried to conceal burst forth to flood over her in a blazing wave, threatening to sear her in their fierce fire.

When he drew back, she sighed in regret. Slowly she opened her eyes to discover his smile had returned. Her lips tilted in response as her heart lilted with the rhythm of its joyous beat. Leaning her head against the firm strength of his chest, she closed her eyes. This must be as close to perfection as any mortal dared to aspire! The melody of the rain on the leaves and the staccato rhythm of his heart beneath her ear was a joyous melody as his arms surrounded her.

Lily did not realize she was humming until Randall whispered against her hair, "Are you singing?"

"I always sing when I'm happy."

"That's the same song you sang for Deirdre the night we arrived."

She smiled as she traced the deep-set dimple in his cheek. Right where she had believed it would be. "I am surprised you remember. You were blistering mad."

"You could drive a saint into a pelter, Lily, with your antics."

"Sing with me, Randall."

"Sing . . . ?"

Catching his hands as she had Deirdre's the night she had first sung with the child, she drew him from beneath the tree. "Sing and dance with me, Randall."

"It's raining."

"Is it?" she whispered as she drew his arm around her. "Odd, for the sun is shining brightly into my heart." She clasped his other hand and began to hum the song. Pausing, she said, "Sing for me, Randall, please."

With the slippery grass beneath their feet seeming as smooth as the finest marble floor and the delicate shower sprinkling them like soft rose petals, he twirled her as he sang the country tune. His voice, deep and filled with laughter, resounded through her, awakening every inch of her to happiness.

She giggled as if she was as young as Deirdre when he spun her away from him and back into his arms. The dance had no pattern, but her feet followed his with ease. As he slowed, his mouth captured hers again, and she remembered how she had danced with him like this so often in her dreams.

And now her dreams had come true.

Lily was singing lightly as she came down the stairs. She paused to take a deep breath of the geranium-scented air. Taking one of the blossoms from the bouquet on the table at the base of the stairs, she wove the stem through her hair.

"Good morning," she called as she came into the breakfast parlor.

No one answered because the room was empty.

Hearing footsteps, she turned. Deirdre looked around the door and smiled. "Aunt Lily, Uncle Randall wants to speak with you right away."

"Where is he?" She tried to keep her voice from revealing how her heart swelled with joy at the idea of being with Randall again.

"Out in front."

"Out in front?" What did Randall have planned now? Patting Deirdre's hair back into place, she said, "Have Cook bring breakfast out while I speak with your uncle. I think she has some of that marmalade you love left . . . if you haven't eaten it all already."

The little girl laughed and ran toward the swinging door that led to the hall into the kitchen. Even before Deirdre had reached it, Lily was retracing her steps. She saw the front door was open and went out onto the steps.

Her smile faltered as she saw Randall's coachman packing his bags into the boot of the carriage which had brought Randall and Deirdre to Knowles Park. When Randall came around the other side, he was wearing the same coat and breeches he had worn the day they met.

"You are leaving?" Lily asked, although that was obvious.

"I told you I needed to return posthaste to my duties in London." He bent to check a wheel, not even giving her the courtesy of looking at her. "Now that I have reassured myself that Deirdre will be properly cared for here, I can do what I should have done a week ago."

Could this be the same man who had held her with such passion in the rain only yesterday? The man who had swirled her about the garden, laughing as rain washed over them as warmly as the brush of his mouth against hers?

Blinking back tears, she knew she had been wrong to try to

change Randall. He clearly preferred his drab, humorless life to the laughter she had tried to bring to him.

"May we expect you for a visit soon?" Her breath caught on the ragged edges of her broken heart. "Deirdre has so much affection for you. She will miss you sorely."

Again he avoided looking at her as he brushed the back of his hand against his hat. "I shall either return at month's end with Deirdre's allowance, or I shall send it by courier."

"A courier isn't her uncle."

"You have a ghastly habit of speaking the obvious, Lily."

"Do I?" She swallowed roughly. She would not cry, for that would betray her to him. Tommy had been right when he said she would one day succumb to the same madness that had misled him! She had been a widgeon to believe she could be immune to love's enticements. Not even hiding in Knowles Park had protected her from a handsome man with bewitching blue-gray eyes. Her voice cracked as she asked, "Have you said adieu to Deirdre?"

"I thought it better that I don't put her through the pain of another parting."

"Her or you?" she fired back, her anger freed by his apparent indifference to Deirdre. The little girl had done nothing wrong but love him.

For the first time, his gaze met hers. She was nearly staggered by the misery she saw in his eyes. He was *not* indifferent to Deirdre's pain. She tried to harden herself to his anguish. Why should she care if he was hurting when *he* was the one leaving?

"You know the child has suffered too much grief already," he said with a deep sigh.

"I don't think you are as worried about Deirdre as you are about Randall Montgomery." Her voice rose, but she did not try to restrain it. "Are you so afraid of love, Randall, that you will run away from it no matter what form it takes? You have lost your sister and your best friend, and for that, I am sorry. But what right does that give you to shut Deirdre out of your life? She loves you."

"I know."

"And so do I."

He flinched as he set his hat back on his ebony hair. "Don't, Lily."

"Don't what?"

Seizing her shoulders, he pulled her to him. His kiss was bittersweet, and as he stepped back, his fingers lingering on her shoulders, she fought the tears she must not let fall.

He climbed into the carriage and closed the door. "Don't ask me to be a hero this time, Lily."

She locked her hands so tightly her knuckles bleached as she watched him drive away, knowing her dream had become a nightmare. She understood too well what he had not said. This time, he was smart enough to know when to turn his back on danger—the danger of losing his heart, so he never had to own to the truth that he might care for Deirdre and for her.

Lily looked up as she heard the door to the parlor open. She affixed a taut smile in place and held out her hand to Deirdre. "Come in, my dear."

Deirdre ran to her and dropped to her knees, clutching Lily's hand. "It isn't true, is it, Aunt Lily?"

"What?" she asked, although she feared she knew when she saw the pallor on the child's face.

"Uncle Randall isn't gone, is he?"

"He has business in London." She selected each word carefully. She would not be false with the child, but she could not be completely honest either. "I'm sure he will give us a look-in as soon as he can."

"No!" cried the little girl. "He told me he would take care of me forever."

"And he shall. Before he left, he spoke to me about school for you and—"

"But he left me! Just like Father did!" She hid her face in Lily's lap and sobbed.

Stroking Deirdre's hair, Lily said nothing as she listened to the child weep. Blast Randall! And bless him, for he had given

Deirdre a way to unleash the agony she had quelled since her father's tragic death. Deirdre needed to mourn that loss, but she should not be crying for her uncle. Blast Randall!

Lily waited until the little girl could cry no more, then drew Deirdre up to sit with her head against her breast. With her lips against the child's golden hair, she whispered, "I shall never leave you until you are ready to leave me."

"Never!"

"When you grow up and fall in love, you may wish to buckle yourself to a fine young man who will want you all to himself."

"What if you get married first?"

Lily smiled gently. "I have no plans to marry, and if I did decide to marry, Deirdre, the gentleman would have to ask your permission first."

"I like that idea," she said, nestling closer.

She let the little girl prattle on about how she would demand that all callers state their intentions before they could speak with Lily. Not that it mattered, for Lily knew she could give her heart to no one now. It had ridden away with Randall when he had driven out of her life.

After a rainy week, the sun finally shone on the gardens around Knowles Park. Deirdre wasted no time in reminding Lily that she had said they would go riding on the first clear day.

"Mayhap this afternoon," Lily said as she paged through a book she had been trying—most unsuccessfully—to read.

"Now!" Deirdre grasped her hands and pulled. "You promised, Aunt Lily."

With a sigh, Lily set herself on her feet. She *had* promised, and if the truth must be known, she was glad for the excuse to get out of the house, where every room seemed to hold the memory of Randall. Quickly, as they had their horses saddled, she found that even her beloved Park offered no escape. She remembered walking with him by the pond, through the roses, along the creek.

Deirdre led the way, and Lily followed, not paying much attention where they rode. When the little girl jumped off her horse, Lily was astonished to discover they were in the midst of a patch of strawberries, each dark green leaf shielding a luscious berry.

"Let's pick some for supper," said Deirdre as she held out two small baskets. She plucked a strawberry and stretched to pop it into Lily's mouth. "Aren't they delicious?"

"How did you know they were here?"

"Heard about them in the stables."

Lily could not help smiling as she took one basket. Perkins must have told Deirdre about the berry patch and found the baskets. She forced aside her melancholy and set to picking the berries with Deirdre. She suspected most of the berries were going into the little girl's mouth, but she hoped to have enough for dessert that evening.

"There are more over there," Deirdre said, pointing toward the slope leading down to the pond. "May I pick them?"

"Of course. Don't go too close to the water."

Lily was rewarded by a sticky kiss on the cheek, and she sat back on her heels to watch Deirdre run through the sunshine. *This* was the life she wanted, a quiet life at Knowles Park. Yet if that was so, why was she so miserable and filled with longing for Randall?

Thinking of him now only proved that she was an air-dreamer. Randall wanted nothing to do with her or the joy they could know. Instead he favored his somber ways where a smile was no more welcome than a Pindari attack. By now, he should be safely ensconced in his town house where he could surround himself with acquaintances who asked nothing more from him than to drink his brandy and use his chairs at the table of green cloth.

Blast him! She should despise him for coming to Knowles Park and staying just long enough to break her heart . . . but she loved the man she had danced with in the rain. It was her misfortune that he did not really exist.

When her back ached with the strain of squatting, she stood and rubbed it. "Deirdre, it is time to leave."

She got no answer.

She whirled to look in the other direction. "Deirdre?"

How had she vanished so completely?

Lily ran down the hill toward the pond. In her ears, she could hear Randall's warning about letting the child play on its edge. Deirdre would not have gone into the water without asking permission . . . would she?

She pressed her hands to her lips as she saw a ribbon caught in the reeds. It was the same color as the ones Deirdre had been wearing in her hair. Relief nearly staggered her when she noted another ribbon farther up the slope, not far from the gazebo.

Lily put her basket over her arm and climbed the hill. Calling Deirdre's name, she tried to ignore the streak of dismay racing through her when only silence answered. Mayhap the child had gone into the gazebo. Although the upper half was covered with latticework, vines had grown up through them. The inside—as she knew so well—could be a quiet haven, so Deirdre might not be able to hear her.

She gasped as she stepped into the gazebo. Swaths of lace were draped over the latticework, deepening the shadows in the corners. On the benches, bouquets of lily of the valley covered the seats in a deep green wave with white froth.

"Deirdre?" she asked, incredulous as she set her basket of berries on the closest bench.

The little girl stepped out of one shadowed corner. "It's a game," she said with an eager smile.

"A game?" Lily asked when the little girl grasped her hands and drew her beneath the center of the peaked roof. "What kind of game?"

"A game of pretending."

Taking a deep breath, she forced a weak smile. She need not ruin Deirdre's day simply because hers had become a disaster . . . as the rest of her days would be now without Randall.

"Deirdre, I was so worried about you. I thought you might have wandered away and hurt yourself. Didn't you hear me calling?"

"I wanted everything to be perfect." She spun around to point at the beautiful lace and flowers.

"But, Deirdre, you should have—"

"Don't you wish to know what kind of game it is, Aunt Lily?" Not giving her a chance to answer, the little girl said, "It's a wedding game."

Her smile wavered, but she struggled to keep her voice light. "Deirdre, this is lovely, but why didn't you answer me? Didn't you hear me call?"

"She heard you," answered a deeper voice.

Lily stared, sure she must be asleep or mad, as Randall stepped out of the shadows. He wore a broad smile.

"You are here!" she gasped.

"I'm glad to see you have not changed." He chuckled. "You still have a tight grip on the obvious."

"But why? You said—"

His hands curved along her face as he drew her closer. "I said many stupid things. Now it is time to do the wise thing."

"And not be a hero?"

"No, by trying to be one," he retorted with a laugh that flowed through her like the sweetest song.

"How?"

Desire glittered in his eyes. "Before I answer that, let me say that you Armstrongs are very much alike."

"Tommy and me?" She knew she sounded silly, but she could not believe what she was hearing.

"And Deirdre. All of you have taught me so much, even though at times I did not want to learn. Your brother taught me about friendship and loyalty." He glanced away to smile at Deirdre, who was watching them with a cheek-splitting grin. "And Deirdre has taught me that an obligation doesn't have to be an ordeal."

She swept the stubborn curl back from his forehead. "And me?"

"You have taught me not to be afraid to laugh and smile and *feel* again." His fingers splayed across her cheek, sending the warmth of his touch deep into her. "Do you think I would have been willing to be a party to Deirdre's game of luring you out here on the pretense of picking strawberries when I first arrived here? You have both taught me there is more to life than responsibilities. So now, in this lovely bower, I shall play the groom while you play the beautiful bride."

As he tilted her lips toward his, she whispered, "It is only a game."

"But this will serve as excellent practice for our real wedding, Lily."

"Real wedding?" She feared her heart could not hold all this happiness, and she did not want to lose a moment of it.

"Why not, my love?" He enfolded her against him.

"I can't."

"You can't?" His eyes darkened to the color of thunderheads as his smile vanished.

She kept her hand on his arm as she stepped back and looked at Deirdre. "Not until I have your permission."

"Oh, yes!" cried the little girl as she flung her arms around both of them.

Randall chuckled. "You have her blessing—"

"Permission," corrected Deirdre with a grin.

"You are getting to be a naughty child!" he said, wagging his finger in her direction. He bent and kissed the little girl on the cheek before turning to face Lily. All humor left his face as he asked, "Will you marry me, Lily Armstrong, and help me learn more about love?"

"Yes," she whispered.

Swirling her about so that her skirts belled out around her ankles, he enfolded her to him. Just before his mouth claimed hers, he whispered, "And there's no time like now to begin my lessons."

The Present
by Cindy Holbrook

A grimy spyglass slid through the bushes, its lens trained upon the elite, aristocratic party that was disporting itself upon Glenning Hall's rolling, well-manicured lawn. To be sure, the gathering must have been called a picnic, though there was a linen-clothed table, gleaming silverware, and servants aplenty to ensure each guest's comfort. Chairs were set out as well. No ants would find their way into this noble frolic.

"Well, do we want the Viscount Montcleif?" a quiet voice asked.

"No," a very serious one replied. "I don't like him as well as the duke."

"Yeth," a third chirped. "The duke!"

"Then we are agreed?" the first asked, clearly the leader. "It is the duke?"

"Yeth, oh yeth. He hath nice eyes."

"That ain't why we're catching him, shrimp!" The voice was scornful.

"Perhaps we oughtn't," the more sober one considered.

"Do you want Aunt crying and moaning again? You want Shannon angry?"

A moment's hesitation ensued. "No."

"Then we gotta do this. Are we agreed?"

Three pairs of small hands clasped each other's in a secret handshake. "Agreed!" The bushes rustled and light footsteps were heard, the sound disappearing toward the neighboring estate.

* * *

Alex Tremain, the ninth Duke of Trenton, rode musingly along the deserted lane, reining in his stallion, Calif, to an amble. It was a pace the animal clearly thought beneath him.

Alex, however, was in the mood to meander. His mind was upon the voluptuous and fulsomely offered charms of Lady Susan Glenning. Now there was a sweet dessert!

Her mama's eye, however, gleamed with the idea of matrimony, and that was one trap that would never snare Alex Tremain. At thirty, he was knowledgeable of all the angles and all the ruses. He'd not be caught!

A muffled sound distracted him. The noise seemed to come from the distance. It sounded like a child crying! Alex prodded Calif swiftly forward, rounding the curve in the lane to discover a golden-haired little girl sitting beneath a large oak. Her face was hidden, her hands covering her eyes. As he approached, she let forth a tragic wail.

"What is it, child?" he asked in concern, directing Calif to stop a few feet from her. "What are you crying about?"

The girl's hands slid slowly from her face. Brilliant blue eyes, clear and dry, peeked up at him. A cherubic smile swiftly dimpled her face. "Hello, Your Grace!"

"I beg pardon?" Alex asked, frowning. How had she known his title? Why was she not crying now? Before he could ask such pertinent questions, he heard a grunt and a rustle.

He looked up quickly, only to discover a heavy net falling directly over him. Of common rope, it smelled distinctly like fish.

A tow-headed boy grinned down at him from a sturdy branch.

"What the devil do you think you're doing?" Alex ground out, attempting to throw off the net.

"We've caught you!" another child's voice suddenly shrilled. A small figure jumped out from behind the trunk of the tree. "We're taking you to Shannon!"

"Yeth, yeth, for Shannon!" the little girl chorused, springing up to hop out a mad little dance of glee.

Calif started at the commotion and neighed. He liked neither the odiferous netting, nor the strange, erratic actions of the small persons before him.

He reared, snorting his complaint. Alex drew firmly in on the reins, yet the netting had become entangled with the leads, diluting his commands. Calif, well into an equestrian fit, reared and efficiently shed himself of the offending netting and Alex as well.

Alex flew through the air, hitting the ground roughly. He thought he heard a snap, and then an exquisite pain shot through his right leg. He groaned and knew no more.

Shannon gazed down at the man who lay silent upon the guest-room bed. His large frame dwarfed it, his length outstripping its mattress. Yet it was the largest bed in the house and would have to suffice.

Twigs and dirt coated the man's jet black hair. A raw cut was scratched across a high, intelligent forehead. Another marred his firmly molded lips—lips that immediately drew a woman's attention. Even in repose they appeared sensual.

Shannon shook herself. What was the matter with her? Rather than staring at the poor man like a moonling, she should be doing something to help him.

She had already cut off his Hessian from his right foot. She had regretted it, and from the superb fit and gleam of the boot, she was sure this stranger would, too. Yet his foot was swelling to terrifying dimensions and his leg looked as if it had been broken.

How had he come to be in such a condition? Shannon wondered. The children had driven up in their small pony cart shouting and crying for her. This poor man had been laid out in the back.

Their stories had been breathless and jumbled. Apparently they had taken the cart out to play and had stumbled across this man. He was fortunate they had come upon him Shannon thought, for his state was desperate. If only the doctor would come soon!

Biting her lip, she leaned over and untied his cravat. Then

forcing herself to be calm, she unbuttoned the first three buttons of his lawn shirt. Her hands tingled as they accidentally brushed the curly black hair upon the stranger's chest. This was closer than she had ever been to a man.

Suddenly a strong hand gripped her wrist. "What are you doing?" a low, harsh voice rasped. Her eyes flew in shock to the man's face. Glittering green eyes, slitted in suspicion, studied her.

She flushed. "I—I was merely undressing—I mean, undoing your shirt buttons. They—they looked restraining."

"What do you want from me?" he growled.

"Want from you?" Shannon echoed, shocked by the rage in the man's eyes.

"Tell me," he demanded. His fingers dug into her skin, shaking her wrist.

"I don't want anything," Shannon gasped.

His eyes narrowed and he stared at her a moment. "You are Shannon, are you not?"

"Why yes, but how did you know? Have we met?"

"Have we met?" he exclaimed angrily. "Stop playing games with me!" With a sudden, powerful jerk on her wrist, he pulled her down to the mattress. His other hand swiftly clamped her shoulder as Shannon tried to right herself with a surprised squeak. "What kind of monster would send children to do her dirty work?"

"Children? Dirty work?" Shannon realized she was inanely parroting the man, but she couldn't help herself. His words and actions were befuddling.

He shook her slightly. "Don't play the innocent. What do you want from me? Is it money? Are you holding me for ransom?"

"No, of course not," Shannon retorted, concluding in a flash that the man was mad. "Now do let me go. You are suffering from delirium!"

The man's eyes flared and a vein throbbed at his right temple. "Like hell I am. It is you who are delirious if you think you will gain anything from me."

"I don't want anything from you," Shannon said, exasperated.

Her own anger was rising and she was becoming healthily tired of this bedlamite's mauling. "Now let me go or I'll scream!"

"You'll scream?" Incredulity washed his face and then the perverse man laughed nastily. "That's rich! Now you're the shrinking violet! What are you trying to do?"

"I am trying to hold my patience," Shannon said through gritted teeth, sure a vein in her own forehead was popping out. "Now, sir, unhand me and I shall try and find a draught for you."

His eyes narrowed. "I'll not be drugged by you, strumpet."

"Strumpet! Ohh!" Her hand swung out and delivered a stinging slap to his cheek. Its mark immediately swelled red across his skin. "Oh my!" She stared at him. He stared back. Rampant shock was clearly the overriding expression upon both faces.

"I—I am sorry, sir," Shannon said stiffly. "Yet I will not tolerate such offensive language. Now if you will release me . . ." The man's hands slid slowly from her shoulders. Still he stared. Gawked in fact!

Apparently he was not accustomed to women lifting a hand to him. Which seemed strange, Shannon thought. With his aberrant behavior he should have been familiar with collecting a few odd slaps a day.

Shannon rose and cleared her throat. "Now, sir, I shall leave you to rest. The—the doctor shall be here soon I have no doubt. He—he will attend to your wounds." The man's steady green gaze pinned her. Shannon flushed. "Very well then." She nodded as firmly as she could and sped from the room.

Shannon did not proceed very far though, for she ran directly into three small bodies as she crossed the door's threshold.

Thomas squealed as she trod sharply on his hand. He had apparently been kneeling down—keyhole level. Michael pedaled backward hastily, only to tumble over Becky who had been pressed up behind him, all the better to hear no doubt.

Shannon made a quick recovery. Drawing herself up in wrath, she glared at the children. "How many times have I told you children not to listen at the keyholes?"

She swung around and smartly closed the door to the guest

room and the maniac it housed. A flush coursed through her. What if the children had overheard the exchange?

"We—we just wanted to know if the du—man was all right," Thomas, the oldest of her three younger siblings said, struggling to an upright position.

"Yeth," Becky, the baby of four nodded, still sprawled on the floor. "Ith he all right?"

"He's not hurt too much is he?" Michael asked, his big brown eyes pools of concern.

"I—I am not sure," Shannon said, feeling desperate. "But on no account are you children to go in and see him. I—I fear he is somewhat delirious and acting very queerly. Now you children go downstairs. I must help Aunt Elizabeth prepare bandages."

Casting them a minatory eye and ensuring that all three looked penitent, she sped down the hall. Faith, when would the doctor come? And could he cure sicknesses of the mind? She was positive that such was her patient's malady, and if the doctor did not arrive soon, she was sure she would succumb to a bout of it herself.

Alex lay back against the pillows and gritted his teeth. "Steady old man," he recommended to himself. "Keep your calm!" Well, keep whatever shred of calm he still possessed after the scene he'd just survived with that vixen.

Where the blazes was he and who the devil was this woman Shannon? It had been no problem to recognize her, for she was a replica of the little girl who had lured him into the trap. Her hair was the same shining gold; her eyes a deep, stormy blue.

Her body, however, was anything but that of a little girl; the curves were womanly and well-pronounced. Faith, whatever this Shannon's game, she certainly had all the feminine weapons at her disposal.

He suddenly tensed. The door to the room was slowly, stealthily opening. A towhead hesitantly peeked around the door. Ah, the boy from the tree!

The miniature culprit entered as well as his other two cohorts.

Wordlessly they solemnly lined up in front of him at the bed's edge.

"What do you want?" he asked, eyeing them warily. His leg throbbed, his head ached, and his cheek still smarted. What new torment must he suffer now?

Still they did not speak, though their eyes grew wide with horror, as if he were an ogre ready to rend them limb from limb.

"Please, Your Grace," the tallest and apparently the oldest finally squeaked, "you oughtn't be angry at Shannon."

"You called her bad names," the little girl said, shaking her head in sad reproach.

"Er—so I did," Alex said, nonplussed. The child gazed at him. Apparently she expected more. "I—I apologize. That, er, was ill done of me."

"You called her *strumpet,*" she said. Alex flushed. "What is a strumpet?"

"A word you should never use," Alex said firmly. He looked at the children and felt as if he was sinking. He should be the victim here, but he was quickly feeling like the criminal. "I—I was quite angry at the time. I, er, lost my temper."

"We didn't mean to make you angry," the middle boy said, his brown eyes full of worry. He drew in a deep breath. "You see, Shannon didn't know anything about—about what we did."

"She didn't?" Alex asked. He studied them. "What relation is Shannon to you?"

"Thister," the girl chirped.

"I see. And what of your father and mother? Do they know of this?"

"No," the oldest said, shaking his head. "They are dead."

"Ah," he said. "I'm sorry."

"But we have Shannon," the boy added quickly, proudly. "And she's enough for anyone."

A chuckle escaped Alex, making him catch his breath as his leg complained of the movement. "Ahh—perhaps you had better tell me what this is all about. Who are you?"

"I'm Thomas," the oldest said. "This is Michael. The runt here is Becky."

"Thomas," Alex nodded. "Why did you capture me and bring me here?

"Well, you were supposed to make Shannon a mother . . ."

"For her birthday!" the little girl nodded.

Alex blinked a few times. "I beg your pardon?"

"You see, Aunt Elizabeth always starts crying about this time," the boy Michael said. "She gets real sad and sighs a lot."

"She does?"

"She gets upset because Shannon isn't a real mother," Thomas continued. He looked down. "She—she says that we children aren't enough."

"Oh no, now that I refuse to believe," Alex said fervently. "I would imagine you are more than enough for anyone."

"No," Michael said, shaking his head, his brown eyes large. "Aunt Elizabeth says Shannon should have children of her own, that we're just brothers and sisters—and that she is throwing away all her prospects."

"All," Becky nodded woefully.

"Shannon's birthday is coming soon," Thomas explained, "and we wanted to give her a real special present. We want her to be a mother this year. So—we decided to get you. We thought you could do it."

"Good God!" Alex exclaimed, stunned.

"Jack in the stables says that you've made plenty of women mothers," Michael said eagerly. "Couldn't you do that for Shannon?"

"Please?" Becky added sweetly.

Three sets of innocent, trusting eyes gazed upon him in sincere entreaty. Alex cleared his throat. "I hate to disappoint you, but I have not fathered any children—at least, that I know of," he added under his breath. "Jack in the stables was mistaken in his information, I fear."

The three young faces fell. Alex eyed them cautiously. It was Thomas that brightened first. "But you could, I am sure! If you tried really, really hard! You're a fast worker. Cook said so."

"Very fast," Becky nodded.

"Faith," Alex groaned. "Is naught but my reputation discussed around here?"

"It is still several weeks before Shannon's birthday," Michael calculated. "Her birthday is the 17th of May and 'tis only April now." He cast Alex a hopeful look. "That should be enough time to make her a mother, don't you think?"

"Faith no!" Alex exclaimed. He looked at the expectant children. "It, er—it takes much longer for the ah—total process."

Thomas frowned, looking at him in frank disbelief. "But we got Sir Rupert at Christmastide and he's made Miss Emily a mother. It only took a month or so."

Alex stared, mad images chasing through his mind. Certainly these children hadn't caught some other man, and. . . . He shook his head to clear it. "I don't know who Rupert is," Alex said firmly. "But he couldn't have done it. No man could."

"Oh no," Michael said. "Rupert's a bunny!"

"A bunny!" Alex exclaimed. His mouth fell open and then he started to laugh. Evidently he was to be in competition with a rabbit!

"So we thought you could do better," Thomas said reasonably. "After all, Rupert isn't anything to you, is he?"

"Sorry old man," Alex shook his head apologetically. "I fear Sir Rupert must take the honors." He studied the children. "How old are you?"

"I am six," Thomas said. "Michael is five and Becky is four."

"I see." Now he knew why their mother had passed away so promptly. She and Miss Emily had much in common. "And how old is Shannon?"

"She is twenty-three," Michael said.

He frowned. "That's a gap."

"She's really only a stepsister," Thomas confided.

"She had a different mother," Michael nodded. "But she is awfully nice. Are you sure you wouldn't want to make her a mother?"

Alex envisioned the shapely, blond-haired beauty, and a surge of desire shot through him. Make her a mother? Yes, he'd like to.

He flushed. What was he thinking? And with children in the room at that!

"I am sorry," Alex said as gently as he could. "That is not the way things work. Besides, I am not sure your sister would approve of your plan. You know your sister would wish to be married if she were going to be a mother."

"Oh yeth," Becky nodded.

"We know that," Thomas said scornfully. "Ladies can't be mothers unless they are married. Others can, Aunt Elizabeth says . . ."

"Like our maid Dora," Michael interrupted. "She wasn't married. She even had twins!"

"But never ladies!" Thomas finished sagely.

"That's why we chose you," Michael said, reaching over and patting Alex's shoulder approvingly. "Jack said that you are a ladies' man. You should be just right for Shannon."

"Because she's a lady," Becky nodded.

The children looked at him, well-satisfied with their grasp of the situation. In fact, it was evident they were quite proud of their master plan. Alex was considering what to say, how to delicately phrase matters, when the door opened.

"What are you children doing in here?" The object of their discussion entered the room, a wrathful look in her blue eyes. "I told you not to come in here!"

Alex looked at the blond beauty and a chuckle escaped him. She stood proudly before them, exuding a rare but natural confidence and power. Only wait! Little did she know what her siblings had in store for her.

"But the duke doesn't mind," Thomas said, his voice wheedling.

"Duke?"

"Yes, he's the Duke of Trenton." Michael nodded.

"Alex Tremain at your service, madam," he said blandly. "I'd rise, but I am slightly incapacitated."

Her reaction was swift. She gasped and paled. "Lud!"

Alex's brows snapped down in aggravation. That was not the reaction he had expected. Most women became quite affable once they learned of his noble estate. Not so this Shannon. The devil! Old Jack in the stable was a very busy man no doubt.

"But you'll like him, Shannon," Thomas said quickly. "That's why we chose him for you."

"Chose him for me?" Her eyes narrowed in suspicion. "What do you mean?"

The three conspirators looked down, guilt rife upon their faces.

"Well, we," Thomas said in a mumble, "wanted him to be a gift, sort of . . ."

"For your birthday," Michael said weakly, since their sister's eyes had darkened dangerously.

"Yeth," Becky whispered, a finger slipping into her mouth.

"Let me understand this. You brought me a man?" Shannon asked in an even, frightful tone. "As a gift!?"

"Yes," Alex said, since the children were speechless and quaking. "They brought me here so that I could make you a mother for your birthday—that was to be the real present. I was just to be the deus ex machina as it were."

Her eyes flew open wide. "You? Were to make me a mother? Oh my God!"

Alex could not contain himself. He roared with laughter. His broken leg, his splitting head, every discomfort he had suffered this day had been worth it, only for the sight of the chagrined, stupefied expression upon the face of the woman before him. It was a sight he was sure he would remember and cherish for the rest of his life.

It was ten the next morning and Shannon sat in the morning room with a cup of tea, hiding. She was hiding from the fact that a wounded duke occupied her upstairs guest bedroom. A duke, mind you, that her siblings had seen fit to capture for the sole purpose of procreation with her. It was not only mortifying, but stupefying. How could they have chosen the Duke of Trenton of all people?

His reputation as a rake and fighter was renowned in this small town. Lady Susan Glenning had seen to that! From greengrocer to smithy, everyone in town had heard Susan's endless tales of the dashing Alex Tremain. He was a member of the Four-in-Hand Club, a top Corinthian, a bruising rider to hounds, and a devil with the ladies!

Furthermore, there wasn't a person in the district that had not been forewarned of his visit or of Susan's nuptial plans for the dangerous duke. And now that very man was upstairs with a broken leg because her siblings had seen fit to net him.

"Shannon, dearest!" a worried voice called, and her Aunt Elizabeth dashed into the room. Silver-haired and blue-eyed, Aunt Elizabeth stood all of five feet and two. She was both plump and matronly. Never having been married, her disposition was that of the romantic. Aunt Elizabeth could sigh and cry with the best of the Radcliffe heroines. What very few realized, however, was that Aunt Elizabeth also possessed a determined streak that ensured she got her way more times that not.

This odd mixture of high flights and firm backbone made Aunt Elizabeth a very volatile and unknown quantity. She could easily drive Shannon up the walls when she so desired, but Shannon also knew that Aunt Elizabeth's love and loyalty to the family were unswerving. Indeed, many were the times that Shannon was grateful for Aunt Elizabeth's support and kindness.

Aunt Elizabeth was in one of her dithers at this time, however, and wrinkles creased her brow. "Shannon, the dear duke won't eat his broth," she wailed, sitting down next to Shannon. "He—he is demanding a beefsteak and a bottle of port. I fear he is in the boughs, but a beefsteak and port surely cannot be beneficial to him. Dr. Chester strictly forbade it. Whatever shall we do?"

Shannon cast her eyes toward heaven. It seemed quite simple to her. "Tell him to eat the broth or nothing at all."

"My love," Aunt Elizabeth gasped, "we couldn't do that; the poor boy could starve."

"I highly doubt it," Shannon said, her voice dry.

"Please, dear, could you not see if you could persuade him to eat?" Aunt Elizabeth's voice was laden with concern, yet something sly flickered within her eyes.

Shannon's own eyes narrowed suspiciously. "Aunt, are you up to one of your tricks?"

"Oh no, dearest. He truly is in a tiff and will not listen to me." Aunt Elizabeth widened her eyes in a good portrayal of innocence, but added eagerly, "And 'deed dear, what could it hurt for you to nurse the poor man and show him how sweet you can be? After all, I know the children were terribly naughty in capturing the man, and that he broke his leg is unfortunate, but now that he is here, what could it hurt to take advantage of it? He is such a fine figure of a man, such speaking eyes, such strong features . . ."

"Aunt Elizabeth," exclaimed Shannon, throwing up her hands in exasperation. "You are as bad as the children. Are you suggesting I try to set up a romance with him?"

"Oh yes," breathed Elizabeth, her eyes turning starry. "What could be more perfect? He is so fine-looking."

"He is also a rake!"

"He needs a good woman. That is all, dearest. Men simply go awry without the love of an understanding, caring woman. You could reform him, Shannon, I just know you could."

"No, Auntie, 'The Reforming of Rake Tremain' is a role that has already been applied for by Susan Glenning. Have you forgotten?"

"That hussy!" Aunt Elizabeth hissed, and then flushed deeply. Aunt Elizabeth rarely used such strong terms. "She is not right for the boy. Anybody can see that! Besides, she cannot hold a candle to you, darling." Elizabeth sighed. "To tell the truth, Shannon, I would so like the duke for a nephew."

"You and everyone else in this world," Shannon said with a laugh. "Despite his wicked reputation."

"I told you—"

"I know, I know, the poor duke only needs the love of a good woman." She stood and patted her aunt consolingly upon the shoulder. "Forget it, dearest." I doubt I'm that good of a woman."

"Oh yes, you are!"

Shannon shook her head. "Please, Aunt, rid yourself of such

romantical notions. I'll not reform him, neither will I play barmaid to his prince."

"Why, 'tis no such thing. Your lineage is excellent."

"He can look much higher than me, dearest, and I am sure he will." Aunt Elizabeth's face fell so ridiculously that Shannon softened. "I will, however, see if I can induce the duke to take his broth, and with that you must be satisfied."

Shannon left the room, shaking her head. She had no doubt that Aunt Elizabeth was already air-dreaming about the great affair that she and the duke would have. Faith, given another hour, she was sure Aunt Elizabeth would have them married and walking down the aisle in St. Peter's Cathedral.

Her mouth tightened and she scowled. Well, if the duke thought the same, he would receive short shrift from her. She was not hanging out for a rich husband. Neither was she a deceiving, conniving woman as he had so hatefully insinuated. Indeed, she wanted nothing to do with the man.

She straightened her shoulders and entered the guest bedroom. The Duke of Trenton sat upright in bed, pillows stuffed behind his back. His green eyes glittered, stubble shadowed his face, and a high color ran through his cheeks.

"I hear, Your Grace," she said in a prim manner, "that you will not eat Cook's fine broth."

"You heard correct, madam," the man said curtly. His frown was thunderous. "You call it broth, I call it pap. I have a broken leg and nothing more. I am a man, not a baby, for God's sake. I will have a beefsteak and a bottle of port, if you please."

Shannon studied the disgruntled, irate duke, and her mouth suddenly twitched at the corners. With his feet surpassing the end of the bed, he certainly was no baby, but his fractious manner was suspiciously akin to that of her little brothers when they were ill.

He glared at her and his brow rose imperiously. "Well?"

She sank into a deep curtsy, meekly bowing her head. "I am quite sorry, Your Grace."

"Indeed," he said nodding. " 'Tis forgiven. Only tell your cook . . ."

"I am sorry," Shannon said less meekly, rising from her curtsy, "but Dr. Chester strictly forbids solid food for a day. Only liquids. You shall have our broth Your Grace, or nothing else."

"I beg your pardon!" the duke said, outraged and clearly shocked at her temerity.

"I said—"

"I heard what you said!" he roared. "That doctor is a quack, and you, my girl, are impertinent. I demand food, not this slop!"

"No, Your Grace," Shannon said, her chin jutting out.

His eye's darkened ominously. "If you do not order it, I shall order it myself."

"You shall not!" Shannon retorted. Her temper hit boiling point. The duke may have been accustomed to his every order being meekly and swiftly obeyed, but as mistress of Meadowlark Manor so was she! "You shall not move from there. The bone must be permitted to set correctly."

"I will not be commanded by a country mouse," he snarled, now truly in a rage, his green eyes glittering under flaring brows. "A country mouse, mind you, whose small brothers and sister were forced to go out and find her a man by snare and net!"

Shannon gasped. She drew herself up to her full height and said with dignity, "You are certainly no gentleman to mention the incident! But then I knew that! Only naive children under the age of seven would mistake you for anything but a rake."

"Fiend seize it all! I am not!" he shouted, sheer outrage clouding his undeniably handsome features. "Only country misses with bourgeois notions would think such. All you've done is listen to gossip mongers with nothing better to do than tear a man's character apart!"

"What character?" she snapped.

"Well, at least I don't spend my life listening to my groom jaw away over some man I don't even know like you and your hellion siblings have done. Faith, what an exciting life you must lead! I ought to grass the blighter."

"My Lord! If this is the language you sophisticated London nobles use in the presence of ladies, I will have none of it!" She turned sharply on her heel to leave the overbearing, obnoxious man.

"Are you going to get me some real food or not?"

She froze, refusing to turn. "I shall not! You may eat that pap, or you may starve."

"Bedamn I will!"

Shannon heard the springs of the bed creak and the sheets rustle. She spun, aghast. The infamous man had swung his splinted leg to the floor and was rising. "Don't!" she exclaimed. "Don't!"

"If I have to . . . ahhh . . ." The duke swayed.

"Oh no!" Shannon ran to him, reaching out to grasp him about the waist. They both stood suspended, Shannon desperately clutching him. Then the man groaned, his arms coming about her to gain support.

"Damn," he muttered. He teetered, Shannon cried out, and together they toppled over onto the bed.

Shannon lay stunned, somewhat beneath him. They were totally entwined, his face just above hers. His breath came in gasps, his complexion white. "Are you mad!" she seethed.

"Must be," he murmured. He grinned weakly and then he stared at her.

"What?" she asked. His eyes were starting to glitter with a strange light.

"Must be mad," he said. Suddenly he lowered his head and kissed her squarely on the lips.

Shannon let out a surprised, muffled yelp, but he did not halt. He increased the pressure, his lips warm and mobile upon hers.

Now Shannon had only been kissed by family in her entire life, and the duke's kiss was nothing, but nothing, like her young brothers' and sister's. His firm, teasing lips sent odd, warm sensations throughout her. She opened her mouth to gasp in a breath of air that she was sadly lacking and—heavens! He took advantage as surely only a rake could!

Discovering, however, that she very much liked the rake's kiss, she clutched at the large man, pulling him closer. It seemed as if she were drowning in sensations. She shivered slightly and moved her lips against his as he had done to her. She shivered again. It was delightful!

He emitted a groan and suddenly drew back. "Gads!"

Shannon opened her eyes, not realizing she had closed them. His were deep and unreadable. She stared at him, still amazed at the feelings running through her.

"I am sorry," he said, looking away.

"Oh," she said, trying to marshal her thoughts. He seemed upset. "That is all right," she said kindly. "You can't help yourself, after all."

"I can't?" he asked, his eyes turning back to her.

"No, it is your propensity, I would imagine," Shannon said, striving desperately for reason. Faith, they had both been going irons and tongs at each other and then, from nowhere, that kiss! It made little sense, except that the duke was evidently a man who simply must kiss women. She focused on that theory. "I mean, I know our prize bull is the same in that he . . . he . . . well . . ."

The duke groaned, rolling away from her. "Oh Gad!"

"Did you hurt yourself?" she asked, rising up on her elbow to study him.

"No, but you and your family have slain me," he said, his hand going over his eyes. Then he started laughing deeply, richly. "Forsooth, you liken me to a bull while your charming brothers and sister have, mind you, likened me to a rabbit!"

"A rabbit?" Shannon gasped. His face was droll, his eyes sparkling as he pulled his hand away. "They didn't!" A giggle escaped her. "Never say so. You—you certainly do not look like a small furry creature to me."

"Ah, but rabbits propagate within the span of two months!" he retorted. "And your brothers and sister decided that if Sir Rupert was bunny enough to do so, certainly I should be man enough to do so! Got to make the mark of your birthday, you know."

Shannon should have blushed, perhaps, or gasped or done any number of maidenly tricks, but she could only laugh. "Oh heavens! How demanding!"

"I know I should be honored by their confidence in my, er, prowess, but I own I have never been considered merely for stud purposes. Faith, it sinks me."

" 'Tis only fair, my lord," Shannon retorted, sitting up to wipe the tears of laughter away.

"How is that?"

"Are not we women chosen as such? Do we have the proper bloodlines? What of our parents and their history? Are we not chosen for our ability to birth and rear children?"

He gazed at her. "Well, that is very blunt."

Shannon flushed. "I am sorry, Your Grace, but we here in the country say it more forthrightly."

His brow quirked. "All of you?"

She grinned. "No, perhaps only some of us. Yet as a mere country mouse, I—"

"Country mouse! Ha!" he exclaimed, raising his hands in feigned surrender. "I take that comment back. Even a duchess has never sent me to such a rightabout as you did!"

"I am sorry," Shannon blushed. "I am not accustomed to dukes, you see."

"Nor anyone else that brooks your orders, I would imagine." Shannon remained silent, for she could not deny the fact. "Very much the way I am," he then said, his voice gentling. "I do apologize. We dukes really aren't such terrible people, despite what your groom reports."

"Oh no," Shannon exclaimed. "I hadn't listened to Jack. I had heard it from—" Shannon bit her tongue.

"From whom?" he asked, his eyes sharpening. She remained silent and he chided, "Come now, I've been sufficiently humbled; I am sure I can take one more lowering comment. Unless you intend to liken me to some other beast of burden."

"No."

"Who was it?" he asked again.

"Susan told me all about you," Shannon confessed. "But you must understand, she did not mean it in a bad way. She thinks you quite dashing and is enamored of you." He raised a cynical brow and she said, "No, truly."

"Don't stop being frank with me now. You mean she is enamored of my wealth." Tremain frowned. "In truth, being chosen for my breeding abilities is by far more complimentary than being chosen for my monetary worth."

At that juncture the door to the bedroom opened, and Aunt Elizabeth walked into the room. She halted immediately. "Oh dear!" she gurgled, her eyes widening as she spied both Shannon and the duke upon the bed. "I do apologize. I am so sorry to interrupt, Your Grace . . ."

"No, dear." Shannon cast the duke a wry look and sprung swiftly from the bed, hearing a groan from him at her swift movements. "It is perfectly all right."

"Er, yes," the duke said, attempting to pull himself into a more orderly position.

"I would not interrupt for the world, but the Glennings are downstairs inquiring after your health!"

"They are?" His tone was not one of pleasure, and he cast a stern glance at Shannon.

"I sent a message to them immediately last evening," Shannon said, shrugging helplessly. "I did not wish them to worry."

"I see." He looked at Aunt Elizabeth, who gazed at him expectantly. "Very well," he sighed. "If Shannon would help arrange me for visitors, I shall see them. There is no way out of it, I fear."

Aunt Elizabeth's eyes brightened. "Very well." She nodded and left.

"Help arrange you for visitors?" Shannon quizzed, even as she went to place pillows behind his back.

"But of course. I am an invalid, after all." He grinned shamelessly at her as she straightened the sheets over him. "A poor, weak, defenseless invalid."

Shannon stepped back to survey him. His eyes were merry and teasing. "Would you need a shave perhaps, Your Grace," she asked, an answering glint in her eyes. "I am sure I could find a razor."

His brow quirked. "And would you know how to shave a man, madam?"

"No," she said sweetly. "But I am sure after a few nicks and cuts I shall master it."

He barked a laugh. "I knew it! No, Shannon, I'll greet my guests unshaven but unmutilated."

Shannon had no time to retort, for they heard the Glennings' approach in the hall. They had made the stairs in record time, Shannon observed.

"Oh, my dear duke," Lady Susan Glenning gushed as she came into view. She stopped to pose within the doorway. Susan was a picture in green satin, her chestnut locks gleaming, wearing a look that blended both concern and feminine lure upon her face. "Whatever happened?" She rushed to his side and Shannon was hard-put not to be mowed down in the process.

"Yes, Duke, what happened?" Lord Glenning asked, entering with his wife upon his arm. Lord Glenning was a beefy man, his wife a faded picture of Susan with a few pounds added. "Heard you took a spill; thought that couldn't be."

Shannon flushed. Tremain did not look at her, but laughed at the earl. "Afraid it is very lowering, but that is exactly what I did. And if it weren't for Shannon's . . . er, Miss. . . ." He stopped and looked at her in enquiry.

In truth they had had no proper introduction. "Miss Aldon," she supplied quickly.

"Miss Aldon's brothers and sister discovering me," he proceeded smoothly, "I truly would have been in a bind."

"Then we must be grateful," Susan said, picking up Tremain's hand and patting it. She turned to Shannon and said warmly, if not condescendingly, "I thank you, Shannon. Why, the thought of poor Alex lying injured somewhere just rends me."

"I am sure," Shannon said quietly, wishing to make an escape as was her wont when around the Glennings. "Perhaps I should find some chairs for you, in order that you may sit while you visit."

"Of course," Susan nodded, smiling dismissively as if to a servant. She immediately turned back to the duke. "Duke, what can we do to make you more comfortable? Have you had a physician's care yet? We shall bring our own London doctor here. We wouldn't want you to suffer inferior care . . ."

Susan's tone all but said that the duke was camped out amongst a tribe of savages. Shannon suppressed her indignation and turned swiftly to leave.

"Do not get the chairs, Miss Aldon," Tremain said before she had taken two steps. "I—I feel weak and am sure the Glennings do not mean to stay long."

"Oh, no! Of course not," Susan breathed in consternation, as if she had not agreed to Shannon's proposal. "We wouldn't want to exhaust you in any manner." She held his hand close to her, drawing it well nigh onto her breasts.

"Indeed not," Shannon agreed. "The duke should not have any, er, excitement." Susan flushed, casting Shannon an angry glance, but she lowered his hand to a more proper distance from her bountiful bosom. "Now, if you will excuse me," Shannon said.

"Where are you going, Duchess?" Tremain asked, his eyes lighting. It was apparent he read her feelings. He winked at her mischievously.

"Duchess!" exclaimed Susan, her mouth falling open. "But how? When? I—"

"It is a joke, Susan," Shannon said. "His Grace is roasting me."

"Oh, I see," Susan said, though her dark eyes narrowed. "He is such a jokester. Alex, you are just too, too amusing."

"Yes, aren't I?" the duke said irrepressively. "You still haven't answered me, Miss Aldon."

Shannon wanted to slay him. She forced a demure smile. "I am going to warm up your broth again, Your Grace. It is quite cold now, and we wouldn't want that, would we?"

He barked a laugh. "Touché, Duchess."

Shannon grinned and exited as fast as possible. Yet it was not fast enough, for Susan's next words trailed after her. "Alex, you naughty man, you shouldn't call Shannon 'Duchess.' People will receive the wrong impression. Her family is of the peerage, but only remotely so. Not like our house, and most certainly not like yours. Now tell me, when can we arrange to remove you to Glenning Hall? I am sure you'll want to move as quickly as you can, rather than stay here."

Shannon gnashed her teeth and fled. She was going to find her devil siblings and rake them over the coals again for bringing the duke, and now the Glennings, into her house.

She found it very difficult to upbraid the children, however, when she arrived in the nursery. Becky had drawn the duke a lively picture—of what no one was certain, not even Becky. Thomas and Michael were constructing a wooden craft of sorts for the duke as well.

"Look, Shannon, do you think His Grace will like it?" Michael asked, hesitancy and worry in his eyes.

She smiled. "Why, I am quite sure that he will."

"We thought he might," Thomas said. He looked down, fingering the cloth that was to be a sail. "We—we didn't mean to hurt him, Shannon, we really didn't. We only wanted to talk to him."

"Well, netting him was certainly a novel way of opening a conversation," she sighed. "It was a rather wild scheme, my dears, and I believe you know how wrong it was."

"We're thorry," Becky whispered. Michael nodded, and Thomas was still unable to raise his head.

"All right," Shannon said, smiling. "We are fortunate that the duke doesn't mean to say anything of what you children did. He told the Glennings he merely fell off his horse."

"He did?" Thomas asked, brightening. "We knew he wouldn't squeal on us. He's a right one!"

"Er, yes," Shannon said. "But let's not do anything to make him change his mind. Let's try and make the duke as comfortable as we can for as long as he is here. I am sure he will be removing to Glenning Hall promptly. The Glennings are visiting with him now." The children appeared so woeful that Shannon almost groaned.

"Mark me, I understand what you children meant to do, but you must forget it. The duke is leaving soon, and there will be no romance between us." She flushed at that, ruthlessly relegating the duke's shocking kisses to the back of her mind. That had not been romance; that had merely been the heat of the moment. She flushed even deeper and said as firmly as she could, "I don't need a husband and I don't need to be a mother. You three are all the children I need."

"Honestly?" Michael's brown eyes studied her worriedly.

"Honestly," Shannon nodded, smiling. "Are we not family enough?"

"But a father wouldn't be so bad to have," Thomas shrugged, looking steadily down at his crafted boat.

A guilty pain shot through Shannon. Perhaps the children would like a father, especially the boys. But she had never found a man that she wished to marry, never found a man that remotely interested her. As much as she loved the children, marrying a man she did not wish to live with was something she could not envision.

"I know you miss your father," she said gently. "But not all men are the same. He was unusual. Not all fathers are like he was. Some children have fathers but never see them. In that respect they are just like you. Now do we really need that?"

"No," Becky said, wide-eyed.

"We rub along well enough, don't we?" Shannon asked anxiously, surprised at how important their answer was to her.

Thomas smiled. "Yes, Shannon, we do."

"Well then," Shannon smiled, a warmth rushing into her. "Let us get to the lessons Vicar Thornton has for you now."

The three children obeyed immediately, if not enthusiastically, and two hours had passed when Aunt Elizabeth came into the nursery. A frown was upon her face.

"Shannon, the duke is awake now and the poor boy is bored to flinders. He does not say so, but I can tell."

"But did the Glennings not stay?" Shannon exclaimed, surprised.

A smile of pure satisfaction crossed Elizabeth's face. "No, Alex routed them!"

"Alex?" Shannon asked.

"He said I could call him that," Aunt Elizabeth said, smiling proudly. "The Glennings were not here above ten minutes and he had them gone. I am sure that Susan intended to stay a lifetime, but she didn't succeed. However, now he has had his nap and the poor boy needs some entertainment. Do go to him, Shannon."

"And entertain him?" Shannon asked dryly. Aunt Elizabeth was desperately trying to appear nonchalant, while the children merely watched her with bated breath. What a clutch of conspirators was her family.

A wicked thought entered her mind. Perhaps if the children could see the duke in the cursing, roaring light that she had witnessed this morning, they'd not be so anxious to claim him as a father.

"Very well," she said, smiling impishly. "Let us entertain him. Becky get your picture and, boys, put that last sail upon your boat. We are going to see the duke."

"Shannon," Aunt Elizabeth gasped. "I—I think it best if you went alone."

"I am sure you do," Shannon said, "but all of us will entertain him."

It was time her family learned a lesson!

An hour later, Shannon sat next to the duke's bedside, dismay in her heart. Her family had not learned the lesson she had desired! Indeed, the duke and the children were well-ensconced, playing a game with paper. If she didn't know better, she could have sworn the duke had done it purposely to vex her. Yet his eyes sparkled as much as the children's and in no way did his enjoyment appear feigned.

"He's done it again, Shannon!" Thomas howled. "He's captured my fox. How did you do that!"

"Strategy, my boy, strategy!" the duke retorted.

"That's the third time he's won," Michael complained.

"Ah, but this last time you boys almost had me," he said. "And remember I've had more practice. Maybe next time you'll win."

"And that next time will have to be later," Shannon said swiftly. "His Grace should rest now."

"Aw!" Thomas said.

"Retht," Becky nodded, and patted the duke on his arm consolingly. Becky was the only one in the family still well-accustomed to naps upon demand.

The duke's brow rose, but he said, "You've heard your sister. It taxed me no end to win you this last time. I am exhausted. I think I'll stop and just rest on my laurels now." The boys laughed loudly and Becky clapped her tiny hands together in delight.

"Now go and prepare for tea," Shannon said, chuckling. At the word *tea* the children brightened and all but dashed from the room.

"And what of me?" Alex asked, his green eyes quizzing. "Must I take tea all by myself?"

Shannon looked at him, nonplussed. "I had thought you would care to rest—have some peace and quiet from the children."

"Faith no," he laughed. "I fear mine is not a solitary nature. I far prefer people and action."

"Indeed," Shannon said in a rather strangled voice, "you—you did well with the children."

"They are an unruly bunch." His laughter was amused, pleasant. Then his eyes sharpened. "You said that oddly. Why?"

Shannon shrugged. "I—I did not think a man of your station would care for the company of children."

His face darkened. "Do you consider me so inhuman as not to enjoy children? What an odd notion you have of me. Don't tell me Susan ever said that. And your man Jack better not have . . ."

"No, no," Shannon said swiftly. "Your preference for children—or lack of it—is not what they talk about, it's only your preference for—" She stopped.

"For women," he finished grimly.

"Well," Shannon smiled impishly, attempting to divert him. "They do mention you have an eye for a good horse as well."

He stared, and then laughed. "Ah, then some of the gossip is true, after all."

Shannon smiled. "I did not mean to offend. 'Tis only that from my experiences men are rarely patient with children."

"Ah, is that the way of it?" he said then, his eyes far too knowing.

She looked away. "Is what the way of what?"

"I wondered how a beautiful woman like you had remained unwed. The men are willing to accept your delectable self, but not the children?"

Shannon's chin rose. "No, that is not the way . . . well, not always."

"But enough times, I'd wager. When did your mother and father die?"

"They died in a carriage accident shortly after Becky was born."

"Faith, so you have raised her practically by yourself. And the boys?" He frowned. "Do they not have a guardian?"

Shannon laughed. "Oh yes, Uncle Bertram. He lives in London and is a proper dear. However, bucolic air depresses him, and he is not one for books and accounting, so he sends his man Jaspers to look over them. We deal famously together."

"I have no doubt," Alex Tremain said dryly. "And when does he intend to take the boys' education in hand?"

Shannon flushed. "Their education is in hand."

"Witness their concept of human propagation."

"Well, I—I did not know they knew so little on that score," Shannon confessed. "Vicar Thornton must deem them too young to learn of such matters."

"The vicar is to teach them?" Alex asked, disbelief rife within his voice.

Shannon was forced to smile at his outraged look. "Perhaps he is not the right one. He is rather old-fashioned. But I can teach them." His look was cynical. "I shall—I shall start studying the matter. There are plenty of books."

"Books! Gads," Alex said. "That should certainly help them. They'll know all the science of it and none of the knowledge. Listen, Duchess, you have two extremely intelligent boys, and if you don't set them straight upon the matter soon, you'll be sorry."

"Certainly not this young, Your Grace!" Shannon gasped.

He grinned. "You'd be surprised how early young boys start questioning the great mysteries of life." Shannon flushed and did not know where to look. "I know this is an improper subject, but since I was specifically captured because of it, I feel I should council you." Shannon felt as if her face was on fire. "After all, you can't have them netting and roping every eligible male around here and dragging them to your doorstep. Or asking them to produce upon demand."

"I know," Shannon said, sighing, "but I believe they are sorry. If only—" She stopped and bit her tongue.

"If only what?"

"Well, you gave them the impression this afternoon that having a father might be fun," she bit out as his eyes sharpened.

"Why, you baggage," he suddenly laughed. "You were hoping that I would scare the children away, weren't you? Confess!"

Shannon smiled wryly. "I had thought that as—as . . . er . . . vexed as you were this morning that—"

"That I'd give the children the sharp edge of my tongue," Alex finished. "What a little schemer you are, Miss Aldon. But you'll have to find another man to disillusion them. I like children, have plenty of nephews and nieces of my own. I'll not be the one to turn them from the thought of having a father."

"Very well," Shannon said, shrugging. "It was only a thought."

"Indeed," he said, frowning. "Having a father could be beneficial for them—and you might find having a husband of certain uses as well."

Shannon stared at him. He raised his brows wickedly and she laughed. "Rogue!" She rose. "Well, I must go attend to tea."

"After the children's will you come and have tea with me? It is a liquid, you know," he added sanctimoniously.

"If you promise to rest until then," Shannon said in concern.

"Rest! That's all I hear!"

"Why of course, dear Duke," Shannon said, sashaying to the side of the bed. She fluttered her lashes and attempted to look as Lady Susan had. She lifted the duke's hand, but held it a distance from her. "Why, we wouldn't want to exhaust you in any way," she breathed in a fair imitation of Susan's drawl.

He laughed softly, but his hand tightened upon hers. "Beware what you are about, Duchess!"

"And really, dear Duke," she breathed huskily, fluttering her lashes. "You shouldn't call me 'Duchess.' People might get the wrong impression. After all, my family is only slightly connected with the peerage."

"Tush, madam, mine is a democratic nature. I am not at all top-lofty."

Shannon laughed. "Only when you are denied anything."

"Of course." His smile was slight, oddly provocative. " 'Tis simple: do not deny me anything."

Shannon flushed, a wave of heat flashing through her. She attempted to drop his hand as though it was a firebrand.

He refused to release it. "Lady Susan knows what she is offering, Shannon."

"I have no doubt."

Their eyes locked, and he gently drew her hand to his own chest. His eyes roved to her lips. Shannon's breathing stopped.

"Whereas . . . you don't," he muttered. He released her hand, looking away.

Shannon blushed and breathed again. She felt as if she had been under a wizard's spell, but he had released her. She was grateful to him for that. Indeed, she was no Susan Glenning and she was most definitely out of her element with the duke. She cleared her throat. "The children will be ready for tea."

He looked at her steadily. "You'll come back afterwards?"

She smiled. "Indeed. Heaven forbid that you become bored. You'd most likely haul yourself up out of bed and drag yourself down the stairs for company."

He laughed. "Yes, just remember that I am an invalid and will need attention these next few days lest I fall into a decline."

Shannon's brow rose. "You are staying that long?"

"Of course. Where should I be able to go?"

"But I thought that Lady Susan—"

"I would not be moved." His look was bland. "After all, 'twas you that warned me of the danger of moving before my leg is set."

"Yes, indeed."

"You do not mind?" he asked. "I shall try not to be too much of a trouble."

She looked at him. She was hosting a lion in the house and he asked if he would not be too much trouble? A smile quirked her lips. "Indeed, of course not. So even-tempered that you are."

He barked a laugh. "Have mercy. Would you truly care to leave me to Lady Susan's tender mercies?"

"They would be more tender than mine," Shannon said pointedly. "You could have beefsteak and port every morning and—and anything else you desired—er, wished."

"All of which could kill me at this time, especially the 'anything else' you so delicately hint at." Shannon flushed. "And it could be even worse than that," he said ominously.

"Worse than death?"

"Yes," he nodded. "I could be entrapped, as down and helpless as I am . . ."

"Helpless?"

He cast her a quelling look. "I could be entrapped by Lady Susan into marriage."

"Ah, that is the fate worse than death?"

"Indeed. Now don't you feel it your duty to protect me? After all, it was your siblings that got me into this fix. Surely you will help me get out of it."

Shannon quirked her head. "Then . . . then you do not think me the scheming strumpet?"

"Forgive me for that," Tremain said. "You were correct; I was delirious. I've never met a less artless person. In fact, you are too artless for your own good. Or is it for my own good?"

Shannon laughed, a warmth flooding through her. The duke trusted her! "Either way, we shall contrive to protect you."

"Ah Shannon, you are a rare and wonderful woman," he said.

"That I am," Shannon replied. "Do rest for now. I shall return later. I'd not want you to fall into the doldrums."

She left him, a smile upon her lips and a smile upon his.

* * *

It was odd, Shannon mused as she surveyed the pristine dinner table set before her, how the advent of a new person into the household could change the atmosphere so promptly and remarkably. The last two weeks had been ideal.

Shannon frowned. Why had she thought of the word *ideal?* Tempestuous, yes, but ideal? Alex Tremain was anything but an "ideal" patient and not by any stretch of the imagination could one say the weeks with the confined duke had been peaceful.

How could they have been? Alex Tremain was autocratic and demanding. He had demanded brandy before it was time, he had demanded he should be able to walk before it was time, and he had demanded his valet upon the instant. Shannon had won the first two rounds after much battle, but the duke had won the last. His valet, Peters, had arrived at Meadowlark Manor without her say.

Yet Peters had turned out to be indispensable to both his master and Shannon. In truth, she had fought against having the valet come merely because she feared he would be one of those sniffing, snobbish London servants that would look down his nose at the simple household of Meadowlark. But Peters was no such personage, and if he was dignified and precise, he was also kind and amenable.

Shannon had discovered that the same could be said about his master. Alex Tremain could demand and command, but he never failed to give something in return. He was almost ceaseless in his demands for her to come and entertain him, yet while she read to him or played cards, he would easily draw her out upon all her daily woes and worries and suddenly make them into laughing matters.

Aunt Elizabeth spent hours devising recipes for "dear Alex," while Cook stood by in eagerness to put them into action. The word *pap* was a terrible, nasty word that was never to be heard at Meadowlark Manor again.

"Dear Alex" would slowly, seriously taste each new creation and then proclaim it "magnificent" or "delicious" or "wonderful." Invariably, just as Aunt Elizabeth was flushed with pride, he would slip in some sly, roguish comment that would send her to blushing and Cook to laughing when it was relayed to her, as it always was.

As for the children, they haunted their guest's sickroom. Alex Tremain and the boys had what appeared to be a strange relationship to Shannon. He ofttimes called them "cawkers" and "silly bantlings," and the boys took no offense. Indeed, they would puff up with pride. The duke would let them go wild, horseplaying and shouting, and then he would but raise his hand and tell them to take themselves off, for he had had enough of their hellish noise. The boys would laugh and immediately obey, only to return an hour later for more.

The whole household had enjoyed the weeks, and Shannon did not wish to consider the void there would be in their lives when the duke left. Perhaps a man in the household was not such a terrible thing, after all.

Then she laughed. The only unfortunate side effect of Alex Tremain's presence was that it drew daily visits from the inhabitants of Glenning Hall. They arrived everyday, yet never stayed long. The entire Meadowlark household saw to that!

Indeed, it was an unspoken campaign. Keep the Glennings at bay! One day the children would see to it, rushing in to sit and gawk at the visitors. The next day Aunt Elizabeth would settle in with her knitting and a surplus of inane chatter. One day even Peters got into the game, announcing not ten minutes after their arrival that His Grace needed his nap; and this when Alex had only risen one hour before.

The sound of rushing feet and excited voices broke Shannon's reverie. Her three siblings dashed in, Aunt Elizabeth directly behind them.

"Well, don't you all look nice," Shannon said approvingly. They were dressed in their best and the boys' curls were still damp from washing behind their ears. "You do the Aldon name proud."

"Tho do you," Becky breathed.

Shannon blushed. She feared she was overdressed in her blue

watered silk. Nothing else in her closet, however, had appealed to her. Besides, tonight was to be a celebration of the duke's getting back on his feet, with crutches, of course, but back on his feet nonetheless. It behooved her to dress properly. "Thank you, Becky."

"Oh yes, dear," Aunt Elizabeth said, her blue eyes bright. "I am so glad you took my advice."

"Aunt," Shannon chided, "your advice was for me to wear my ball gown!"

"Well, this is just as nice, I am sure," Elizabeth returned kindly.

Shannon laughed, and then she noticed Thomas hid something behind his back. "Thomas, what do you have there?"

"The duke's crown," Thomas said, proudly sticking out a brightly painted pasteboard circlet for her inspection. "Alex is King for the Night."

"Very good." Shannon smiled. "I am sure it will lend much dignity to the occasion. Now, let us all find our places. Peters will be helping Alex—I mean the duke—down soon. We are going to place the duke at the head of the table, of course. 'Twill be easier for him. Aunt, you shall sit on his right side and I'll sit on his left. Thomas, you and Michael sit next to Aunt Elizabeth, and Becky, come and sit next to me."

They had just managed their seating when Peters appeared at the door. Tall, thin, and as meticulously dressed as his master, there was a gleam in his eye as he announced, "The Duke of Trenton." He stepped aside and Alex entered upon his crutches.

Shannon gasped. Her gasp was drowned by the rest of her family's. She had only seen Alex Tremain in rent clothes or nightshirts. She had only seen him as the invalid, the informal man.

Tonight a different man stood before them, a far more dangerous and compelling man. The duke wore full evening attire. His intricately tied cravat gleamed white against the stark black of his tailored jacket. A single green jewel glittered at his throat, matching the green of his eyes. Alex stood poised upon his crutches and surveyed the tongue-tied observers with obvious amusement. "What is the matter? Have you never seen a man walk before?"

"You look pretty," Becky said. Even a female babe like Becky was affected! Her blue eyes were wide with wonder. No doubt very much like mine, Shannon thought wryly.

"He ain't pretty, tot," Thomas exclaimed. "Men ain't pretty. You look dandy, Alex," he added properly.

"Dressed to the nines," Michael nodded.

Alex's green eyes glittered and he smiled. "Did you think that I would not come properly attired for this august celebration?" His eyes fell upon Shannon and they seemed to flare. "Now there, Becky," he pointed toward Shannon, "there is pretty; even beautiful, I would say."

Shannon flushed. "Thank you, Your Grace." She could not think what else to say, even as she could not tear her eyes away from him.

"Now, Alex dear," Aunt Elizabeth said in excitement, "you are to come and sit here at the head of the table."

"Er, yes," Shannon said, trying to reclaim her smitten wits. "And the children have something prepared for you as well."

"They do?" Alex asked, swinging his crutches forward and haltingly approaching the chair that Shannon held for him.

"Thomas." Shannon waved her brother forward as Alex lowered himself into the chair.

Thomas eagerly stepped up, a grin splitting his face. He jabbed the paper crown out. "Your Grace, we crown you King for the Night."

"Thank you, Sir Thomas," Alex said gravely, ducking his head down in order that Thomas could place the crown upon him. He laughed, straightening it. "Faith, I do hope Prinny doesn't catch wind of this. He'll have me for a traitorous usurper."

"Your loyal subjects shall not betray you," Shannon laughed, slowly adjusting herself to this new Alex Tremain and feeling more comfortable, though she still found it hard to draw her eyes away from him. She lifted a decanter of wine and smiled impishly at him, "Would you care for wine, Your Grace?"

His brows shot up and a pleased smile crossed his lips. "Wine?

Saints above, I truly am king! Not only to be offered wine, but to have it poured from your own sweet hand! My cup overfloweth!"

"And you can have brandy later," Michael informed him. "Shannon said so."

"I can?" Alex gazed at her. "Truly gracious tonight, Duchess. I am not sure I can handle such treats."

"I thought I'd best change my tune now that you can walk," Shannon teased as she leaned over and poured wine into his glass.

"Yes, you don't have a captive anymore. You can't cut the orders and expect me to just lie there and take it."

Shannon's hand shook, for his tone was low and warm. The wine dribbled over his glass. She swiftly pulled the decanter back and passed it to Aunt Elizabeth.

"Oh my, isn't this wine excellent!" Aunt Elizabeth exclaimed after she poured a glass and sipped it.

Shannon hid a smile. Aunt rarely drank wine and as a judge could only be considered lacking. Shannon cast Alex a twinkling look, positive that the wine they now tasted was far inferior to those to which Alex was accustomed.

"Indeed it is, Aunt Elizabeth," he said, sipping with a smile. "The best I have had for a long time." Shannon chuckled at his diplomatic touch. "A toast!" he proclaimed. "Lift your glasses high. To my loyal, faithful subjects, who have saved me from the gates of death." The children began to giggle. "Subjects who have gently, ever so gently, nursed me back to life," he cast a wry glance at Shannon, who pulled a face at him, "and to whom I am grateful."

"Here! Here!" Thomas said, banging his milk glass on the table.

"Long live the King!" Michael cheered.

"Yes, long live the King," Aunt Elizabeth giggled, drinking fully from her glass. She set it down empty on the table. She leaned forward and said as the food arrived, "Tell me, dear Alex, what do you intend now that you are walking?" She poured herself another glass of wine. "Do you mean to go back to London? I have not seen London for years. Has it changed much?"

"London never changes, Aunt Elizabeth," Alex said dryly. "You may have more people and more noise, but London remains the same."

"Ah, but it can be such an exciting place," she sighed gustily, turning wistful eyes to Alex. Shannon's own eyes narrowed. What was Auntie talking about? She had never mentioned wanting to see London before.

"Why then, you must come and visit me upon my return," Alex said dutifully.

"Could we! How wonderful of you to invite us."

"Now, Aunt . . ." Shannon said, amazed at her aunt's duplicity.

"London!" Thomas's voice squeaked. "Oh boy!"

"We really can?" Michael asked, eyes bright.

"Why certainly," Alex said, smiling. "It is about time you boys saw more of the world." He looked quizzically at Shannon. "That is, if your sister wishes the visit."

"We wouldn't want to impose," Shannon said slowly.

"I have a town home large enough to sleep an army and servants. What would be the imposition?"

"Indeed what, Shannon?" Aunt Elizabeth asked, her eyes glittering from both wine and excitement. "After all, you have me as chaperon. What could be more proper?"

A choking sound came from Alex as he swiftly lowered his glass from his lips. Shannon rolled her eyes. This from the woman who apologized for interrupting when she discovered her niece and a rake upon a bed!

"We shall have to see," Shannon said, trying not to blush.

"Aww, that means no," Thomas complained.

"No, it doesn't!"

"Perhaps Shannon is worried, Your Grace," Aunt Elizabeth said, an odd light in her eye. "Worried that she'll not be properly dressed for London. You must tell her all about the ladies' fashions. We wouldn't want Shannon to be thrown into the shade by all those London beauties."

"Aunt . . ." Shannon directed a stern gaze upon her.

Alex's eyes sparkled and he smiled widely at Shannon.

"Never, Auntie. No matter what the other women wear, Shannon's natural beauty will outshine them all."

"Thank you," Shannon said blushing. She lowered her voice. "You have at least saved me the expense of a new wardrobe."

"I hear that, my dear," Aunt Elizabeth said. "But you must have a new wardrobe."

"Just for a visit to London?" Shannon asked, amazed.

"Well, you wouldn't want to appear the country dowd in front of Alex's friends, would you?" Aunt Elizabeth said innocently. "After all, Alex knows many, many prominent people, I am sure."

"Ah, so I am to be a mushroom, am I," Shannon said in a teasing voice, "trying to use all His Grace's connections?"

"I am sure he wouldn't mind," Aunt Elizabeth said blithely, polishing off her second glass of wine and setting it down promptly on top of her fork. The fork bounced into the air to land on Michael's plate between the potatoes and the peas. "I mean, Alex must have men friends, eligible parties for a lady to meet. You do, don't you, Alex? I mean, proper men that Shannon would be able to meet and consider an attachment toward? They are not all like you, are they?"

"Aunt Elizabeth!" Shannon sputtered, stunned.

"But dear, Alex doesn't mind, I am sure," Elizabeth said, smiling sweetly. "He knows what I mean. After all, since you and he have not taken to each other, I see no reason why he can't introduce you to a man that would take you. I mean, be taken with you."

"Aunt Elizabeth, that is enough," Shannon said, flushing. Aunt Elizabeth merely smiled and drank her wine. Shannon, catching the strangled expression upon Alex's face, swiftly resorted to her own.

"Zeus, do you think you could, Duke?" Thomas exclaimed. "Could you find Shannon a man to make her a mother?"

"Thomas," Shannon said warningly, "I told you to forget that scheme. I do not need a man, I mean a husband! And don't you dare start thinking up any other revolting schemes either. Look what happened last time!"

"Yes," Alex drawled. "You got me."

"But we like you!" Michael said.

"Yeth." Becky nodded.

"We do, even if you don't want to make Shannon a mother," Thomas added munificently. An odd, muffled snort came from Aunt Elizabeth.

"Saints preserve me," Shannon said, raising her eyes toward heaven and then casting a wry glance toward Alex, expecting to see amusement there. Alex refused to look at her, however, and instead quaffed his wine quickly.

Frowning, Shannon forced her attention back to the children. "Thomas, did I not explain to you that it is not proper to carry on such conversation, especially in a social setting?"

"Which conversation?" Thomas asked, truly confused.

"Why, upon whether a man would like to . . . oh, never mind," Shannon said in sheer exasperation and embarrassment. How could the conversation have gotten so out of hand? Easily, she thought angrily. All one needed was three Aldon children and a tipsy aunt!

"I only meant since the duke won't make you a—" Thomas stammered to a halt at Shannon's glare. "Well, then can't he find someone who will?"

"By proxy as it were," Alex murmured lowly. Shannon choked. "Now that is enough you, young cawker. Your sister has told you to stop talking upon the matter, so desist."

"Yes, Your Grace," Thomas said penitently.

"And I do not want you approaching the duke on this subject later," Shannon said knowingly. "You can stop thinking about going to London as well."

"Awww!" Thomas wailed as did the other children.

"But Shannon dearest . . ." exclaimed Aunt Elizabeth.

"No more discussion," Shannon said, pressed. "Let us talk on something else." The children stared at her with stricken eyes. Aunt Elizabeth's were reproachful. Alex sat back and sipped his wine, watching her steadily. "Perhaps," she said desperately, "if the weather is fine, we can go on a picnic tomorrow."

Smiles slipped back onto the children's faces as they planned the adventure. The three adults at the table, however, were oddly silent.

The meal finally drew to a close and Shannon sighed with relief. She told the children to go on ahead and ready themselves for bed, glancing at Alex worriedly. He looked tired and strained.

"Well," Aunt Elizabeth said, rising with a sway. "I am sure this was fun." She blinked her eyes like an owl. "I believe I'd b-best retire." She hiccupped and meandered to the door. Shannon and Alex watched her in wonder. She turned then, her hand clutching the door for support. "Alex dear, if I insulted you in any way I ap-apologize. You know I would not mean to . . ."

"No, of course not," Alex said. "And you didn't insult me, Aunt Elizabeth, you only spoke the truth, after all."

"I am so-o glad," Aunt Elizabeth sighed heavily. "For though I like you the best, perhaps you could find someone that Shannon would like the best. Oops, sorry, Shannon dearest, I—I know I should not talk like that! Please don't be angry," she said, almost teary-eyed now. " 'Tis only that you'd make such a w-wonderful w-wife and mother. I—I don't want you to miss that, l-like I have."

"I understand, Auntie," Shannon said flushing. "Now don't worry; go to bed."

"Night, children," Aunt Elizabeth said, waved her hand in the air, and tripped from the room.

"Well," Shannon said, sucking in her breath, "that was quite an entertaining meal. I fear, Your Grace, that you are king of an unruly rabble."

"And you, the mistress of them," he said, reaching for his crutches. He paused. "I mean, the queen of them."

"Oh, never mind," Shannon said impatiently. "Being delicate at this juncture is quite unnecessary, since my family is anything but." She walked to his chair and pulled it back in order that he could lift himself onto his crutches.

As Alex rose, he swayed. "Faith, I am weaker than I thought."

"It took all your strength just to survive a meal with us," Shannon said, still irate. She hovered next to him, lest he need her aid.

"Come now, Duchess, they mean no harm. You were a bit too severe with them, don't you think?"

Shannon opened her mouth to retort angrily, but then she clamped it shut and sighed. She looked at him apologetically. "I suppose that you are right."

"You truly do not plan to deny them a trip to London, do you?" Shannon was silent, trailing behind him as he moved toward the door. He stopped and studied her. "Well?"

"No, I don't think so," Shannon finally said. "If it is not an imposition to you."

"I told you it would not be, so what is your objection?"

"I do not trust the venture. I simply cannot have the children behaving in London as they do here. Why, they'd be bartering me off on every street corner, I have no doubt."

"Oh, gads!" Alex exclaimed, a chuckle escaping him. "I can just see them dropping nets out the windows on unsuspecting passerbys."

Alex and Shannon looked at each other and broke into laughter. Alex literally shook with it. Unwary, he lost the balance on his crutches and began to fall over. Shannon, gasping and laughing, swiftly reached out to hold and support him. "Do watch it, Your Grace," she chuckled. "Or is it my King?" She giggled as Alex's pasteboard crown slid drunkenly over one eye. She reached up to nudge it back into place.

"Thank you." He laughed. "You have saved me from falling on—er, at your feet."

"But according to Aunt Elizabeth, that is exactly where you ought to be," Shannon teased. She fluttered her lashes at him, expecting him to laugh with her.

His eyes darkened. "Watch it, Duchess. I am getting healthier every day." As if to prove it, he dropped a crutch, letting it clatter to the floor. His newly free arm came about her and his lips came down upon hers.

Shannon merely sighed and moved closer, returning the kiss strongly, eagerly. In truth, ever since the first time he'd kissed her, Shannon had been secretly hoping for this, just one more kiss from Alex.

Yet the one kiss turned into more. It was as if the touch of his lips ran to the very core of her. Heat flashed along her skin and she shivered as his hand caressed her back. Alex groaned slightly and his hand slowly slid down to caress her—

"Excuse me, Your Grace," a prim voice said from behind.

Shannon gasped and pulled back. Turning, she discovered Peters standing at attention directly behind them. Flushed, well-kissed, and embarrassed, Shannon quickly withdrew her arms from around Alex's neck. She hadn't even realized they had sneaked up there.

"Damn," Alex muttered. His eyes were dark and murky. "Saved, Duchess, by a subject evidently more loyal to you than me." His green gaze roved over Peters's emotionless face. "Even though I pay his wage."

"I came to help you back to your room, Your Grace," Peters said, his eyes focused upon the ceiling.

"I just bet you did." Alex's voice dripped sarcasm.

"Alex, you will need his help you know," Shannon said in a muffled voice.

He looked down upon her. A smile warmed his face and her heart. "I like being called Alex by you." Then he sighed and his eyes twinkled. "But it seems a sad trade; my valet taking me to my room rather than you."

"Rogue," Shannon said. She stepped back quickly, a sudden flush rising to her cheeks. What would have happened if she had assisted him all the way back to his room . . . to his bed? A sudden fear wracked her. She knew what she would have wanted to have happened. She bit back a despairing moan and said, unable to look at Alex Tremain, "Good night, Your Grace." She spun quickly away from him.

"Shannon?" Alex asked, confusion in his voice.

"Take care of him, Peters," she said swiftly and dashed from the room, finding the stairs and taking them by twos to reach the safety of her room.

She closed the door and leaned against it. Her eyes were wide, shocked. She wanted Alex Tremain, rake that he was, to make love to her! What kind of brazen woman was she? She slowly walked over to her bed and sank down upon it. No, what kind of fool was she? She didn't just want Alex Tremain to make love to her; she wanted him to love her. She wanted him to love her and to be with her every day—forever. Good Lord. She wanted to marry him!

Alex lay quietly, lazing in the sunshine upon a blanket. He watched Shannon and the Aldon children as they played by the small pond on their property. A bedraggled, giggling Becky clutched at Shannon's hand. Both females were clearly enjoying the antics of their two brothers who had shoved their newest little boat off for a maiden voyage, only to have it sink three feet from them. They were now wading in the water, peering suspiciously about for the wreckage.

What a fine family they were, Alex mused. An odd twinge passed through him. When he left, what would happen to them? Who would take care of them? He ignored the fact that the family had evidently survived very well to this date. He knew that as the children grew there would be many difficulties. The boys were in need of a firm hand and a more worldly education. Becky would be in need of male guidance as well as female.

And Shannon herself? Well, Aunt Elizabeth had the right of it. Shannon Aldon needed a husband. Someone that would help raise her siblings and give her more children. Suddenly, as he watched the laughing group, he imagined another little boy in the picture, black-haired like him but blue-eyed, and a little girl, with Shannon's blond hair, but with his green eyes . . .

Alex blinked. What the devil was he doing? He forced himself back to the subject at hand. Shannon needed a husband, and he was just the one to find her one. He knew the type of man she needed, and he could steer her in the right direction, use his connections. He didn't want her to fall in love with the wrong man, and there were plenty of them out there.

Shannon turned and waved at him. She dropped Becky's hand and walked toward him. Laughter lit the blue of her eyes and sunshine created a blazing halo of her blond hair. He blinked again. Yes, he'd best find her a husband and fast!

"Heavens," she gasped as she unceremoniously plopped down next to him on the blanket. "I'd best not allow Thomas and Michael to pursue careers as sailors. The great British fleet would definitely be in jeopardy. This is the fifth boat they've made and sunk this month!"

Alex chuckled, though his mind remained fixated upon his prior decision. He caught a slight waft of Shannon's soft perfume and decided to approach the issue immediately. "You know, Shannon, I shall be leaving soon."

"I know," Shannon nodded, looking away. "The Glennings have had all they can bear with you staying here. They become more persistent everyday."

"I do not intend to stay long with them. I plan to return to London."

"You must miss the London life," she returned, her voice quiet.

He grimaced. Miss London? After the pleasurable time he had spent here? The woman must be daft. "No, I do not miss London at all."

Shannon's eyes turned to his, an odd vulnerability in them. "You do not?"

He grinned. "London life pales compared to the outrageous life you have served me here at Meadowlark Manor. Faith, I've gone from captive to invalid to crowned king. It fairly makes my head spin."

Shannon laughed as he knew she would. He liked to hear her laugh, deep and honest. He liked to see the way her eyes tilted up with amusement, just as her full warm lips did. Unconsciously he leaned closer to her—closer to those smiling, inviting lips. "I must return to London in order that I may prepare my house for you."

Her eyes widened. "For me?"

"Yes, for you." He clasped her hand. "Aunt Elizabeth is right, Duchess. You would make a wonderful wife. You should be in a man's life to make it happy, warm, and caring." He was lost in her clear, vibrant blue eyes; eyes wide and a little stunned. "And the boys," he murmured, his voice turning husky despite himself, "they need a father. Little Becky needs a daddy to protect her from all those loose fish that will swarm about her when she grows up."

"Really?" Shannon whispered.

"Yes," he said, leaning closer, his eyes upon her lips. His thoughts scattered and he didn't think what he was saying although he still said it. "When you come to Town, I will find you a husband. I have many friends, surely . . ."

Shannon's eyes suddenly shot sparks and it seemed she choked. "You'll find me a husband," she squeaked, "amongst your friends!" She sat up swiftly, taking those inviting lips far away. "You odious, odious man!"

Alex blinked, as if shaken from a trance. Shannon was looking daggers at him, as if he were some slithery creature from beneath a rock. "What? I am merely offering to help you!"

"You, too, are now to join the throng of those wishing to barter me off," Shannon exclaimed. "Poor, poor little Shannon must have a husband! And now the great Duke of Trenton condescends to help. My, how generous. He will offer up one of his friends as sacrifice. Ask them to do what he will not do!" Shannon leaned into him, her snapping blue eyes but inches from his. "Understand this, my high and mighty Lord Duke, I do not need your help! I will find my own husband without you, and I am sure he will be a far sight better than any man you know!"

Rage flared through Alex at this. She was telling him that she did not need him. She was telling him that she could have other men! "Is that so, madam?" he said coolly. "Just where are all these men you are talking about? I see no line of courtiers at your door." He grabbed up her hand, holding it tight when she tried to pull it away. He eyed it scornfully. "I see no ring of engagement here."

A pain flashed through Shannon's eyes and Alex felt it in his own heart. She snatched her hand away, and it flew up as if she meant to slap him. Then she put it back into her lap. Her face became frozen. "It is too bad you will be leaving today, else you would have the pleasure of seeing all my admirers, Your Grace.

I can and will have a man. I shall merely have to set my mind to it." She rose swiftly, looking down at him tauntingly. "Yes, you have decided me. I will set my mind to the acquisition of a husband!"

"Your mind?" Alex snorted. He grabbed up a crutch and, gritting his teeth, rose. "It shows what you know! It won't be your mind these imaginary men of yours will be wanting, but your luscious body!"

"Libertine!" she hissed, paling.

"Shannon," he said, suddenly regretful of his crude remark. He reached out an apologetic hand. "I should not have said that."

"No, Your Grace," Shannon said tautly, stepping back from him. "You have spoken but the truth as you see it. After all, that is all you care for, is it not? The use of a woman's body? Never mind her thoughts and feelings."

"I get no complaints," he retorted, nettled.

"You don't stay long enough to hear them!"

"Dammit, Shannon," he said angrily, reaching out to grasp her one shoulder. "Stop ripping up at me. There is no need to argue."

"Of course not, for you are leaving this afternoon, are you not?" He flushed. Never had a woman told him to leave her! Most schemed and connived just to keep him by their side. And now this country nobody was showing him the door!

"And don't worry about me," Shannon continued. "I will find a husband who will love me for my mind and not because of my appearance. A man that I can respect and—and trust!"

"Unlike me, you mean?" Alex asked, his grip convulsing on her shoulder.

"You, Your Grace?" Shannon raised her brow. "I was not talking about you. After all, you do not figure in this discussion, do you? We were talking about men that might marry me, were we not? You are not in those ranks, are you?"

Alex gulped. The woman was a vixen! "That's right! Since you want some proper, respectable pattern card of dullness, not a real honest-to-God man . . ."

"A real honest-to-God man?" Shannon quizzed, her voice

dripping scorn. "Ha! Say that to me when you have become really honest with yourself and with me. Until then I wish never to see you."

Shannon's hands flew up and broke his grip on her shoulders. Her movement was so precipitous that Alex teetered, unbalanced. "Go back to London and that raking life of yours, Your Grace. It is certain that you won't have me around to kiss on the sly whilst you try and find me a husband in public. Faith, I want no husband of you. I mean, no husband from you." Flushing deeply, Shannon picked up her skirts and tore off.

"Shannon!" Alex called, furious. "Shannon, come back here!" He hobbled after, but almost tripped. "Shannon, dammit!" he bellowed. "You can't leave me here like this. I am crippled."

Shannon spun and yelled, "You most certainly are crippled, and 'tis not just your leg."

"Wasp!" he shouted. Then he sighed, for he saw nothing but the back of her. Breathing a curse, he eased his body back down to the blanket. Impossible woman!

"What happened!" Thomas called, running from the pond, worry upon his face. He immediately sat down next to Alex.

"Did you have a row?" Michael asked as he joined them.

"Shannon ran," Becky observed, finding a place on the blanket.

"Your sister and I disagreed on a certain matter," Alex said tersely. "She is the most stubborn, proud, shrewish—"

"What is the matter?" Thomas interrupted, evidently unimpressed with Alex's cataloging of his sister's faults.

"I beg your pardon?" Alex asked, brought up short from his tirade.

"What did you disagree about?" Michael asked patiently.

"I was merely trying to get her to agree to the London trip and to meeting some of my friends, only those that would be suitable parties for her, of course."

"Thutable what?" Becky asked.

He sighed. "Husband material."

"Oh," Thomas said in strangled tones. "Then you . . . you truly don't want to make her a mother yourself?"

"Er, no," Alex said, ruthlessly ignoring the surge of hot emotion that ran through him at the question. "I am sorry. I just wouldn't make a good father, Thomas, or a good husband. Your sister Shannon knows that."

"We understand," Michael nodded, forcing a weak smile. "Shannon says she's the same way—except she wouldn't make a good wife."

"She's wrong," Alex snapped. "She'd make an excellent wife."

"If she's wrong," reasoned Michael, "couldn't you be wrong, too? Maybe you'd make a good husband, too."

It took all of Alex's strength to shake his head in the negative and extinguish the look of hope in Michael's eyes. "No, Michael, I am not wrong. I would make a terrible husband."

A weighty pause ensued. Little Becky finally reached out to pat his sleeve with her tiny hand consolingly. "It's all right, Your Grace. We like you anyway."

"Yeah," Thomas said staunchly. "Just because you can't make Shannon a mother or be a father, doesn't mean we don't like you! We do. We really do."

Alex stared out across the Glennings' rose garden as he leaned against the stone wall that encircled the veranda. What was the matter with him? A ball was in progress inside, yet here he was outside.

He shook his head wryly. Some of the *ton's* brightest and wittiest were inside, yet tonight he found them all decidedly flat. He should return to London, he thought; perhaps that would interest him. He sighed. The prospect of London life did not excite him either. What was he to do with himself?

"There you are, Alex." Lady Susan Glenning's voice was light as she drifted out and across the stone floor. "Hiding, are you?"

Alex turned, forcing a smile to his lips. Susan was stunning in a golden silk gown, her magnificent bosom perfectly framed by a low décolletage. "You must forgive me, my dear. I fear I am very dull company tonight."

She moved slowly, provocatively toward him, her heavy perfume cloying in the night air. "In the doldrums, are you?" Without hesitation she wrapped white arms about his neck and pressed her full, lithesome body against him. "Well, let me see if I can't help raise your . . . spirits," she laughed huskily. Standing on tiptoe she kissed him.

Alex returned her kiss swiftly, almost feverishly. Yet he did not feel anything. Why the hell didn't he feel anything? He slowly withdrew from her. "Susan, we had best not. Someone might see us."

A pout pursed her lips. "Preaching propriety now, Alex? I'd not have thought it from you."

"Only think of the fuss if your mother were to catch us," Alex joked, forcing a rakish smile to his lips.

Susan's eyes darkened. A knowledge entered them as well as a pain. Alex wondered if he weren't seeing the real Susan Glenning for the first time.

"And you wouldn't want that, would you, Alex? Mama might demand you marry me, and that is something you would not wish to contemplate, is it?"

Alex grasped her hands quickly as she pulled them swiftly from around his neck. "I am sorry, Susan. I've been terribly clumsy, have I not?"

She nodded, her eyes bright.

"And very stupid," he added softly. "You are a charmer, Lady Susan."

"But not charming enough," Susan said, her smile brittle. She pulled way from him and walked towards the entrance. Turning, she said, "I believe you should return to London, Alex, after the week's end, of course."

"Certainly," Alex said, bowing.

He stood frozen, staring after Susan with vacant eyes. Yet another woman had asked him to leave. What kind of fool was he? Did he never do anything but hurt women? Where had his much-publicized skill with the fair sex flown? Well, Duchess, he thought wryly, I'm not the ladies' man you thought I was.

He heard a slight rustle from the bushes not far from him.

Alex turned, scanning the night. He saw nothing. Sighing, he forced himself to return to the festivities.

"Shannon, dear," Aunt Elizabeth said, as she walked into the library where Shannon sat behind a desk and a mound of ledgers. "Cook is terribly upset, near tears in fact. What is this about you taking her to task for spending too much?"

"She is," Shannon said, refusing to raise her head from the accounts. "The latest butcher bill is frightful."

"But you know Cook is frugality itself," Aunt Elizabeth said gently as she sat down in the chair across from Shannon's desk.

"She was not this month."

"Indeed, we were entertaining, and entertaining a duke at that. What were we to do? Serve poor Alex chicken feed?"

"No, however, 'poor Alex' is no longer here and we must tighten our budget. We need no longer entertain nobility, thank God."

Elizabeth sighed. "I know, 'tis a shame. I miss Alex so much. Do you not?"

"No, I do not," Shannon said succinctly, slamming a ledger shut.

"I would have thought he would at least come and visit us."

"Why should he? After all, he has women to chase and pleasures to pursue. Did you really think that we would figure in his life after he was well?"

"Perhaps if you had not refused to see him before he left. It was uncivil of you dear—"

"Uncivil?" Shannon rose swiftly, her hands firmly planted on the desk. "Fustian! It was he who had been uncivil! Indeed, I do not care to see him ever again. Is that clear Aunt Elizabeth? I am tired of hearing about 'poor Alex' this, and 'poor Alex' that. The man is not 'poor' anything, so please desist in talking about him. I will thank you not to use his name in my presence again!"

Shannon stormed from behind the desk and rushed to the door. She discovered the exit glutted with three children. She checked, putting her hands on her hips. "And that goes for you three as well, do you hear me? I am sure you have overheard the entire conversation since you are forever eavesdropping. 'Tis a habit that shall get you in trouble one of these days!"

"But we weren't . . ." Thomas objected.

"No," Shannon said angrily, waving away his defense. "I do not want to hear any of your excuses. Now pardon me. I must see to the rest of the household chores."

Shannon charged forward and her siblings parted in the wake of her rage. Silence filled the room as all eyes remained fixed upon the place where Shannon had last been.

"We didn't mean to eavesdrop," Thomas said morosely, treading softly into the room to sit at Aunt Elizabeth's feet. "Really."

"I know, dear," Aunt Elizabeth sighed. "You must forgive Shannon; she is sadly out of sorts these days."

"She always seems angry," Michael observed disconsolately as he sat on the carpet next to Thomas.

"Always." Becky heaved a sigh and plopped down beside them.

"Yes, well, she misses the duke, I believe," Aunt Elizabeth said. "But she's too stubborn to admit it."

"Why won't she?" Thomas asked.

"Because she is in love," Aunt Elizabeth explained. "And you must forgive adults when they are in love, for they will act very oddly and, generally, very stupidly. Shannon's not all to blame, mind you. I could just kill Alex! Never coming to see us."

"I know," Thomas nodded. "So we went to see him."

Aunt Elizabeth's blue eyes sharpened. "You did?"

"Well, we sort of saw him," Michael clarified. "He was at a party . . ."

"He was looking grand," Thomas interjected.

"Then Lady Susan came out," Michael continued.

"She kithed the duke," Becky said, her face balling up in disgust.

"Why that shameless—er, never mind," Aunt Elizabeth said. "Then what happened?"

"He kissed her back," Thomas reported.

"Oh dear," moaned Aunt Elizabeth.

"But he only kissed her for a little while," Michael amended.

"Thank goodness!"

"And then Susan got all mad and told Alex he should leave after the week's end," Thomas said.

"Oh no!" Aunt Elizabeth's face fell. "If he leaves, we will never get the two of them back together. Shannon is being idiotic and stubborn. And Alex—he's supposed to be a ladies' man for goodness sakes! And instead he is acting like a clod pole. Why, he should break down her defenses and tell her she is his! He should . . ." She stopped and blushed as she saw three pair of young eyes watching her with interest. "Er, never mind. The nub of the matter is that we must do something if we are ever going to get Alex and Shannon back together. And do something before he leaves for London."

Thomas frowned. "We could catch the duke again. Would that help?"

"Not likely," Aunt Elizabeth snorted. "It's Shannon we'd have to get to . . . oh my, oh yes! I have the answer! We shall catch both of them!" Her eyes sparkled. "Now listen children . . ." Her silver head bent down and the three children crawled in closer as plans were whispered and a campaign formed.

The next morning Shannon looked up from the eggs she was considering without interest. Aunt Elizabeth breezed into the room and Shannon winced. Her aunt was in an obviously ebullient mood.

"Good morning, Shannon," Elizabeth said as she sat down. "Dearest, we simply must go and hunt some more herbs. We are shockingly low. I thought this morning would be a perfect time to gather them."

"I would like that, but—"

"Now Shannon, you have worked long enough. You are looking pale. The fresh air will work marvels on you, I am sure."

"But—"

"I do not want to hear any 'buts' from you, my dear. Now I

have thought of the perfect place to start. I am positive we will find some around the old hunting lodge."

"What?" Shannon exclaimed. "But that is so far out. Why not—"

"No, dearest," Aunt Elizabeth said firmly, pouring her tea and ignoring Shannon's confusion. "I am positive it must be the hunting lodge. Now do hurry and eat: there is much to do."

Shannon stared at her aunt who was busily applying herself to her breakfast. She shrugged in resignation. Aunt Elizabeth was in one of those moods which defied reason. Shannon chewed morosely on the rest of her toast. Now the day would be wasted going to the hunting lodge merely for herbs. Nothing would be accomplished today, it appeared.

Alex was out taking his morning ride through the woods. He rode along the path he took every morning since returning from Meadowlark Manor. As he turned around the familiar bend, his heart beat faster. Michael was sitting beneath the tree where Alex had first met the younger Aldons. He sat quietly, his legs stretched out before him.

"Michael," Alex called out happily. "How are you, my boy?" He swiftly reigned to a stop and dismounted. "Is everything all right?"

"Yes, Your Grace," Michael nodded.

Alex thought he heard a rustle overhead, but he refused to look up. "And how is—" Before he could complete his sentence, he heard a very obvious giggle, and then a familiar, odiferous netting enshrouded him.

Alex bit back a quick smile. God, he didn't even mind if it smelt like fish. "What are you doing?" He feigned a sternness and began to struggle halfheartedly as the children attacked him from all angles.

Shannon turned and gasped as the solid wood door to the old hunting lodge slammed shut behind her. "Aunt Elizabeth!" she called, and turned to shove at the door. It refused to budge. What had caused it to shut anyway? There was no wind today. "Aunt Elizabeth, are you out there? I can't get the door open!"

"I know, dear." Aunt Elizabeth's cheerful voice came through the wood. "I have it barred from this end. It's for your own good, dearest."

"What is for my own good? Open the door!"

"No, Shannon. Now do be a good girl and settle down!"

"Aunt Elizabeth, don't jest," Shannon shouted, hammering her fist against the sturdy wood. "You can't mean to lock me in here!"

"Yes, I can," came the pleasant reply. "Now I must go, dear, and see how the children progress."

"Aunt Elizabeth, are you mad?" Shannon yelled. Silence answered her. She pounded a frustrated tattoo upon the door.

Faith, her aunt had finally lost a tile! Pulling back a smarting hand, she turned a fulminating glare upon the lodge. Shannon's eyes widened. Her traitorous aunt had asked her to enter the old lodge and ensure that it was still in proper condition. As a whole it was, if one ignored the extreme clutter of old furniture, the lodge being the graveyard for the Aldon outcasts throughout time.

Yet in the center of the eclectic mélange now sat a large table covered with a gleaming white cloth. Upon it rested a bucket of ice and a bottle of champagne. Next to that were fruits, nuts, and chocolates.

"What on earth?" Shannon muttered, walking over to survey the table. Whatever was Aunt Elizabeth planning? Was she, Shannon, supposed to eat fruit and sip champagne for the day? Ridiculous. Her eyes narrowed as she spied two glasses for the champagne. Who was the second glass for? A ghost?

Her hands going to her hips in indignation, Shannon turned to scan the room, intent upon finding an escape. The only windows to the lodge were high and small—and boarded over! Aunt Elizabeth hadn't missed a trick, she thought angrily. Shannon emitted a disgruntled huff. There was nothing to do but to make herself comfortable and await the whims of Aunt Elizabeth. Faith,

Alex had joked about her unruly family. He'd be in whoops over this fresh start!

A severe frown turned her lips down at this thought. She had done it again. She had allowed a thought of Alex Tremain to enter her mind. It was happening all too commonly. In truth, it seemed to happen every minute of every day. She had to stop it!

Deep in contemplation on how she was going to eradicate the thought of Alex Tremain from her mind forever, she clutched the bottle of champagne to her chest, snatched up one of the glasses, and wandered about until she found a large chair amongst the array that still had all its legs and some cushioning.

An hour passed and Shannon had polished off one glass of champagne and had plucked out all the strawberries from amongst the fruit. She was no further on her plan to banish Alex from her mind than before. She was rummaging through the rest of the fruit when she heard a sound from behind.

She turned, apple in one hand, champagne glass in the other. The door swung open. "Well, it's about time," she said in exasperation, ready to do battle with Aunt Elizabeth.

Aunt Elizabeth did not appear, however. In her place a large, disheveled figure stumbled into the lodge, barely missing an ottoman that must have been seventy-five years old.

"Alex! Good gracious—no!" Shannon squealed, for the door behind him was closing. The apple flew in the air and the champagne glass shattered on the ground as Shannon charged to the door. Her hands slammed against the wood just as she heard the bar thump down on the other side. "No, oh no!" Shannon wailed, pounding dementedly against the door. "Aunt Elizabeth, don't you dare! Don't you dare or I will never forgive you!"

"What's the matter, Duchess? Is your plan going awry?" Alex's deep, taunting voice came from behind.

Shannon stiffened. She gave one last angry slam to the door and turned slowly, casting him a dark look. "It was not my plan. And why didn't you help?! Now we are locked in here."

"I am sorry, but my hands are tied," Alex said with a shrug of his broad shoulders. "Literally."

Shannon drank in the sight of him. He was tousled, with dust on his face, twigs in his dark hair, his hands behind his back. She swallowed. He looked so very good to her.

"Now what is this about, Duchess?" he asked. "I would have preferred it if you had just asked me to come and visit you."

"I—ask?—oooh," Shannon steamed. "You are truly an arrogant beast! I told you, I had nothing to do with it. This is another benighted plan of the children and Aunt Elizabeth's! I know you will find it hard to believe, since you are always so positive that every woman is fainting for your attentions."

Alex's eyes darkened and Shannon pedaled back as he stepped toward her. It appeared as if he would speak, but then he turned and scanned the room. His eyes immediately fell upon the opened champagne bottle and fruit.

"Champagne in the middle of the day? Tsk, tsk, Duchess."

Shannon flushed. She crossed her arms and scurried across the room, putting distance between them. "Aunt Elizabeth's idea, I believe. At least, I don't believe the boys would have thought of it. Unless you taught them, that is," she added, quite unworthily.

Alex's brow rose. "I refrained, Duchess. Though what you intend to teach them, the Lord only knows. They'll be the only ones going up to Oxford still thinking that humans can birth children in two months."

She spun on him, enraged. "How dare you!"

"Of course I dare!" he said, his face unreadable. "I am, after all, the disreputable Rake Tremain, am I not?"

Shannon flushed and opened her mouth to retort, but thought better of it. There was an odd energy coming from Alex that she could not define.

"I swear I will kill my family," she muttered, looking away from the appealing vision of the Duke of Trenton. She thought she heard a small chuckle from him, but when she glared at him, his look was innocent.

"I will be glad to assist you in their demise," he said more mildly. "But in order to do so, I would need you to undo these bonds."

Shannon studied him cautiously. To aid him, she would have to diminish the comforting distance between them.

"They do rather hurt," he said with a sigh.

"All right." Shannon traversed the room slowly, hesitantly. "I—I am sure the boys did not really mean to hurt you. They—they just miss you, I believe," Shannon stammered as she stood before him. Their eyes met and held for a charged moment.

Then he turned, presenting his tied hands to her. "I find I miss them as well."

"You do?"

"Yes." His voice was muffled. "Poor children. They only want a father. I should have come to visit them. Then this would not have happened."

"Yes, yes, that is true," Shannon said, her mouth becoming dry. "And I was no better." She forced herself to reach out to the bonds. Strange, they did not seem that tight. Indeed, they—they weren't even tied! "What. . . ."

"Shannon, let me be their father!" Alex spun on her. Before she could speak, he had pulled her close, his lips fastening to hers in a demanding kiss.

Shannon stiffened a moment. He was a rake! Then she groaned and, forgetting it all, flung her arms about him. She let her body melt into his and returned passion for passion.

Alex's lips left hers and traveled to her ear. "Let me, Shannon. I could be their father, I know I could."

"Yes, yes," she said dizzily, not thinking as his lips nuzzled the side of her neck and sent chills playing along her spine. "And I—I think I could be a d-decent wife after all," she gulped, a delicious shiver shaking her.

Alex pulled back. There was a warmth in his eyes that Shannon had not seen before. A warmth that she knew she would willingly commit her life to keep. "Duchess," he laughed. "You'll make a wonderful wife, a glorious wife, a—"

Shannon pulled his face to hers to kiss it wildly. "Hmm, yes," she finally murmured. "I believe I could acquire the knack for this wifely stuff."

Alex's laughter rumbled through them both, so enwrapped

with each other were they. "Madam, much more practice and you will far outstrip me."

Shannon smiled. "That sounds promising, Your Grace, and ever so enjoyable."

He laughed and hugged her close. "I love you, Shannon Aldon, I truly do." He drew back and there was a concern, a fear, within the green depths of his eyes. "I know I've caused you to have doubts about me. I've been a fool, acting the rake for you. And then to be such a gudgeon as to tell you I'd find you a husband."

Shannon could not bear the pain in his eyes. "But you did find me a husband, the very one that I wanted."

"Truly?" he asked, his voice husky.

"Truly," Shannon nodded. She smiled wryly. "I've waited for you for so long, but then the way that it all happened, you being captured by the children. It was just too mortifying to admit they had found me the right man."

"Only think of me," he laughed. "I wanted you from the moment I woke up and saw you. It didn't help to have your brothers and sister offering you to me, in matrimony of course. It was hellish. And you seemed as if you didn't care."

"I cared," Shannon said softly. "But I couldn't believe that you were interested in me, an unsophisticated country girl, seriously interested that is. I—I didn't want to be just a passing fancy."

"Not passing, love," he said softly. "Always my fancy, always." He leaned down and kissed her. Her head fell back and she welcomed his kiss. The gentle flame flared brighter, and his hands were at the buttons of her dress when he stopped, jerking away. "Damn!" he said with a ragged breath. "Sorry, Duchess! Get away from me! We're not making you a mother yet. Not until I get you safely leg-shackled and you can't get away."

Shannon stood motionless, gasping in air. "Of course," she said dazedly. She looked up at him and was lost. "Oh dear," she murmured. Her body leaned toward him of its own volition. She wanted him to kiss her again; nothing else seemed to matter. She couldn't tear her eyes away from his lips.

Alex slowly backed away from her. "Now, Duchess, you've got to help me here! I—I am not practiced at being noble."

"Oh yes," Shannon said, gulping. She may have been practiced, but at this moment her practice had made her anything but perfect. She never knew one could have such an overpowering urge to. . . . She spun from him and ran toward the door.

"Let us out, Aunt! You've got to let us out! Please!" There was no reply, and Shannon turned to Alex, her eyes locking on his, her breath becoming shallow. "I wonder how long they intend to leave us here?"

He laughed weakly, running his hands through his hair. "I don't know, Duchess, but if it's much longer, it will be our undoing." His eyes restlessly roamed the lodge, landing on the table again. "Gads, it's pure seduction."

"And all done by a spinster aunt and three children," Shannon said, shaking her head. She started to laugh despite herself. Alex's eyes spoke and he joined her. Laughing uncontrollably, they walked toward each other. Shannon, giggling, reached out her arms to him.

He choked on his laughter and stopped dead. "No," he said, suddenly stern. He raised a hand to ward her off. "You stay away from me, do you hear, Shannon Aldon?"

Shannon blinked, for it had been so natural for her to go to him. Then she smiled impishly. "What an unusual role for you. I am not sure I like this, Saint Alex."

"Don't push me, Duchess," he growled. "I want to do this right."

Shannon bit her lip. "So do I . . . but what are we to do? If they leave us here much longer . . ." She spun and began pacing, weaving her way amongst the furniture. "All right, we are two mature adults, able to control . . ."

"Stop pacing," Alex said in an odd voice. "I like watching you too much."

Shannon checked and turned to him, knowing her smile was fatuous, but not caring. "And I like watching you . . ." They stepped toward each other but then halted.

"Damn," Alex said. "I can't stand this."

"I know," Shannon exclaimed, never having experienced such a frustration as this before. "Didn't Aunt Elizabeth think what might happen with the two of us left here all alone with nothing to separate us?"

"Since when did your aunt ever care about separating us?"

Shannon latched onto a curio table and set it in the middle of the lodge. "You stay on your side and I'll stay on mine, and we'll build a wall between . . ."

Alex stared at her as if she were insane. Then he shouted a laugh and grabbed up a rickety rocking chair. "Duchess, only the Aldon mind could concoct such a notion. 'Tis brilliant. When we get out of this, I am going to marry you and then . . ."

"I know, I know," Shannon said, quickly shoving a stuffed chair into the line. "Just don't say it. Get that armoir over there!"

Four hours later a band of three children and one older lady sneaked toward the hunting lodge.

"Do you think they made up by now?" Thomas whispered.

"I'd bet a monkey on it," Aunt Elizabeth said rather inelegantly. They reached the lodge's door and all laid a well-honed ear to the wood. Not a sound reached them.

"Shannon, dear," Aunt Elizabeth called, hesitantly rapping on the door. "Alex?" Ominous silence prevailed. Aunt Elizabeth, a fear entering her, slowly unbarred the door. What could be the matter?

Aunt Elizabeth swung the door wide and exclaimed. Becky squeaked and the boys' jaws dropped. A mammoth structure met their stunned eyes. A mountain of furniture rose before them, running down the width of the lodge and towering to the ceiling.

"Heavens," Aunt Elizabeth said weakly.

Alex appeared from one side of the furniture wall and Shannon from the other. As the two cleared the furniture, Alex snatched at Shannon and dragged her close. He planted a ruthless kiss upon her lips, bending her back over his arm.

"Good gracious," Aunt Elizabeth gasped.

Shannon jerked away from Alex, pushing him back. "Go! Leave me!" The children's faces crumpled and Aunt Elizabeth moaned in disappointment. "I don't want to see you until—"

"I know, I know!" Alex said fiercely. "Hello, Aunt, children." He charged past the flabbergasted observers. "Is my horse here?"

"Y-yes," Aunt Elizabeth stammered, running to keep up with him.

"Calif's all right," Thomas said, trailing behind as did Becky and Michael.

Alex discovered Calif within a few yards and flung himself into the saddle. Only then did he look at the wide-eyed, fearful band that stood watching him. "Goodbye, children, Aunt!"

Becky's face clouded over and a tear trickled down her nose. "You're leaving?"

"It didn't work," Thomas wailed.

"Oh, no," Aunt Elizabeth cried. "Don't go, Alex! Shannon, do something. Don't let him go."

"Don't detain him, Aunt," Shannon said sternly, coming up from behind them.

"But we don't want the duke to go," Becky whimpered.

"I do," Shannon said, "and speedily, I pray."

"But we want him to . . ." Thomas began.

"I know," Alex said, barely holding Calif in check, since the large stallion had become restive. "You want me to make Shannon a mother. Well, I won't . . . not until she marries me. I'll not have the lady any other way."

"What?" Aunt Elizabeth gasped.

"You heard me Auntie, and that was a terrible thing to do to us, you know! The children wouldn't know the torment you put us through, but you—you should be ashamed."

Aunt Elizabeth flushed. "Well, you are both so stubborn."

Alex's eyes flashed to Shannon and lightened even as she smiled widely at him. "That we are. I insist on marriage or nothing else. I am off to get a special license as fast as I can."

The children squeaked in delight and jumped up and down with pleasure. "After all," Alex laughed, "your sister is a lady, and I want to be her proper husband. Now take care of her." He blew Shannon a kiss. "Goodbye, Duchess."

Shannon waved to him. "Hurry, Alex, hurry."

He directed a dangerous look at her and let Calif have his head. The large stallion sprung forward and they were gone.

Thomas tugged at Shannon's skirts to gain her attention, since she remained transfixed, staring after Alex. "You really mean it? You are marrying him?"

"Yes, dear, I am," Shannon nodded. "Now are you happy?"

"Oh yes," Thomas said. "He'll be our father then?"

"Yes," Shannon nodded.

"And he'll make you a mother, right?" Michael asked.

Shannon flushed. "I would imagine so."

A choking sound came from Aunt Elizabeth. Shannon cast her a quelling frown.

"Well, dearest," Aunt Elizabeth said with studied innocence, "I, er, would imagine so, too."

"He'th our duke, then?" Becky asked happily.

"Yes, dear," Shannon said, laughing. "He's our duke."

"Gee!" Thomas said, bouncing on his toes and beaming. "I'm glad we caught him."

"He hath nice eyes," Becky sighed.

"He was a good gift," Michael nodded proudly.

"Yes," Shannon said, smiling broadly. "I am glad we caught him, he has nice eyes, and he was a wonderful gift."

A Change of Heart

by Lynn Kerstan

The crash reverberated through the house, rattling the china and resonating in Philip's aching head. He gritted his teeth and waited for the second door to slam, reconfirming his wife's displeasure.

Elaine was moving more slowly than usual, although her pregnancy had not begun to show except in those details which might be apparent to a lover. He could only imagine what those were.

When the second clap echoed from upstairs, Philip knew that she'd reached her room and was settling in for a good sulk. He pushed away the remains of his breakfast and poured the last bit of lukewarm coffee into his cup.

What was it, precisely, that set her off this time? For his life he could find no pattern in the offenses he gave without intention.

Could it have been the marmalade? He'd buttered her a piece of toast and slathered it with thick orange preserves, only to have his offering fly past his head, land smack up on the silk wallpaper, and slide unhurriedly to the carpet.

She preferred honey, he was roundly informed. How could he fail to remember? Hadn't she begged him to employ a beekeeper to supply the fresh honey she craved?

He sighed. In fact, Elaine *had* preferred honey—until last week. Then she announced a decided inclination for the tart marmalade he favored. So many of her tastes changed, by the minute it seemed, that he had long since despaired of keeping track of them.

Communication had dwindled to rare pleasantries and frequent spats. They no longer slept together, not since she twigged the consequences of admitting him to her bed . . . which was, to his way of thinking, rather like closing the barn door after the horse escaped.

More likely she was punishing him for the crime of making love to his wife without taking precautions. It had never occurred to him to do so, nor had she asked. But perhaps he ought to have suggested it. Apparently Elaine held him solely responsible for her unwelcome pregnancy.

She had banished him, not to his own room which adjoined hers, but to a smaller bedchamber at the end of the hall. By her report, he made noises in the night which disturbed her sleep—noises so loud they could be detected through thick walls and solid oak doors. Like the old story of the princess and the pea, he reflected without humor.

He had sympathized with Elaine's plight before conducting a test with the aid of his valet and a footman, who sacrificed several nights of sleep to assess his nocturnal habits. His Lordship did not precisely snore, they were agreed. On occasion he emitted a soft, rumbling sound, but it was scarcely audible even when they approached the bed and bent down to listen.

He did not tell Elaine. There was no point. If she wanted to keep him at a distance, she'd only find another excuse.

Under the circumstances, it had become impossible to determine when she was up and about, or if she required his presence. One morning she expressed annoyance at his failure to take breakfast with her, so the next day he dutifully waited in the breakfast room for nearly three hours, his stomach soured by the smell of kippers and kidneys and sausages wafting from the sideboard, only to learn that she had requested a tray in her room.

After that, he enlisted the neutral—meaning male—servants to spy for him. They were the only ones he trusted, because women tended to band together when one of their own was breeding. Now he knew her plans ahead of time and took pains to be at her disposal whenever he reckoned she might want him. But for all his efforts, the frequency of their quarrels had not lessened. They simply wrangled about sillier things.

A discreet rap at the door was followed by Barrow's hesitant entrance. Everyone walked on tiptoe when Elaine was in a temper. The butler glanced at the streak of orange goop on the wallpaper and prudently busied himself at the sideboard. "How may I be of service, milord?" he inquired in a solicitous voice. "More coffee, perhaps?"

Dear God, Philip thought with a jolt of shame. His own servants felt sorry for him! He could only imagine the gossip belowstairs, what with the slamming doors and Elaine's usually sweet voice growing shrill as she berated him for his latest transgression.

Things could not continue this way. He must take action. Do something. But what?

"Yes, I would like a pot of fresh coffee," he said.

"At once, milord." Barrows sounded disappointed. "Nothing else?" Turning, he peered down his long thin nose as if hoping to espy his employer's backbone.

Humiliated, Philip cast about in his mind for a way to redeem himself. At the least, he could muster sufficient pluck to seek advice. "Dispatch a message to Lady Crayton," he said decisively. "If it suits her convenience, I should like to meet with her at eleven o'clock."

"Very good, milord. I'll see a horse readied, or do you prefer the carriage?"

"I'll ride. And, Barrows, perhaps you'd better send a maid to Lady Halsey. She is not feeling well this morning."

Barrows nodded. "Alicia went to milady's chamber but was turned away. Shall I have her try again?"

Philip swallowed a groan. "That won't be necessary. I'll have a look-in."

With a decidedly sympathetic expression on his face, the butler left him alone with his thoughts.

Maybe Imogen would have some notion what he should do. His mother-in-law's heartening support never failed to raise his spirits, but of late he'd hesitated to seek her out. Elaine seemed to resent his visits to Black Oaks and rarely wanted to accompany him, as if she'd cut off her parents the way she'd excised her husband. Odd, that. He knew she idolized her scholarly father, and he'd always envied the close relationship she shared with Imogen.

Perhaps because he'd never had one to speak of, mothers had always been of particular interest to him. His own died when he was an infant, and his stepmother diligently ignored his existence. Now, continuing that melancholy theme, he was taxed with a wife who did not want to be a mother.

When a petite maid appeared with coffee, he managed a smile of thanks and tried not to wince as she gave him the same pitying look he'd seen on Barrows's face.

Even Imogen did not seem suited to her role as loving mother, he reflected, probably because he'd danced with her at fashionable balls for several years before meeting her daughter. They looked much alike, Elaine and Imogen, both tall and slender with golden eyes and hair the color of champagne.

What had become of his quiet, shy, absurdly eager-to-please bride? What had happened to the marriage of convenience that began with such promise, exploded into such passion on the wedding trip, and deteriorated into a series of rows and slamming doors?

Granted, Elaine had already surprised him by virtually transforming her personality in the space of a heartbeat—most notably on the day they were married. As they left Black Oaks, she remained quiet and tense until the coach turned onto the main road. Then, to his astonishment, she untied the ribbons of her bonnet and tossed it out the window with a flourish. Her wide, happy smile was unlike any smile he'd ever seen. At that moment, willy-nilly, he'd fallen in love.

"I'm free," she said breathlessly. "Oh, Philip, I am free at last. And what a wonderful time we shall have. I still cannot credit that you are taking me to Paris!"

"It was your mother's suggestion," he confessed.

Her mood darkened briefly, as if a small cloud had passed across the sun. "Yes, Imogen would want me out of England," she said matter-of-factly. "But how glorious to travel at last. Shall we go directly to the coast? Shall we sail tonight, Philip? Oh do tell me we'll sail tonight."

Having quite different plans for their wedding night, featuring an enormous bed in the country house he'd borrowed from a friend, he shook his head. "That would be impossible, what with the distance and the tides." Not that he'd any clue what the tides were doing, but she accepted his explanation and settled back against the leather squabs.

"Well, tomorrow then. We'll have an early night so we can start out immediately when the sun comes up."

The bridal night continued well into the next day, and two more after that. Once again Elaine surprised him, this time with her eager passion, and his own ardor was frankly astounding. He suspected that was when his seed took hold in her body, because the wedding trip had to be cut short when she spent mornings bent over a basin and afternoons sleeping. So rarely could they venture from the hotel that he'd insisted, over her vociferous protests, on bringing her home.

Only her health mattered, he told her.

"Only your heir matters to you," she replied viciously.

Since then, they'd been at war—Elaine on the attack, he trying to appease her, both of them fiercely unhappy.

When a footman arrived with Lady Crayton's reply, Philip was tempted to head directly for the stable. The thought of another quarrel with Elaine made his head throb, but he couldn't leave the house without assuring himself that she was all right. Feeling vastly older than his twenty-seven years, he slouched up the curving stairs to her room.

From experience, he knew to knock and step inside before she ordered him to go away. She invariably did so, but he could never be sure if she expected him to obey or wanted him to persist. It was simpler to dodge the question altogether.

Elaine was seated at her dressing table, staring into the mirror. Her gaze lifted momentarily, noting his arrival, before resuming the intense study of her own reflection. He closed the door behind him and leaned against it, needing the support, casting about for something to say that wouldn't set her off again.

"Who is this person?" she asked after awhile. "I'm looking at her, and I don't know her. She has my hair and my eyes. But she says things that don't come from my brain or my heart, although I hear my own voice speaking the words. *Shrieking* the words. Who is she, Philip?"

He had no idea. Elaine had been so many different people since they met that he never knew what to expect. This introspective woman manifested a whole new personality, one he didn't recognize. With effort, he lifted himself from the door and moved behind her to massage her shoulders.

For a moment she leaned back, accepting the caress with a low noise in her throat.

"I'm sorry about the marmalade," he said. "I thought that's what you wanted."

The corners of her mouth lifted. "So did I, until you gave it to me. These days I seem to want the opposite of everything I'm offered. Have I gone mad, do you think?"

"I . . . what do you want me to say?" he murmured uncomfortably. "Certainly you're not mad, but I cannot understand what is happening. Nor do I seem to do anything that pleases you."

"And you are trying, aren't you?" She rested her head against his chest. "I know that you are. But all the big things are wrong, and you've made it impossible for me to fight them, so I squabble about things that don't matter. I cannot seem to stop myself."

He cleared his throat. "What big things do you mean, Lainie? I don't understand."

"I'm certain you do not," she said with a bitter edge to her voice. "You are exactly where you want to be, on the estate you are restoring with the money from my dowry, while your dutiful wife produces an heir in record time. You have everything you married me to acquire."

Their gazes locked in the mirror. "You agreed to this marriage," he said gravely. "Are you telling me that you were forced into something you did not want?"

She bit her lip. "Does any woman truly wish to marry a man she scarcely knows? Find herself incarcerated ten miles from a house she's hoped to escape all her life? You promised me a long wedding trip and a London Season."

"So I did, and meant it, but you know why we had to come

home and why I cannot take you to London. Besides, what is the point of going there now? You already have a husband."

"I'd have preferred to choose one for myself."

His fingers clenched on her shoulders. "Then why did you consent to a marriage of convenience and accept my proposal?"

"Philip, had I not married you I'd have died an old maid. Don't you realize that?"

"How so? You are the loveliest woman I've ever seen." His face reddened. How few compliments he'd given her in their brief marriage. "Had you made your debut you'd have been ranked an Incomparable, and with the generous dowry your father offered, even a blind man would have come to scratch. I'm only grateful I didn't have to compete with every eligible male in London for your hand."

"Have you never wondered why you did not?" she inquired too sweetly.

"I . . . no. Your mother was certain we would suit, and you had no objections—none I knew of. It seemed an ideal match. Imogen assured me you wished to live near your father, and I was determined to restore Glenhaven because it once belonged to my mother's family. After my brother, God rest him, squandered everything that wasn't entailed, I had no choice but to marry an heiress or abandon my dream."

"Did it occur to you that I might have hopes and expectations of my own, Philip?"

He frowned. Young women of his acquaintance devoted themselves to leg-shackling a presentable spouse equipped with a title. True, he was a mere viscount, but dukes, marquesses, and earls didn't grow on trees. If Elaine's parents thought him acceptable, he'd assumed he was, but it appeared that she entertained loftier ambitions. "You never told me what you expected, and I thought you pleased with the marriage. Especially after our first days . . . and nights . . . together. Evidently I have failed you, but I cannot credit you have come to despise me because of an abbreviated wedding trip and the impossibility of a Season this year. London and Paris will always be there, after all."

"But will *I* ever be there with them? Suppose I'm carrying a daughter? Will you not keep me imprisoned until I produce an heir? And a spare? How old will I be when you permit me to escape this backwater?"

"Imprisoned? By God, Lainie, I've no wish to hold you anywhere against your will. When this child is born and your health restored, no doubt some accommodation will be made for travel. Most children are reared by nurses and governesses, after all."

"So they are," she said unhappily. "It's so unfair. The children are deprived of parents, or the parents are chained to their offspring." With a sigh, she propped her chin on her wrists. "I only wanted a little time for myself and some excitement. Just after we were married, I wanted time with my husband. Now a tiny stranger has taken control of my body and my life. I want the child, Philip, and I want you, but I resent you both for what you've done."

"We did it together," he reminded her.

"That maddens me above all things, because I've no one to blame. Although," she observed candidly, "I'm taking it out on you. Do you suppose we could forget everything for a few hours and enjoy ourselves? A ride in the country or a bit of shopping in Exeter? Anything to get out of this house."

He smiled. "Of course, but our excursion must wait until after lunch because I've made an appointment to see your mother. She's expecting me within the hour."

Elaine's lips tightened.

"Would you like to come along?" he added swiftly. "You could visit your father."

"Papa spends mornings dictating correspondence to his secretary," she snapped. "And when you return, there won't be time for an outing, so forget I suggested it. Just go about your business, Philip, and don't keep Imogen waiting. She hates that."

Imogen Bartell, second wife of the Earl of Crayton and many years his junior, delighted in surrounding herself with handsome men. They flocked to her like birds to nectar, and wherever she chose to sit or stand became the center of the room.

New on the Town, Philip had been exceptionally vulnerable to the easy charm with which she held court. Shy, somewhat reclusive by nature, and inept at small talk, he'd always found large social gatherings uncomfortable. But he soon relaxed in the glow of her welcome.

It was no secret that Imogen took lovers, although her liaisons were conducted with discretion and confined to young men of high rank and staggering good looks. Few expected her to remain faithful to a stay-at-home spouse, and only the most spiteful tabbies begrudged the countess her fun.

Philip thanked his stars that her favor had never fallen upon him, for of course he could not have married Elaine if he'd bedded her mother. But Imogen rarely indulged impecunious younger sons, so he enjoyed a light flirtation from the outer circle of her admirers.

Only when he came into the title did she look at him with speculation and beckon him closer. Perhaps the new viscount would like to meet her daughter. He agreed immediately with surprise, because until that moment he'd no idea there was any such creature.

Imogen, wearing a russet morning dress trimmed with lace, greeted him in a parlor designed to complement her unusual coloring. Everything was arranged, as always, to enhance her beauty, with the curtains drawn to a precise angle so that light streamed over her glorious hair but left her face slightly shadowed.

She remained seated on the striped silk divan and lifted her gloved hand for his salute. "My dear Philip, it is a pleasure to welcome you this morning. I so enjoy having company."

He brushed her wrist with his lips. "You are kind to receive me on such brief notice."

"Nonsense. The country grows tedious, I'm afraid. Soon I must be off again, and we shall have no opportunity for these pleasant cozes. Now sit in that large chair which I had brought in especially for you and tell me what has sent you into the mopes."

"Is it so obvious?" Heat climbed up his neck. "Or perhaps

you are simply playing the odds, because I seem to be in a perpetual muddle these days." He sank onto the comfortable leather chair. "I am exceedingly embarrassed to solicit your advice yet again."

"But to whom else should you apply? It is only natural that you come to me, for who knows Elaine better than her own mother?"

"I see that you've guessed what bedevils me," he observed wryly.

She smiled. "Scarcely a stretch of the imagination. That same affliction has brought you to my parlor with some regularity these last weeks."

He gave her a worried look. "Am I betraying Elaine by talking with you behind her back?"

"Ah, Philip, what can you tell me I don't already know?" She lifted a hand. "Not that Elaine confides in me of late, for she is determined to assert her independence, but be assured that whatever you say is in strictest confidence."

"It must be," he said earnestly, "because I dare not give her another reason to be angry with me. She has enough of those already."

"Dear me. What have you done?"

"Devil if I know." He shot her a rueful look of apology. "Everything I say or do sends her into the boughs. Not to mention what I leave unsaid or undone. When she isn't railing at me, she weeps, or sulks alone in her room. I am at wit's end, Lady Crayton."

"Good heavens, so you must be to address me formally. Had you forgotten my name is Imogen?"

"These days I have difficulty remembering my own name." He smiled crookedly. "To my wife, I am Perfidious Viper, Selfish Swine, Pitiless Tyrant, or Barbarous Lout."

Imogen looked thoughtful. "I had hoped Elaine would take control of her temper when she wed. She seemed so pleased with our arrangement, and with her bridegroom. Not once during your betrothal were we treated to the sort of display that had become all too commonplace at Black Oaks."

"She has always been volatile?" He frowned. "I had no idea."

"Oh, you mustn't imagine we have concealed some dark family secret, Philip. Lord Crayton and I are even-tempered, so what turmoil Elaine created in our household was all the more apparent. And she was certainly on her best behavior during your courtship, as any young woman would be."

"I'd scarcely describe those few days as a courtship. Now I am certain we should have taken more time to become acquainted."

"For what reason?" Imogen tapped a long manicured fingernail against her chin. "You seemed to have no doubts, and I warrant you that Elaine did not. Do you now regret the marriage?"

He sat upright. "Absolutely not. But you have relieved my mind. I feared she felt somehow constrained to accept my suit."

"How so?" Imogen folded her hands. "Lord Crayton and I are not ambitious parents. As you recall, the financial settlements were all in your favor, and Elaine's rank surpasses your own. Indeed, Philip, you brought nothing to the marriage but yourself. Elaine might have set her sights higher, but I arranged an introduction because I thought you would suit." She smiled. "I still believe that."

"Then why can we not get along? What must I do to make her happy?"

"Elaine has the lamentable habit of wishing to be where she is not, doing impractical things unsuited to her station. When she begged to be sent away to school, we reluctantly complied with her wishes, but even under the strict tutelage of Mrs. Beesome and her staff the child managed to slip her leash again and again. One summer afternoon I was walking with friends in Brighton and looked over to see her running barefoot along the strand, flying a kite. I'd thought her at Black Oaks with her father, but she convinced Mrs. Beesome that her parents wished her to spend the holidays with a friend. As we learned, it was not the first time she'd imposed on the families of her schoolmates. Naturally we had to withdraw her from the Academy."

A holiday at the beach with a chum seemed prodigiously more

agreeable than spending the summer with one's father, but he could scarcely say so. And of course Elaine should not have disobeyed her parents. "She wants me to take her to London for the Season," he said darkly.

"We have already discussed that," Imogen reminded him. "No woman in a delicate condition is permitted to show herself in public. It is simply not done."

He wasn't altogether sure why. Elaine was carrying a child, not a communicative disease. Nonetheless, Imogen knew the ways of Society and the forms of correct behavior far better than he.

"Do you wish my honest opinion, Philip?" she asked in a diffident tone. "Be certain before you answer."

A desperate man was in no position to hedge. He nodded vigorously.

"Very well then. If your situation is to improve, you must be firm with Elaine. As you've seen, catering to her whims only incites further rebellion. She must learn that the husband is master of his house and of his wife."

Philip was careful not to change expression. Imogen's relationship with the lenient Earl of Crayton rather contradicted that theory.

"I do not mean to suggest you become a brute or a dictator," she continued, "but so long as you allow Elaine to have everything her own way and exert yourself to please her, she will keep you dancing through hoops."

"It is difficult to oppose a woman carrying one's child."

"Yes, and she is taking full advantage of that. I have a suggestion, and while it will not seem at all the thing, I beg you to consider it. You are too close to the situation now. If you put some distance between the two of you and regather your strength, you'll return to Elaine with more perspective. Tomorrow I intend to set out for London, but Crayton, as usual, prefers to remain at Black Oaks. You would be a most welcome escort."

He was stunned. "Leave Elaine?"

"We speak of only a few days, Philip. She will learn that you are not subject to her every caprice, and absence, they say, makes the heart grow fonder. Certainly you cannot continue as you are."

"I do have business in London," he mused, "but I cannot think this is the time to precipitate a quarrel."

"You mean *another* quarrel. So far Elaine has things all her way, and a confrontation will become more difficult as her pregnancy advances. If you are ever to take a stand, Philip, now is definitely the time."

"Perhaps." He ran his fingers through his hair. "I'll think on it, Imogen, but you should proceed without expecting me. It is one thing to anger my wife, and another to hurt her. I wouldn't do that for the world."

"Sometimes one must be cruel in order to be kind," she said placidly. "I shall expect you at ten o'clock."

Philip bowed and took his leave, reflecting that Elaine was not the only Bartell woman accustomed to getting her own way.

Dr. Joseph McGuiness was lifting his bulk into a pony cart when Philip came up the elm-lined road to Glenhaven. Kicking at his horse, the viscount made the last few hundred yards in Newmarket time. "What's wrong?" he demanded, his voice strident with panic.

The doctor gave him a reassuring, patient smile. "Your wife is perfectly fine. Blooming, I would say. Positively blooming."

"What the devil does that mean? And why are you here if she's blooming?"

McGuiness looked puzzled. "By your own instructions, my lord, I stop by whenever I'm in the neighborhood. One of the workmen repairing the barn roof fell and broke his leg, so I took the opportunity to—"

"Yes, I understand. Thank you." Philip wiped his brow with his sleeve. "You found no problems when you examined my wife?"

"Beyond her reluctance to be poked and prodded, none at all. Everything is proceeding normally."

"Easy for you to say." The viscount scuffed his toe in the dirt.

"How can any man know what a woman goes through at a time like this? Or why she behaves as she does?"

Settling back, McGuiness rested his hands on his bulging stomach. "Of course we cannot. Until I met and married my own dear Madame, I was woefully unqualified to treat expectant mothers."

"I wasn't aware you had children," Philip said politely, intent on restoring his shredded dignity.

The doctor released a sigh. "We were never so blessed, although Madame bore three sons by her previous husband. Two, alas, died in the war, and the other resides in Provence with his family. Madame was trained from childhood as a midwife, and usually delivers the babes while I assist. For some reason most aristocrats do not trust midwives, and I assumed you felt the same. Be assured, had I any concerns about Lady Halsey I would ask you to permit Madame to examine her and preside at the birthing."

"I shall speak to my wife about this, Dr. McGuiness. I've no idea how *she* feels, but I have no objections whatever. Quite the contrary."

"A wise decision, my lord. May I add that you appear somewhat . . . distressed? Possibly Madame could answer some of your own questions and ease your mind. Would you like to meet her?"

"Yes," Philip said immediately. "Tell me when."

The doctor smiled. *"Now* would be an excellent time, if you have no pressing engagement. Madame is a superb cook, and it is the country habit to have a large midday meal. Will you join us?"

Philip's gaze shifted to the window of Elaine's room. "I should look in on Lady Halsey."

Chuckling, McGuiness took up the reins. "A good Provençal luncheon lasts for several hours. We shall expect you."

Elaine was napping, her maid informed him, so Philip set out for the doctor's cottage a few minutes later.

The scent of onions and garlic assailed him as he entered the small, neat house. Dr. McGuiness welcomed him affably and led him straight to the kitchen, confiding that his wife's name was Marie although she preferred to be addressed as Madame.

Like her husband, Madame McGuiness was large, comfortable, and easy-going. Before he knew it, Philip was seated at a trestle table with a bowl of thick fish stew, chunks of crusty fresh-baked bread, and a full glass of white table wine. After the disaster at breakfast, he was hungry, and the couple kept up a stream of light conversation while he ate his fill.

Well into his second glass of wine and more relaxed than he'd felt in weeks, he found himself blurting his woes to the sympathetic pair. He got the distinct feeling they'd heard it all before.

Madame was heartily amused by his complaints and dismissed them with a wave of her hand. A few blessed women seemed to waltz through pregnancy, she advised, but most mothers-to-be experienced the symptoms he described—to a greater or lesser degree.

Well, perhaps not greater. The viscountess, like many highly bred ladies, was doubtless ignorant of matters any farm girl would have learned in childhood. In Madame's opinion, ignorance led to apprehension, and from there to downright terror. And because they were trained to conceal emotion, aristocrats had a harder time of it from beginning to end.

"Feelings will out," she explained. "Imagine your wife holding back a river of scalding water with her hands. It will seep through in one place, break through in another—there is no way to dam it up. And you, my lord, will invariably be burned."

That, he decided, summed it up pretty well. "So how can I help her?"

Madame nodded with approval. "Patience. Endurance. A bounty of attention and affection. Pregnant women experience heightened sensitivity in their bodies and, if I may be so bold, they also develop a prodigious appetite for sexual gratification."

Philip choked on a swallow of wine. "That has not been my experience," he divulged sheepishly.

Chuckling, Madame passed him a fresh napkin. "They also feel unattractive, once the seed is planted."

His head shot up. "Elaine is beautiful, as always. I cannot detect the slightest change in her . . . her body."

"Not yet," the doctor remarked. "But soon."

"Alors, what you cannot see your wife already senses," Madame warned. "Every part of her is at war with every other part. I cannot explain it, for this is something only a woman will understand. She craves your touch even as she pushes you away. She needs you to persist, because that will show how much you desire her."

Philip massaged his temples. "So far I have attempted to go along with everything she says she wants—within reason, because some of her demands are wholly unreasonable. Are you telling me I should *demand* my . . . er . . . rights? Would that please her?"

"A bit of seduction is more in order," Dr. McGuiness suggested laconically. "As I recall, you were wed only a few months ago. Scarcely enough time to weary of each other in the bedchamber."

Philip could heartily agree, at least from his point of view. "The thing is," he ventured, "she is so young to be a mother. Only nineteen."

The doctor and his wife looked at one another with raised eyebrows.

Joseph McGuiness cleared his throat. "I think there must be some mistake. Correct me if I am wrong, Madame, but we had been wed two years when the young lady was born."

"You have the right of it," Madame said decidedly. "It was the same year Clara Ruggers lost her own babe. Clara was wet nurse to your wife," she explained when Philip gazed at her in stunned surprise. "Let me see. By all reckoning that would make Lady Halsey three-and-twenty."

"How can that be? I was sure . . ." Philip's voice faded off. He couldn't recall Elaine ever discussing her age, but he'd gotten the impression from somewhere that she was eighteen when they married, nineteen now. "My mistake," he said uncomfortably. "She looks so young."

"And lovely," Madame agreed. "We all feared she would never

marry, and what a shame that would have been. Now here she is with a handsome husband, a child on the way, and her beloved father close to hand. She has everything she could possibly want."

"I wonder." Philip crumpled his napkin and laid it on the table, feeling a bit woozy after the wine and spicy stew. "Madame, you have been most kind. I beg you to attend to my wife and trust you'll inform me if there is any reason, however slight, to be concerned."

"*Cela va sans dire.* A husband kept in the dark is of no use whatever. Only remember, all your troubles, like the pain of childbirth, will seem as nothing when you hold the babe in your arms."

"Pain?" He swallowed hard. "No one told me about that. Well, I've heard there was some, but . . . ah . . . how bad is it?"

"Bad enough," Madame said flatly. "When it is nearer time, we shall discuss it."

"We'll discuss it now. I don't want Elaine to suffer. Find another way."

She laughed. "There is one way in, which you know about, and one way out. Whatever your attributes, my lord, the child is a good deal larger. Pain is inevitable, but it is perfectly natural and your wife will endure as women have done since the beginning of time."

"Dear God."

"If it is any consolation," Dr. McGuiness put in, "the husband usually suffers more than his wife."

Madame scowled.

"You cannot deny it, my sweet. Agony of the soul. Guilt. He wants to relieve her suffering and cannot. He would change places with her and knows it is impossible. You will experience these things, my lord, as *men* have done since the beginning of time."

Philip surged to his feet. "What about laudanum? Surely that would help."

"If you insist," Madame said with a grin. "But none for your wife. She will have work to do."

For a moment Philip stared at her blankly. Then he laughed. "It appears you have two patients, Madame, and I begin to think I'll be the more troublesome."

"Sans doute, but for now it is enough that you care and that you do your best. We shall help any way we can."

"And think on this," Dr. McGuiness added serenely. "I have never witnessed a birthing so swift and painless as the one which brought Lady Halsey into the world. If she is half so fortunate as her mother, you have nothing to worry about."

As he rode away, Philip felt a good deal better and a great deal worse. Did any man anticipate the consequences of a night of passion? Obviously not, or the human race would be extinct.

If only he'd gotten to know Elaine better before getting her with child. If only they could share this terrifying, exciting, confusing time together. But it was too soon.

It was too late.

Sweat beaded on his forehead. The thing was done. Two virtual strangers had conceived a new life and could only go forward, through what promised to be an excruciating ordeal, to its conclusion.

And then—*three* virtual strangers, one wholly dependent on the other two. Dear God.

He slumped in the saddle, feeling all the weight of a lifetime commitment, hoping that by some miracle he could measure up.

Elaine wielded the pruning shears with a vengeance, clipping rosebushes into naked sticks while the gardener watched with dismay from a safe distance. Eventually he wandered off, unable to bear the annihilation of his cherished plants. There would be few roses this spring if Lady Halsey continued to amputate every hopeful branch and twig.

Heedless of the destruction she was wreaking, Elaine lopped off anything remotely brown and withered. It had been years since she tried her hand at gardening to alleviate the boredom that sometimes overwhelmed her at Black Oaks, and she'd forgotten the results of her futile attempt to grow cabbage, cauliflower, and peas.

Still, flowers were not precisely vegetables, and someone once told her rosebushes had to be cut back if they were to flourish. Years of neglect had reduced the garden to a morass of weeds and overgrown shrubs, but if Philip intended Glenhaven to be her new prison, she would decorate it with the roses she loved and tend to them herself.

The afternoon was warm for early spring. Perspiration streaked her brow, and she wiped it off with the hem of her skirt. There was no reason to be concerned with her appearance now, although hours ago she'd chosen the crisp sprigged muslin dress with care because Philip had promised to take her shopping.

After a brief nap she'd come down to lunch feeling almost attractive, and even managed to enjoy poached salmon and buttered rice without being sick to her stomach. Surely he would return in time for their excursion.

By two o'clock she'd abandoned hope. Yes, she had told him to forget the whole thing, but at the time she was angry and didn't know what she was saying. By now he should be used to that. And she distinctly remembered telling him how much she longed for a treat.

What in blazes would keep him at Black Oaks all this time? She took another devastating whack at an innocuous rosebush. Imogen, of course. No doubt he'd shared a long private lunch with his mother-in-law while his wife waited for him to come home. The perfidious snake.

She suspected that he'd never recovered from the disaster of their wedding trip. Imogen had warned her time and again to maintain strict privacy when her body was dysfunctional, because men were repulsed by female maladies like the monthly bleeding. A clever woman made sure her husband was never exposed to any fleshly imperfection.

Unquestionably, retching into the nearest container fit that definition.

At the Paris hotel where they spent their wedding trip, and on the boat which carried them across the Channel after the honeymoon ended so abruptly, there was no place to hide. Philip saw her at her positive worst, day after day, and even held the basin while she disgorged her latest meal. The humiliation still sent shivers up her back.

No wonder he preferred the company of fastidious Imogen, who had probably never vomited in her life.

Once home, Elaine made certain Philip would not be witness to the nausea which swamped her most evenings and every single morning . . . until just recently. She was afraid to believe the sickness had passed. Dr. McGuiness assured her that it often vanished after the first months of pregnancy, but however much she longed to sleep in Philip's arms, she couldn't take the chance he'd awaken to the repugnant sights and sounds of her distress.

She had nightmares of not reaching the basin in time. Of spewing the contents of her stomach all over him.

Better to sleep alone and dispatch Philip out of earshot to a distant bedchamber. It was for his own good. One day, when she knew him better and had control of her mercurial emotions, she'd find a way to explain.

But, oh dear Lord, she was so lonely and afraid.

Her mother had nearly died giving birth. Imogen often told the story of her ordeal—with unnerving relish—after securing her daughter's promise to keep secret the agony she had endured. Elaine supposed she ought to be grateful. At least she knew what to expect. As for her father, he was informed only that his wife breezed through the delivery. Men preferred to remain ignorant, and shrewd women obliged them.

"Elaine?"

Startled, she looked up. Philip stood by the French doors which opened onto the garden, beaver hat in hand, his cravat limp and his hair disheveled. As always, her heart raced at first sight of the quietly handsome man with warm brown eyes.

He stepped forward, eyeing the pruning shears warily. "Am I disturbing you?"

The shears fell to the ground from numb fingers. "Of course not." Her lips quirked in a grin. "I'm not much of a gardener, and expect I'm doing everything wrong."

"It will be lovely, I'm sure."

After the brief, hesitant exchange, silence fell between them like a boulder.

Elaine moved a cautious two steps forward. Philip did the same.

"Did you have lunch?" he inquired politely.

"It was quite nice," she said. "I'm sure Cook will fix you a plate. If you like."

"I've eaten, thank you."

There was another long stretch of awkward silence. Then Philip crossed the space between them, pausing several yards from where Elaine stood wringing her hands.

"You look . . . splendid," he ventured in a husky voice. "Have I botched it up again? That gown was not designed for pruning bushes, but I thought you no longer wished to go into town."

"I changed my mind, but you had no way to know that."

"I should have *expected* it," he said. They both laughed.

"You might have come back in time," she pointed out. "I decided to be ready, just in case."

The tips of his ears went fiery red. "Had I known . . . ah, forgive me, Elaine. Will tomorrow be soon enough? We can spend the whole day doing whatever you wish."

A smile lit her face. "Truly? The whole day? Shall we plan it together?"

He took another long step, and then another, until they were within arm's reach. "I'd like that very much. And never mind what you've heard about men and shopping, because I'm sure to enjoy it. Besides, you'll be needing a complete new wardrobe."

Inadvertently she glanced down at her slim stomach, imagining it distended and ugly. "Yes," she said dully, "I will."

He frowned. "Did I say something wrong?"

"Not at all, Philip. You only spoke the truth. Soon the dresses I have will no longer fit, but how any seamstress can rig out an expanding balloon escapes me."

He couldn't think of a response.

"She'll need to be terribly inventive," Elaine hastened to add. Men loathed female afflictions and she'd been foolish enough to remind him of what to expect. It was bad enough anticipating the repugnance in his eyes when he saw her swollen to bursting point like an overcooked sausage.

"Elaine?" he said in a bashful voice. "May I ask you something?"

Her mouth went dry. "Yes. Of course. Anything."

"Do you still . . . perhaps I should say did you ever . . . find me . . . attractive?"

She caught her breath. How could he doubt it? "Always," she managed to squeeze between taut lips.

"Then what have I done to drive you away? You won't let me touch you or hold you or kiss you. I want to, Lainie, more than I can find words to express. Please tell me the truth. Is there anything I can say or do that will bring us together again?"

"Oh Philip." His pain shook her to the heart, but no explanation could clarify her jumbled feelings. She didn't understand them herself. Wordlessly she held out her hand.

After a moment he took it, and sheer force of desire drew them together.

"I've missed you," he murmured, bending his head until their lips nearly met.

She barely had time to shove him back before the nausea engulfed her. Dropping to her knees, Elaine retched uncontrollably onto the nearest rosebush while tears streamed down her cheeks. She clutched her stomach, unable to grasp the handkerchief he offered in stoic silence. He let it flutter to the ground.

After a moment she heard him stomp away, bellowing for a servant.

What had become of him?

Elaine knew only that Phillip had saddled the wildest horse in the stable and thundered off hell-for-leather after the incident in the garden. She glanced again at the clock. Nearly midnight. Could he have returned to Black Oaks . . . and Imogen?

Ears perked for any sound that would let her know he'd returned, she sat on the edge of her bed nibbling dry toast and sipping tea, still trying to settle her unruly stomach. When he ventured upstairs, she'd know it, because the floorboards creaked and his firm stride was unmistakable. Many was the night she'd listened for the sound of him passing her door, wondering if he'd pause and knock. Come to her.

Wondering why she'd ever told him not to. If she dozed the afternoons away, it was because she rarely slept at night, always hoping he'd . . . what? Demand his rights? Want her so much he'd refuse to take no for an answer? But if he made the attempt, as he often did the first few weeks, she'd probably send him away.

How had she come to be at war with Philip and her mother and the unborn child—not to mention herself?

Feeling suddenly cold, she went to her dresser and pulled out a heavy shawl. It didn't help. The cold was inside her, bone-deep. Somehow, she must explain to Philip. Make amends with him.

She'd hurt him terribly these last few months, but never so much as this afternoon when he tried to kiss her. She'd wanted that kiss and the low male voice murmuring words of love and pleasure in her ear. But when he wrapped his arms around her and bent his head to touch her lips, her stomach rebelled violently.

She couldn't imagine what had caused such a reaction. Philip rarely wore cologne, and she'd always liked the faint scent of lemony soap on his skin. No, this was something else, and it had overwhelmed her.

Whatever produced that mortifying display, it was not distaste for his touch. Wrapping the shawl around her shoulders, she decided to track him down. Perhaps he was somewhere in the house, and if not, a search party should be organized. Her heart began to thump. On that accursed stallion, in that mood, something terrible might have happened to him.

Panic turned to disgust when she flung open the library door and saw Philip tilted back in a chair with his ankles crossed on the large teak desk, raising a whisky bottle to his lips.

He regarded her from bloodshot eyes. "Ah, m'gentle wife. Mother of m'child. Do come in."

Elaine slammed the door behind her. The wretch wasn't hurt.

He was foxed. "Oh pray, don't get up on my account," she said sweetly.

Since he'd made no move to rise, the viscount looked puzzled.

Elaine stalked to the desk and glowered at him.

He smiled back genially. "Yes, I am toes over forelock, and what of it, wife? Not many things a man can do in his own house these days. Tell me, is he permitted to drown his misery in a bottle without being called to account?"

Her mouth, open to object, snapped shut at the word *misery.*

"What, speechless? For once I have done something quite deliberately to merit a broadside, and you have nothing to say?" He downed a long swig of whisky. "As always, you baffle me."

She had never seen him like this. She was the *reason* he was like this. But try as she might, no word could get past the constriction in her throat. Helplessly she sank onto a chair and closed her eyes. If she could find words to explain and manage to say them, would he understand?

"It wasn't you," she finally croaked.

"Indeed? Then who, pray tell, *was* it?" His feet came off the desk and hit the floor with a thud. "Are you telling me something I don't want to hear? Bloody hell, Elaine, is that why you cannot bear for me to touch you? Are you carrying another man's child?"

Her eyes flew open. "Certainly not!"

"Makes sense to me," he continued as if she hadn't denied it. "That why Imogen was so anxious to marry you off?"

"Don't be an idiot. You know very well I was a virgin on our wedding night."

His brow wrinkled. "Ah yes. So you were." He gazed at her fuzzily. "What were we talking about?"

Drunken lout. Leaning forward, she planted her elbows on the desk. "Philip, do you remember what happened this afternoon?"

"Ummm—something bad. Then I went riding. Then I got squiffy."

"You wanted to kiss me," she said patiently, "and I wanted to kiss you, too, but I threw up on a rosebush."

"That was it!" He tried to snap his fingers and failed. "Tell you what, Elaine. Cools a man down when a lady casts up her accounts because he kisses her."

His words made little sense, but the pain behind them was clear as water. Absurdly, she wanted to smooth his ruffled hair.

"Didn't mean to be impertinent," he slurred, "but somebody—I think it was the doctor—told me that women in a delicate condition want to be kissed and touched, so I thought maybe you did too, but I was wrong. Always wrong with you, Elaine. I don't mean to be, but I am."

"Philip, you mustn't blame yourself. I'm always wrong, too."

"Then we *are* in a pickle. If you are wrong and I am wrong, there's nobody left to be right. But I have a plan. Been thinking about it all night. Wanna hear it?"

She didn't think so, but nodded and watched him settle back with his arms folded across his chest.

"I have decided that we should get away from each other for a bit," he said in a studied voice, as if he'd been rehearsing. "To that end, I've made arrangements to leave in the morning." He squinted, trying to read the ormolu clock on the mantel. "It's *already* morning, by God."

Elaine's heart gave a lurch. "I don't want you to go."

"You don't want me *here,*" he reminded her. "Look, I tried to write it down in a letter." He pushed several sheets of paper across the desk.

She picked them up. At some point Philip had sloshed whisky on the letter because the edges were curled and the ink had run. "I can't read this," she said.

Leaning forward, he snatched the pages from her hand. "Then I'll read it to you. 'Splains everything." He cleared his throat. "Dear Elaine, the duck sails at dawn."

With a baffled look, he scrutinized the paper and repeated the phrase.

"Most enlightening," she said, clinging to her temper.

He regarded her owlishly. "I don't think *duck* is right."

"Philip, never mind the letter. Just tell me."

"It was all in here," he grumbled. "Thought it would be easier to explain if you wasn't listening. But here you are and I don't know what to say."

Her fist hit the desk. "Devil take the letter. Why are you leaving me? How can you even consider it?"

He sat back and studied the wood-beam ceiling. "Did you ever wonder why I decided to restore Glenhaven instead of Halsey Manor? Well, I'm not wanted at the family estate, Elaine. Never was. My stepmother loathed me—don't know why—and m'father considered me a bloody nuisance. They sent me away to school when I was seven years old, and I dreaded holidays at home because they'd shut me in my room out of their way. The dowager is welcome to Halsey Manor, and when she turns up her toes, I still won't go back."

"Oh, Philip."

"Our child will never be unwelcome at his home, Elaine. Think on this while I am away. If you'd rather dance in London, give me the babe when it's born and we shall separate." He swallowed a long draft of whisky as if he wanted to rid his mouth of the words he'd just said.

Stunned, Elaine could only gape at him. Of its own accord, her hand moved to her flat stomach.

"You need to be alone with the baby for awhile," he said bleakly. "I don't 'spect you know it's really there, but it is, Lainie. There's another person growing inside you, and no matter how much you want it to go away, it won't. When it comes out into the air, I vow this baby will have a home and at least one parent to love it. If you cannot live with me, I'll go away. And if you don't want our child, I'll give it all the love I can. But for God's sake, Lainie, don't punish the baby because of me."

Her throat tightened. "I cannot bear for you to go away, Philip. How will that solve our problems?"

"We speak of a few days, m'dear, and I've already sent word the town house is to be opened."

"London," she breathed. "You are going to London. Oh please, take me with you."

"That is out of the question." He came, unsteadily, to his feet. "Have you heard nothing I've said? A few days of separation will give you time to reflect on our future together. If there is to be one."

She made a low, unhappy sound in her throat.

His eyes gentled. "I shall never stop hoping for that, but for a short time let us both lick in private the wounds we've inflicted on each other. Besides, you could not make the journey to London in one day, and your mother does not wish to stop overnight."

Horrified, Elaine surged from the chair. "What has Imogen to do with this? Never tell me she is accompanying you."

His gaze slid away. "Rather the opposite. She has requested that I escort her, with the roads so uncertain this time of year."

"Has she now? Just like that, out of the blue?" Elaine's lips curled. "I wonder why."

He shrugged.

"Tell the truth, Philip. Imogen put you up to this. She suggested we separate and insisted on an immediate departure so I couldn't change your mind."

His jaw hardened. "Your imagination has run wild. This arrangement is convenient for Lady Crayton, nothing more."

"What a fool you are!" She wrapped her arms around her waist. "Or perhaps I am the fool. Has she yet to seduce you, Philip, or have you been lovers all along?"

He stared at her blankly for a moment. "By God, wife!" he erupted, jabbing a finger at her. "You dare accuse me of infidelity? Your mother of consorting with her son-in-law? You insult all of us, yourself included, with such humbug. I'll hear no more from you this night." He pointed to the door. "Go to bed. Now."

Elaine felt as if he'd slapped her. Clutching the shawl to her breasts, she stumbled across the room. Her hand was on the latch when he spoke again, so softly she could scarcely make out the words.

"It isn't true, Lainie."

She glanced at him over her shoulder, unable to decipher the taut lips, clenched fists, and troubled brown eyes. A long breath later, she nodded and stepped into the hall, careful to close the door gently.

"Not yet," she whispered, startling a passing footman. Sensing her distress, the young man lent his arm for the journey to her lonely room.

In spite of the fire and the thick goosedown quilt, Elaine shivered as she curled in the center of her bed, still listening for her husband. The house was eerily silent, except for the blood pounding in her ears and the tiny whimpers which escaped her throat. Please, Philip, she begged again and again. I'm sorry. Forgive me. Don't go.

It was hours before a nearly imperceptible voice tickled at her awareness. "I won't leave you," it seemed to say.

She coiled around the presence, certain that exhaustion and fear had produced this hallucination but unwilling to let it escape. The voice did not speak again, nor had it ever, she decided after awhile. Still, instead of reaching out for what she'd always wanted, for the first time Elaine turned inward. She remembered the things her husband had said before blindsiding her with the news he was going to London with Imogen.

The child. How was it she'd never accepted the existence of this tiny scrap of life growing inside her? It was part of her but separate, wholly dependent and yet a complete soul. In wonder, she felt the beginnings of peace. And with a jolt of pain, the realization that her baby's only impression of its parents consisted of illness and quarrels. Only Philip had ever spoken of wanting it. Only Philip ever said words of love.

That must change. The child should hear gentle, soft voices of welcome. She crossed her hands over her belly and cleared her throat.

"Hello, my darling," she said aloud, feeling a bit silly. "My name is Elaine and I'm your mother."

There was no response. Not that she expected any, of course.

"So far I suspect you don't much care for me," she persevered, determined to be honest. "You were bounced around a great deal when I was sick, and you must worry that I wish to be rid of you along with my breakfast every morning, but truly I do not."

With a start, she realized that was true. She wanted the child far more than all the other things she'd longed for. She'd resented the new life inside her because she'd not been allowed to choose for herself, but now, consciously and deliberately, she made her choice. There seemed no reason to say it aloud. She was certain the baby understood.

But there were other issues to address. "Nor do I wish to be rid of your father, sweeting, in spite of our quarrels. Those were of my own making, because Philip already loves you very much. He is much wiser than I, as you'll find out when you are born. Try to be patient with me, because I expect you'll hear a great many unpleasant things before I learn to be the mother you deserve. Know that I will try very hard from now on."

She continued to speak words of reassurance and love for a long time, promising she would confront Philip before his departure and convince him she'd already learned the lesson he wanted to teach her. But near dawn she fell asleep, and by the time she awoke at noon, he was gone.

Once the pain of his departure had settled to a dull, steady ache, Elaine resolved to become the perfect wife.

How hard could it be? She had faults, but who did not? She would simply eliminate them. It was possible there were virtues, concealed until now, but she would develop them.

A few days, he'd said. Not much time, but she could do it. When Philip returned, he would find a totally new woman . . . one he could love . . . and there would be no more talk of separation.

Dr. McGuiness had advised her to take long walks, so she bundled herself against the chilly air and headed for the garden. Best to get over the rough ground first, she decided, steeling herself for a strict examination of conscience. It took rather longer than she'd expected.

There were, Elaine was chagrined to discover, a devil's litany of vices in her repertoire.

How very like Imogen she was—selfish, manipulative, devoted to her own pleasures, and determined to bend her husband to her will as Imogen had done with Papa. Lacking her mother's devious charm, however, she'd gone at Philip with a virtual sledgehammer. It was a wonder he hadn't left her months ago.

Elaine resolved there and then her child was a boy. She could not bear to think of another self-absorbed Bartell woman growing inside her. A boy would take after Philip. He would be generous, loving, and strong. Turning inward, she sought an affirmation of her decision, but the babe remained stubbornly noncommittal.

How odd that she'd never considered Imogen a bad mother. Actually, she never thought of her as a mother at all. She was a dazzling creature who swept in now and again with a boxful of presents. She related enchanting stories about princes and dukes and balls and masquerades. Always she was the center of every tale, the focus of attention, the brightest star in London's sky.

Convinced that society could not function without Lady Crayton, Elaine didn't begrudge her mother's long absences. She simply longed for the day when she'd be old enough to join her.

She'd begun to fantasize in the nursery about her first Season, and even at the advanced age of two-and-twenty she'd fallen asleep to the imagined music of a waltz and the vision of herself dipping and swaying in the arms of a handsome aristocrat.

But there was never a Season, for one reason or another. When Elaine turned seventeen, Imogen went to Paris in the spring. The following spring it was Rome. Every April she set out for Europe, proclaiming that London had grown unhealthy for a lady of her delicate constitution.

"You will make your debut next year," she promised. Always "next year."

Not that Elaine lacked for suitors, because Imogen took care to provide a surfeit of them. In the fall, they appeared with monotonous regularity, one each month from September until Christmas, lured by the scent of an enormous dowry. Some were handsome, a few conversable, all of acceptable rank. They were universally poor.

Now that she lined them up in her mind, Elaine discerned

another trait they had in common. Every last one of them resided in some obscure backwater of England.

She calculated that she'd rejected fourteen proposals, surely a record for a maiden not officially "out." Papa usually complied with Imogen's wishes, but he never allowed her to pressure Elaine into marriage. When she said no, the suitor was gone the very next day.

Only once had she seriously considered an offer. Robert was exceedingly handsome for a cleric, with broad shoulders, lush black hair, and eyes that smoldered with dedication to the new parish he hoped to serve for the rest of his life.

It was located on the Isle of Man.

Even so, Elaine contrived to be alone with him whenever she could, hoping he'd steal a kiss. The astonishing new urges in her body were frightening and delicious. With a touch he might have resigned her to life on a remote island, but he quoted interminably from the Bible about the qualities of a virtuous woman until she'd memorized every line. After a week, she sent him packing.

A good thing, too, she reflected, because Imogen next, miraculously, produced Philip Grant, Viscount Halsey.

Still twitching from her unexpected female response to the hapless cleric, she was wary of her immediate attraction to this rather solemn young lord. While Imogen presided over a tea tray with her customary charm, Elaine tried to decipher the peculiar light in the viscount's brown eyes. She scarcely heard a word he said that first afternoon, although now the conversation replayed itself to the last syllable.

It occurred to her that she ought to tell her son about his parents' first meeting. After scanning the garden to be sure no one could hear, she began to speak aloud.

"Would you like me to tell you about your father? I do hope so, because I almost never have anyone to talk to, and the day I met him was very special.

"You should know what he looks like so that you will recognize him. He is tall. His hair is brown, flecked with gold like his eyes, and he's quite handsome although I cannot explain why. Nothing about him is out of the ordinary, but altogether he is quite extraordinary. Well, you must see for yourself, but I could never tire of looking at him.

"He spoke with Papa that same evening and proposed to me after breakfast the next day. I'm afraid it wasn't terribly romantic. He wished to restore Glenhaven, needed the money my dowry would provide, and was frank about his intentions. Ours was to be a marriage of convenience, if I would have him, and he promised to do everything in his power to make me happy."

Elaine continued to stroll as she talked and suddenly found herself in front of the ill-fated rosebush. Someone had removed the evidence of her disgrace and cleared the weeds from its root. Absently she fingered a brown twig.

"I have not made him happy, sweeting. From the beginning he was everything I wished for, but I didn't realize it. When I told him I wanted . . . well, demanded . . . a Season in London, he consented immediately. And after that I forgot all about him and thought only of my grand debut. The same way I've tried to ignore you, I'm afraid."

As she stroked the rosebush, Elaine noticed a tiny green lump protruding from the dry stem. New life already. By May, there would be flowers.

"I don't think I'll have changed very much before he returns," she admitted. "There is a great deal more work to do than I'd imagined. But I do love you, sweet child, and I love your father. Be patient with me."

As if the babe had any choice, she reflected on her way into the house. Children and parents, like husbands and wives, were stuck with one another.

Every week brought a letter from the viscount with a new reason why he could not come home. He was exploring the possibility of investing in a shipping line, and the friend who owned the company predicted he would double his money within two years. Naturally he had to be cautious, weigh the advantages and risks, examine the books. He hoped she was well.

Elaine knew that Philip had always felt guilty about living off her dowry, and she wanted his new venture to succeed. Still, she missed him terribly as the child began to grow inside her. At night her breasts ached, and her stomach had begun to swell. Few of her dresses fit comfortably, but she was too lethargic to make the trip into Exeter for new ones. She existed for the baby, and Philip's return.

After awhile, it began to appear he would never come home.

The letter that arrived on the tenth of April spurred her to action. His business was concluded, but Imogen had asked him to remain a few more days. The Crayton Ball was the highlight of the social season, and this year the Duke of Wellington had accepted an invitation. Since her husband would not be there, she required a host, and only her son-in-law would do.

Elaine's patience had run out. She knew how persuasive Imogen could be, and how enticing. If Philip thought he was going to stay in London indefinitely, he had another think coming.

Lady Halsey resolved to make her long-postponed debut at the Crayton Ball.

Elaine paused just inside the library door, not certain her father was aware she'd knocked and entered. The Earl of Crayton was huddled over a paper-strewn desk, spectacles balanced on his thin nose and a magnifying glass in his hand, frowning as he examined a tiny square of blue tile.

"Hullo, Papa. Have I come at a bad time?"

He looked up, clearly startled. "Elaine! What a delightful surprise."

"Don't get up," she begged as he reached for his cane. Hurrying across the room, she planted a warm kiss on his forehead.

Not satisfied with that, the earl hugged her tightly. "It's going to rain, Puss. I can always feel it in my bones. Now sit down and tell me how you are doing."

"I am well, Papa." Perching on the edge of a wing chair, she folded her hands in her lap so he wouldn't notice how they shook. As many times as she'd lied to her father, it never got any easier.

"And I hope you are wrong about the weather, because tomorrow I leave for London."

The earl pushed his spectacles up his nose and regarded her keenly. "Indeed? Is that wise in your condition?"

"Not you, too," she groaned. "Honestly, I'm being cosseted to the point of strangulation by everyone except Dr. McGuiness, who assures me there is no reason to lead other than a perfectly normal life. And Philip agrees, for I have a letter asking me to join him in London. It seems he is forced to remain there longer than expected for reasons of business."

"You cannot travel such a distance alone, child. I shall go with you."

He'd made a noble effort, but failed to conceal his reluctance. "Of course you will not," she said with a grin. "I intend to travel in style, with footmen and outriders. Not to mention Alicia, who is in alt at the prospect of going to the metropolis. She contends that her training as a lady's maid is wasted in the country."

The earl lifted an eyebrow. "In the same way you feel your training as a lady has gone for nothing, Puss?"

Heat rose to her cheeks. Her vague, scholarly father rarely made personal observations, but evidently he saw more than she gave him credit for. "I have always been curious about London," she admitted, "and Philip promised me a Season, but that is now impossible. Still, there is no reason we shouldn't enjoy a few days seeing the Town."

"I don't like you traveling without an escort. Why did he not take you with him a month ago?"

She bowed her head. "We quarreled, and I refused to go. Where did I acquire such an execrable temper, Papa? You and Imogen are always so calm."

The earl winced as he always did when Elaine used her mother's given name. Imogen insisted on that form of address. "Calm is not a word I associate with Lady Crayton, although she contrives to give that impression in public. And since she also contrives to be in public most of the time, it's no wonder you have been gammoned."

"Not completely," Elaine said with a chuckle. "Nevertheless,

Imogen manages to control her temper, which I have not. Poor Philip has suffered my vile disposition far too long, but I intend to make it up to him."

"So you shall, Puss, by giving him the greatest blessing a man can hope for." He leaned forward, templing his hands. "Are you happy in this marriage?"

Caught by surprise, she blushed hotly. "Of course I am. Philip is kind and generous and . . . a great many other things. I *am* pregnant, after all."

The earl laughed, but his eyes were somber. "Perhaps sooner than you'd hoped." He waved a hand when she started to object. "There is no shame in wanting to enjoy the pleasures of the young, Puss. You should have made your curtsey to the Queen and danced until your slippers were worn through instead of keeping your old father company in this rustic outpost. And I should have insisted that your mother take you to London, or taken you myself. In truth, I was too pudding-hearted to oppose Imogen's will and too selfish to relinquish the pleasure of having you with me."

Elaine felt tears well in her eyes. "I was happy to be with you, Papa."

He nodded. "We did have fun together when I was agile enough to prospect for artifacts. Do you remember the day you came home with the pretty tiles you'd found?"

She brightened. "I was seven years old. You were so excited you practically turned cartwheels."

"I knew from the records there had been a Roman villa on the property and searched in vain until you found it. You were the best of helpers, meticulously brushing away the dirt and marking quadrants with sticks and string like a born scholar. I was very proud of you. But the last few years I've closeted myself in this room, analyzing and writing descriptions of faded Roman mosaics no one gives a groat to read about. I neglected to take care of you and see to your welfare, Elaine, and I am very sorry."

"Oh, Papa, don't say such things. You make me feel like the most selfish creature alive."

"That pinnacle is reserved for your mother and me," he corrected dryly. "My own faults are legion, but do not be too harsh with Imogen. Her life was difficult until we met, and I cannot blame her for escaping a brutal family by marrying me, even though I was twenty years her senior and not at all interested in the things she cared about. Perhaps each of us thought we could change the other, but as you see, that has not happened. I am still a stick in the mud, while she is the light of society. We are happier living apart."

"Do you regret the marriage, Papa?"

"Regrets are futile. We both reaped what we contracted for, after all. I was mesmerized by her beauty and charm, while she was captivated by my fortune and title." His smile was unutterably sweet. "How can I regret what accorded me a precious daughter? You, Elaine, are the finest thing either of your parents ever did."

"Mama doesn't think so," she objected, unaware that she'd called Imogen "Mama" for the first time in her life.

"Not yet," he agreed softly. "There are a hundred reasons for that, Puss, none important in its own right, but they submerged her better instincts. You must not despair of her, as I do not. She was upset to find herself with child within weeks of our marriage and blamed me for her condition. I expect women generally do that. My first wife had produced your stepbrother Roger to inherit the title, so I expect Imogen hoped to be let off the hook. But I was rather an ardent lover in those days, and nature took its course. Imogen never quite accepted the reality of being a mother, although she doted on you the few weeks she spent here at Black Oaks every year. You cannot have forgotten that."

"I thought she was magic and wanted to be exactly like her—charming and gay and beautiful. I thought when I was old enough she'd invite me to London and I'd take the *ton* by storm as she had done. But that never happened. She didn't want me with her." Years of hurt made her voice tremble.

The earl removed his spectacles and wiped the lenses with a crumpled handkerchief. "She didn't want a rival, Puss. Imogen is terrified of getting old. She couldn't bear to stand next to you in a receiving line, where your young fresh beauty would show up the wrinkles beginning to trace around her eyes and lips. If she presented a daughter of eighteen or nineteen, well, even the most spongy-headed aristocrat can do simple mathematics."

A fierce anger gripped her. "Did she think to hide me away forever? But of course she did. She even served up potential husbands just as anxious to keep me in quarantine, and you offered an enormous dowry to make certain one of them would have me. How could you, Papa, when you knew all along what she was about?"

He peered at her myopically. "She found you a good man, Puss. Had you caprioled through a hundred London Seasons you'd not have come across a better."

Elaine sank back in her chair, much struck by that observation. "I'd have liked to have found him for myself," she protested ineffectually.

"You should have been given that opportunity. I should have seen to it. Perhaps you will learn some lessons from your parents' failures and do better with your own child."

She rested her hand on her stomach, once again aware of the sublime responsibility that was hers. "I shall remember your advice," she said fondly. "But I would have no other father than you."

"Thank you for that, my dear. And when the time comes, as it will, when your mother needs your love, try to forgive her. Imogen will not slide gracefully into old age."

Elaine's eyes widened. "How horrified she must be to think of herself as a grandmother."

He laughed. "She is determined not to think of it at all, but we must all face the truth sooner or later." The earl reached out a hand, and Elaine took it, feeling warm and protected. "The trouble with Imogen, Puss, is that she thinks she can only succeed by exploiting her beauty. That is my fault, because beauty attracted me to her and rescued her from poverty. She does not yet know that her unique personality will more than suffice, however many the wrinkles etched on her face. One day, take my word, she'll find herself accepted by the *ton* for her charm and wit, more popular than she is now, and cease being jealous of you."

"You still love her," she said in wonder.

"In my way. You are a woman now, Elaine—have been for longer than your parents are willing to admit—so it is past time we speak frankly. I know that Imogen takes lovers. Ours was a marriage of convenience on her part, infatuation on mine, and I never deluded myself that she would be faithful. If I have buried myself in Roman ruins, it is because I did not want to watch the inevitable. But I will always be here when she needs me. I only hope to live long enough for that to happen, and meantime, I wish her happy."

"Oh, Papa." She took the handkerchief he offered and blew her nose vociferously. "You must be a saint."

"By no means. I'm an old man set in his ways who was foolish enough to marry a young wife. Whatever Imogen's faults, she gave me a daughter, and now you will give me a grandchild to dote on. I am rewarded beyond my dreams."

"How strange it is, after all these years, to speak like this. We've wasted so much time, Papa." Her gaze lifted to his. "Why is it so very difficult to speak the truth and say what we feel?"

"A mystery for the ages, Puss. Don't make the same mistake with your husband, and you must take the initiative because the male of the species is woefully tongue-tied. It is difficult enough for us to acknowledge our feelings to ourselves, let alone admit them to anyone else." He cleared his throat. "So, when will you depart?"

It took a moment for Elaine to adjust to the change of subject. Evidently this astonishing exchange of confidences was over for now, but she'd find it easier to confide in her father in the future.

At a time when she wasn't lying to him, of course. "We set out at dawn. Philip would prefer I not stop at an inn, so I hope to make the trip in one day." She stood, favoring him with a wink. "If it rains as your bones predict, we'll take shelter until the storm passes."

With effort, the earl pulled himself erect and came around the desk to embrace her. "See that you do. And if you stay in London very long, write to me."

"I shall. Now I'm going upstairs to rummage through Imogen's closets. She forgot a few things and wants me to bring them along."

"How can a woman who travels with two baggage coaches have forgotten so much as a hairpin? Ah well, I am pleased she is ready to welcome you to London at last. Have a good time, Puss, and convey my regards to your mother."

Elaine spent the next hour combing through Imogen's extensive wardrobe, selecting gowns she thought might fit her while Alicia folded them into the portmanteau they'd brought along.

"These are years out of fashion, milady," she objected with each new addition to the pile. "Should've been given to the poor."

Elaine tossed her a filmy gauze ballgown. "As if the poor had occasion to wear such things. I haven't time to have a dress made up before the Crayton Ball, so you must help me decide which of these can be made over. I'm certain you can transform one into a stylish confection."

The maid regarded her dubiously, and her doubts grew when they returned to Glenhaven. The viscountess was slightly taller than her mother, with broader shoulders and, now, a bulging stomach. Only one dress, in an unflattering shade of tangerine, did not stretch at the seams, although the skirt ended where her ankles began. By the time she tried it on, Elaine was a little desperate and refused to see how her belly swelled beneath the high-waisted bodice.

"I can sew ribbons and lace at the hem," Alicia conceded when it was apparent only the tangerine dress would do.

Next they confronted the problem of shoes. Elaine could barely cram her feet into any of her mother's slippers but finally selected a pair that nearly matched the gown, making up her mind to endure the blisters. Nothing came without a price, and she would appear at the Crayton Ball if it meant cutting off her toes.

It was nearly midnight before the altered dress and accessories were packed away, along with a few of her own things in case Philip allowed her to remain in London past the first explosive encounter. He was always generous with pin money, and since she never went anywhere to spend it, she could afford an overnight stop on the way and the best hotel in London when she arrived.

She had decided to surprise Imogen and Philip by appearing after the receiving line had dispersed, when the dance was well underway. Actually, that was her only chance to set foot in the ballroom, because if Imogen got wind of her plans in advance, she'd be hustled back to Glenhaven under guard.

"Was all of London invited to the Crayton Ball?" Alicia practically hung out the window of the hackney, which had been mired in the crowd of carriages and onlookers for more than an hour. "It's like a fair, milady. People are selling oranges on the sidewalk. Look! There's a man eating fire."

Without interest, Elaine glanced at the street performers before leaning back with a sigh. "I expect they've all come for a glimpse of Wellington."

"Oh my. Will you dance with him?"

"Don't be absurd, Alicia. I am far beneath his touch, and besides, it will be a miracle if I manage to walk in these shoes." Her mother's slippers pinched her swollen feet and the hair arrangement she'd so admired in the mirror at the Pulteney seemed plastered to her scalp. She felt like an overweight mushroom with no business whatever at a fashionable ball.

Ten minutes later, the hack pulled up to the brightly-lit mansion on Grosvenor Square and a liveried footman presented himself to assist her to the curb. Elaine doubted she could have made it on her own.

"Give my regards to the Duke," Alicia called in a shrill voice.

As the footman led her up the wide marble steps to the door of Crayton House, Elaine reflected that Alicia was experiencing the curiosity and fascination she could not muster in herself. She scarcely noticed the elegant marble facade of the family mansion she'd dreamed about but never seen, nor the impeccable servant who took her cloak.

Seconds later she was engulfed in a surging tide of the fashionable elite, all bound for the upper floor. She had no choice but to go along.

"Crushes" were more pleasant in theory than practice, she decided as a wave of perfume and sweat swept over her. Luckily, there was no room to faint. Her feet scarcely touched the floor as she was borne upstairs and down a wide hall before being spewed into the ballroom. Disoriented, she pressed herself against the wall, arms folded protectively across her stomach.

No one paid her the slightest attention. She heard music, and if she stood tiptoe, she could make out the heads of dancers near the center of the room. A young man sporting shirtpoints to his eyebrows stepped on her foot and apologized brusquely as he threaded past.

So this was a posh London ball. Elaine smiled thinly. It could be that Imogen had done her a favor by keeping her in the country all these years. Thoroughly disillusioned and feeling very much alone despite the crowd, she focused her waning energy on locating Philip.

Gingerly at first, then getting into the spirit of things, she elbowed herself toward the dancers, fully expecting to see her husband cutting a gavotte with his mother-in-law. Instead, she found herself nose to cravat with a distinguished gentleman in impeccable black-and-white evening dress who regarded her kindly from bright blue eyes.

"How d'you do," he said in a pleasant voice.

"Not well at the moment," she replied curtly, trying to look past him to the dancers. "Take no offense, sir, but I am searching for my husband."

He made a nearly imperceptible gesture and suddenly the crowd melted away, leaving the two of them in a space at the edge of the dance floor. "Perhaps I can help you. What is his name?"

She glanced at him sideways. "Philip. He's tall, with brown hair."

"Then I confess a touch of envy," the man said with a crooked smile. "Many was the time I wished to be tall, and my own hair went gray in my youth."

"I am sorry to hear it, sir, but I expect we all wish for things we cannot have. Now if you will excuse me—"

He grasped her elbow gently. "Not until you have told me your name. One rarely meets a wife so anxious to find her own spouse."

She couldn't help but laugh. "I am Elaine Bartell Grant, and my husband is Lord Halsey. Perhaps you and I will meet again, but for now pray forgive me. It is most urgent that I find him before . . . well, never mind. Goodbye, sir."

Taking swift advantage of the space that had materialized around them, she slipped past a fountain burbling with champagne, rounded a pillar, and felt claws dig into her arm.

"What in God's name are you doing here?" Over a wide, false smile, Imogen's eyes blazed with fury.

Elaine could only stare in dismay at her mother, wishing the floor would open and swallow at least one of them.

"Wicked girl!" The smile never left Imogen's face. "How could you disgrace me like this? Look at you. Big as a house, wearing that foul dress. For shame."

Elaine wanted to point out exactly who bought the foul dress in the first place, but all the blood seemed to have pooled in her cramped feet. Lightheaded, she could do no more than hold herself upright and endure Imogen's tongue-lashing.

With half an ear, Philip listened to Lord Mumblethorpe chirp the praises of a young woman he wished to meet. The chit in question was guarded by a formidable mother, and Mumblethorpe required a proper introduction. Bored, more with the Crayton Ball than the infatuated stripling at his side, Philip scanned the room for Imogen.

He'd done his duty by her, including two dreary hours in the receiving line, but surely his presence was no longer essential. If he slipped away now, he'd never be missed.

Mumblethorpe plucked at his sleeve. "There she is. My goddess. Just by the champagne fountain."

Glancing over, Philip saw a cluster of bemused spectators observing what appeared to be a "scene."

Imogen loomed at the center, a sham smile carved over her flashing teeth. Next to her, eyes huge and terrified, Elaine gazed helplessly at her mother.

He caught his breath. Elaine! She looked ready to sink through the parquet floor. Slicing through the crowd, his eyes focused on her pale cheeks, Philip broke into Imogen's low-voiced tirade in a tone sure to be heard by the gawking bystanders.

"My dear Elaine! You have made it after all, in spite of yesterday's rainstorm. I am so pleased." Unclasping Imogen's hand from his wife's arm, he moved between them and brushed a kiss on Elaine's cold cheek. "You cannot imagine how worried we have been since word of the accident."

Her mouth opened and closed soundlessly.

The viscount fired a look at Imogen, warning her not to contradict his improvised story. "As you see, Lady Crayton, the message was accurate in spite of your fears. It was indeed the baggage coach which lost a wheel and plunged into the ravine. Your daughter is perfectly safe."

"So it appears." Imogen eyed Elaine with barely concealed malice. "But you needn't have come here to reassure us, child, weary as you must be after such a difficult journey."

Philip forced himself to smile. "How could she do otherwise? Elaine's concern for her family matches your own, Lady Crayton. Remember how you were bent on canceling this ball and launching a search when the news arrived? But you could not know the trust I place in Mr. Ryson, who carried word of the accident. A thoroughly reliable man. No one else would do to escort your daughter to London, and Mrs. Ryson has been with her all along. Has she not, my dear?"

Gulping, Elaine nodded.

"So there's an end to it," he said briskly. "I'm only sorry your lovely new ballgown is now buried in the mud along with the unfortunate baggage coach, but how clever of you to borrow another dress at the last moment." Seizing her arm, he drew her relentlessly away, still speaking in a voice loud enough to be heard by the curious throng. "You must tell me of your adventures, my dear. I'm sure no one will mind if we seek a bit of privacy."

Philip continued his rambling monologue as he led her to the French doors which opened onto the terrace, aware that Elaine remained on her feet only because he supported her.

"Hold onto me," he whispered when she stumbled.

Pulling herself erect, Elaine summoned a dazzling smile and turned its brilliance on her mother, who regarded her with slitted eyes from across the ballroom. Then, like a duchess, she swept onto the marble terrace, smiling at the other couples enjoying the cool air as she aimed for the darkest corner.

Towed in her wake, Philip watched her sink onto a wrought-iron bench concealed behind a potted tree.

"Well-done," he said admiringly.

"I could say the same to you, Philip. Baggage coaches and mud and borrowed gowns, not to mention Mr. and Mrs.—was it Ryson? Wherever did you learn to tell such a bouncer?"

He grinned. "I *was* rather good, wasn't I? Do you think they believed it?"

"To be sure. For a time, even *I* was convinced that my lavish entourage had met with disaster in a rainstorm. But am I truly such an antidote? Imogen said that my appearance shamed her, and you were at some pains to account for this lamentable dress."

"Only because I have observed that, whatever the crisis, a lady's concern quickly turns to how she looks. That gown is long out of fashion and does not fit you well, but even in rags you would be beautiful."

"Neatly said, Philip, but you need not spare my feelings. I am quite recovered now." She drew out her fan. "How does anyone endure the suffocating heat in that ballroom without swooning? 'Tis a wonder the guests don't wind up the evening in a great heap on the floor."

"A London Season requires stamina and, I fear, a profound tolerance for unpleasant odors. Perhaps now you understand why this is not the place for a woman in a delicate condition."

"Ah, now comes the lecture. Go ahead, husband. Ring a peal

over me for disobeying you and traveling to London on my own. Will you be shocked to learn I stayed one night at an inn and another at the Pulteney Hotel?"

He regarded her in the moonlight. In spite of her upraised, stubborn chin, she looked apprehensive and her eyes glistened with unshed tears. Gently he touched her nose with the tip of his finger. "There will be no scolding from me, Elaine. Not so long as you've come to no harm."

Her lips curved. "Other than the humiliation of making a spectacle of myself in front of all your friends."

"That did not happen, I assure you."

"Only because you saved me from absolute disgrace." One tear escaped, streaking down her cheek. "Thank you, Philip. It was more than I deserved."

"I should do other than stand with my wife?" He pulled out his handkerchief and wiped her face tenderly. "Wherever you go, whatever you do, I will always defend you in public, Elaine. If we are to quarrel, we shall do so privately."

"Like now?"

He shook his head. "Are you spoiling for a fight? I won't oblige you, at least on the subject of your sudden appearance tonight. From the beginning you made your wishes clear, but I failed to understand how very important a London Season was to you . . . perhaps because I'd long since wearied of balls and routs and musicales, and the constant jostling for position, and the tedious gossip."

"At least you had the opportunity to become jaded," she complained.

"Yes. And I'd forgotten what great fun I had in the early days. You have every right to experience that excitement for yourself, Elaine. I want you to. One day, when the time is right, you will cut a dash and I shall see London through your eyes. But for now you are carrying our child and your triumph must wait. Forgive me, I cannot be sorry for that."

"Nor am I," she said. "And I did not come to London for the Season or the Crayton Ball, Philip. I came for you."

His brows drew together. "How so? I told you in my last letter that I'd return after the ball. Indeed, I have already packed, and intended to set out in the morning."

"Each of your previous letters contained an excuse for another delay, Philip. I began to think you did not wish to come home."

"What the devil would keep me in London when my wife and child are in Devonshire?"

She shrugged delicately. "Imogen?"

"Dear God, Elaine! You cannot still believe—"

She cut him off with a wave of her hand. "No, I do not, if I ever did. When I accused you that awful night, I was not thinking rationally. You are too honorable to betray me with my own mother—"

"With anyone," he corrected swiftly. "If it matters to you, I have seen little of Imogen since we arrived. On occasion our paths have crossed, but for the most part I've avoided *ton* parties."

"Truly?" She emitted a watery giggle. "I'd imagined you dancing with her through every ballroom in the city."

"I've danced with her precisely once, to open this ball, and she'd have dropped me in a heartbeat had the Duke of Wellington arrived in time to lead her out. Since he is generally late, as he was tonight, she insisted I wait in the wings to play understudy."

"Then what have you been doing all these weeks?" Her gaze lowered. "Was it such a beastly prospect, coming home to your shrew of a wife?"

"If I answer that honestly, you will think me a coward, Elaine."

She blinked. "Then don't answer. Although I expect you just did."

"You misunderstand." Heat rose to his face. "I am not used to explaining myself because no one has ever cared to listen, but let me try. The night when I was vilely drunk, I said a number of foolish things. It was inexcusable of me to fling ultimatums in your face and accuse you of disavowing our child. If I kept finding reasons to postpone my return, it's because I owed you an apology and was sure I'd muss it up." He splayed his arms. "Most of all, I feared you might be happier at Glenhaven without me."

"I was miserable without you."

"You were miserable when I was there."

Her nose wrinkled. "You were not responsible for that. The blame is all mine, Philip, but I am trying to change. And do you know, I have not once been ill since you left."

"Indeed," he said stiffly, "I am delighted to hear it."

Heat rose to her cheeks, but she couldn't repress a tiny chuckle. "My, that did *not* come out as I intended. Truly, I was sick at heart without you, but my stomach has managed to settle itself at last."

He stared over the top of her head into the torchlit garden. "It was obvious that I upset you, but I'd no idea that I was the cause of your physical difficulties. Had I realized your health suffered from my presence, I'd have taken myself off directly." His voice was flat. "Perhaps I *should* have known, since you forbade me your bed, but until my attempt to kiss you, it was not clear to me."

"Oh Philip," she said after a moment. "What a mull I've made of everything. Will you sit down and permit me to explain?"

"Dare I get so close?" he asked between his teeth.

"Impossible man. I have hurt you badly, and now you need a little of your own back. Well, you shall have it, and apologies by the score, only listen to me first."

He looked mulish.

"You will laugh," she promised, "and feel quite as silly as I did when I learned the truth. Please. Sit with me."

Jaw clenched, he lowered himself to the edge of the bench, as far away from his wife as possible. "Very well. What is the truth? If not my kiss, what caused you to be sick?"

"Garlic."

He blinked.

"Well, it might have been the onions," she confided, "or even the fish. I'd have tried to narrow it down, but the consequences wouldn't have been pleasant."

"What the devil are you talking about, Elaine?"

"Don't imagine this was easy to figure out. I could not think what had caused such a violent reaction to your kiss, nor bring myself to ask Dr. McGuiness, but of late he has been accompanied by his wife when he examines me. It's so much easier to discuss intimate matters with another woman. Madame remembered the fish stew she'd prepared for lunch that day and that you ate two bowlfuls."

"What of it? Besides, you *like* garlic. I distinctly recall that in Paris—"

"I wasn't pregnant then," she interrupted. "Not very, anyway. Madame has observed the symptom now and again, so she made up a batch of fish stew and offered me a taste, with the same result. We are not certain which ingredient is responsible, but I'd wager it was the garlic made me ill. Certainly not you, Philip. Never you."

He doubled over with laughter. "All this turmoil and distress," he said when he could find his voice, "because I had bad breath?"

"So it seems. I told you that you'd laugh."

"But why didn't you explain in a letter?"

She poked him in the chest with her finger. "Because I thought you'd be home any day, wretch. Until I began to worry you would not come home at all."

After a moment, he slid along the bench and took her in his arms. "I had plain roast beef for luncheon, Lainie, and no dinner. May I put your theory to the test?"

"Oh yes, Philip. Please."

Elaine felt a great many things when he kissed her, with evident passion, for a long breathless time. Loved. Desired. Secure. And beautiful. For some reason, that seemed very important.

"Will you come to bed with me tonight?" he asked in a husky voice. "I promise not to snore."

Her smile was dreamy. "You have never done so, that I recall. And you will not snore tonight, Philip, because I intend to make sure you don't go to sleep."

"Ah Lainie," he said, kissing her again before tugging her from the bench. "I hear a waltz. Come dance with me."

She placed a hand on his shoulder. "I'd like that."

"Not here on the terrace, sweetheart. Inside, where everyone can see us."

"I can't go back in there," she wailed as he drew her toward the open doors. "Philip! I have already made a cake of myself in this dress. *Philip!*"

He paused, took both her hands, and looked deeply into her eyes. "Elaine, you are my wife. I am very proud of you. I want to show you off. We shall waltz together at the Crayton Ball, and you'll be the loveliest woman there. Everyone will envy us, and when the dance is over, we shall make a grand exit with our heads held high."

"I don't think I can," she whimpered to no avail. Seconds later he was spinning her around the dance floor as if they were the only couple in the room.

Elaine quickly forgot her appearance, and all her apprehensions vanished in a blur of happiness. She was waltzing at London's poshest ball in the arms of a handsome, dashing gentleman. Her lifelong dream had come true. No, a better dream than she'd dared to imagine because it was *Philip* holding her and gazing into her eyes with unconcealed love.

The child was dancing, too. She was certain he heard the music.

Imogen released a long sigh. Her ruin was complete. Everyone knew.

It was almost a relief that the charade was over. Soon her child would produce another child, and in a few months the countess who had reigned over Society for two decades would be a gr—

The word would not complete itself, even in her mind.

How happy they were, Elaine and Philip. All the light in the room seemed to follow them as they danced. Only once had she seen a man look at a woman the way Philip was looking at his wife, and she had not thought about that moment for more than twenty years.

It was when she told the earl they had conceived a child.

All her life men had admired her, but that glow in her husband's eyes was the only time she'd felt loved. It had scared her to death. She did not want to be loved by an old man.

William was handsome, even at forty-two, but she was nineteen and on fire with dreams of a London triumph. The light in his eyes disappeared when she told him he'd spoiled all her plans for the future, and she was careful never to look at him too closely after that. What if he still loved her?

What if he didn't?

Surely he did not. She rarely saw her husband, scarcely spoke to him, and had taken more lovers than she could count. What man could love a faithless, indifferent wife? She did not deserve to be loved.

"May I have what remains of this dance?"

Startled, Imogen looked up at the Duke of Wellington. He swept her onto the dance floor before she could think to respond.

"Your daughter is charming," he said, "and very like you, although not so beautiful."

She felt heat rise to her cheeks. "Only because Elaine is . . . expecting a child, Your Grace."

"I noticed, but that is not what I meant. There is a style and a grace a woman only achieves with experience of life. Every year Lady Halsey will grow lovelier, as you have done."

Imogen gave him a skeptical smile. "I think you were too long on the Peninsula, Your Grace. You have come home laden with Spanish coin."

He barked the sudden, raucous laugh that never failed to astonish his companions. "Too long indeed, Lady Crayton, but what I said was pure gold and plain-spoken truth. I have just turned fifty and am certain that it is a better thing to be a wine that improves with age than a comet which streaks brightly but so very briefly across the sky."

Her lips curved. "How is it you have contrived to be both, Your Grace?"

Again the laugh rang out. "By God, you *are* a charmer. On Thursday next I host a dinner party at Apsley House. Tell me you are not already promised forth."

"I rarely make promises of any sort," she said mischievously.

"Very wise. There are more than enough obligations we cannot escape without committing to new ones. But I shall set a place for you on my right, just in case."

Her gaze caught Philip and Elaine as they nodded to each other and left the dance floor hand in hand. "You realize," she said haltingly, "that you could find yourself dining with a gr . . . grandmother."

"How I envy you. Because of the war I missed watching my boys grow up, and they were virtual strangers on my return to England. We shuffle along fairly well now, but Arthur is only twelve and Charles younger than that, so it will be many years before they give me grandchildren to dandle on my knee."

With surprise, Imogen realized that the waltz had come to an end.

The Duke did not release her. "We had only half a dance," he complained. "I claim the next by right of possession."

Smiling, Imogen allowed him to lead her into a set forming for the cotillion. Nothing had changed after all. The most fascinating man in the room . . . in all of London . . . desired her company. The young man to whom she'd promised this dance looked suitably bereft. Sally Jersey shot her an envious glance. And every gentleman she met in the exchange of partners regarded her with the adoration she'd come to expect.

But all she could think of as she moved gracefully through the figures was the love in Philip's eyes when he danced with his wife. She wanted to see that same love directed at her, and only one man had ever cared for her so much.

She had thrown away the most valuable thing ever offered to her. Was there any way she could get it back after all this time?

As she made her way from partner to partner, Imogen decided that she would forego a summer in Brighton this year. She had a sudden longing to reacquaint herself with her husband, still remarkably attractive in his sixties . . . which no longer seemed quite so old.

And of course she must remain at Black Oaks through the fall, to be sure of welcoming her first grandchild to the world.

"Thank you," she said to the Duke when the music ended, "for a great deal more than this dance. I don't suppose you'd care to be a godfather?"

"Indeed I would," he declared. "You may expect me at the

christening, if your daughter approves, and I look forward to meeting your husband."

She laughed, feeling genuinely happy for the first time since she could remember. "So do I. The two of us have been strangers far too long. Is it not wonderful to have so many good things to anticipate, Your Grace? In truth it rather astounds me, but I can hardly wait to be a grandmother."

Christening Day

by Joy Reed

Viscount St. Damien raised his arms, then lowered them suddenly, sending a wave of water splashing over the side of his bath basin. His mother jumped back with a gasp of laughter. "Only see what he has done, Hester," exclaimed the countess. "I'm wet from head to toe. Arthur Edward Guilford St. Damien, that was not at all a gentlemanly thing to do, upon my word. I would be quite annoyed with you, my dear, had you not the excuse of being too young to know better. He certainly does love water, doesn't he, Hester?"

The nurse, a stout, dark, middle-aged woman with a capable air, cast an indulgent eye at her infant charge. "Indeed he does, the little lamb," she said. "Never happier than when he's in his bath. I believe I might leave him there all day and he'd never make a murmur about it. Ah, and just wait till he's a bit older, Miss Elizabeth—my lady, that is, as I should say. Before you know it he'll be toddling down to the river to chase after the ducks and get himself covered with mud. Babies grow up tremendous fast."

The countess nodded, but she was no longer smiling. It was the morning of her son's christening day, an occasion for rejoicing if there ever was one; but the day that had promised so much had already been spoiled by a quarrel, as senseless as it was upsetting, which had arisen between herself and her husband at the breakfast table. In consequence, the countess was feeling very low. She watched as the nurse took a warm towel from the rack in front of the fire and brought it over to the baby in the basin. "If you'd hold the towel for me, my lady, while I take him out—thank you, my lady. There you go, love," she told the viscount, as she wrapped him snugly in the towel. "We'll have you all warm and dry again in two shakes of a lamb's tail."

"Can I hold him, Hester?" said the countess hopefully. For answer, the nurse put the baby, towel and all, into her arms. He at once let out a wail, and she began to walk up and down the room, patting him gently on the back as she walked. "There, that's quieted him," she said with satisfaction. "I believe I'm getting the way of it at last, Hester. I never dreamed there was so much to taking care of babies." She had slowed her steps as she spoke, and the baby let out another wail, causing her to quicken her pace once more. "Perhaps I spoke too soon," she said, looking down at her son ruefully. "He seems to cry a great deal, doesn't he, Hester?"

"Aye, more than some, my lady, but not so much as others I've known. Why, you yourself cried full as much as he when you was a babe, Miss Elizabeth—my lady, that is. I recall many a night I had to walk the floor with you before you'd settle down to sleep." The nurse seemed to sense the countess's downcast mood, for her voice took on a comforting tone reminiscent of that lady's own nursery days. "Never you mind, my lady: they all of them outgrow it sooner or later. It's just a matter of time till he does, too. Though there's no denying it's trying while it lasts. We had a bad night of it last night and no mistake."

The countess nodded, stifling an urge to say that she was very well aware of it. She and her husband were presently residing at Rosehill, one of the earl's several properties, which was situated in the country about a half-day's journey from London. Rosehill was a large house dating from the early years of the previous century, and the nursery on the uppermost floor was separated from the principal bedchambers by no less than three doors, a flight of stairs, and a long corridor. The infant viscount had good lungs, however; even in her bedroom, with doors and windows closed and bedcurtains drawn, the countess had been able to hear quite distinctly the sound of his voice rising and falling, dying away and then starting up again. It had been impossible for her to sleep with that thin, faraway wail in her ears.

After tossing and turning for nearly two hours, she had got out of bed again, put on her dressing gown, and tiptoed upstairs to the nursery. In the back of her mind lurked a fear, all the worse for being unacknowledged, that her son was undergoing some neglect or abuse at the hands of his nurses. But when she had peeped cautiously around the door, she had beheld a scene that set all her half-admitted fears to rest. Ellen, the wet nurse, squatted beside the hearth, heating something in a saucepan over the fire, while Hester Smithson, once her own nurse and now her son's, sat perseveringly rocking the cradle which contained the wailing baby. Ashamed of her suspicions, the countess had tiptoed away again and gone back to bed, but still it had been a long time before either she or her son had been able to sleep. Nor were they the only restless ones: at intervals throughout that long, long night, the countess had heard footsteps in the room next to hers where her husband slept. She had deduced that the viscount's crying—or some other cause—was keeping the earl as wakeful as herself. In the early hours of the morning, when at last the crying had stopped and she was lying tensely awake, praying the silence would last, she had heard the earl's steps approach the door that adjoined his rooms to her own. She had pushed back the bedclothes and sat up in bed, looking toward the door. But the earl had not come in; after a moment his steps had moved away, and the bedroom door had remained closed. It had been closed now for more than six weeks.

That closed door was a source of considerable anxiety to the countess. In some ways it was an anxiety that ran deeper than her fears about the viscount's well-being. There could be no doubt that the earl was proud of his son; she could clearly recall the moment when, her labors concluded, he had been admitted into her bedroom to see his newborn son for the first time. She had been lying in her bed, unutterably weary but also unutterably happy, watching as the smiling doctor put the baby in his father's arms. It had been an oddly touching encounter. The viscount had entered the world roaring at the top of his lungs, but his roars had ceased as soon as the ordeal of birth was over; he was wide-eyed and quiet now as his father stood looking down at him. The earl's face had been reverent as he touched one tiny hand and watched it close instinctively over his finger. "He's so small," said the earl in a hushed voice. "So small, but so perfect. I can't believe he's really ours, Beth. Our son . . ."

The countess had said, rather tartly, that after twelve hours of labor she herself was quite convinced of the reality of the experience. The earl had laughed and sat down on the edge of the bed. "My poor Beth," he said with a smile. "I should think not indeed. But a noble effort on your part, my dear—worthy of more than any words of mine can express. I can express it better without words, perhaps." Laying the viscount in her lap, he had then taken her in his arms and kissed her, undeterred by the presence of the doctor, the dowager, the nurse, and a couple of giggling maidservants. His pride and pleasure had been very evident on that occasion, and they had continued evident in the weeks that followed. Not a day went by without him visiting the nursery at least once, and often more than once; and he had interested himself in the details of his son's progress in a way that was rare among the generality of men, if the countess's friends were to be believed.

She had at first been gratified by his interest, but lately her gratification had been alloyed by a suspicion that his interest in his son surpassed his interest in herself; at times she found herself growing jealous of her own child, which was plainly ridiculous. But ridiculous or not, it was a fact that the kisses which the earl had bestowed on her that day represented the utmost intimacy that had passed between them since the viscount's birth. As the weeks had gone by, the bedroom door had remained unbreached, and the countess was beginning to fear it might remain that way permanently.

She had been at first surprised and then hurt by the earl's neglect. That aspect of their marriage had always been highly satisfactory, as indeed had been their marriage as a whole, and nothing in the earl's past conduct had given her reason to suppose he found it less satisfactory than herself. Theirs had been no marriage of convenience, but a bona fide love match, as well she knew; the Earl of Carlton might have taken to wife any number of young women both better born and better dowered than herself if his sole purpose in marrying had been to obtain a son and heir. The countess simply could not believe that, having obtained one, he had no further use for her.

She was more inclined to attribute his present neglect to the change which motherhood had wrought in her appearance. Pregnancy had not damaged her figure so much as she had been led to fear, but there had undeniably been changes, and the changes were not limited to her figure alone. Even now, as she walked back and forth across the nursery with the viscount in her arms, she could not escape the evidence: the chimney glass over the fireplace gave back a faithful image of her own face, wan and worried-looking, with dark circles under her eyes from lack of sleep. The countess averted her eyes from her reflection with an inward sigh. She was a blue-eyed blonde with the fair skin that usually accompanies such coloring, but it had seemed to her lately that she looked not merely fair but downright colorless. She had never felt more colorless than she had the night before, when she had sat at one end of the dinner table and watched her husband laughing and talking with Mrs. Blackwell at the other.

The Honorable Mrs. Charles Blackwell was a widow of about the countess's own age, and a lady of undoubted fashion. She was a vivacious brunette with dark eyes and blooming cheeks, who was celebrated throughout London society for her consummate horsemanship. Mrs. Blackwell was often to be seen riding in the park on some high-spirited steed or driving herself about in her famous phaeton-and-four; she was as often to be seen at balls and assemblies, besieged by gentlemen eager to dance with a lady known as much for her wit as her beauty. She had arrived at Rosehill the day before, one of a party of guests who had come to attend the viscount's christening.

It had been the first time the countess had seen the other lady in some months. Her pregnancy had been a difficult one, which had prevented her taking part in the most recent London Season, and at her doctor's advice, the earl had taken her to Rosehill early in April to spend the final weeks of her pregnancy in the more healthful surroundings of the country. Throughout those weeks, right up to the day of her *accouchement,* the earl had remained with her at Rosehill and had showed a touching solicitude for her welfare. He had never once left her until her delivery was safely accomplished, and even then he had only absented himself for a day and a half to make an overnight trip to London to deal with some matters of business. That had been during the previous week.

The countess had watched him leave and welcomed him back without any particular disquietude, but something had happened at dinner the night before which had made her wonder about the exact nature of the earl's business in London. During the meal the conversation had turned to the subject of horses and driving. There had been a great deal of good-natured argument about whether it was a greater pleasure to drive oneself in an open carriage or be driven in comfort by a coachman in a closed one. Most of the ladies had taken the latter position, but Mrs. Blackwell had been outspoken in favor of the former, and at one point in the conversation, she had appealed to the earl for support. "*You* must agree with me, Carlton," she had said with a smile. "Why, only last week you were driving your own curricle when we—"

Some movement on the part of the earl had caused her to break off in mid-sentence and glance at the countess at the other end of the table. The countess, by exercising enormous self-control, had forced herself to go on eating her ragout as though she had not heard, but she had seen the quick, guilty look which the earl had cast in her direction. His next words, spoken to Mrs. Blackwell, she could not hear, but the lady's reply had been quite audible. "Of course, my dear . . . how maladroit of me." The countess had gone on eating her ragout, but it might have been dust and ashes for all she tasted of it. Her head was buzzing with the most unpleasant conjectures.

Those same unpleasant conjectures had accompanied her when she retired to her room later that same evening and had kept her company during the sleepless night that had followed. Even the next morning, as she had sat drinking tea and nibbling toast in her boudoir, she had found herself unable to forget that suggestive exchange between her husband and Mrs. Blackwell. She had just resolved, for the twentieth time, to put the matter out of her head for the time being, and was pouring herself a second cup of tea, when a knock on the door nearly surprised her into dropping both cup and pot. Her dressing woman went to the door to admit the visitor, who proved to be the earl. He was wearing a dressing gown of dark blue silk over fawn-colored trousers and Hessian boots, with his dark hair swept back in the fashionable Titus cut. He seemed rather ill at ease as he came into the room, but a smile appeared on his face when he saw the countess at her breakfast table. He looked so very handsome, and so much as he had looked on certain other mornings during the earlier, happier days of their marriage, that she had found herself smiling back at him and offering him a cup of tea. He had accepted with a word of thanks and sat down across from her at the table. The countess had settled back in her own chair to watch him drink it and to reflect with satisfaction that she had chosen to wear that morning a new and particularly pretty lingerie cap trimmed with lace and blue ribbons. She had been so happy to have him visit her once more, even if it was only for tea, that for a time she had forgotten her suspicions.

But as they sat drinking together in companionable silence, the sound of laughter and the pounding of horses' hooves came drifting through the open window. The countess looked out and saw a party of guests on horseback passing by on the lawn below, on their way back to the stables after an early morning ride. Chief among the party was Mrs. Blackwell, clad in a smart black riding hat and crimson habit. She was riding by the side of Lord Raybourne, a longtime friend of the earl's who was also at Rosehill to attend the christening festivities. At the moment, he and Mrs. Blackwell appeared to be in the midst of a race; side by side they galloped their horses across the lawn, urged on by cheers from the others of their party.

Mrs. Blackwell was slightly in the lead, and as she passed beneath the countess's window, she looked back at Lord Raybourne and laughed exultantly. The sound grated unpleasantly upon the countess's ears. It reminded her of the words she had overheard at dinner the night before and of her suspicions about the earl and Mrs. Blackwell. Once her thoughts were turned in this direction, she found it impossible to think of anything else until at last, in desperation, she put thought aside altogether and began to talk, speaking a little too quickly and a little too brightly in an effort to distract herself from the same obsessive subject.

"Well, and today is St. Damien's christening day," she said. "It's difficult to believe he's already six weeks old, isn't it? And yet, in some ways this has seemed the longest six weeks of my life."

The earl took a sip of tea before answering. "Yes," he said, "it has been a long six weeks." He looked as if he might have said more, but the countess had already hurried on.

"Your mother insists that he wear your old christening dress, Carlton," she said, "and she gave me a receipt last night for a traditional drink—a christening caudle—that she wants us to serve at the fête this afternoon. It seems that every St. Damien for the past two or three centuries has had this same caudle served at his or her christening. I got the distinct impression from your mother that the sacrament wouldn't be effective without it!"

The earl smiled a little ruefully. "My mother does tend to put a high value on tradition," he said. "Sometimes an excessively high value. I know she can be difficult at times, Beth. If there's something you would rather do differently, just tell me—I'll have a word with her and try to make her see reason."

"Oh, I don't think that will be necessary, Carlton," the countess assured him. "I don't mind if St. Damien wears your old christening dress—in fact, I agree with your mother that it is a very nice tradition. And I don't suppose the caudle will be any difficulty either, though you never know with Henri. I haven't mentioned it to him yet, but I must speak with him later this morning to arrange the details about the fête. I can give him the receipt then."

Unasked, the countess went on to tell her husband a great deal more about the christening, the fête, and her plans for the day, talking so fast and so fluently that he had no time to put in more than a word on any given subject before she had moved on to another. Such loquacity was not usual with her; already the earl was looking at her quizzically, and she despised herself for the weakness that kept her chattering on and on about trivial domestic affairs rather than speaking frankly about what was really troubling her. She was tolerably sure that the earl would tell her the truth, if asked, but a fear that it might be a truth she did not want to hear kept her chattering on about strawberries and champagne punch.

"I had planned to serve tea in the belvedere," she told him, "but your mother thinks I ought to put the orchestra in the belvedere and serve tea on the terrace, so that we can move into the house if it should start to rain. She says alfresco meals are never satisfactory . . . and of course, if it *should* rain, the terrace would certainly be the better plan. But it doesn't look the least bit rainy right now, and the belvedere would be such a nice central location for the refreshment tables. What do you think, Carlton?"

The earl had just finished pouring himself another cup of tea. He gave the countess a look, half-impatient, half-amused, as he stirred sugar into his cup. "My dear, I don't care," he said. "If you really want my opinion, I would advise you to settle it as you like and not fret yourself about all these details."

The countess had not expected the earl to take an overwhelming interest in the location of the refreshment table. Her question had been more or less a rhetorical one; what she had really been seeking was reassurance at a deeper level, and his casual recommendation to "settle it as you like" was like a slap in the face. She had been on edge ever since the party on horseback had passed beneath her window, and now her overstretched nerves seemed suddenly to snap. "No, I know you don't care," she shot back. "Not about me—not about the fête—it's all a matter of indifference to you, and I ought not to have bothered you with my worries, I know. A mistake on my part, but you needn't fear I'll do it again, Carlton. You've made your feelings very clear."

The earl looked at her in amazement, his teacup halfway to his lips. The countess looked back defiantly, but already she was regretting her words; there was a sickish feeling in the pit of her stomach as she waited to hear what he would say in reply. As it happened, he said nothing at all. He merely set down his cup with quiet force, got up from the table, and left the room without vouchsafing a single comment. The countess, watching the door swing shut behind him, felt dismally certain he would not approach her again for at least another six weeks.

After spending several minutes vainly trying to assure herself that the whole incident had been the earl's fault, not hers, and that she was quite within her rights to snarl like a fishwife when he persisted in behaving with such provoking indifference, she, too, had left the table and gone to her dressing room. Her dressing woman was waiting there, and the countess had more time to brood on the same subject as the dresser fastened her dress and arranged her hair. As soon as her toilette was complete, she had gone upstairs to seek solace in the nursery with her infant son.

And solace she had found there, though not exactly of the kind she had been seeking. The viscount's company at present was more demanding than sympathetic, but it had at least the advantage of keeping her too busy to dwell on her private woes. She walked up and down the nursery, patting him on the back and addressing him in a confidential manner. "Today is your christening day, St. Damien," she told him, pausing in front of the chimney glass to let him inspect his own solemn reflection. "We will take you to the church this afternoon for the ceremony, and then have a lovely party here at home afterwards. I do hope you will be on your best behavior and show all our guests what a splendid, well-mannered baby you really are."

"Ah, but it's good luck for babes to cry at their christening," said the nurse from the recesses of the clothespress, where she was getting out fresh baby linen. "I've known mothers who gave them a pinch as they brought them up to the font, just to be on the safe side."

"Oh? Well, that's different, then. Feel free to cry all you like, St. Damien," said the countess. Seeing that the nurse had his clothing laid out and was waiting to dress him, she carried him over to the table and watched the nurse powder him, diaper him, and dress him in clean clothes. He objected strongly against these proceedings, but settled down into relative calm as soon as they were over. "Has Lady Carlton sent the christening dress over from thc Dowcr House?" asked the countess, leaning down to tickle one bootied foot. "She told me last night she would see you got it sometime this morning."

"Aye, her ladyship brought it over herself an hour or so ago," said the nurse. "It's over in the press, fresh-ironed and ready to put on."

"The ceremony is at two o'clock. That means we must leave here by half-past one at the latest," said the countess, laying a heavy stress on these last words. Hester Smithson was a thoroughly dependable nurse, but as a woman she had a definite failing in the area of punctuality, and the countess hoped a gentle reminder now might avert trouble later on. "I think it would be best if you started dressing him at one o'clock, Hester. That would allow plenty of time, just in case something should go amiss, you know."

"Aye, I'll do that, my lady," said the nurse cheerfully. "He and I'll both be ready at half-past one, never you fear."

"That's that, then," said the countess. She leaned down to kiss her son's brow and remained leaning over him as she spoke. "I must take leave of you now, my love," she said. "This will be a busy morning for me. I'm afraid I shan't have time to do more than look in on you between now and this afternoon." The baby gazed up at her with furrowed brow as though trying to make sense of her words, and the countess laughed. "He doesn't look as though he approves, does he, Hester? I'm sorry, St. Damien. It's very remiss of me, but I'll try to make it up to you later, after our guests are gone." She kissed him again, once on the forehead and once on the tip of his nose, and then left the nursery insensibly cheered by this one-sided interview.

The countess's morning proved even more hectic than she had anticipated. When she came downstairs, she found the ground floor in a state of uproar, with maids and footmen, valets and waiting women rushing to and from, and her appearance was greeted by a barrage of questions from several different people who all seemed intent on talking to her at the same time. Patiently she assured them that she would attend to them all as soon as she could and made her way to the small parlor where she dealt with household business. As soon as she was seated within the parlor, she admitted her petitioners one by one and heard them out in an orderly fashion.

First came the head gardener with questions about the floral decorations for the fête. He was an elderly man, slightly deaf, whose service at Rosehill dated from the days of the dowager countess, and his loyalties clearly remained with his former mistress; the present countess had considerable difficulty countermanding her mother-in-law's orders that the terrace be readied to accommodate the refreshment tables. "No, the refreshments will be served in the belvedere," she told him in a raised voice. "In the *belvedere*. It will need to be swept, if it isn't already, and the tables brought in. For decorations I had thought to have garlands festooning the roof and pillars—white flowers, you know, and lots of greenery. And we will also need flowers to decorate the tables." The gardener departed, acquiescent but grumbling, and was succeeded by an important-faced kitchenmaid who announced in a voice of doom that the cream had turned and what was Monsoor expected to do about the chantilly? The countess directed that a footman be dispatched to the nearest farmhouse to beg or borrow cream at any cost. "And if they haven't any to spare, Henri will simply have to omit the chantilly; there's no help for it."

A little later the same maid reappeared and announced that cream had been obtained, but that the chef had caught the kitchen boy in the act of dipping a none-too-clean finger in the lobster salad. "Monsoor was that angry, my lady," said the maid with relish. "Threw a saucepan at Tommy and called him all sorts of terrible names in French. And Monsoor wants to know if we're to serve the lobster anyway?" The countess passed a hand over her brow and said that, assuming the contaminated portion was removed, she saw no reason why the remainder might not appear at the fête.

A few minutes after the kitchenmaid had departed, the countess's housekeeper burst into the parlor. She was a large, mild-looking woman in her middle years, with a temper as mild as her appearance, but it was evident this morning that she was laboring under an unusual agitation. Her cheeks were bright red, and she was breathing so hard that it was several minutes before she could make herself understood; when she was able to speak at last, it was to inform the countess that she was resigning her position of housekeeper as of that minute. "No decent woman ought to have to endure such abuse as I have endured this morning from that—that *madman* in the kitchen," said the housekeeper in a trembling voice. "Why, he nearly killed poor little Tommy for putting a finger in the salad. And when I tried to intercede for the boy, I was called such dreadful names—at least they were in French, but I know quite well they were dreadful—in short, my lady, I don't have to endure such abuse, and I'm very sorry if it's putting you out to quit you at such short notice, but I will not be treated in such a way and by a *foreigner*."

With sinking heart, the countess flagged down a passing housemaid and sent her off for a pot of tea. She then begged the indignant housekeeper to sit down and, by plying her with cups of tea and soothing words, was able by degrees first to calm her and eventually to convince her to stay on in her service, with the understanding that she herself would speak to Henri and extort an apology from him if possible.

No sooner had the housekeeper curtsied herself off than Henri himself appeared. He was a small man with a short, square-cut black beard and a pair of bright black eyes which served as a sort of barometer of his mood; the countess observed with trepidation that on this occasion they were snapping with barely repressed fury. She had a very good idea of how the ensuing interview was likely to go when Henri commenced it by pulling off his white cap and stamping on it with both feet.

"C'est affreux! Les imbéciles—ils me rendent fou," charged Henri, clutching his head in his hands and rolling his eyes in a way that lent credibility to this last statement. *"Impossible, impossible.* I can do nothing with such *imbéciles* to assist."

The countess took a deep breath and steeled herself for the

ordeal ahead of her, which she foresaw as a lengthy one. With many sympathetic murmurs and words of encouragement, she managed at last to get Henri calmed down enough to speak English, so that he might tell her in greater detail where exactly the impossibility lay. Henri replied that, in addition to the kitchen boy's delinquencies and the incredible stupidity of the kitchenmaids deputed to assist him (fit only to peel *les pommes de terre*), he was experiencing great difficulty with *les bonbons,* owing to *la humidité* of the wretched English climate.

He went on to say that he very much feared that the quantity of champagne ordered for the fête would prove insufficient and hinted darkly at private depredations on the part of his rival, the butler, to explain this lamentable state of affairs. The countess disregarded his accusations against the butler, a staunch Methodist of rigidly abstemious habits, but to the rest of his plaint she gave full and sympathetic attention.

When at last Henri had come to the end of his list of grievances and was beginning to repeat himself, she judged it time to step in. The best method of dealing with Henri was not to make light of his difficulties, as she had learnt through bitter experience; instead, she shook her head and looked very grave.

"Indeed, it does sound an impossible situation, Henri," she said. "I don't wonder you're upset. Whatever shall we do? I suppose the fête will have to be put off until another day . . ."

It was unnecessary to say any more. Henri, balked of opposition in one direction, promptly swung round to the other and set out to prove to the countess that the situation was not impossible at all. The difficulties that had been so insurmountable a moment before became, as he assured her, mere trifles: annoying, *sans doute,* but nothing to seriously tax the abilities of a genius like himself. "To put off the fête for *le petit vicomte*—no, no, madame, it is not to be thought of," he told the countess earnestly. "I will look upon it as a challenge to my abilities and contrive something, you will see. And truly, the challenge will not be so very great. For the dinner, you comprehend, it would be a different matter, but for a mere tea—bah! *Cette petite affaire* will arrange itself very well."

The countess expressed herself suitably grateful. Henri smiled modestly, laid a hand on his heart, and made her a very long speech in which he mingled much self-praise with a pious resolve to overlook, for her sake, the foibles of his intellectual inferiors. The countess thought this an appropriate moment to make mention of his treatment of the housekeeper. Henri assured her that he had not used the housekeeper with undue severity, given the provocation, but readily agreed to apologize, saying that, apart from a tendency to meddle in affairs not her own, she was a *bonne femme* whom he would be sorry to think he had seriously offended. He had by this time talked himself into such a mellow mood that the countess decided to push her luck a little further and present him with the receipt for the dowager's christening caudle.

"Qu'est-ce que c'est?" demanded Henri, looking at it suspiciously.

"It's a receipt for a caudle—a drink that is traditionally served at christenings," said the countess, affecting an ease she did not feel. "Lady Carlton—the Dowager Lady Carlton—wishes that it be served to the guests along with the other refreshments."

Henri ran a practiced eye over the receipt. "Eggs. Milk. Sugar," he read, enunciating each word with great clarity. "Sherry. Mace. Nutmeg. But this—is not this the receipt for *le lait de poule*—the eggnog?"

"It is very like eggnog, I should think. But this particular drink is called caudle, and I understand it is quite traditional at christenings."

"But *le lait de poule*—the eggnog—madame, it is *June.*"

"Yes, I know, Henri, and I don't imagine many people will care to drink it in such warm weather. But it would please Lady Carlton very much—and Lord Carlton and I, too—if you would make it for the fête this afternoon."

Henri continued to scowl down at the receipt. His mood clearly hung in the balance, and the countess held her breath, fearing a return to his former rage. His good humor held, however; after a minute he shrugged his shoulders and gave her an indulgent smile. "Ah, *les Anglais,*" he said. "With you English, I comprehend well that the tradition is everything. Yes, madame, I will make you your *lait de poule*—though for me, I should prefer *le champagne.*" Once more Henri looked down at the receipt, and a spark of interest began to glow in his dark eyes. "And it may be that I can improve it, so that it is not so very *mal à propos,*" he said. "With a *soupçon* of lemon, perhaps, to cut the richness—"

"Oh, no," said the countess in distress. "Lady Carlton says that the receipt must be followed exactly, Henri."

"Bah! What does that one know of cooking? *Un soupçon* of lemon, I say, and a small adjustment in the spices would much improve it."

"Truly, Henri, I think you had better follow the receipt. Lady Carlton says—"

The Dowager Lady Carlton's injunctions were brushed impatiently aside. "Madame, trust me," commanded Henri. "I know what I am about. *Madame la vieille comtesse*—she will adore it."

All the countess's expostulations were in vain; Henri merely smiled, scooped up his cap from the floor, and bade her a cheerful *bonjour,* assuring her as he went out that he would set to work immediately concocting a new and supremely delicious caudle which would ravish the tastebuds of all who sampled it. The countess put her hands to her throbbing temples and wondered if it were too late in the day to claim indisposition and take to her bed.

Fortunately, even the worst morning must draw to an end at last. By early afternoon the countess's domestic difficulties had been largely ironed out, and the preparations for the fête were either complete or in a fair way to becoming so. She made a last-minute inspection of the belvedere and garden to verify that the gardeners were following her own instructions rather than those of her mother-in-law, and then went upstairs to change her dress.

For the christening ceremony and the party afterwards, she had chosen a blue-flowered muslin to be worn with blue kid slippers and an artlessly elegant straw cottage bonnet ornamented with cornflowers and blue ribbons. The dress was a new one and had been ordered in a great hurry only a few days ago when the countess had suddenly realized, in the midst of her other preparations, that she had nothing suitable to wear.

An urgent express had been dispatched to the London dressmaker whom she had patronized in the past; the dressmaker had responded nobly, and the bandbox containing the finished dress had arrived at Rosehill on the previous afternoon. The countess had been busy with other things when it arrived and had not thought it necessary to try it on, feeling confident that Madame Paquet had fulfilled the commission with her usual éclat. But such, unfortunately, proved not to be the case. Possibly the dress had been cut to the wrong measurements, or possibly (and much more likely) the countess's measurements had changed since they had last been taken; when tried on, the dress was found to be uncomfortably snug. "I must still be a few pounds above what I was before," said the countess, surveying her reflection with chagrin.

Her dresser nodded in gloomy concurrence. "Yes, I wouldn't be surprised, my lady," she said. "Do you want me to put out the green instead? It's not so à la mode as this, but since it ties rather than buttons, there shouldn't be a problem with the fit."

The countess thought of the beautiful Mrs. Blackwell and resolved to be à la mode if it killed her. "No, I'll wear this," she said. "It's pretty, even if it's not very comfortable. And do my hair in curls, Potter, if you please. I wish I had thought to have it put in papers for this afternoon, but there wasn't time, of course."

After the dresser had arranged the countess's hair and tied her bonnet under her chin in a crisp bow, the countess again surveyed herself in the glass. The hectic morning just past had tinged her cheeks with color, so that she looked not quite so wan, and the blue silk lining of her bonnet set off her fair hair and made her eyes appear a deeper, brighter blue. There was really no fault to be found with her appearance except for her expression, which was noticeably strained—almost as tight as her dress. The countess turned away from the mirror with a sigh.

Gathering up her gloves, reticule, and parasol, she stepped into the hall, just as an ear-splitting shriek broke forth from the floor above. The countess rushed upstairs to the nursery and found, to her dismay, that the nurse was only now engaged in wrestling the red-faced viscount into his christening robes. Her reminders about the need for punctuality had clearly been wasted breath; the clock already stood at half-past one, the hour when the party should have been departing for the church. Beside the nurse stood the wet nurse, clicking her tongue and waving a rattle over the viscount's head in an effort to distract him from his fury; the dowager stood at her other hand, dispensing unwanted advice and generally making matters worse. "Here, woman, you've gone and tied his bonnet too tight," she said as the nurse fumbled with the bonnet's satin ribbon ties. "No, no, not like that—step aside now and let me attend to it."

Elbowing the nurse aside, the dowager took charge of the bonnet and tenderly tied it over the head of the howling baby, who continued to howl with unabated fury even after it had been adjusted to her satisfaction. She picked him up in an effort to soothe him, and his howls promptly redoubled. "Poor angel . . . I daresay there's a nasty pin sticking you somewhere," she said, pretending to address the baby but directing an accusing look at the nurse.

"Indeed there is not, my lady," said the nurse indignantly. But the dowager was already undressing her grandson and could not be content until dress, petticoat, and diaper had all been removed and a search had been made for the nonexistent pin. This took a considerable time, and when it was done, it was of course necessary to dress the unhappy viscount all over again in his festive garments; his screams had reached a fever pitch by the time the last button was buttoned.

"Come, come, my angel," crooned the dowager, attempting to cuddle the outraged baby, who lay stiff in her arms shrieking like a siren. "There, there, my sweet. You can tell he's more comfortable now," she told the countess confidentially. "Poor little babe, you're much happier without that nasty pin, aren't you?"

To the countess's ears the baby's screams sounded as loud as ever, but the dowager said firmly that he was quieting, adding that it was only want of proper management that produced these little fits of temper in an otherwise exemplary child. The countess returned no answer and followed her mother-in-law out of the nursery in the wake of her son's howls.

When the nursery party reached the bottom of the stairs, they found the earl waiting for them with watch in hand. He did not reproach them for their tardiness—the viscount's screams echoing inside the marble-lined hall made speech impossible in any case—but it was clear he was unhappy about it. Without speaking he led them outside to the waiting carriage and handed them in one by one.

The dowager entered first and made a great to-do settling herself and the viscount on the rear seat. The countess should have entered next, but she hung back and let the nurse go on before her. As the earl helped Mrs. Smithson mount the carriage steps, she scrutinized his face, wondering if he were still angry about their disagreement at breakfast. In her heart of hearts, she felt he would be quite justified if he was, for she was by now very ashamed of her behavior on that occasion. Even if the earl had been in the wrong, that was no excuse for expressing herself so vehemently—and looking back, the countess was no longer quite so sure that he *had* been in the wrong. She had, in short, made up her mind to apologize if a suitable opportunity arose; and it was in hopes of gaining such an opportunity that she had waited till last to enter the carriage.

As soon as the nurse was settled, the earl stepped down from the carriage and came over to the countess. Here was the opportunity she had been waiting for, but when it came to the point, her courage failed her, for there was so much noise all around them that she would have had to shout to be heard. The viscount was still crying loudly inside the carriage, provoking comment in some form or other from nearly all of the guests who were gathered under the portico awaiting their own carriages. In the case of the ones with children, this comment invariably took the form of anecdotes beginning, "When *my* child was christened . . ." The comments of the childless ones were more variable, but generally agreed in finding the whole situation extremely funny.

The earl was looking harassed as he took the countess's arm and led her toward the carriage. His movements were hurried, yet she observed that he looked down at her once or twice as though wanting to say something, and when they reached the carriage, he hesitated perceptibly before handing her in. His hesitation happened to coincide with a lull in the viscount's crying. Encouraged by this momentary calm and by the signs of relenting which she observed in the earl's manner, the countess was just plucking up her courage to speak when a couple of guests detached themselves from the group under the portico and came over to where she and the earl stood. One was Lord Raybourne, the gentleman who had been racing Mrs. Blackwell that morning, and the other was Mrs. Blackwell herself.

"That son of yours has a good set of lungs on him, Carlton," said Lord Raybourne, slapping the earl genially on the back. "Downright deafening at close range, ain't it? I say, old fellow, if I was you, I'd let the infantry go on ahead and follow after with Susan and me. We was just saying that you looked as though you could use a spot of peace and quiet—and even Susan's babbling would seem like peace and quiet compared to that din." He grinned provocatively at Mrs. Blackwell, who made a face at him and turned to the earl.

"Yes, Carlton, you are very welcome to come with us," she said. She was wearing a rose-colored gauze dress with a wide Gypsy hat tied over her dark ringlets, and the countess felt a pang of jealousy to see how bewitchingly beautiful she looked. "Don't pay any attention to what Raybourne says about my babbling," Mrs. Blackwell continued with a smile that included the countess as well as the earl and Lord Raybourne. "I'm not half so much a babbler as he is. And I will be too busy to babble in any case—I'm driving my new grays today, and they are a handful." She looked with pride toward the end of the carriage sweep, where a groom was struggling to restrain a team of high-bred grays. "If Lady Carlton can spare you, Carlton, then by all means come along with Raybourne and me, and watch me put them through their paces. I'll do my best not to overset us on the way—and I can practically guarantee getting you to the church on time!"

The earl looked at Mrs. Blackwell, then at the countess with an air of indecision. The countess stared back at him stonily. The sight of him with Mrs. Blackwell had wholly dispelled her penitent mood, and she would have sooner cut out her tongue than apologize to him now. It was just as she had supposed: he obviously preferred Mrs. Blackwell's company to her own, and the only reason he was hesitating to go with her now was out of consideration for appearances. Very well, the countess told herself angrily, very well; if it was permission he was wanting, he would get it, and with interest. She would show him he was not the only one who could deal out rejection.

"Yes, Carlton, you go on with Mrs. Blackwell," she said in a voice cold as ice. "If she can get you to the church by two o'clock, you can at least explain to the Vicar why the rest of us are late."

The earl looked at her a moment, nodded unsmilingly, and turned away. Taking Mrs. Blackwell's arm, he began to walk toward the phaeton-and-four at the end of the drive. Lord Raybourne took Mrs. Blackwell's other arm and fell in beside them. The countess watched them walk away, then got into the carriage and settled down to enjoy as best she could her rather hollow victory.

The countess had strolled out on the lawn to say goodbye to a party of departing guests. They were a trio of maiden ladies whose home lay some distance from Rosehill, and all three of them assured her that only their elderly coachman's dislike of driving after dark could have forced them to leave such a charming party at such a ridiculously early hour. The countess thanked them, wished them a safe trip home, and watched them walk away with a smile of satisfaction on her face. All the bustle of preparation was over; the fête had been in progress for several hours now, and rather to her own surprise, everything seemed to be going very smoothly.

The christening at the parish church had not been an unqualified success, but the countess felt it might have been much worse, given her own mood and the mood of the chief participant. The viscount had cried more or less continuously during the ceremony and had objected most strenuously to the proceedings at the baptismal font, but as soon as they were over, his howls had subsided, and he had ended by falling asleep in the dowager's arms on the drive home.

There had been another tense moment at the beginning of the fête, when the guests had gathered about to toast the newly christened viscount. The countess had watched apprehensively as her mother-in-law had lifted a cup of caudle to her lips and taken a cautious sip. A look of surprise had appeared upon her face; she had taken another, longer drink and nodded approval.

"Very good," she told the countess, "even better than I remembered. I daresay it's your living in the country that accounts for it. Both Carlton and his sister were christened in Town, and it stands to reason the milk and eggs wouldn't have been so fresh as they are here. Nothing like the country for fresh milk and eggs." The dowager took another drink and smacked her lips appreciatively. "You ought to try it, Elizabeth," she said. "That On-ree of yours makes a decent cup of caudle, even if he can't do a thing with an honest boiled joint of mutton."

With her worries about her mother-in-law out of the way, the countess had been able to concentrate on making the fête a success, and as she looked about her now, she thought contentedly that its success could no longer be in doubt. Everywhere she looked she saw happy guests talking and laughing, eating and drinking, and enjoying the beauty of their surroundings. Despite the dowager's fears, the day had turned out warm and sunny, with only a light breeze off the river to keep the warmth from becoming sultry. There could not have been more perfect weather for an alfresco party, and the setting was as perfect as the weather.

Rosehill was not the earl's principal residence, but it was undoubtably his most beautiful, a square Palladian villa of white stone set high on a hill, surrounded by green lawns sloping down to the banks of a lazily flowing river. The roses that gave the house its name had not yet come into full flower, but the laburnums were in bloom, as were the syringas and lilacs. A dense hedge of them ran down one side of the lawn, screening the orchestra from view, and the lilacs' subtle perfume mingled with the music of oboes and horns, clarinets and bassoons, to fill the air with a mixture of scent and sound delightful to the senses.

There was more to delight the senses inside the belvedere, a square, white, open pavilion situated halfway down the slope of the hill, where liveried footmen were dispensing lobster salad, cakes, ices, and other elegant, insubstantial fare. The gardeners had decorated the belvedere in accordance with the countess's orders, and it made a pretty picture with flowered garlands twined about its columns and draped in lavish festoons from its roof. Guests drifted in and out, or stood in clustered groups nearby, the ladies looking rather like butterflies in pastel summer dresses and flower-trimmed hats. Even the dowager had been inspired to put off her weeds for the day and array herself in a riotous slate-gray lutestring.

From where the countess stood, she could see her mother-in-law's gray-clad figure sitting on a bench in the shade of a giant elm not far away. On the bench beside her was a beribboned basket in which lay the sleeping viscount, and the dowager beamed with pride as she accepted the compliments of a group of guests who had gathered about to admire him. Most of the group were women, and the countess smiled to see her unconscious son with his circle of female worshipers; her smile faded a little, however, as she caught sight of another group a little farther along the lawn. Mrs. Blackwell was seated here, surrounded by her usual court, and among the blue-jacketed figures gathered around her, the countess recognized her own husband. The earl was at the very center of the group, along with Lord Raybourne and several other privileged gentlemen. To judge from Lord Raybourne's gestures and the earl's smiling nod of collaboration, the subject under discussion was once again Mrs. Blackwell's epic drive to the parish church. It was a subject that had already been much discussed at the fête that afternoon. The countess had had to listen several times to the history of her rival's triumphs; she had even been forced, out of politeness, to add her congratulations to those of the others, but her thoughts had been very bitter. They were bitter now as she watched the earl laughing and talking with Mrs. Blackwell and Lord Raybourne beneath the trees. Instead of rejoining her guests on the lawn, the countess unfurled her parasol, placed it over her shoulder, and began to walk down the graveled path that led to the river.

Before she had gone far, she was hailed by a gentleman who had just emerged from the belvedere. "Hullo, Beth," he called, strolling across the lawn to join her.

"Hello, Will," said the countess, and stood still until he had reached her side. She recognized him as Sir William Walcott, a cousin of the earl's and a well-known character in London society. Among fashion's devotees there was none more slavishly devoted than Sir William: his dress was a point of pride with him, and he made it the study of his life to be always turned out in the very latest style, however extreme that style might be.

The first time the countess had met him, she had taken one wondering look and written him off as a dandified rattle with small taste and less wit. That had been several years ago, however, and since coming to know him better, she had found herself gradually revising her first, unfavorable opinion. Sir William might be something of a sartorial peacock, but a kind heart beat beneath his bright-hued waistcoats, and his intellect was nowhere near as negligible as his rather rattling manner made it appear. As the countess's acquaintance with him had grown, she had learned to respect the native shrewdness that underlay some of his seemingly aimless remarks. He was besides, an amusing companion with a ready store of *on-dits* at his tongue's end, and she was not sorry to find herself in his company, even in her present unsociable mood.

"You look dashed pretty, Beth," said Sir William, who had meanwhile been looking her over approvingly. "Pretty as a flower. A regular spring beauty, by Jove."

"Thank you, Will," said the countess. "You're looking very—er—springlike yourself." She could scarcely keep her countenance as she spoke, for Sir William had chosen that day to array himself in garments that were unconventional, to say the least. His topcoat was fashioned of bright grass green kerseymere and featured long tails, an exaggerated peak at each shoulder, and an exaggerated point at each lapel; with it he wore a pair of very full Cossack trousers, striped in two tints of yellow and gathered in snugly at the ankle with rosettes of green and yellow ribbon. His hat, which he was carrying rather than wearing, was as unconventional as his other garments, being a light-colored straw with a small brim and shallow crown: a startling departure, in all respects, from the dark-hued, high-crowned beaver that was the usual gentleman's headwear.

The countess's expression was not lost on Sir William. "You don't like it either," he said mournfully. "Thought it was a pretty neat get-up myself, but I'm dashed if I can find anybody else who thinks so. Carlton's mother told me a minute ago that she liked to see a man with a decent leg show it, instead of swaddling himself in petticoats like a girl. I mean to say, *petticoats!*" Sir William looked down at his voluminous trousers and shook his head sadly. "Terrible woman, my Aunt Carlton. Tried to tell her these Cossacks are all the go back in London, but I might as well have saved my breath. You've got my sympathy, Beth: don't see how you stand it, living in the same house as that woman day in and day out."

"She can be rather difficult sometimes," admitted the countess. "But she resides at the Dower House, you know, so that we do not actually live in the same house. And I think she has been a little easier to get on with since St. Damien was born."

Sir William said he was very glad to hear it, though he himself had noticed no sign of improvement. "But I didn't come over here to talk about my Aunt Carlton," he went on. "I was just getting ready to take a stroll down to the river. Saw you were headed the same way and thought I'd ask you if you'd like to come along with me and feed the ducks." He held out his hat as he spoke, showing the countess its interior filled to the brim with rout biscuits. "Always used to feed the ducks when I was here as a boy," he explained. "Thought as long as I was here I'd like to do it again, for old time's sake. I've got plenty of fodder here for 'em if you'd like to come, too, Beth."

"Thank you, Will, I would like that very much," said the countess. She accepted Sir William's proffered arm, and together they began to walk toward the river.

As they walked, Sir William chattered on in his usual light, inconsequential manner. "You've a nice day for your fête," he said. "Usually rains buckets on these affairs. That, or it's hot as the blazes and no shade in sight. Your Henri's done himself proud with the food, too. Demmed good lobster, demmed good champagne—demmed good everything, in fact. What's that stuff you're serving in the silver bowl—some kind of fancy French milk punch?"

The countess explained about the caudle, laughing as she described the dowager's self-deception. Sir William listened attentively. "Caudle, is it? Never heard of the stuff. But there, I'm a bachelor and wouldn't know these things. Mean to say, might have had it when I was christened myself, but I wouldn't be likely to remember that, of course. Anyway, a dashed good party, Beth. Everybody looks as though they're having a good time."

These words caused the countess's merriment to subside as quickly as it had come. She thanked Sir William politely but thought unhappily of her husband, who was having such a good time flirting with Mrs. Blackwell. Sir William, meanwhile, was rambling on about something else. "Took a look in on St. Damien a few minutes ago," he told the countess. "He's a fine little fellow, Beth—not bad looking at all when he ain't screaming. Looked like an angel or a cherub or a what-d'ye-call-it, there asleep with his thumb in his mouth. Wouldn't know it was the same baby as earlier . . . funny how they can be all nice and quiet one minute, and screaming their heads off the next. Don't seem to be much in between at that age, does there?"

The countess agreed with feeling that there did not. They had reached the river's edge by now, and Sir William led the way around a clump of willows, out onto a small stone pier that extended a way into the river. Laying his hat upon the railing, he took several biscuits from the hat, broke them into pieces, and began tossing the pieces into the water. Half a dozen ducks immediately came paddling over to snap them up. At Sir William's urging, the countess also took a biscuit, but it crumbled away unheeded between her fingers, for she found more diversion in watching her companion's efforts to distribute his largess equably among the feathered mendicants gathered below.

"There you go—no, not you, sir, you've had more than your share already. That's right, old fellow. Plenty for everybody if you'll wait your turn. None of that, now." Sir William looked severely at a pair of ducks who were squabbling noisily over a large piece of biscuit. "You forget yourself, ma'am. Let grandpa, there, have that one, and there'll be another for you, just as good—see now, what did I tell you? There, that's the lot."

Tossing the last bit of biscuit into the water, Sir William picked up his hat again; he carefully brushed it free of crumbs before setting it on his head. "A pretty place, this," he said, looking around him with a pleased expression. "When I used to come here as a boy, I always thought Rosehill was the prettiest place in the world. And the funny thing is, I still think so. Looking at it from here, it looks almost too beautiful to be true, don't it?"

"Yes, it does," said the countess. She leaned against the railing of the pier, looking back at the scene she and Sir William had left behind them. The lower slope of the lawn was hidden from view by the willows surrounding the pier, but she could see the upper lawn with its trees, shrubs, and flower-decked belvedere, and beyond that the house itself. Rosehill was a house always remarkable for its beauty, but it seemed to the countess that it had never appeared more beautiful than it did at that moment, surrounded by the verdure of late spring and set against the background of a deep blue sky. The snowy clouds drifting overhead were no whiter than its white stone walls.

"Yes, Rosehill is very lovely at this time of year," she said aloud. "I can remember how beautiful I thought it when Carlton first brought me here, after we were married." The contrast between her feelings on that long-ago day and the way she was feeling now struck her as eminently depressing; she pushed the thought aside, however, and spoke on with determined cheerfulness. "And now St. Damien will grow up here," she said, "and more than likely take it all for granted! I often think what a lucky baby he is, to grow up in such beautiful surroundings."

"Pretty lucky baby all around, if you ask me," said Sir William soberly. "Lucky to be born to all this, of course, but even luckier to have you and Carlton as parents. I've known Carlton since he wasn't much bigger than St. Damien is now, and I can tell you he's one in a million—in fact, I'm not sure you could find two of his stamp if you was to spend the rest of your life looking. Carlton's a quiet fellow, of course—he don't go running on and on about his feelings, like some I could name, but when he talks about you, Beth, or about the baby, there—well, you can tell how much he thinks of you both. And it's not just the way he talks—you can tell from the way he acts, too, which is more than you can say about some of these fellows that go around spouting love poetry every time they open their mouths. A very decent fellow, Carlton—really decent, I mean, and that's a pretty rare thing nowadays. Not to say you ain't decent yourself, Beth. You're all of that and more—Carlton's demmed lucky to have you. It's a terrible thing, the way some of these young married women go on." Here Sir William paused to sigh and shake his head, with the air of a dowager deploring the manners of the present generation.

"You mayn't believe me, Beth, but upon my word, it's getting so you can't so much as pay a lady a compliment without her taking it into her head you're trying to set up a flirtation with her. I tell you, a fellow has to watch his step these days, and that's a fact."

The countess nodded, but her thoughts were on something other than Sir William's words. Her attention had been caught by the earlier part of his speech, in which he had praised the earl's virtues as husband and father. She could not doubt that Sir William believed what he said; he had spoken with obvious sincerity, and his long acquaintance with the earl gave his testimony a weight that was difficult to discount. At the same time, the countess could not forget the words she had overheard at dinner the night before. She glanced at Sir William's profile, wondering if she dared take him into her confidence about her suspicions. In the end she did not quite dare, but she thought she might achieve the same object, in a more roundabout way, by bringing Mrs. Blackwell's name into the conversation and seeing how he reacted to it.

His remarks about young society women gave her a good opening, and she smiled at him as she spoke, keeping her tone light. "I think with most young married women it is a case of the attention going to their heads," she said. "A great many men who would never go near an unmarried girl think nothing of flirting with a married one. Just look at Mrs. Blackwell: I never saw an unmarried girl with half as many admirers as she has—although, being a widow, I suppose she falls into a slightly different category. Do you consider widows more or less dangerous than matrons, Will?"

Sir William looked surprised. "Susan Blackwell? No, I wouldn't consider her dangerous at all," he said. "A demmed nice woman, in fact, though there's no denying she's a bit of a dasher. I daresay you're thinking about her racketing around with Raybourne and that set, but I don't think there's any harm in that. Pretty understandable, really, considering the circumstances. But maybe you don't know much about her circumstances—you and she were never what you could call close, were you, Beth?"

"No," said the countess, "we are acquaintances, no more. I rather think Carlton knows her better than I do."

"A pretty sad story, really. She was married to old Blackwell out of the schoolroom—sold off, rather, I *should* say, for that's what it amounts to. Blackwell was sixty if he was a day, but there were mortgages and gaming debts and two or three younger girls to provide for . . . in short, Blackwell was willing to come down handsomely, and that was all that mattered.

"I hear she fought the match pretty hard, but once it was a done thing, she kept her part of the bargain all right. There was never a whisper about her all the time she and Blackwell were married. And when he died a couple of years back, she kept her mourning for him the same as if she'd been really fond of him, which couldn't hardly have been the case. Just here lately she's been running a bit wild, it's true, but I think that's natural under the circumstances. Her mourning's over, and she's got her freedom and a dab of money—and probably, too, there's a little of what you was talking about, Beth. The beaux have been flocking around her pretty thick, and it wouldn't be surprising if it's turned her head a bit. But I'd say she's pretty sound at bottom for all that."

Sir William's voice was matter-of-fact, but the countess felt as though she had been reprimanded. "I see," she said. "I didn't know, Will. That *is* a sad story . . . poor Mrs. Blackwell. I think it is perfectly barbaric that a young girl could be forced into a marriage of convenience like that."

"Aye, so it is," said Sir William. "But I must say, I've seen one or two marriages of convenience that turned out a deal better than most of your so-called love matches. I guess when you get right down to it, there ain't many marriages of any sort that you could really call ideal. Living in London's enough to make a person pretty cynical on the subject of matrimony. But then, when I come down here and visit you and Carlton, I start thinking there might be something in the business, after all."

There was a large lump in the countess's throat, which prevented her from making any immediate reply. "Thank you, Will," she said at last. "That is a high compliment indeed. I only wish you may not be overstating the case."

"It's no more than the truth, Beth. You'll laugh when I tell you, but there are times I think I wouldn't mind taking the plunge myself, if I could be sure it will turn out half as well for me as it has for you two."

Sir William's naiveté made the countess smile, yet there was something very moving about his simple faith in the integrity of her marriage. Almost in spite of herself, she began to take a more hopeful view of the situation than had been the case an hour before. Perhaps the earl's interest in Mrs. Blackwell did not go beyond flirtation—or if it did, perhaps matters had not yet gone so far that they could not be retrieved through some effort on her own part.

She winced as she recalled how she had snapped at him that

morning, then snubbed him that afternoon when they had been getting ready to drive to the church. Almost she felt he might be excused for preferring Mrs. Blackwell's company to her own, but she resolved that in the future he should have no such excuse: from this day forward her conduct would be irreproachable. And she would begin now, this very afternoon, by seeking out the earl and apologizing for her misconduct with a humility that would win his heart—or rewin it, rather, from the allurements of Mrs. Blackwell. Having taken this resolution, the countess found her mood was very much lighter; she laid a hand on Sir William's arm and spoke with affectionate gaiety. "Indeed I will not laugh, Will," she said. "I have often thought you would make some lady a very good husband if ever you chose to marry. Only it would have to be the *right* lady—you must take your time and choose carefully, Will. I don't think there are many ladies around who would be good enough for you."

Sir William looked both pleased and embarrassed. "Oh, I don't know about that," he said. "I suppose I'm no better or worse than most fellows. But if I ever do decide to take the plunge, I know what kind of lady I'll look for—mean to say, I've got a dashed good example right in front of me." A gallant bow accompanied these words, and the countess laughed, but allowed Sir William to take her hand and carry it to his lips.

And at that moment, the earl came around the clump of willows at the end of the pier.

The countess was seething with resentment as she and the earl walked across the lawn toward the house. She felt it typical of the way things had gone that day, that he should have arrived at the river's edge just in time to witness Sir William's impulsive expression of gallantry. It had all been a piece of the most disastrous ill timing, and equally disastrous had been her own behavior at the critical moment.

Instead of greeting her husband calmly, with the assurance of a clear conscience, she had started guiltily and snatched her hand away with a haste that must have confirmed his worst suspicions.

And suspicions he plainly had, though he had concealed them fairly well in front of his cousin. The countess did not think Sir William had noticed anything amiss in the few minutes they had all been together. The earl's manner had been reserved, but not excessively so, and she herself would have made little of his reserve if she had not had fixed in her memory a clear picture of his face in that first, unguarded moment when he had come round the willows to see Sir William kissing her hand.

After exchanging a few civilities with his host and hostess, Sir William had excused himself and strolled off to rejoin the party. The earl had stood watching him until he was absorbed into the group around the belvedere, then had taken the countess by the arm and followed after. He had not said one word to her, either then or later in the afternoon, when the fête was drawing to a close and they stood side by side to bid farewell to their parting guests.

Even now, with evening falling and the festivities quite over, the visiting guests all departed, the houseguests returned to the house to change for dinner, and they themselves bent on the same errand, it was clear he intended to treat her to another dose of the same chilly silence. The countess's heart swelled with indignation. She felt it was very unreasonable of him to take this attitude about an innocent kiss on the hand when he himself was guilty of conduct so much worse. The thought gave fuel to her indignation; and, quite forgetting her good intentions about apology, humility, and so forth, she launched into the attack.

"I would like to know what you meant, Carlton, by behaving as you did down by the river this afternoon," she said coldly. "Poor Will—if he didn't take offense at the way you treated him, it's only because he's too good-natured for his own good. You barely said two words to him—and then, the way you looked at him when you first came onto the pier! You looked ready to murder him, and me, too, only because he was kissing my hand, for heaven's sake. I can assure you there was nothing in it, Carlton. As a matter of fact, he was complimenting me only a moment before on my womanly virtue. It seems some gentlemen nowadays still put a value on that commodity."

If the earl felt the sting in these words, he gave no sign of it. "I don't doubt it was innocent, Beth," he said. "I only thought it rather ill-advised. It takes so little to start gossip—and to neglect your other guests by going off alone with one gentleman has rather an odd appearance, you must admit."

The countess was in no mood to admit anything of the sort. It was on the tip of her tongue to retort that *he* had thought nothing of neglecting *his* other guests to flirt with one fascinating widow, but in the end she decided it would be more dignified to make no response at all. The earl likewise said nothing more, and they entered the house and went upstairs to their separate bedchambers without saying another word to each other.

As soon as the door was shut behind her, the countess gave vent to her temper by yanking the bellrope for her dressing woman and by stripping off her too-tight dress and hurling it into the far corner of the room. This somewhat relieved her feelings, and by the time her dresser arrived, she was calm, at least externally. "You can have it," she told the woman, who had gone over to pick up the crumpled blue-flowered muslin. "I shan't want it again, or the bonnet, either."

"Thank you, my lady," said the dresser, folding away her new acquisition with jealous care.

The countess walked over to her wardrobe and began to flip through the dresses hanging there. In the next room, she could hear drawers opening and shutting, and the earl's voice speaking to some unidentified person, presumably his valet. "No, not that one, dammit," he was saying. "Bring me the blue one—never mind, I'll get it myself."

The countess listened and found consolation for her own bad mood in reflecting that the earl's appeared to be no better. Presently the dresser finished with the flowered muslin and came over to join the countess in front of the wardrobe. "Which were you thinking to wear tonight, my lady?" she said. "The blue sarcenet?"

"No, I'll wear this," said the countess with sudden inspiration. She reached into the wardrobe and took out The Dress.

The Dress was a closed robe of lilac-pink silk, simple in line and sophisticated in cut. It had been made for the countess in the spring of the previous year, before pregnancy had begun to proscribe her wardrobe and social life, but she had never publicly worn it. The one time she had ventured to appear in The Dress, on the evening of a dinner party which she and the earl had been holding in their London house, the earl's reaction had been less than enthusiastic. "Are you going to wear that?" was all he had actually said, but it had been enough to tell the countess that her costume did not please him, and after laughing at his subsequent feeble efforts to convince her to the contrary, she had gone upstairs and changed into something else. "But tonight I really shall wear it," she muttered to herself, stroking the shiny folds of lilac-pink silk. "And if he doesn't like it, so much the better!"

"What's that you say, my lady?" asked the dresser.

"Nothing, Potter. Get out my jewel box, if you please. I'll wear the pearls, I think, and the pearl and diamond eardrops."

While the dresser was busy with this errand, the countess continued to fume about the earl's unjust behavior until she was seized by yet another brilliant inspiration. He had as good as said that by going off alone with Sir William she had been guilty of indiscretion. Why then should she not show him how wrong he had been by giving him a sample of behavior that was *really* indiscreet? "Why not, indeed," said the countess through her teeth, and set at once to making a toilette that would be in keeping with her new character.

The Dress was admirably suited to such a purpose, having already a deep décolletage front and back, but she recklessly decided to make it even lower by the removal of some drapery about the corsage. While her dressing woman was effecting these alterations, the countess prowled about her bedchamber searching for further inspiration. Rouge, heavy perfume, and sheer pink silk stockings she judged to be useful and appropriate adjuncts to her costume, and she might even have gone so far as to damp her petticoat, had she not conceived the still better notion of dispensing with one altogether. Hair tousled *à la méduse* completed the picture; and the countess, surveying herself in the glass, felt satisfied that she looked quite the epitome of feminine indiscretion.

"And I shall flirt with all the gentlemen and drink a great deal of wine and behave just like all those other young married women Will was talking about," she vowed to herself. "It is intolerable that Carlton should criticize my conduct when he has been behaving so much worse himself. It's his fault, every bit of it, and if he doesn't like it, he has no one but himself to blame."

Fortified by this reflection, the countess threw her shawl over her shoulders and headed for the door, but her steps slowed as she neared the threshold. It still lacked fifteen minutes of the dinner hour, which was rather early to go downstairs; on the whole she felt it would be better to make a late appearance at dinner, partly for dramatic effect and partly to escape the possibility of a confrontation with the dowager, who would almost certainly take exception to the way she was dressed. How then to dispose of the remaining quarter of an hour? The sight of a silver porringer, coral teething ring, and several similar gifts lying on a nearby table suggested one idea, which the countess was quick to seize upon, feeling as she did that she had rather neglected her son that day. Gathering up the gifts, she continued on her way out the door, but instead of going down the main staircase, she turned and went along the hall until she reached the narrower flight of stairs that led to the nursery.

She found her son in the act of taking his evening meal at the wet nurse's breast. "If you're looking for Mrs. Smithson, my lady, she stepped out a minute ago," said the wet nurse as the countess unburdened herself of the baby gifts and came over to where she sat. "Hester most generally goes out for a breath of fresh air and a bite to eat while his lordship's at nurse." With a smile, she looked down at the baby at her breast. "He's a hungry one tonight, my lady, and no mistake. All the excitement this afternoon's given him an appetite, seemingly."

"It has been an exciting day for him," agreed the countess. She watched with interest and a certain amount of envy as the nurse expertly detached the viscount from one breast and shifted him to the other.

"Aye, he's had a busy day of it," continued the nurse, once these maneuvers were complete. "A busy day, but then so have we all. What with the christening at the church, and then your party for the gentlefolks here this afternoon, all fine as fine can be, as Jem was telling me when I came in downstairs not an hour ago. And there's still the party for the staff tonight in the servants' hall, which we've all been looking forward to. Jem's ma is coming over from Skyler later on to watch my own little one, so he and I can both go. Ah, you're finished, are you?" she said, addressing the viscount, who was at last showing signs of satiety. "Looks like he's had his fill at last. High time, too, considering how long he's been at it!"

"I'll take him if he's done, Ellen," said the countess, reaching out to take the viscount from his nurse.

Ellen started to put him in the countess's arms, then hesitated. "I don't know if you should, my lady," she said dubiously. "He's just eaten, you know, and babies being babies—well, you wouldn't want him to go and spoil your pretty dress."

"I don't care if he does," said the countess. She spoke quite sincerely, for in the quiet, homey atmosphere of the nursery it did not seem to matter very much what she wore, or did not wear, to dinner; she would not have been sorry for an excuse to forgo dinner altogether and remain where she was for the rest of the evening. Taking the baby from the nurse, she sat down in the nursing chair and began to rock. The viscount lay quietly in her arms; only his eyes moved as he considered her features with drowsy interest. The countess looked down at his small, sleepy face and felt her heart contract. Until that moment she had been thinking of her conflict with the earl as a strictly private quarrel, affecting only themselves, but the baby in her arms was a sobering reminder that others besides themselves might be affected by its outcome.

If she and the earl continued on their present course, the viscount was doomed to grow up in a household where master and mistress lived virtually separate lives—or worse yet, to grow up with the stigma of parents who were publicly separated. As she thought over the day just past, the countess could not feel such a possibility was unduly far-fetched, and since she had by this time worked herself into a thoroughly melancholy mood, she found it easy to take her imaginings a step further and imagine herself and the earl divorcing amid a flood of scandal and public outcry. Once the earl was free, he would naturally lose no time marrying Mrs. Blackwell, while she herself would be forced to live abroad or to slink about on the fringes of society, an object of pity and contempt to those who had been wont to envy her in the past.

It was an exceedingly dismal picture, but the countess told herself firmly that she would prefer even life as a divorcée to a marriage that was marriage in name only. Her resolution quailed a bit, however, when she looked down and met the viscount's wide, unblinking gaze. Even if the earl no longer cared for his wife, he unquestionably cared very much for his son and heir, and it was unlikely that he would allow the viscount to be raised away from Rosehill. The countess envisioned him in the years ahead, passing through all the stages of babyhood and boyhood with only servants to care for him—kind, well-meaning servants, to be sure, but incapable of a mother's love or a mother's solicitude. It was an idea that brought tears to the countess's eyes.

She was so intent on these melancholy musings that she did not hear the nursery door click open and then quietly swing shut. It was only when she heard the wet nurse say, "Good evening, my lord," that she looked up with a start and saw the earl standing just inside the nursery door.

It was evident that he had not expected to find her there. Consternation was written large on his face, and for a moment it appeared as though he might turn and leave without saying anything at all. But this was only for a moment; he soon recovered himself and, with a polite "good evening" to the wet nurse, walked over to where the countess sat.

"Good evening, Beth," he said. He had changed his blue coat and light trousers for formal black evening clothes whose somber hue was relieved only by the white triangle of starched stock and shirtfront. The countess felt a rush of involuntary pleasure to see how handsome he looked in this dress, but her pleasure quickly changed to pain at the formality of his address. "I came up to see St. Damien," were his next words, spoken with what she could not but feel a pointed emphasis. To make the emphasis still clearer, he kept his eyes on the viscount as he spoke, carefully avoiding meeting her gaze.

The countess's throat was too choked to make any reply. She merely nodded and, like the earl, fixed her eyes on the baby in her arms. The viscount was by now nearly asleep, lulled by the gentle motion of the rocking chair. His eyelids fluttered and drooped shut, opened again, then slowly closed. With his eyes still closed, he yawned soundlessly and snuggled himself a little closer against the countess's breast. A moment passed, and she supposed him asleep, but the next moment he yawned again and let out a resounding burp, which caused his eyes to fly open once more. For an instant he regarded her with sleepy surprise, then the vestige of a toothless smile appeared on his face, almost as though he were apologizing for his previous solecism. The effect was so droll that the countess could not help smiling. Instinctively she looked at the earl to see if he, too, had observed his son's actions.

This time the earl's eyes met hers squarely, with no attempt at evasion. He was not exactly smiling, but he looked as if he were trying not to; after a moment he abandoned the struggle and smiled reluctantly. The countess felt a sudden lightening in her heart. Forgetting all her anger and heartburnings, and the whole vexed question of whose fault was the greater, she spoke impulsively, "Carlton, I'm sorry—"

"I'm sorry, Beth," he said at the same time. They both stopped, started to speak, and stopped again, confounded by their own mutual eagerness to apologize. The countess laughed out loud in sheer nervous relief; the earl laughed, too, more quietly; and the wet nurse smiled indulgently at them both from the window seat where she sat sewing. The earl was the first to speak when at last they sobered. "Truly I am sorry, Beth," he said. "What I said this afternoon, about your going off with Will—I didn't mean to criticize, my dear. I'm afraid I wasn't in the best of moods at the time and said more than I really meant. But you must believe me when I say that I never doubted for a minute it was all perfectly innocent."

"Not even for a minute, Carlton?" said the countess wickedly. Her spirits had made an amazing recovery, and she could not resist teasing the earl a little, now that they were on speaking terms again. "I think you must have had *some* doubts, my love, or you wouldn't have been so stiff to poor Will, there on the pier. And the look on your face when you saw him kissing my hand—I was sure you were going to call him out or at least throw him in the river!"

With a self-conscious smile, the earl admitted to having entertained some such idea but assured the countess he had done so only briefly. "I think myself it was a sort of temporary insanity—and God knows today's been enough to drive anyone half mad. Ever since breakfast it seems things have gone from bad to worse . . ."

Conscious of her own guilt in this regard, the countess looked at the floor. The earl hesitated a moment before going on, rather diffidently. "About what I said at breakfast, Beth—you misunderstood me, I think, when I spoke about not caring. I do care, very much, about you and about him." He looked down at the viscount, now sleeping peacefully in the countess's arms. "When I said I didn't care, I only meant I didn't care about the party. I'm afraid men in general don't care about such things as much as women. But if I'd known it was so important to you—"

"Carlton, you shall not apologize," said the countess, quite overcome by this display of forbearance. "I am excessively ashamed of the way I behaved this morning. Oh, Carlton, I am so sorry. . . . I think I must have been a little mad myself, to have made such a fuss over such a trifle."

The earl said philosophically that madness in some degree seemed to be the common lot of new parents. "But whether it's cause and effect, or a prerequisite condition, I couldn't presume to say," he finished with a smile. The countess laughed shakily, and he laid his hand on her shoulder, a simple gesture that had all the poignancy of an embrace. "I know these last weeks have been a strain on you, Beth," he said gently. "I've been under a bit of strain myself, if it comes to that. But I'll try to be more patient after this and make allowance when necessary for the pressures you're under."

"And I shall see that it *won't* be necessary," said the countess resolutely. "No matter how much strain I'm under, that's no excuse for taking it out on you. But these last few weeks *have* been rather dreadful. I've been so worried about St. Damien's crying, and about other things, too . . ."

"He's not crying now, anyway," said the earl, surveying his offspring with a critical eye. "At the risk of being proved wrong, I'd say he was pretty well out of it for the evening."

"Yes, and I must put him in his cradle and go on downstairs if I'm not to be late to dinner," said the countess. With the earl's help she got to her feet, then paused, looking at him with a smile. "Would you like to put him in his cradle, Carlton?" she whispered, offering him the small bundle in her arms.

"I'll probably bungle it and wake him up," he whispered back, but took the bundle into his own arms willingly enough. The countess stifled a giggle as the earl, moving with extreme care, carried the baby to his cradle and lowered him gingerly into it, as though depositing therein some highly explosive substance. The viscount stirred but did not waken, and the countess came over to help the earl tuck the blankets around him.

"He looks quite angelic, doesn't he?" she said softly, as they stood side by side looking down at their son's small sleeping form. "I daresay every mother thinks her child beautiful, but it really seems to me that St. Damien is an unusually handsome baby. I do believe he's going to be dark like you, Carlton." She reached up to touch the dark wavy hair that spilled over the back of the earl's shirt collar.

The earl turned his head to smile at her. "He's got your eyes, though—blue as blue," he said.

"Silly, all babies have blue eyes—or almost all. Hester says his will probably turn dark when he's older."

"Is that so," said the earl, rather absently. He was looking down at the countess as if pondering further speech. "How long—" he began, and then stopped.

"How long before his eyes change? I don't know, but Hester probably does. I'll ask her next time I see her."

"No, not that. How long . . . how long before you're recovered from your lying-in? Completely recovered, I mean."

"What you really mean, I suppose, is how long it will be before I recover my sweet temper," said the countess, pretending great indignation. "I cannot say with any certainty, Carlton, but I hope it won't be *much* longer. And in the meantime I will faithfully promise not to snap at you unless it's strictly necessary!"

The earl smiled but looked a little embarrassed. "No, that's not what I meant either, Beth," he said. "I was speaking of your recovery in a physical sense. The doctor said it might be a couple of months before you were ready to—well, to resume marital relations, you know."

"Oh . . ." The countess let out her breath in a long-drawn sigh as the meaning of the earl's words dawned upon her. A great many things that had been inexplicable before were now suddenly explained; and she could only wonder that an explanation so simple and obvious had not occurred to her sooner. But there was too much else to occupy her thoughts to give her leisure for meditating on her own lack of acumen. She was very happy to learn that the earl's absence from her bedchamber had not been voluntary, as she had supposed, and if she could have been sure he had also been absent from Mrs. Blackwell's, her happiness would have been complete. This assurance was denied her, but even so, the thought of Mrs. Blackwell did not depress her quite as much as before: having been mistaken in one part of the earl's conduct, she was willing to hope she had been mistaken in the other as well.

All these reflections passed through the countess's head in a matter of seconds. She waited a moment before speaking, however, lest her answer smack too much of an unladylike eagerness. "Indeed, Carlton, I believe I am recovered *now,*" she said delicately.

"Are you?" The earl looked down at her searchingly. The

countess found it difficult to meet his eyes, from which evasiveness he seemed to draw the wrong conclusion. "You mustn't feel I'm badgering you, my dear," he went on, in a softer voice. "If you need more time, you have only to tell me. I am quite willing to wait another week or two weeks—as long as is necessary."

The countess found his concern so touching that her eyes promptly filled with tears. It was not the first time she had felt like weeping that day, but it was, beyond doubt, the first time she had felt like weeping for joy. With a sigh at her own lachrymose sensibilities, she blinked back her tears and smiled at the earl. "I don't deserve such a considerate husband," she said, "and truly, on this occasion your consideration is unnecessary, Carlton. I am quite well now—very well indeed."

"My dear, are you certain? There's no hurry, you know—and I wouldn't want to do anything to jeopardize your health."

The countess sighed again, but this time it was a sigh of exasperation. "I'm not going to beg you, Carlton," she said severely, "but yes, I am *quite* certain."

The earl began to laugh. He put an arm around her shoulders and drew her closer, so that his mouth was against her ear. "Tonight?" he whispered.

"If you like," said the countess demurely. It was quite exciting, she reflected, to be making assignations with one's lover in this delightfully disreputable way—and the fact that one's lover in this case happened also to be one's husband did not lessen the enjoyment one bit.

The earl's enjoyment appeared to be equal to her own; with a grin, he again bent to her ear and whispered a few words to the effect that he did like, very much. The countess blushed, shook her head, and looked warningly toward the other end of the room where the wet nurse sat. The earl looked guiltily in the same direction, but seeing Ellen busy with her sewing, he took advantage of the moment to kiss his wife lingeringly on the nape of the neck. This mode of kissing had always affected the countess strongly. She opened her mouth to rebuke the earl, but all that came out was a soft "oh" of pleasure. When he failed to follow up his advantage, she was as much disappointed as relieved;

turning her head, she saw that he was fingering the clasp of her necklace with a peculiar look on his face. "What is it, Carlton?" she asked.

The earl did not answer directly, but went on fingering her necklace as though trying to make up his mind. "I wonder if you might come with me to my room for a minute, Beth," he said at last. "There's something I wanted to show you, here before dinner."

The countess eyed him suspiciously. There appeared to be no double entendre in his words, but a glance at the nursery clock gave her another cause to demur. "I don't think I can go with you now, Carlton," she said. "I should be getting downstairs to the drawing room right now, and so should you—in fact, we ought really to be there already."

"It will only take a minute," said the earl, smiling in a way that tended to strengthen her suspicions. He refused to be more explicit, however. All the countess's teasing established only a few additional bits of information, to wit: 1) that the thing he wished to show her was a surprise 2) that it was a surprise with which she had no prior acquaintance, in any form, and 3) that it was a surprise which ought ideally be bestowed upon her before, rather than after, dinner. By now very much intrigued, the countess agreed to accompany him, and paused only to kiss the sleeping viscount before heading for the door. The earl followed suit, and together they left the nursery and went down the stairs to his bedroom.

The earl's apartments at Rosehill were a set of large, handsome rooms, fitted out with as much splendor as was consonant with masculine tastes. There were hangings of deep blue velvet at bed and windows, a Wilton carpet on the floor, and some half-dozen very large, very solid pieces of mahogany furniture. The largest and most solid of these, the bed, stood high on carved lions' feet in the center of the room, and lions also figured largely in the Carlton coat of arms embroidered upon the bed's canopy and upholstered headboard.

While the earl went into his closet to get the surprise, the countess stood looking around her with interest. She had had little occasion to visit the earl's rooms at Rosehill in the past, and none at all recently, so that they had now almost the charm of novelty. In a few minutes the earl emerged from his closet carrying a small wrapped package, which he placed in the countess's hands with a ceremonious bow. "Is this the surprise?" she said, turning it over curiously in her hands.

"Yes, that's it," said the earl. "Go on and open it."

Obediently the countess tore away the wrapping paper to reveal a square, flat, velvet-covered box. "Heavens, Carlton," she said, "this looks rather an *expensive* surprise."

The earl only smiled and told her again to open it. She did so, half-prepared for what she would find, but even so, a gasp escaped her when she saw the contents: a necklace of sapphires set in silver, each stone encircled by a ring of small diamonds. There were matching earrings as well, and the countess's fingers shook as she lifted one from the box to examine it more closely. "Oh, Carlton, how beautiful," she breathed. "But why . . . when . . . ?"

"The why's pretty obvious, I should think," said the earl, looking very gratified by her reaction. "I felt the birth and christening of our firstborn was an occasion worthy of commemoration. And the when's pretty obvious, too—I bought them last week when I was in London, of course. Do you really like them?"

The countess assured him rather incoherently that she did. "This is a surprise indeed, Carlton! I never dreamed you had such a thing in mind."

"Did you not? I tried to keep it pretty dark, but I wasn't sure how successful I'd been, especially after Susan Blackwell's gaffe at dinner last night. Both she and Raybourne were in on the secret, you see—they were in Hamlet's at the same time I was, looking for an engagement present—"

"Engagement present?" exclaimed the countess.

"Yes, it seems that after all these months Raybourne's finally persuaded the lady to have him. They won't mind my telling you, I'm sure, though you mustn't let it go further at present—the formal announcement won't be for another week or two. Well, I wished them happy, of course, as soon as they'd told me why they were there, and while we were all standing around talking, I happened to mention why *I* was there—thinking that one good confidence deserved another, I suppose. But I ought to have known better than trust either of those two with a secret. Neither one of 'em's exactly a model of discretion. I nearly had an apoplexy last night when Susan started chattering away about seeing me in Town the week before. I got her stopped before she could say anything too incriminating, but still it was a pretty near-run thing. It's a mercy you weren't paying attention, Beth, or you might have heard enough to put two and two together."

The countess said weakly that she had always had a poor head for mathematics. "I can assure you that you surprised me completely, Carlton," she said in an unsteady voice. "Such beautiful sapphires—and given for such a beautiful reason. I wish I wasn't already dressed that I might wear them to dinner tonight."

The earl looked contrite. "I did mean to give them to you earlier," he said. "Only what with one thing and another . . . well, we needn't go into all that again. I'm sorry, Beth. But you still might wear them tonight if you wanted to—that's the whole reason I made such a point of giving them to you now rather than later. It wouldn't take a minute to change them for your pearls."

"I'm afraid this color wouldn't do them justice," said the countess, looking down at her dress. Such a lot had happened since dressing for dinner that she had all but forgotten that remarkable garment. The sight of her own nearly naked chest reminded her in a hurry, however, and she was much embarrassed, on looking up, to catch the earl just withdrawing his eye from a study of the same subject. "No, I fear this color wouldn't do your sapphires justice," she said again, in some confusion. "If it wasn't already so late, I'd change into something else, Carlton. I know you don't like this dress."

"Don't I?" said the earl. He gravely surveyed the countess from the top of her tousled blond head to the tips of her lilac satin sandals. His expression did not noticeably change, but the gravity of his manner was somewhat impaired as he continued, "On the contrary, my dear, I like it very well. If I objected to it before, it was solely on humanitarian principles."

"Humanitarian principles?" repeated the countess, eyeing him askance.

The earl nodded solemnly. "Yes, I can't reconcile it with my conscience, to let my wife go about in public looking as enticing as you look now," he said. "Every man who sets eyes on you would be thinking—well, pretty much what I'm thinking now, I expect. The only difference is that they, poor devils, can never do a thing about it, and I can—and right this very minute, too, if I like."

Once more the earl's gaze swept the countess from head to toe. The corners of his mouth curved upwards in a slow, dangerous smile; before she realized her peril, he had caught her round the waist and pulled her into his arms, nearly knocking the jewel case from her hand in the process.

"Heavens, Carlton," said the countess mildly. She got no chance to say more, for the next instant she found herself being kissed with an ardor that rendered her speechless, and very nearly breathless as well. Once she had been reduced to this tractable state, the earl plucked the jewel case from her hand, tossed it atop his dressing chest, and drew her into a yet closer embrace. "After all, you *are* my wife," he said, running an insinuating hand down her back.

The countess did not attempt to deny it. "But we will be late for dinner, Carlton," she said. "In fact, we're late already. And with guests in the house—"

"Let them wait," said the earl, silencing her with another kiss. "Let them wait, every man jack of them. After all, it's my dinner—my house, too, if it comes to that. And if I feel like disrupting the established order now and then, who's to say me nay?"

The countess recognized the futility of arguing with her husband in this masterful mood. She sought to temporize, however, as he began to maneuver her, without overmuch subtlety, in the direction of the Carlton lions. "I suppose it will not matter if we are a little late, just this once," she said, "but I *was* looking forward to tonight, you know."

Between kisses, the earl assured her that he was looking forward to it quite as much as she was. "Don't think you'll escape me tonight merely because you indulge me now, ma'am," he told her sternly. "I've missed you very much these last few weeks. Now that I've got you to myself again, I intend to make up for lost time."

With all her objections thus summarily disposed of, the countess could do nothing but submit, which she did with a very good grace. "Well, since you put it that way, my love," she said, reaching up to untie the earl's cravat, "I suppose you really cannot begin too soon . . ."

The earl and countess of Carlton were rather late for dinner that evening, but their lateness inconvenienced no one. After waiting twenty minutes for host and hostess to appear, the dowager countess had taken matters into her own hands and decreed that dinner be served without them. She had even invented an excuse for their absence: as the junior countess was trying to slip unobtrusively into her place at table, her mother-in-law fixed her with a steely eye and inquired loudly if she were recovered from her fainting spell?

The countess took the hint and assured everyone that she was feeling much better, a statement to which her glowing cheeks seemed fully to attest. But the others at the table were too busy exclaiming over her sapphires (worn with a most lovely dress of cerulean blue sarcenet) to take notice of the blush that accompanied her words. The earl's gift was very much admired, and by no one more than the Honorable Mrs. Blackwell; with great pride she informed the countess that it had been she herself who had suggested sapphires when he had been hesitating among the offerings in Hamlet's shop, and that she congratulated herself now that her suggestion had been a good one. The countess agreed and said, smiling, that she understood congratulation was due Mrs. Blackwell in another direction as well, causing that lady to laugh and look archly at Lord Raybourne.

It was altogether a most lively and enjoyable dinner party. Conversation flourished throughout the meal, and the food was exceptionally good, even for Henri; so good, in fact, that when the dessert course was finished, one earnest gourmand got to his feet and proposed a toast to the genius responsible for such a delectable repast. There were many willing glasses raised, but before they could be drained, Sir William Walcott intervened. "I don't mind drinking to Henri," he said. "Best chef in England, in my opinion, and that's not excepting Prinny's Carême. But it's only right we drink to St. Damien first, seeing as he's the one who brought us together tonight."

"Amen," said the earl softly. He lifted his glass and smiled across the table at his wife.

"Amen," she said, smiling back.